THE DECEIVED

THE DECEIVED

TOMM A. BOYER

PUBLISHED BY

LIGHTHOUSE MANUSCRIPTS LLC

Lighthouse Manuscripts™

The Deceived

Published by Lighthouse Manuscripts LLC
12020 Sunrise Valley Drive, Suite 100
Reston, VA 20191

Scriptures are the King James Version – Public domain.

This is a work of fiction. Names, places, characters and incidents used or referenced in any
manner in this work are either the product of the author's imagination or are used fictitiously,
and any resemblance to any actual persons, living or dead, businesses, companies,
organizations, events or locales is entirely coincidental.

ISBN: 978-1-7358723-0-8
Library of Congress Control Number: 2020921007

Printed in the United States of America

For more information, email: info@lighthousemanuscripts.com

Acknowledgement & Dedication

Thank you Shawna (Boobie), Sean (Champ), Chris (Ace), and Rocky
for allowing me to spend many weekends to complete this book.
I truly appreciate your jokes, laughter, and support.

◊◊◊

I also thank my family and friends ("the Ville") who always showed me
support, especially the many strong and godly women in my life, including my
Mother (Tiny), Cindy, Linda, Charlotte, Gwen, Joyce, and Sheena. Proverbs 35:31.

◊◊◊

A special thanks to my past mentors and role models, who either inspired me by
their lives or by their words, including, James, Otis, Ronald, Richie, Tyrone, Colin,
Herschel, Darren, Darryl, Greg, David C, and my entire Prout Drive crew.

◊◊◊

This book is dedicated to my former HT Youth Group. Your youthful spirits
and humor always made my day and our events were the best.

◊◊◊

This book is also dedicated to Paul. Just like, Joshua, the main character in this book,
Paul was a church organist and minister of music. But to me, he was an inspirational
father figure and friend. Paul, thank you for your words of hope and music of praise.
Now, you share your wonderful music in Heaven with no limitations.

◊◊◊

Dad, thank you for teaching me how to work hard and stay focus despite
distractions or what others think. We rarely agreed and you were never
around, but I still learned a lot from you. For that, I thank you.

◊◊◊

*"Finally, brethren, whatsoever things are true, whatsoever things are honest,
whatsoever things are just, whatsoever things are pure, whatsoever things are lovely,
whatsoever things are of a good report; if there be any virtue, and if there be
any praise, think on these things." – Philippians 4:8 (KJV)*

'I will forever love and think on the *Lovely* of this world.'

Chapters

'Good bringeth forth good, evil bringeth forth evil'

1

Shouts of Praise

Sunday morning.

It was chaos. The church's large beautiful cathedral ceiling and the colorful pane glass windows along the high walls only amplified the sounds of the screams, the yelling, and the noise of objects falling to the ground. The heavy dark smoke was visible in the air. Everyone pushed each other frantically to get out the nearest exit. Most covered their mouths with their hands, shirts, or tissues as it got harder to breathe. The large sanctuary now appeared to be too small for the filled church, way above capacity.

Joshua looked toward the altar. He stared in disbelief as he witnessed a group of people fighting. The ministers from the pulpit attempted to break it up. They were the only ones oblivious to the imminent danger. Joshua looked around, confused. He wondered, *What was happening, and why?* He jumped off the organ seat and ran to help break up the fight. As Joshua moved forward, he saw in his periphery a shadow coming up from behind him. He could feel its dark presence, its evil intentions. He turned his head to get a better look at what approached him, but the dark shadow was too fast. It was already at his back, and hovering over top of him. Before he could move or react, Joshua was struck on the head. He fell to the ground. His vision went dark.

* * *

Joshua woke with a sudden jump. He quickly reached for the back of his head to the spot where he had been struck. Joshua looked around and realized he was home, in his bed. It was just another dream. The same reoccurring dream he'd been having for the past few weeks.

It was another hot Sunday morning in Philadelphia, Pennsylvania, 89 degrees, and it was only 9:30 a.m. It was the sixth day in a row that the temperature was expected to get over 100 degrees. No wind, no clouds, and only one air conditioner in the living room used to cool the house. It was a two-bedroom shotgun-style home that was larger than a trailer home, but fell just short of the square footage of a typical rancher. The house possessed significant maintenance issues. Both the roof and the ceiling were in dire need of repair. As a result, a small amount of mold on the ceiling was just over the kitchen area that looked like old dirt and grease stains. But more concerning for Joshua's mother, Denise Williams, was the low water pressure that provided less-than-satisfactory showers and weak-flushing toilets. Joshua felt the low water pressure was more of an embarrassment than a concern, and mostly when guests were over at the house. Joshua's best friend, Monty, always joked that the bathroom's plunger got way more use than Joshua's toothbrush.

"Josh! Get up, now! I cannot afford to be late this Sunday!" yelled his mother from the kitchen.

Mostly everyone called Joshua Alexander Williams by his shortened name, Josh. However, Joshua hated his full name. He felt it sounded too biblical; but being called Josh was tolerable.

It took Joshua approximately five minutes of struggling to get out of bed. He was still thinking about his dream.

Joshua finally walked into the kitchen and in the presence of his mother. She looked at the clock hanging on the wall.

"Only five minutes after I called! This must be a world record. Wait. Did you brush your teeth?" asked Denise.

Joshua did not respond. He just turned right back around and into the bathroom. Like every Sunday morning, Joshua looked extremely tired. He avoided looking in the mirror to see his zombie semblance: long downward-sloping face, slightly reddish eyes with a little bit of puffiness underneath.

It was time for church, and Joshua was the organist and minister of music at his uncle's church, New Lighthouse Temple. To get ready, Joshua had a fairly good routine for not having enough time to get a shower. His mom called it the "quick wash." He would brush his teeth and then wash his face three times: once with hot water to open up his pores, a second with warm water and soap, and last a fresh rinse with cold water to tighten his skin. Next was a separate towel for his underarms and then he'd put on deodorant. Now and then, he added a fourth step: using eye drops to get any red out of his eyes from smoking weed the night before. He smoked weed about once or twice a month, and usually with Monty. Joshua did not consider smoking a few puffs of marijuana a bad thing. To him, this was only a minor sin, and technically it was a drug that helped people, and many other people he knew in the church did things worse than that. Yet, Joshua still did not want his mom to know. Over time, he'd learned that the allergy brand of eye drops worked better at getting the red out of his eyes than the regular drops. In severe cases, when the eye drops would not work, he would look directly into a light bulb or at the sun, which immediately helped remove the red from his eyes. But he knew this fix was not the safest or smartest thing to do.

Joshua walked back into the kitchen, looking refreshed.

"Do we have time for breakfast?" asked Joshua.

"You can put some frozen waffles in the toaster. But you must hurry up. It's my first day ushering, and I can't be late," said Denise.

"Are you sure you want to usher? You stand on your legs all day for work at the grocery store. Standing all day for church as well doesn't sound like a good idea," said Joshua.

"Boy, stop worrying about your mother. You need to worry about whether you brushed properly, with those, I can't believe they're not two sticks of butter teeth of yours. You cannot sit in front of everyone on that organ with your teeth looking all yellow," joked Denise.

Joshua just smiled. But if Monty had been there, Monty would have been cracking up in laughter for a few minutes. Denise would always come up with funny jokes. Joshua felt her jokes were corny, but they were just embarrassing when said in front of others.

"Well, I think you need to worry about how long you will be standing on your feet in those extremely tight Nanny McPhee heels. We don't go to one of those Catholic churches where service only lasts an hour, remember," said Joshua.

"Boy, get on your shoes, and make sure you floss your teeth too," said Denise, as she became impatient.

Joshua just smiled again. And then, for some reason, he noticed her heels one more time. But this time in more detail. Denise could step with the best of them in a pair of high heels. However, the shoes she had on today were not new or even the most polished. The core of them was sturdy, but the tips were slightly worn. But you could not tell that by the way she walked in them. He shrugged to himself, not sure why she would want to wear them in the first place. After he ate, Joshua got dressed and they made their way to the service.

As usual, people packed into the church this Sunday like sardines in a can. Since the central part of New Lighthouse Temple was old and antiquated, it had a retrofit air conditioning system that, for the most part, did its job. But for one of the hottest days of the year, they would also turn on the four large spinning fans. The ushers also passed out manual hand fans. Denise proudly took her position in the back as the greeter; which for most churches, a greeter is the entry-level usher position. Ushering can be stressful, especially at a church with a large congregation such as New Lighthouse Temple. The usher is looked at, patiently or impatiently, while he or she searches through the packed pews for the right number of open seats. Hopefully, the usher does not give away a seat already taken by someone, possibly in the bathroom or maybe dropping their kid off in children's church. If an usher does choose an undesirable seat, then he or she must start the search all over again. But as a church greeter, you just stand and wait for the doors to open, smile, and say:

"Welcome to New Lighthouse Temple! Thank you for coming this morning," said Denise as her first action as the new church greeter at her brother, Pastor Williams' church.

"Sister Denise Williams! Thank you! You look good in the black and white," said Sister Wendy Marshall. Wendy was an old-time member. She had been with the church since it started and even had a thing with Denise's brother before he was married and became a Pastor.

"Where's your son, Josh?" asked Wendy.

"He's already on the musicians' stage. I cannot believe we finally made it here on time," said Denise.

"On the stage already? Hallelujah! That must be a first!"

Denise laughed as well. She then placed her hand lightly on Wendy's arm and said, "Girl, tell me about it. It takes the power of God to resurrect that boy from sleep on Sunday morning. Lord knows, if he didn't play for this church, we would never make it here before the sermon."

When Joshua was young, his uncle, Jerome "Jerry" Williams, simply known to everyone as Pastor Williams, taught him to play the piano. Every Saturday, Pastor Williams would take Joshua with him to the church while he practiced his sermons. Joshua would sit behind the old piano, which was no longer in the church, and just bang on the keys. Eventually, the keys he played started making purposeful sounds and subsequently turned into excellent melodies and chords. Pastor Williams realized the love Joshua had for music and spent time teaching him gospel chords. Sometimes, Pastor Williams focused on the music lessons so much that he'd forget about preparing for his sermons.

This relationship was good as Joshua was unaware of the identity of his father. Some thought, this was the result of Denise's promiscuity when she was younger. Years prior, she'd disappeared for weeks or even months at a time. However, Pastor Williams was confident that Denise, for reasons unknown, wanted to keep this person a secret. In any event, Pastor Williams had spent as much time as he could with Joshua. He gladly took up the big brother role to help out his sister. So, when times were tough for Joshua and Denise, they would stay with Pastor Williams and his wife, Angela. Because of this, Joshua always felt like he owed his uncle something. Even when he did not feel like it, he would push himself to church service and play the organ. Albeit, the musician's fee of $125 a week also incentivized this habit.

Wendy continued the conversation. "Sister Williams, Josh has come such a long way from banging on that old, out-of-tune piano. I love hearing him play. How old is he now?"

"He turned eighteen just last month," said Denise.

"Wow, and still so young. God has his hand over him. There is something special about that boy. I can just feel it. How does he feel about you working in the church as an usher?" asked Wendy.

"Yes. It is a blessing to see Josh play. But I don't think he likes seeing me in this tight outfit greeting all the people he knows," said Denise as she laughed. "Must be somewhat embarrassing to him," she added.

"Well, pay him no mind. Your beautiful smile greeting us is like sunshine this morning," said Wendy.

"Thanks, Sister Wendy."

Denise did have one of the best smiles. She was attractive but not strikingly beautiful. But her smile and bubbly personality made her even more appealing. She could light up a dreary room with her presence and her pearly white teeth. Obviously, she brushed hers more than Joshua. But, anyone speaking to her would never know that she had struggled for so many years. She'd endured lost jobs, poor health, and almost losing it mentally, all while raising a son by herself, who at most times was ornery. But she still managed to remain positive. She credited it to her faith in God. Joshua attributed it to the fact that she had no other choice. In Joshua's opinion, they had little to no options.

About a year ago, Denise had suffered a severe heart attack. They'd had no other choice but to move in with Pastor Williams while Denise recovered. Joshua was grateful they had a place to go, but he still did not like it. Living under the roof of his uncle, a pastor, meant many strict rules that he had to follow. Pastor Williams would always tell Joshua, "You don't have to agree with my rules, but you sure will respect them." Joshua obliged while they lived there. But he was thrilled when Denise fully recovered, and they were able to get their own place again. The thought of losing his mother brought some restraint to Joshua's previous ungodly language and nefarious actions. He became more respectful and appreciative. The last thing he wanted was to become the reason his mother suffered another heart attack. But, that did not stop him from smoking joints with Monty.

Denise looked up at the stage and saw Joshua overshadowing the organ with confidence, perfect posture straightened back. The rest of the church band—lead guitarist, bass player, drummer, saxophonist, and bongo player—were warming up. Joshua looked slightly in his mother's direction to see her, but not to make any eye contact. He then warmed up by playing the key scale, getting in rhythm with the band. He noticed her outfit one more time.

Since Denise did not have a lot of money, her new black skirt and white blouse for ushering were not exactly stylish or expensive. She'd gotten both from The Bargain Outlet just eight miles from the house they were renting. It was located in the same shopping center where she worked. After Denise had recovered from the heart attack, she was blessed with an assistant manager training position at the local Penn Fresh Supermarket. It paid a decent wage, but the benefits were even better, especially if she passed the management training. After training, an assistant manager position paid $45,000 to $60,000; while a manager position paid $60,000 to $90,000, not including the quarterly bonuses. If she completed the training, the benefits package included a low co-pay and low deductible with health, dental, and vision for the employee and any dependents. After having a heart attack at her previous job with no insurance, and now with mounting medical bills, she realized the priority was medical insurance. She joked that the next guy she dated better had a job with benefits.

Assisting Denise again, Pastor Williams had cosigned for her to get the place they lived in now. He did it partially out of his love for his sister, but the other part was because of his wife, Angela. Angela was a kind soul, but she got tired of both Denise and Joshua living there. After being told what to do, Joshua's attitude and under-the-breath responses, did not help.

The church doors opened again. "Monty!" said Denise, greeting Joshua's best friend as he entered the sanctuary.

Monty walked into the church with his father, mother, and little sister that followed behind him. Monty's father always made Monty enter a room or building first. It was his way of teaching Monty to be a man, or, as Monty's father called it, "letting your presence be known" to others in a room. Every time Joshua went over to Monty's house, Monty's father would say, "When you shake a man's hand, you always get in his space, look him square in the eyes, and squeeze his hand with all your might!" He would also tell Joshua that in life, it was better to be respected than liked. If Joshua had received these speeches a hundred times, Monty must have gotten them over a thousand.

One time in high school, Joshua witnessed Monty running into their social studies class a whole ten minutes late. Monty had been on the opposite side of the school in the hallway flirting with a senior named Samantha. To Monty's surprise, she became more engaged with their conversation after the class bell rang. So, Monty continued to talk to her as if he did not hear the bell or, possibly, didn't care. That was until Mr. Shafer, the wood shop teacher, yelled at them to get to class. When Monty got to social studies, he immediately ran up to the teacher, Mr. Roberts. Before Mr. Roberts could say anything, Monty invaded his space, looked him square in the eyes, and said, "Mr. Roberts, I truly apologize for my tardiness to your wonderful class. Due to the unhealthy offerings and limited options at the cafeteria today, my body, against my will, required the lengthy services of this institution's bathroom facilities. Please forgive me." With anyone else, that would have been immediate detention. But with Monty, Mr. Roberts just told him to take his seat. Mr. Roberts had known Monty was lying, but he gave the respect Monty wanted, and without punishment.

Monty's mother, Harriet, walked up to Denise and greeted her with a hug. Monty quickly walked away.

"Looks like our boys had another late night," said Denise with a smirk at Harriet.

"Yes. Monty's grounded," said Harriet.

"Well, Josh may be too. I just haven't gotten to that yet," said Denise as she shook her head, looking back up at Joshua. Joshua saw and responded with a look of admitted guilt.

"Enjoy the service!" said Harriet.

"You too!" said Denise.

The day's service was just like others at New Lighthouse Temple. It was a Pentecostal church with a standard Sunday program that included prayer, hymnal, scripture reading, praise and worship, choir, announcements, choir (again), offering, and sermon.

Aside from the "shouting" breakouts and the long-winded members who did or said more than their task on the program specified, services went smoothly. If things did get out of control—for example, Brother Kenny jumping hysterically and screaming at the top of his lungs right after everyone else was done shouting—Pastor Williams would grab the microphone and start singing a slow worship song. Joshua was prepared to find the right key and play louder than usual to drown out Brother Kenny or whatever else was happening. Things would get back under control soon enough. It gave Pastor Williams and Joshua a connection that Pastor Williams appreciated.

The offering portion was usually the loudest time of the service. In addition to the choir singing, the congregation would join in singing as well. The choir would always sing a familiar song, and Joshua would lead off singing and playing. Because of this, Joshua and the musicians had some autonomy in how they played. This flexibility created more excitement: harder claps, louder stomps, and more spontaneous shouting. For the most part, everyone shouted the same, feet seemingly to run in place, head bounced up and down. But, if the shouts were wild, the kids, especially the older ones, would laugh or even mock them. This day was no different, and so far, the church service was filled with the Spirit of God.

In Joshua's periphery, he'd seen his mother waving her hands high in the air, praising God. He knew she was thinking about her new job and the opportunity she had. They still had their problems, but he was comforted by seeing her praising God.

Joshua took a deep breath, exhaled, waited a moment, and the scripture Psalm 34:3 came to his mind. He then sang.

"O magnify the Lord and exalt his name!" sang Joshua.

Without missing a step, the choir and the congregation immediately joined on the next beat, "Oh Hallelujah! Oh Hallelujah!"

Joshua accompanied the song with the organ and the band joined. A few church members broke out in a praise shout, including Denise. Despite attending many church services together, this was the first time that Joshua had seen his mom shout. It was very unorthodox, to say the least. But it motivated Joshua to play even faster, adding in new chords not typical of his play. The drummer and bass guitar player followed, playing harder and faster, increasing the beat's pace. The congregation followed with harder claps, louder stomps, and louder singing as Joshua led the praise:

"O magnify the Lord and exalt his name!" sang Joshua.

"Oh, Hallelujah! Oh, Hallelujah!" sang the church.

Joshua looked around the church in appreciation. When his eyes made their way to the area where his mother was standing, he noticed a crowd gathered in one spot. They were hovering over someone. He could not see if it were his mother. But when he looked around, he did not see her anywhere. He stood up from the organ seat while still playing to get a closer look. At that moment, he saw his mother's heels pointed up to the ceiling. The same ones that he had joked about earlier. Three people stood over her, praising God with the assumption that she'd experienced a "slain in the spirit" phenomenon. They were unaware that she had passed out, or even why. To them, her condition was unknown. But a fourth person, a woman, looked over Denise with fear. She furiously waved a paper fan over Denise in an attempt to cool her down, while simultaneously waving her other hand for others to come help. Joshua's face showed the same fear, and he missed his lead into the next chorus. The congregation did not miss a beat and continued the song.

"Oh, Hallelujah! Oh, Hallelujah!" sang the church.

Joshua stopped playing, but uncertainty kept him on the musicians' stage. The rest of the musicians kept playing. Joshua looked over at Monty, who had a better view of the situation. Monty also looked concerned. When Monty saw Joshua looking at him, he waved Joshua off the organ to come over and check on his mother. Joshua stepped down from the musician's stage and ran to the back of the church toward her. As he got closer, he was able to see her whole body more clearly. As he approached, things started to look worse. Denise's arms and legs were making random jerking motions. Her torso was erratically shaking. Joshua could see her eyes were now lost in a set direction. He had just missed the initial clutching of her chest. However, he was fully aware of what was happening. Joshua had seen this before, approximately a year ago. Late one night, he heard his mom making gasping noises in her room. He got up to check on her, and when he had opened the door, Denise was shaking violently.

Joshua finally reached the back of the church. Denise's body had stopped jerking. Her arms rested. Her eyes were fixed. Joshua stood over his mother's lifeless body. He knelt to the ground and screamed a cry that no person ever wants to hear. He grabbed her by her arm and body and pulled her in toward his chest.

"Help!" yelled Joshua. "Help! Somebody, please help!" The congregation stopped singing, and the musicians stopped playing.

"Help! Somebody, please help!"

Pastor Williams and the other ministers ran to the back to meet Joshua. The congregation turned toward them to see what had happened.

"Uncle! Help her! Please!" exclaimed Joshua. Joshua's heart raced and pounded within his chest.

Everyone watched the expression on his face turn from fear to terror. He then grimaced as he forcefully held back the desperate cry.

Pastor Williams was in shock, suspended looking at his sister on the church floor. His attempt to say or do anything failed.

"Please help! Ask God to save her again! Please ask God to save her again!" cried Joshua.

Pastor Williams was still frozen and remained speechless. One of the female church members ran over and checked her pulse.

"I'm a nurse," she said.

The nurse gently grabbed Denise from Joshua's hold, placed her back on the ground. She checked her wrist and neck for a pulse, and then listened to her mouth for breath or any signs of life. She performed CPR. Denise's body did not respond.

"Uncle. Why aren't you helping her?" asked Joshua, looking confused and hurt at Pastor Williams.

The nurse continued with the CPR.

"Answer me. Why aren't you helping her! Why isn't God helping her!" yelled Joshua, confused.

After numerous attempts at CPR, the nurse got up, backed away from Denise and said quietly, "I'm sorry. She's gone."

Most church members gasped in horror. Others were too shocked to make any verbal expression.

"Well, pray! Pray that she comes back!" exclaimed Joshua, his mind frantically grasping for any sign of hope.

"It's not that simple, Josh," said Pastor Williams.

"Where's all the faith you talk about?" shouted Joshua.

Pastor Williams did not respond.

"Where's all the faith you all talk about!" exclaimed Joshua as he looked at the rest of the ministers and deacons.

"Where's God now? Where is He?" yelled Joshua as he grabbed Denise's upper body and pulled her back into a hold against his chest.

"Josh . . ." said one of the deacons as he approached.

"Get away from her! Get away, I said!" yelled Joshua as he held his mother even tighter.

Pastor Williams squatted to the floor, saddened.

Joshua could no longer hold back the tears. His head dropped onto his mother's shoulder and he began to cry.

2

Works at Hand

Two years later, Tuesday morning—four days before the community revival.

Clouds blanketed the sky, and the wind's strength was enough to turn the leaves. Everyone in the neighborhood knew that turning leaves was a sign of imminent rain.

"Good morning!" exclaimed the shopper.

"Good morning," said Joshua.

"I hope you have some umbrellas," said the shopper.

"We do. There is a standing rack full of them right in front of the checkout lanes," said Joshua.

During the past week, it had rained four out of seven days. It was not severe, heavy rain, but enough to become a primary topic of discussion for small talk.

It was Tuesday, and Joshua was picking up a few pieces of noticeable trash and debris in front of the Penn Fresh Supermarket, which was now Joshua's place of employment. It was the same supermarket that had hired his mother, Denise. He was usually off on Tuesdays, as he worked nights and weekends as the assistant manager. After working in the store for about a year and completing the necessary training, he'd gotten the position. It had been the same training that his mother was completing before she died. Joshua learned very quickly that nights and weekends in a store experienced both quick bursts of high customer traffic and periods of little to no traffic. Most executives believed this fluctuation was an excellent way to train assistant managers to become managers. But the rest of the employees would say that it was just the managers' way of using their seniority to avoid work on nights or weekends.

The store opened at 5:00 a.m. and closed at midnight. A conditional approval set by the city for all retailers in this jurisdiction restricted any retailer from operating a full twenty-four hours. Penn Fresh and many other chain retail stores tried fighting this collectively so that they could all operate on a twenty-four-hour basis. But this was to no avail. They all gave up when a proposed redevelopment of the old run-down mall on the Boulevard and Lexington was denied a twenty-four-hour operation application. The development proposal included a new Walmart Supercenter. If Walmart could not get the approval to operate twenty-four hours, then no one could.

Joshua paid close attention to this application, as, being the night manager, he would most likely have to work even later into the night. This potential change in work hours posed three problems for Joshua: (1) his late nights hanging out with Monty would go from very few to never; (2) time seemed to drag on even longer during later hours; and (3) the later hours would open the store to a higher chance of getting robbed, or Joshua having to deal with a group of disorderly kids, possibly a group that he knew. For example, the Lucky's bar, located across the street, and also the Stage Night Club, a couple of blocks down the road, both closed at 2:00 a.m. They would undoubtedly bring in an unruly crowd.

The store manager, Rick, saw Joshua in the front of the store. He walked over to Joshua.

"I appreciate you coming in this morning, Josh," said Rick.

"No problem," said Joshua.

"Nate will be here at eleven a.m., and we want to be ready and make sure the store looks good. He is very meticulous."

Nate was the district manager. He was in charge of eight Penn Fresh stores in the city, overseeing the managers of each of those stores. Nate was also the previous store manager when Rick was just the assistant manager. They both had worked at this store for many years ever since it was a U-Save. A few years ago, the parent company of Penn Fresh Supermarket acquired a bunch of U-Saves in the Philadelphia market, and a few just over the bridge in New Jersey. The Penn Fresh Corporation kept many of the employees. Most of them were kept due to the union contract Penn Fresh had to assume, and others were held for their perceived talent. But a few weeks after the acquisition, they were pleased with both Nate's and Rick's performance.

"I already started working the front lot, and when Billy gets here, I will have him sweep the side and loading dock area." Billy was the young part-timer working through school.

"Good," said Rick.

Rick listed out to Joshua all the tasks that needed done. Gondola shelves stocked with no empty facings. Swept and mopped floors in the prep areas. Deli bowls fully turned, so all items, like the macaroni and pasta salads, appeared fresh and just put out. All the employees were wearing proper attire, including black shoes and shirts fully tucked into their pants. The front-end area had at least three cashiers and two baggers. Rick continued with his list.

". . . and make sure Billy is on top of the carts in the lot. The last thing we need is for Nate to pull into a parking spot only to be blocked by one of our damn carts!" exclaimed Rick.

"Got it!" said Joshua.

Nate arrived on time, and things went like clockwork. They first toured outside, inspecting the parking lot and the building.

"Look at all that mud and dirt splashed against the sidewalk and along your building wall. This rain has been doing a number on your store," said Nate.

Even though Rick did not mention it, Joshua had a feeling that he had to step up and shine in front of Nate today. So, he took a deep breath, exhaled, waited a moment, and then said, "No worries, Nate! I will take care of it."

Joshua immediately got on his walkie-talkie and radioed Billy in the back room.

"Billy?" said Joshua.

"Yeah, Josh. Over," said Billy.

"Call Facilities. See how soon they could get the power washer out here to clean up the exterior of our store. Over," said Joshua.

"Will do. I will let you know. Over and out," said Billy.

They went inside to tour the store. It took a considerable amount of time as they went through each aisle, looking at and commenting about every single shelf. They eventually made their way back to the meat section. Nate's eyes pierced through one of the coffin cases that had a collection of various hams.

"Make sure you go through these and get rid of any out-of-date products," said Nate.

Joshua had gone through all of them the night before. But from previous experience, he'd learned that perception, and not reality, is everything, especially in business.

After Joshua's mother, Denise, passed away, the Penn Fresh Supermarket was more than happy to help with funeral expenses. Denise worked hard, and she had such a likable personality. She was deemed an "up-and-comer" by Rick and Nate. When Denise was in training, there was only one minority female store manager in the whole company. Some employees in the company felt that having more minorities in management would be great for Penn Fresh's diversity image. A few others voiced that it would be, in their words, "unfair equal opportunity bullshit." But most felt that Penn Fresh could not successfully operate in minority or diverse neighborhoods without minority managers that knew the residents, demographics, and psychographics of the community. Denise did not care about any of that. She just wanted a good job with benefits.

When Rick called Joshua about a potential job working in the store after Denise's death, Joshua remembered his mother's first day of work. Rick had hired her as a deli assistant. Her direct boss, the deli manager, gave Denise the task of making premade hoagies and stocking them in the case for the customers. Denise was excited. She first placed a bottom row of hoagies in a horizontal line from the right edge of the case to the left. Then she stacked as many hoagies as she could in vertical columns, also known as soldier course style, from edge to edge. It left just enough room for her to add one more horizontally stacked row at the top. It gave the case an impressive presentation. Forty-five minutes into the official lunch period, there were only three hoagies left in the case. Denise was so proud. When the lunch rush was over, those same three hoagies remained. Denise assumed she would receive recognition for her creativity and accomplishment. Unfortunately, this was not the case. Denise and the deli manager received a scolding by Rick for allowing only three hoagies to remain in the case for the rest of the day.

Rick explained, "You never leave a case looking so empty like that. Even if those three hoagies were made fresh, to the customer, it looks as if those are the last of the bunch and old. No one wants the last of anything!" Rick further added, "And if they were selling so much, why didn't you go back and make more? So, yes, it is great that you almost doubled our hoagie sales for the same lunch period compared to yesterday. But if you made more hoagies, you'd have tripled it!" said Rick.

Denise replied, "Okay. Tomorrow, we will triple it." And they did. At that moment, Rick knew he had a winner with Denise.

Joshua could see Billy near the restrooms.

"Yo, Billy!" Joshua yelled.

Billy came running to the group.

"Go through these hams and throw out any that are expired. And if any are one or two days from expiration, let me know how many and which ones," said Joshua.

Nate and Rick looked at each other with satisfaction. They walked back to the manager's office.

"Josh, give us a moment," said Rick.

"Sure. I'll go through the hams with Billy," said Joshua.

"Sounds good," said Rick.

Rick closed the door of his office. Nate sat in Rick's chair.

"I love Josh's sense of urgency. He didn't even wait for us to finish the tour to start handling things," said Nate.

"Yes. He is a lot like his mother. Not as creative, but definitely a hard worker," said Rick.

"Do you think he is ready to take over this store? They just moved up the opening date for the new store seven eighty-one."

"Him. What about me? What if *I'm* ready to open a new store or not?" asked Rick, lacking confidence.

"I think you both are. I made the official recommendation to corporate. I fully support you becoming the manager of the new store and Josh becoming the manager of this one. It's only a matter of time and clearance from human resources," said Nate.

"Night and weekend sales increased over two and a half percent, and shrink is down almost one hundred basis points since he's been assistant manager. And I finally can leave the store at night with someone I can trust. I think he is ready," said Rick with confidence.

"Good. I will keep pushing it up the ladder," said Nate.

* * *

Late after work, Joshua took a long hit of a joint. He and Monty were sitting in Joshua's car a few doors down from Pastor Williams' house. Joshua had moved in with Pastor Williams and his wife, Angela, after his mother died. The house was located on Prout Drive, a two-lane street that had good-sized row homes. This section of the city was predominately African American, but just ten blocks to the south, it was split culturally. The east side was mostly Italian, and the west side was predominantly Irish. For the most part, they all got along and walked each other's streets with no problems. However, a few physical and mental borders, which everyone knew, transitioned the different ethnic areas, such as Horace Bridge to the north or Pine Street to the south. But that did not stop anyone from shopping at stores or going to restaurants out of their cultural zone. If you wanted a great cheesesteak, D'andro's Steaks was the only place to go. But when it came to city or neighborhood issues, each respective neighborhood group liked to keep their opinions and neighborhood meetings separate from the others. Pastor Williams had found that out the hard way when he wanted to start his church, New Lighthouse Temple, at the most prime location in the neighborhood, at the corner of the Boulevard and Prince Street. He'd put two adjacent properties under contract. The first was an existing Baptist church that was for sale and had been around for many decades, and the second was a large residential lot right next to the Baptist church. Pastor Williams planned to semi-renovate the large, extremely high-ceilinged Baptist church, and then also add a one-level building next door for additional rooms and offices. It would be two separate buildings, connected only through one short indoor walkway. He had a few contractors confirm that only one opening, the size of a large doorway, would need to be cut into the existing church to make it properly work. The Baptist church property was already zoned as institutional, but the residential property would need a special exception permit granted by the city. When he went to the city council with his proposal for the new church, they told him to first meet with all the major neighborhood groups in the area and get their opinions. And if they supported his new church and the permit's approval, then the city council would most likely vote accordingly. Following their direction, Pastor Williams set up a late-night neighborhood meeting and invited all the respective groups. In addition to the mailed invitations, he called the president of each group to make sure they would attend. It also provided a good rapport with them in advance of the meeting. Even with the beautiful architectural renderings, the planned inspirational message about how the New Lighthouse Temple church would be a lighthouse to the community, refreshments, and even a few pre-committed church members planted in the audience to provide vocal support if no one gave it organically, he could not prevent the disaster that unfolded.

About fifty people showed up. However, once everyone realized that all the other cultural community groups had been invited to the same meeting, about two-thirds left before the meeting started. The remaining third just kept interjecting during the presentation with their immediate thoughts. If one group felt one way, the other groups would automatically be against it, and vice versa. And with every long pause, someone would yell out something like, "Why do we need another church?" Those seemed to come mostly from Mrs. Tucker. She lived across the street and was opposed to the church, as she knew it would be more noise and a parking nightmare on her block. The night ended badly. However, Pastor Williams did not give up. He conducted subsequent separate meetings for each group, and the remaining eleven meetings that it took went exceptionally well. He also spent a lot of days and late nights on the streets handing out gospel tracts, speaking to random people about the grace of God, giving coffee or food to the homeless, and being one of the most active participants of the neighborhood watch group, thus gaining the respect of each community group. Due to his efforts, each group's president, along with many residents, vocalized strong support for Pastor Williams and the new church during his *special exception* public hearing. The city council voted unanimously to grant the application without any debate. And just like he'd committed, New Lighthouse Temple did become a lighthouse to the community.

Joshua took another hit of the joint.

"Bruh, stop being greedy!" exclaimed Monty.

"Whatever, man. I'm the one that had a long day," said Joshua.

"I can't believe you are still working at that grocery store. I couldn't do those hours," said Monty.

"Man, I couldn't do your wallet," joked Joshua as he laughed hysterically. Monty joined with a sarcastic laugh, but then suddenly stopped to signal that Joshua's joke was not funny.

"Wasn't today your day off? I hope they give you a better bonus for that bull," said Monty.

"Well, I might get something. I think they are making plans for me," said Joshua, waiting for some response from Monty. But, Monty said nothing and changed the subject.

"You know I met up with Rachel last night," said Monty.

"Oh my god. Please do not tell me you had her in this car. Front seat or back seat?" asked Joshua.

"Both," said Monty as he laughed.

"Dude, you are disgusting. I'm not sitting in your car ever again!" exclaimed Joshua.

"I'm just playing, man," said Monty.

"You're such an idgit. It's getting late. I better get in this house," said Joshua as he chuckled.

"There you go calling me an idgit again. Why don't you say idiot like everyone else?" asked Monty.

"So, are you admitting that everyone calls you an idiot?" asked Joshua as he laughed hysterically.

Monty did not verbally respond but gave Joshua an evil look. Joshua ignored the stare.

"Idgit, idiot. It's the same thing, bruh. I just like the way idgit sounds. It sounds way better than just idiot," said Joshua with a smile.

"You better get your butt in your uncle's house before you hear him say, 'You don't have to agree with my rules . . .'" said Monty.

". . . but you sure will respect them!" said Monty and Joshua together as they both laughed.

Joshua walked into the house. Pastor Williams' dog, Rocky, greeted Joshua. Rocky was a sprollie, which was a springer spaniel–border collie mix. He had lots of energy, but other than an occasional playful bite, he was harmless. But with his loud, ear-piercing bark and the false but effective beware of dog signs in the front and back of the house, placed by Pastor Williams, no potential intruder or robber would think twice about this house as an option.

Joshua walked from the foyer into the living room.

"Look who's back. You left the house before I could speak to you," said Pastor Williams. He was sitting in the living room on his recliner watching Live News 10 on the television.

Joshua just smiled while he petted Rocky. Rocky followed him into the room as he wagged his tail.

"I'm not used to seeing you out of the house so early. Where did you go?" asked Pastor Williams.

"I had to work."

"On a Tuesday and in the morning?"

"Yeah, they really needed me."

"Does this mean you will be off on the weekends?"

"No. Well, not yet anyway," said Joshua.

"You know the church really misses you," said Pastor Williams, visibly and vocally displaying disappointment and sadness as Joshua has not been inside a church since his mother's funeral.

Joshua sighed. "Not right now, Uncle Jerry," said Joshua.

"Look. You know I'm the last person to push you to do something you don't want to do. I just remember how you enjoyed playing," said Pastor Williams.

Joshua remained silent. Pastor Williams realized his efforts were pointless. He tried to lighten the mood back up.

"We have to find a new organist. If I have to endure more Sundays of Brother Mark on that piano taking five minutes just to find the right key, I'm going to go crazy!" exclaimed Pastor Williams.

Joshua laughed. He remembered how Brother Mark had sometimes tried to accompany him during service on the electric piano that sat next to the organ, where the old piano used to sit. He'd taken a few formal piano lessons as a kid, but not many, and it showed.

"Does he still only know how to play in the two keys of C and D flat?" asked Joshua with a grin.

"Still the only two. Man, the service was amazing yesterday. I gave a great sermon," said Pastor Williams.

"Of course, you did," interjected Joshua sarcastically.

"And then when I started the altar call song, ready to reel them in, here goes Brother Mark trying to find the right key," said Pastor Williams. Pastor Williams changed his voice to make a few off-key notes while acting like he was playing an air keyboard with one finger, similar to someone who never took a typing class.

"So, the altar call mood was good, huh? What song did you sing?" asked Joshua, revealing some sign of nostalgia.

"'Here I Am to Worship,'" said Pastor Williams.

"Key of E?" asked Joshua as he heard in his head the first few music chords that he would have played to catch up to Pastor Williams in the song. He played a few more in his head before he stopped and went back to petting Rocky.

"Where's Auntie? I didn't see her car outside," asked Joshua.

"Out shopping. She's getting stuff for the community revival on Saturday. She said she was going to get some church decorations and kitchen supplies. But she took Sister Ruth, so I know they just went to look at hats and dresses," said Pastor Williams.

"I can't believe the community revival is this Saturday already. A whole year went by that quick. Time flies," said Joshua.

New Lighthouse Temple's community revival was an annual event that Pastor Williams had started about four years ago, two years before Joshua's mother died. It was open to the public. The first part of the day was more like an outside block party. Loud church music filling the streets, lots of food, face painting and balloon creations for the kids, clothing and household item donations, and raffle fundraisers. Last year, Pastor Williams had managed to get three professional football players to the event. The evening was a simple service inside the church, facilitated and performed mainly by the church's youth and teenagers. They would bring in guest choirs, praise dancers, and poetry speakers. Against the desire of a few church board members, everything was free, and they did not take up an offering during the revival. Pastor Williams felt the possibility of bringing in new lifetime members was worth the loss of money that day. The following Sunday, church attendance and people wanting to become members proved that to be true.

"Will you be able to make it to the community revival?" asked Pastor Williams. He'd hope Joshua would say yes.

"With work, I don't think so. Aren't you worried about—"

Pastor Williams immediately interrupted Joshua. "Don't say it. Don't speak it into existence."

They were talking about the two recent church fires, which occurred just within a few days of each other. The first one was at an old abandoned church, Ebenezer AME. The building had been abandoned for many years, and most people thought the fire was probably due to an electrical or building issue. But, yesterday, one large, prominent active sanctuary, Church of the Living God, caught fire. Even more unfortunate, the morning news purported that an unidentified man had been stuck inside the church during the fire, and firefighters were unable to rescue him in time.

"Are you watching the news to get an update?" asked Joshua.

"Yes," said Pastor Williams.

Joshua went in the kitchen and made himself a sandwich.

A few minutes later, he heard, "Breaking news!" from Live News 10 reporter Talia Jones on Pastor Williams' television. "We have an update on the latest church fire, a second fire that has now rocked the community, and only days after the fire of another nearby church just a few blocks away. The man who lost his life in the recent blaze has been identified as John Copeland, one of Church of the Living God's trustees and its bookkeeper."

Pastor Williams turned up the volume as the story continued. Joshua

27

continued to fix his snack, but his ears were attentive.

"A spokesperson from the church said a recent church renovation with building code upgrades and a quick response time from firefighters, being only blocks away, prevented the church from being completely destroyed. Unfortunately, one of their very own still lost his life," said Talia Jones. The story continued.

Once the church fire news segment was over, Joshua could hear his uncle's silence. He knew the thoughts that were going through his uncle's head. Could my church be next? Should I cancel the community revival? Joshua knew he had to say something to comfort his uncle or take his mind off his current thoughts and the fires. He took a deep breath, exhaled, waited a moment, and then went back into the room. At that moment, Joshua knew it was better to help take his uncle's mind off the fires.

"You know, I never thought to ask, maybe because I was so young, but whatever did happen to that old church piano I used to play?" asked Joshua with an upbeat tone.

Pastor Williams smiled, forgetting what he'd just watched on TV and eagerly jumping at the chance to reconnect with Joshua, even with a small conversation.

"No matter how many times we got it fixed, that piano always stayed out of tune, didn't it," said Pastor Williams as he laughed.

"Yes. I always had to avoid hitting those four broken keys. It was harder than it looked, especially when you would change the key on me," said Joshua with a smile.

Pastor Williams responded with excitement. "After our membership started climbing, we were finally able to afford the organ. Pastor Stevens from Mount Sinai Church of God in Christ kept telling me, 'Until you have enough money to afford a B3 Hammond organ, keep playing that old piano.'" Pastor Williams laughed again. "We donated it to

Mercy Retirement. They had it repaired and restrung. I believe it's still there today." Rocky barked as the front door opened. It was Angela, Pastor Williams' wife.

"Hello, Josh," said Angela.

"Hey, Auntie," said Joshua.

"Ask her if she bought anything for me," said Pastor Williams.

Joshua looked down at all the bags she had in her hands and raised a questioning eyebrow. Angela anticipated a petty comment from her husband as soon as she walked in the door with the bags. So, she immediately responded.

"Before you do that, ask your uncle if he fixed the dishwasher yet," responded Angela.

Pastor Williams had been avoiding calling the plumber. He told her that he did not want to spend the money when he had the experience to do it himself. But the reality was he just kept forgetting to get on the internet and find a self-help video to help him fix it.

"I am on it, Boobie," said Pastor Williams, calling Angela by his nickname for her. "I blocked time out this weekend." Angela looked at him with a smirk. Joshua felt this was his cue to leave.

"Alright. I'm going upstairs to my room," said Joshua.

"Good night, Josh," said Angela.

"Don't forget tomorrow!" Pastor Williams called after him as Joshua walked up the stairs. But as soon as Joshua's hand grabbed the stair's railing, he was already disconnected from the two and their conversation. Unfortunately, Joshua did not hear that last important part, and Pastor Williams did not repeat it.

"You are not going to remind him that Bishop Hines will be here tomorrow morning to help with planning for the community revival?" asked Angela in confusion.

"Nope. He's going to learn today." Pastor Williams laughed.

3

A Soulful Fellowship

Wednesday morning—three days before the community revival.

Joshua looked toward the altar and saw a group of people fighting. The ministers were trying to break it up. Those were the few in the church oblivious to the imminent danger. Joshua then looked around confused, wondering, *What is happening, and why?* He got up off his organ seat to run down to the altar to help break up the fight. As he moved forward, he saw in his periphery a shadow coming up from behind him. He felt its dark presence, its evil intentions. He turned his head to get a better look at what was approaching, but the dark shadow was too fast. It was already at his back, hovering over him.

This time, Joshua was able to discern the being, but only marginally better than in his other dreams. Its movement toward him was fluid, like it was floating on water, unobstructed by any objects between them. Its form was not a defined human body, but it was not animalistic either. Joshua could see some type of head on top of this form, a dark outline of a face, maybe cloaked or transparent. He saw no nose, no eyes, only the semblance of a mouth. It gave Joshua an evil grin. Joshua's eyes widened as he was struck in the head.

Joshua jumped up from his bed, heart racing. He could not believe that he was having this same old dream again. He'd stopped having them right after his mother died, but they'd started again the night of the Ebenezer AME fire. But this was the first time that he had been able to see this dark being up close in his dream with a little more detail. He wondered what it meant.

The sunlight through the window blinded his eyes as he awoke. He'd forgotten to close the blinds before he went to bed. He also heard laughter coming from downstairs. He realized that he'd forgotten that Bishop Hines was coming to the house at 11:00 a.m. to help his uncle with preparations for the community revival. Squinting his eyes, Joshua leaned over to his nightstand to grab his cell phone and look at the time: 11:30 a.m. And if there was any person in a black church across America that was always on time, it was Bishop Hines. If church service were scheduled to start at 10:00 a.m., he would make sure it started by 9:59. He did not care if only four people were in the church. If it even slightly appeared that there would be a delay in the start of the service by the worship leader, Bishop Hines would come out from the back office and start the service himself. If that happened, the following church staff meeting would not be pleasant for anyone. Right or wrong, Bishop Hines felt that his strict rules weeded out those who were not truly committed to serving God or the church. Therefore, Joshua knew he had no choice but to get up. Even more potentially awkward, to get out the house, he would have to go down the stairs that dropped right into the living room area where Pastor Williams and Bishop Hines would most definitely be sitting.

Joshua reluctantly got out of bed. He proceeded to the bathroom to do his "quick wash," with some allergy drops in his eyes just in case. As Joshua walked back to his bedroom, he paused at the top of the steps. He looked down at the rail, the steps, and the first-level wood floor, but something seemed different. Joshua waited a few seconds and confirmed the weird feeling.

He shrugged off the feeling, and when he got back in his room, he put on the same jeans he'd had on yesterday and grabbed two shirts that were on the floor. He gave each shirt a sniff test to determine which one was cleaner, or, for Joshua, which one was less smelly than the other. His nose picked a winner, the white shirt with thin blue vertical stripes. It looked better with the jeans anyway. He walked out of the room and approached the steps. When he put his hand on the rail and galloped down the steps, he heard the voices clearer as he approached the bottom. He had a quick thought of how awkward his late appearance would be to their conversation; his name must have already been mentioned by now. He thought, Either Uncle Jerry or Aunt Angela surely said, 'He's upstairs sleeping in late, like always.' As he reached the bottom step, he decided to embrace the situation with the hope of making it less awkward by speaking first.

"Hello, everyone!" yelled Joshua. He spoke before he could fully see everyone, but he waited for the banter to start.

"Look at this. The dead walks the earth," said Pastor Williams in a sly, raspy voice.

Joshua thought of how his mom would always say only God could resurrect him from his sleep. He felt a brief pang of sorrow, thinking about his mom.

He quickly glanced around the room and saw Pastor Williams, Aunt Angela, and Bishop Hines; in his periphery was an unknown woman. He did not get a good look, but before he could entirely turn his head, his Aunt Angela said, "Hello, Josh!"

Bishop Hines continued with the greetings. "Morning, Joshua."

Bishop Hines was one of the very few people that called Joshua by his given name. When Pastor Williams had been a just member and minister of Bishop Hines' church, International Covenant Ministries, he told Bishop Hines that he wanted to go into the ministry. Unlike most of the other ministers in Bishop Hines' church, Pastor Williams was always on time and attended every single service and meeting. He was also in charge of the church's maintenance and did most of the repairs and upkeep himself, saving the church lots of money. Because of this, Bishop Hines was very fond of Pastor Williams, so much that Bishop Hines took more time to mentor him in the ministry than any of his other ministers. This relationship paid off for Pastor Williams.

When Pastor Williams started his own church, Bishop Hines fully supported him, both spiritually and financially. Bishop Hines helped him secure the construction and mortgage loan and provided a hefty stipend so that Pastor Williams could be a full-time pastor from the very start. Even though he did not ask for it, Bishop Hines did not start seeing any money back from all of this until Pastor Williams started the community revival. Pastor Williams was so happy to send the first official "love offering" from New Lighthouse Temple to Bishop Hines' church. Angela assumed this was the primary reason why her husband always spent so much time with Joshua. Even though Pastor Williams never said it, Angela thought Pastor Williams wanted to mentor and groom Joshua to take over the church when he got older or help him start his own, just like Bishop Hines did for him.

"Good morning, Bishop Hines," said Joshua.

"Joshua, I would like you to meet Lauren Alexander. She is attending our church's School of Theology. She is extremely intelligent and like a daughter to me. And I must say, she is one of the few people that has been able to keep me in proper check with my ministry and missions work," said Bishop Hines. Bishop Hines was obviously immensely proud of her.

Joshua looked over and saw Lauren. She sat at Pastor Williams' desk, but was positioned in the chair so that she was parallel to it. Her legs were free, but not fully turned to the group.

When they arrived, she had intentionally sat in this manner, so that she could look on her cell phone without appearing to be rude, but also be able to turn toward the group, in full degree, and at any given moment, to join in on the conversation.

Joshua looked at her with a glance and smiled. "Hi. It's very nice to meet you, Lauren."

She smiled back and said, "Hi."

"Joshua, Lauren has the same last name as your middle name: Alexander," said Angela smiling with intention.

"That's nice," said Joshua. He did not know what else to say.

He quickly looked away before anyone noticed his expression of unexpected amazement at an attractive woman being in the house with them today. Even though Lauren was sitting down, Joshua could tell in that quick glance that she appeared to be very athletic. She had on a light yellow sundress with a pattern of blue and white flowers. Her back was straight, chest forward, and eyes wide open, all signs of confidence. The dress showed a fairly good neck and upper chest line, but it was not too revealing. It showed her youth, but it was appropriate for traveling with Bishop Hines. He was immediately attracted to her, and it surprised him. He could tell that she was different from other girls he'd previously dated. He was intrigued by her presence and wanted to know more about her. But at the moment, the focus was on Bishop Hines being there. So, he disregarded his feelings.

"Uncle Jerry mentioned you added a theology school of some sort to your church. How's it going?" asked Joshua.

"It's going very well," said Bishop Hines. "We were able to acquire a large tract of land at a reasonable price and built a forty-thousand-square-foot dual-level building. We have about three hundred students enrolled this year."

Now, Pastor Williams had done more than just mention this school to Joshua. He spoke to him about it weekly. Also, Pastor Williams did not mind Josh working at the grocery store, as it was paying more money than expected. But he still needed help at the church and felt Joshua could excel in a gospel music ministry.

"What type of classes are taught at your school?" asked Joshua, looking to Lauren.

"Well, I am getting my master's in divinity," said Lauren.

"Sounds impressive. I work at Penn Fresh. So, I guess I am getting my master's in groceries," said Joshua.

Everyone laughed. Lauren smiled.

"Does that mean you know how to control your shrinkage?" asked Lauren with a raised eyebrow.

Joshua chuckled. Everyone else was either surprised or confused by her response. Pastor Williams was both. He knew nothing about retail and was wondering what she meant by it.

"My shrink is down one hundred basis points," said Joshua.

"Sounds impressive," said Lauren.

"What? Your shrink is what?" asked Pastor Williams, looking at Joshua confused, thinking it was a sexual joke.

Joshua immediately responded, "Oh. In retail, it is another term for stolen items or products that you have to throw away. It can really hurt your bottom. I mean, your bottom line!" Joshua shook his head in embarrassment from his misstatement. Lauren laughed. Joshua attempted to clarify his statement more. "From your bottom line, I mean, your profit or loss. Lauren must already know my store is in a tough area," said Joshua.

In his mind, Joshua was still shaking his head. He felt slightly embarrassed. Lauren was obviously smart and articulate. But Joshua was shocked that she would use that retail joke in front of his uncle or even Bishop Hines. He also felt very intrigued. His thoughts about her confidence were confirmed. Her presence in the room even stood out from that of Bishop Hines. That revealed a lot, as Bishop Hines had a commanding presence. His height at 6'4", deep voice, and wealth of knowledge on just about every topic from religion to history to physics made him stand out in any place. Joshua thought, for Lauren to compare to that, maybe even exceed it, there must be something extraordinary about her. Was it her presence that he'd felt when he was upstairs?

"Are you ready?" Bishop Hines' voice interrupted Joshua's thoughts.

"Yes, Bishop. Josh, we are going to head over to the church. We'll be back soon," said Pastor Williams.

"Community revival planning?" asked Joshua.

"Yes. Plus, the Bishop has come up with some rather good ideas to counteract the negativity and community fear as a result of the recent fires," said Pastor Williams.

"Counteract?" asked Joshua.

"The fires already have many churchgoers concerned. If more churches are set on fire, then more people will be afraid and possibly stop coming to church altogether," said Bishop Hines.

"And with more fires, more people will lose a sense of security in our building, maybe even start losing their faith," said Angela.

Lauren chimed in, "You have so many churches in this community. Eventually, if not already, questions will start regarding who is doing this and, more importantly, why? It could start pitting church against church, member against member," said Lauren.

"Yes. The enemy is at work, and he does not take a day off, and neither can we. Too much is at stake," said Bishop Hines.

Joshua's eyes and mind were wide open now, especially with Lauren's comment. *Who could be setting these fires, and why? What if they* need-

36

ed to cancel the community revival? So many people looked forward to it. So many lives had changed because of it.

"Josh. Can Lauren stay here?" asked Angela.

"Sure. I don't care," said Joshua.

At this moment, Joshua remembered that he'd forgotten to brush his teeth. He thought of a way to run back upstairs for a quick brush and mouthwash rinse without being too obvious.

"Okay. I will let Rocky back in the house," said Pastor Williams. Rocky was outside in a makeshift caged pen area that Joshua had built for him.

Everyone left, except Joshua and Lauren. Pastor Williams reopened the door and let Rocky in the house. Joshua bent down as Rocky ran to him to lick his face.

"He is a really cute dog," said Lauren.

"Thanks," said Joshua. "I will be back. I'm going to go wash my hands and face." He petted Rocky again, which was more of a thank-you for giving him the perfect excuse to go back upstairs.

Joshua ran up the steps, skipping every other step. Lauren pulled her laptop out of her bag and sat at the kitchen table. Joshua came back downstairs, teeth thoroughly brushed, and sat down at the table with her. He pulled out his cell phone. Lauren noticed the strong mouthwash smell still on Joshua. Joshua saw her looking at him and smelled it too.

"You smell, umm, interestingly fresh," joked Lauren.

"Nothing like getting rid of doggy breath," said Joshua.

Lauren laughed. Joshua smiled.

"Did you forget the Bishop was coming here this morning, or do you just love sleeping in late?" asked Lauren.

"Both," Joshua replied. "Bishop Hines is just like another uncle to me. But I was not expecting new company."

"You mean female company?" asked Lauren.

"Wow. You sure know how to put a person on their heels. How am I supposed to respond to that?"

"Wait. You wear heels?" Lauren said with a smile.

Joshua laughed. "Probably not as good as you."

"No one wears heels as good as me," said Lauren.

Joshua paused for a few seconds. He thought about his mom: how she used to get dressed up for events, including church; how the basic black-and-white usher outfit was not her style, but she even wore that well. He then thought about the heels she was wearing the day she died, how Joshua saw them pointing up in the air as she lay on the church floor from her heart attack.

Lauren interrupted his thought. "Hello? Cat got your tongue?"

Joshua quickly disregarded his current thought and came up with a witty response. "I was just imagining you walking in heels down a modeling runway. But then, you got near the end and stumbled in front of everyone." Joshua laughed.

"You think you're funny," said Lauren.

"From hearing your laugh, it sounds like you think I am too," said Joshua. He then took control of the conversation before Lauren could respond. "What are you working on?" asked Joshua as he pointed to her laptop.

"My thesis paper," said Lauren.

Joshua knew Lauren was young, but maybe older than him if she was getting her master's degree. He made a subtle attempt to uncover her age. "A master's, right? I'm not asking your age, but . . ." said Joshua with an incomplete sentence, to not offend her.

"Then don't," said Lauren with a stoic face.

Joshua was stunned by her response. Worried he had just made a huge and regrettable mistake, he had no clue how to respond. Lauren knew it.

"Relax, Joshua. I'm only kidding," said Lauren. Joshua breathed a sigh of relief.

"It was hard, but I was able to get my bachelor's degree in three years instead of four," said Lauren.

"Now that's definitely impressive," said Joshua enthusiastically.

"Thank you. We are on break, but I want to accomplish as much as I can on my thesis during this time off," said Lauren.

"Like an essay?" asked Joshua.

Lauren chuckled. "Sort of, but a lot more research, a lot more sources, and definitely a lot more pages," said Lauren.

"What is it on?" asked Joshua.

"It's a lot. But I can tell you my draft thesis statement, at least. That is if you want to hear it," said Lauren.

"Sure. Whatever that is," said Joshua.

"Again, it's incomplete and just a draft," said Lauren.

Joshua noticed how she had just lost her confidence. "Just say it. I promise it won't change what I already think of you," said Joshua.

Lauren knew that statement on the surface could mean good or bad. But since he'd kindly smiled while he said it, good was the most likely choice. She felt more comfortable in sharing her thesis statement. She grabbed her laptop, pulled it closer to her, and read.

"Okay, here it is: 'Many church pastors or spiritual leaders, knowingly and unknowingly, deceive their members and visitors by not teaching the entire Bible. Although these omissions may keep Christians grounded in the belief and hope for a better life, it limits their true realm spiritual growth. This positively and negatively affects the church by . . .'

"Well, that's all I have so far for the statement. But I have been doing the actual research for quite some time," said Lauren.

"Again, impressive," said Joshua, using the same phrase. This time Lauren gave Joshua a stern look, as she assumed he was being facetious. But he was genuinely impressed and intrigued by her thesis statement, even though he did not fully understand it.

"Seriously, it is, Lauren. But what do you mean by, what did you say?" Joshua paused, trying to remember. ". . . True realm and things in the Bible not taught by churches?"

Lauren responded, "The true realm is just another word for the spirit realm, beyond what our eyes can see. Christians mostly refer to it as the spirit world, but it is just the place where the dead and other spirits and our God Almighty reside."

"Interesting," said Joshua. He meant it. He'd never heard someone talk about where spirits reside after death like this.

"Some believe that there is a line between our world and the true realm, and humans typically get close to that realm in their dreams. But that is all just speculation and theory," said Lauren.

Joshua responded without even thinking of his mysterious dream. "You are talking nonsense to me right now. What does all of that have to do with the Bible and churches?" asked Joshua.

"Did you know there are passages in the Bible that show how people used to talk to the dead regularly?" asked Lauren, excited.

"You mean talk to actual ghosts? I highly doubt that." Joshua was skeptical, yet intrigued.

"Yes, Joshua. Actual spirits that were once living human beings that passed away," said Lauren.

He finally realized that she kept calling him Joshua instead of Josh, just like Bishop Hines. Bishop Hines was the only person he allowed to call him Joshua. Given Bishop Hines' presence and good intentions, Joshua was okay with it, but it was more toleration than acceptance. However, hearing Lauren say Joshua sounded different. He thought It felt appropriate, even soothing. Joshua then responded.

"I've been taught that ghosts aren't real, or that it is something like witchcraft or demonic spirits. Isn't a person's soul either in heaven or hell or resting somewhere like purgatory?" asked Joshua.

"You remember Saul in the Bible?" asked Lauren.

"Which one? Weren't there two or more Sauls?" asked Joshua.

"Wow. You remember your Bible. You continue to impress me, Sir Joshua," said Lauren with a little laughter.

"I did sit through a thousand sermons as a kid and had to pay attention waiting for them to start preaching in a music key for me to join in on the organ," said Joshua.

Joshua was referring to when the charismatic vocal preacher spoke in a musical key, which many churchgoers viewed as the Spirit, or Anointing of God, speaking through the preacher. Joshua loved to accompany any minister on the organ when this type of preaching occurred. He would always put creative chords together to match the tune and statement of the minister. And if he did miss some keys or play something wrong, no one would ever notice, as they were too focused or hypnotized with the preacher's message. It just sounded good in the background.

"Yeah, but when was the last time you've been in a church service?" joked Lauren knowing he'd work weekends.

Joshua paused for a minute with the thought of his mother's funeral, but he responded.

"I work. But probably around the last time you were there," Joshua said with confidence. Joshua was right. Lauren may have had strong church acumen and biblical knowledge, but he could tell she was not a regular churchgoer.

"Wait, what? I went to church all my life as a kid. I attend a church college, and I am getting my master's in divinity. You don't get more

41

church than that," said Lauren.

"Hey, I am not saying that you don't ever attend church. But I've been in church all my life as well. You just don't fit the profile of someone who has the patience to sit in a long Sunday morning service, then attend a late evening service, Tuesday night Bible study, a Thursday church meeting, then Friday night praise service, and then do it all over again the following week. Even the way you sat in my uncle's chair showed me how you don't like to be fully engaged in a conversation if it doesn't interest you," said Joshua.

Lauren smiled as she knew Joshua was right. She loved to learn, but as she got older, she hated the politics and protocols of the church. The more she learned about herself and the Bible, the more she felt her divine purpose was outside of the four walls of a church, either learning or actively helping others in need.

She nodded and said, "That's fair. But back to what we were talking about: Saul the King. In the Old Testament, there was a point where he was having a hard time being king. He wanted to get sound advice from the former judge named Samuel," said Lauren.

Joshua interrupted, "Yes. I remember hearing about Samuel."

"The problem was Samuel was dead. So, guess what Saul did?" asked Lauren. Joshua responded without thought.

"What did he do?"

"He went to a psychic to raise Samuel's spirit from the true realm and speak to him," said Lauren.

"Samuel's ghost? Are you telling me that he spoke to Samuel's actual spirit?" asked Joshua.

"Yes," said Lauren.

"Did the Bishop tell you that or did you read that in a book or something?" asked Joshua suspiciously.

"If you mean a separate book written by some theologian, then no.

It's in the Bible, First Samuel, Chapter Twenty-Eight."

Joshua grabbed his cell phone and went to the chapter on his King James Bible app.

"Go ahead. Read if you don't believe me," said Lauren.

Joshua read as she sat quietly, looking at his face. His eyes slightly squinted, looking fierce, but focused. And his posture was straight, a sign of confidence to her. However, this was more likely from the habit of always sitting in front of a church during entire sermons. That was a post where you could not appear to be tired or appear slouching. She watched his eyes so intensely into the reading. His chest was rising and lowering slowly with every breath. He looked calm, but she could tell he was excited.

Joshua got to the eleventh verse, and then read:

11 Then said the woman, Whom shall I bring up unto thee? And he said, Bring me up Samuel.

12 And when the woman saw Samuel, she cried with a loud voice: and the woman spake to Saul, saying, Why hast thou deceived me? for thou art Saul.

13 And the king said unto her, Be not afraid: for what sawest thou? And the woman said unto Saul, I saw gods ascending out of the earth.

14 And he said unto her, What form is he of? And she said, An old man cometh up; and he is covered with a mantle. And Saul perceived that it was Samuel, and he stooped with his face to the ground, and bowed himself

15 And Samuel said to Saul, Why hast thou disquieted me, to bring me up? And Saul answered, I am sore distressed; for the Philistines make war against me, and God is departed from me, and answereth me no more, neither by prophets, nor by dreams . . .

Joshua read in amazement. He thought, *This was in the Bible the whole time, and no one ever mentioned it to me? Someone in the Bible is talking to a real ghost, and that ghost is talking back.* But he glanced back up and paid more attention to verse thirteen, where the woman "saw gods ascending out of the earth." He began wondering, *Who are these other "gods," and why were they ascending from the earth? And God no longer answered Saul by prophets or dreams. So, God can communicate to you through your dreams? What about my reoccurring dream?*

"That's crazy!" exclaimed Joshua. "The only time I ever heard about Saul was when a minister was preaching about David and how . . ." Joshua then continued in a loud voice, mocking a preacher's charismatic sermon with pauses and breaks in between each phrase, "When God . . . says, it's your time! It's your time! Saul disobeyed God . . . and failed! But David . . . obeyed! And succeeded! Can I get an Amen church! I can't hear you!"

"Amen!" shouted Lauren.

"I said, can I get an Amen!" exclaimed Joshua.

"Amen!" shouted Lauren again.

Lauren got up and started mimicking a praise dance shout. Joshua joined in by stomping his foot hard on the kitchen floor with a fast-paced beat, and then playing an air organ while making the organ music with his voice. Their fun went on for about thirty more seconds. Joshua noticed Lauren was starting to sweat, and it made her skin glisten. He loved her skin tone: the smooth transition from her face to her neck, from her neck to her chest. She saw him looking at her and smiled.

Rocky barked a few times. Then the front door opened, and everyone rushed back into the house with Pastor Williams first in the door. He noticed the loud noise and movements of Joshua and Lauren. They had stopped one second too late and were awkwardly noticed by everyone. Joshua and Lauren immediately stopped their fun and attempted to calm down as if they were doing nothing. But, Pastor

Williams saw Lauren sweating and out of breath, and Joshua looked guilty of a crime. Bishop Hines saw as well and raised his eyebrow at them. Angela noticed too.

"Well, at least they didn't kill each other," said Angela as she walked through the room.

"Well, only one of us would remain standing," said Lauren in an ominous tone.

"Yeah . . . in heels!" added Joshua.

Lauren and Joshua started laughing hysterically. The rest of the group looked at them in confusion. Then they looked at each other to see if anyone else got the inside joke.

Joshua and Lauren glanced at each other with the same thought, *They were not gone long enough to complete their agenda.*

"Why are you back so early?" asked Joshua.

"Your uncle forgot the keys to the church," said Angela.

"I could have brought them over," said Joshua.

"Yeah, but now it's lunchtime," said Pastor Williams. He was embarrassed that he'd forgotten the keys. He felt even more disappointed that the day planned with his longtime mentor, Bishop Hines, was not as organized as he'd hoped.

"We have lunch already prepared," said Angela as she started pulling out food from the refrigerator and oven.

Joshua got a text. It was from the store manager, Rick, his boss:

[12:37 PM] Things went well yesterday. We have a lot to talk about when you come back to the store.

Joshua replied:

[12:38] Sounds good.

They all sat at the table. Bishop Hines said the grace.

"Oh Lord of mercy and truth, the alpha and omega, the great I am, we are grateful today by the blessings that you bestow upon us daily.

We thank you for forgiving us of all of our sins; and we thank you for the food we are about to receive that has been wonderfully prepared for us. Bless this house and bless those today that do not have anything to eat. In Jesus' name, we pray. Amen."

"Let brotherly love continue," said Pastor Williams.

"Let brotherly love continue," said everyone, except Lauren. She looked at Joshua, confused.

"Oh. It's just a longtime tradition that my uncle and our family have after saying grace. It's a scripture," said Joshua.

"Yes. Hebrews chapter thirteen. I just never heard it said with grace," said Lauren.

"I added that last part about not having food to eat for that man that was outside of your church," said Bishop Hines.

Now it was Joshua's turn to look confused. "Is he talking about Zeke?" asked Joshua.

"Yes," said Pastor Williams. "But he was not directly outside of the church. He was at the end of the block, talking to himself."

"Zeke was talking to himself?" asked Joshua, concerned.

"Yes," said Pastor Williams.

"That is weird. I've never seen him do that before," said Joshua.

"Me neither," said Angela.

Ezekiel Wilson, known as Zeke, was a homeless man that had been in the neighborhood for years. They had a few others, but Ezekiel was the most familiar. He had always been a well-dressed man that came across as very smart and articulate. He'd previously worked at the Shields Iron Factory for many years. Every time Joshua saw him, Joshua would always say, "Hey, Mr. Zeke. How are you doing?" and Ezekiel would reply, "Hey, Josh. Just busy taking over the world. You do the same." Due to a few bad stock investments and then being laid off from the factory, Ezekiel lost everything. He walked up and down the streets aimlessly, wearing the same clothes day after day. One day, Ezekiel walked out in front of a car and was hit. He said he did not see the vehicle, but everyone thought it was a suicide attempt. The car slowed down and swerved away just in time to avoid completely running him over. However, the impact broke one of his legs pretty badly. Ever since then, he'd given up on himself and society. He walked the streets and the Boulevard, back and forth, without a purpose or direction.

"You should invite him, and the other homeless, to the community revival," said Bishop Hines.

"We do. We invite them to our monthly soup kitchen as well. A few others show up all the time, like this homeless couple named Amelia and Robert, but not Ezekiel," said Pastor Williams.

"I've known him for years. He's a nice guy. But you can't change a man that doesn't want to be changed," said Joshua.

"You're right. But it is still up to us to make the offers and also pray for him. Prayer changes things," said Angela.

"God didn't give up on us. Therefore, you should not give up on this Zeke," said Bishop Hines.

"We should pray to the universe for his soul," said Lauren.

"Pray to the what?" asked Pastor Williams.

"The universe. It's part of the true realm," Joshua said hesitantly, as more of a question to Lauren than a response to Pastor Williams.

"True what?" asked Pastor Williams, now even more frustrated.

"Universe and true realm," repeated Lauren.

"Listen. Don't bring any of that witchcraft nonsense into my house. If you are not talking about Jesus, then I rebuke you!" said Pastor Williams angrily as he stood up from his chair and the table.

Joshua and Lauren started laughing hysterically.

"Wow. He really put the rebuke on you, Lauren," said Joshua, laughing even harder. It was hysterical to Joshua as Pastor Williams had done that to him many times before, especially as a kid.

"Calm down, Jerry. Sit back down and at least listen to the girl first," said Angela in a calm, slow voice.

Pastor Williams reluctantly sat back down, yielding to the request of his wife.

"Jesus is Lord. Now you say it, Pastor Williams," said Lauren.

"Say what?" asked a suspicious Pastor Williams expecting a trap.

"Say, Jesus is Lord," said a patient Lauren.

"Jesus is Lord," said Pastor Williams.

"See, no witchcraft here with you or me. We both are in the Spirit of God," said Lauren.

Pastor Williams looked confused. Bishop Hines chimed into the conversation to help clarify.

"By you both saying Jesus is Lord, she just confirmed that neither one of you are possessed, working in witchcraft, or attempting to destroy the Kingdom of God. Some believe that Satan, or his workers, cannot say the words, Jesus is Lord," said Bishop Hines.

Lauren continued, "Pastor, do you believe in God, Jesus Christ, and salvation by the Grace of God?"

"Absolutely," said Pastor Williams.

"So do I. But, do you believe in aliens?" asked Lauren.

"No!" said Pastor Williams.

"Why not?" asked Lauren.

"Cause it's not in the Bible," said Pastor Williams.

"DNA cloning, airplanes, same-day delivery service, and popsicles are not in the Bible either. But aren't they real?" asked Lauren.

"That's different," said Pastor Williams.

"If the Bible isn't large enough to hold everything done or created in the past, present, and future for just Earth, how do you expect that it could include the same for millions of planets and galaxies thousands of light-years away?" asked Lauren.

"Let me get this straight. Are you saying that you believe that aliens are out there in space?" asked Pastor Williams as he looked up and pointed to the ceiling.

"No. I am just saying, as big and complex as our universe is, wouldn't you be foolish to think our planet is the only one that could sustain life? I will not limit our great and powerful God and say that I know for sure that he did not create life on one of the other millions of planets out there. Just last week, the Chinese confirmed that they are receiving radio frequency bursts or signals from outer space. Where are these sounds coming from, and who is sending them?" asked Lauren.

"Well. Again, the Bible does not say anything about that," said Pastor Williams.

"In Genesis, the Bible talks about the 'firmament.' Do you know what that is?" asked Lauren.

"It's the sky. I mean it's the separation between sky and space," said Pastor Williams, unconfident.

"Maybe. But if what you say is true, isn't it interesting that this separation that God created, mentioned in Genesis, makes objects from outer space burn up with extreme heat when entering Earth's atmosphere? Three thousand degrees Fahrenheit, to be exact," said Lauren.

"And, so what?" asked Pastor Williams.

"It sounds to me that God put a protective force field around the Earth. And why would He need to do that if there were nothing in space that should have us worried? Everything has a purpose, from our nails, to our eyebrows, to trees, to everything God has created. Nothing was done or made by accident," said Lauren.

"Interesting thoughts, Lauren," said Angela.

"All I care about is going to heaven, and how many souls on this earth I can help save to bring with me," said Pastor Williams.

Lauren responded, "I am so glad to hear that. All I care about is the truth. For all we know, Earth could be God's seventh time creating life."

"Lauren has another great point. Everyone at one time thought the Earth was flat, and the Earth was the center of the universe; most of them were Bible-believing, God-fearing men," said Angela.

"And you see how she keeps me and all of the teachers at our school on our toes," said Bishop Hines. There was a long pause of silence. Pastor Williams got up from the table and got a glass out of the cabinet to get water from the refrigerator.

Joshua felt the awkwardness of the disruption. He attempted to wittingly interrupt the silence.

"Oh my god! I could eat a horse right now! Can we eat?"

"Josh, your language!" exclaimed Angela with an angered look.

"Sorry, Auntie. Please forgive me. Let me say that again. I am so hungry. May we please eat?" asked Joshua in a more respectful tone. Lauren chuckled.

Pastor Williams looked at Lauren and Joshua, and then at his wife, Angela, with a look of disapproval. They continued to eat with intentional small talk. Lauren enjoyed the meal.

"I'm stuffed. Thank you so much for the meal, Mrs. Williams," said Lauren, smiling.

"You're very welcome, Lauren. We enjoyed your thoughts and company," said Angela.

"Same here. However, I must go to the library and study. Are you ready to go, Bishop?" asked Lauren.

"Sure. I have a couple of mission work conference calls for the rest of the day, but we can start with the community revival planning again tomorrow. This time real early, Pastor," said Bishop Hines as he gave Pastor Williams a stern look.

"Works for me," said Pastor Williams.

"I'll walk you out," said Joshua as he looked at Lauren.

Joshua led Bishop Hines and Lauren out the door. Bishop Hines continued to the car.

"You made a typically uninteresting day very interesting," said Joshua as he smiled.

Lauren smiled back. "Well, you made a typically boring day very fun," said Lauren.

Joshua felt connected to her. He felt the attraction, but he knew it was more profound than that. It was as if his soul could feel her soul. He wanted to kiss her, and it felt like he should kiss her, but they'd just met. He said to himself, *Josh, calm down. You don't even know her.* He started sniffling from his allergies. His nose was about to drip. But, before he could use his shirt to wipe it, Lauren interjected.

"Don't you dare use your shirt! That's nasty!" she exclaimed. She pulled out a tissue from her purse. But instead of her handing it to him, she took it upon herself to wipe his nose. Joshua was stunned.

"Wait. Did you just wipe my nose?" asked Joshua.

Lauren was shocked herself. She'd just cleaned off Joshua's nose with no advance thought. Her action was automatic. She thought, *Oh my goodness. How could I just do that?* She felt embarrassed, but she played it off as if it was Joshua's fault.

"The wind is blowing. I didn't want that crap flying on me, you germ boy," said Lauren. She handed him the used tissue and reached in her purse to grab a fresh one that she gave to him as well. "Just in case you need another," she said.

"Thanks. Can I get your number?" asked Joshua.

"Well, I already have yours. The Bishop gave it to me along with your uncle's phone number the last time he was here. It was just in case I couldn't reach him," said Lauren. Joshua could not remember when Bishop Hines had been there last. It sounded strange, but he was distracted by the anticipation of what she was going to say next.

"I'll text or call you tomorrow afternoon when I take a break from writing. Is that okay?" asked Lauren, unsure of herself.

Joshua was thrilled; he couldn't suppress his grin. He did not want her to leave without having a way of contacting her. But, he also did not want to look like he was a creep or stalking her either. He reminded himself to remain calm and stay cool.

"Sure. That sounds good," said Joshua.

Bishop Hines blew the car horn with two short, quick beeps.

"All right. I gotta go," said Lauren.

"Goodbye," said Joshua.

"Goodbye," she said with a smile.

Lauren walked to the car. As she opened the door, she looked back at Joshua. He smiled at her, and she smiled back. He turned around and walked back into the house. Before he got fully into the house, though, he stopped in the foyer. He felt some type of heaviness in the next room. Before Joshua took another step into the house, Pastor Williams called for him.

"Josh! Hurry up and get in here," said Pastor Williams.

"Yes, Uncle?" asked Joshua as he walked into the living room.

Pastor Williams was sitting at his desk.

"Listen. I know I am not your father, but I just want you to be careful around Lauren. I don't think it would be a good idea for you to hang around her," said Pastor Williams.

"Why? Because you disagree with her or think she believes in aliens?" said Joshua with a chuckle.

"No. She just doesn't seem rooted or grounded in Jesus Christ," Pastor Williams said firmly.

"Well, the Bishop doesn't mind her around," Joshua pointed out.

"Just be careful. I know a bad influence when I see one," said Pastor

Williams, ending the discussion.

Joshua ran up the steps, skipping every other step up to his room. He lay down on his bed, thinking about Lauren. He could not believe how much fun he'd had with her in such a short time, and how he felt completely comfortable around her, and he didn't even know her. She actually wiped my nose. She must feel comfortable too. He remembered how he could feel her soul next to his. It was like their souls were communicating, getting to know each other, or maybe they already knew each other, and they were reconnecting. Either way, he could not wait for her break tomorrow to hear from her again.

Pastor Williams looked at Angela. "I don't like this one bit. Why is the Bishop bringing this young girl around anyway? Who is she?"

"Honey, I don't know who she is or why she is hanging around the Bishop. Only the Bishop knows that. Maybe you should ask him. But I do know your desire. You cannot expect Joshua to be something that he does not want to be himself. He is his own person. God may have something totally different planned for him, maybe even more than you think," said Angela.

Pastor Williams shook his head in disagreement. The house phone rang, so Pastor Williams answered it instead of her.

"Pastor speaking," said Pastor Williams.

"Pastor. It's Officer Reese," said Officer Joe Reese.

Pastor Williams was familiar with all the officers at Station 98, especially Officer Joe Reese. Pastor Williams and Officer Reese were close friends. This friendship spawned from the two working to rehabilitate criminals and from Pastor Williams being part of the neighborhood night watch group.

"Hey, Joe. How can I help you?" asked Pastor Williams.

"Do you have time to stop by the station tomorrow morning?" asked Officer Reese.

"I might. What's going on?" asked Pastor Williams.

"It's regarding the fires. There is something strange going on that our investigators cannot explain. I thought you might be able to help puzzle it out," said Officer Reese.

"I'm not sure how I can help, but I will try," said Pastor Williams.

"We are hoping you can. Because if not, other churches and the community revival may be in great danger," said Officer Reese.

Pastor Williams could hear the urgency in Officer Reese's voice. He knew it was important.

"Okay. I will be there," assured Pastor Williams.

"Thanks, Pastor. See you tomorrow," said Officer Reese.

Pastor Williams hung up. He had a concerned look on his face.

"What's wrong?" asked Angela.

"Joe just said we all might be in danger," said Pastor Williams.

"Danger?" asked Angela as she looked at him, stricken.

4

Unlawful Grace

Thursday morning—two days before the community revival.

It was 9:30 a.m. when Pastor Williams and Bishop Hines walked into Station 98. They had just come from eating breakfast at the Liberty Diner. They were dressed more relaxed than usual. Station 98's front desk officer, Suzie, hardly recognized Pastor Williams with his khaki shorts and flip-flops. She was going to make a joke about them going to the beach, but she knew Pastor Williams could be too serious at times, let alone find a good joke funny.

"Hello, Pastor," said Suzie.

"Hello, Suzie," said Pastor Williams.

"Please sign in," said Suzie.

"It's pretty quiet around here," said Pastor Williams as he signed in the visitors' log.

Looking behind the counter, Pastor Williams could only see two officers at their desks, and one over near the breakroom getting coffee. No one was talking, and the phones were not ringing off the hook like the last time he had been there.

"It's quiet right now. But that was not the case last night. Just give it a few minutes; things will start picking up," responded Suzie.

"The enemy never sleeps," said Bishop Hines.

"Ain't that the truth!" exclaimed Suzie. "I just wish he took a long nap now and then. God knows I need one myself," joked Suzie. Bishop Hines laughed. To no surprise, Pastor Williams did not.

"I'll buzz up Reese," said Suzie.

Pastor Williams and Bishop Hines sat down on the bench along the wall. But, as soon as they'd sat down, Officer Reese came out from the back to greet them.

"Thanks for coming in, Pastor," said Officer Reese.

"No problem. Anything for the community. You remember Bishop Hines, right?" asked Pastor Williams.

"Of course. Always an honor, Bishop Hines," said Officer Reese.

"Nice to see you again, Officer Reese," said Bishop Hines.

"The Bishop is assisting me with the community revival preparation. Do you mind if he joins us today?" asked Pastor Williams.

"Not at all. I am sure the Bishop will be interested in this as well. And the more thoughts on this, the better."

"Is this regarding the recent fires?" asked Bishop Hines.

"Yes. Come on back," said Officer Reese.

Officer Reese led them past the front counter down the hallway, then past a few of the station's interrogation rooms, all the way to the end of the hall. Officer Reese opened the door and stopped to allow Pastor Williams and Bishop Hines into the room first. A man in a suit, with a visible badge on his belt, was already in the room. He was standing in front of two chairs situated in front of two giant computer monitors. Officer Reese proceeded with the introduction.

"Pastor and Bishop, I'd like you to meet Agent Carson with the Bureau of Alcohol, Tobacco, Firearms, and Explosives, also known as the ATF. He is the lead investigator of the task force investigating the church fires," said Officer Reese.

"Pleasure to meet you both. Please sit," said Agent Carson as he pointed to the two chairs. Pastor Williams and Bishop Hines both sat down while Officer Reese and Agent Carson stood.

"I am certain you are aware of the two recent fires, correct?" asked Agent Carson.

"Of course. Who isn't?" said Pastor Williams.

"Do you suspect foul play?" asked Bishop Hines.

"We don't know what to suspect, Bishop," said Officer Reese.

"The two fires were along the Boulevard. The highest traffic corridor through this part of the city," said Agent Carson.

"Yes. The Boulevard is a prime location for any type of business. They step all over each other when a property becomes available," said Pastor Williams.

"Including churches," said Agent Carson.

"Yes, including churches," Pastor Williams agreed. Pastor Williams was not sure if that was a jab at him by the agent. But it reminded Pastor Williams that his church was on the Boulevard as well, and he'd fought vigorously for his location.

"The good thing is we have a significant amount of traffic and street cams along this corridor and can see just about everything that's going on," said Officer Reese.

"So, you have street cameras on the churches that caught fire?" asked Bishop Hines, as he pointed at the two computer monitors.

"We do. They have good-quality footage, including multi-angle positions," said Agent Carson.

"That's great. So, why don't you already have a suspect?" asked Pastor Williams, bewildered.

"That is the thing, Pastor. The cameras didn't pick up anything at all," said Officer Reese.

"My team combined all the footage we had for each church in a split screen with the different angles, and then we did a quick time-lapse for each," said Agent Carson. He grabbed a small remote that controlled the computer monitors and videos. "First, I will show you the videos that we have of Ebenezer AME's church."

Agent Carson pushed the play button on the remote, and the left monitor's video started playing. The large monitor screen was split into four sections. The top two videos on the screen were of cameras positioned right in front of the church. The other two were of the street intersections on the east and west sides of the church.

Bishop Hines pointed at the top of the screen. "How are you getting these two videos?" asked Bishop Hines.

"These top two are cameras on telephone poles across the street from the church," said Officer Reese.

"I assume the bottom two cameras are of the two intersections on the opposite sides, or the east and west blocks of the church, right?" asked Pastor Williams.

"Correct," said Agent Carson.

"What time does this video start?" asked Pastor Williams.

"The videos are from approximately six hours before the time the accounted witnesses stated that they saw smoke and fire coming from the buildings," said Officer Reese.

"Our video tech sped them up for a viewing time of ten minutes, including when the firefighters arrived on the scene," said Agent Carson.

Pastor Williams and Bishop Hines began watching the first set of videos. After six minutes of remaining quiet and intensely watching the video, they noticed no one had gone in or out of the church. Dark gray smoke appeared, coming from the church, then flames. They saw that no one left or ran away from the church, either.

"What about the back door?" asked Bishop Hines.

"There is no back door. Can you rewind the video before the flames?" said Officer Reese. Agent Carson rewound the video and paused it right when the smoke started. Officer Reese further narrated, "This church only has two entry points that are both close to the street's frontage. The first is the main door," said Officer Reese as he pointed on the monitor. "And the second is here, which is just an emergency exit door on this side, but it's still near the front."

"This church has been abandoned for quite some time. The property looked like trash, even before the fire. So, everyone in the neighborhood just assumed it was something electrical that started the fire," said Pastor Williams.

"The building is incredibly old and mostly made of brick and stone, such as the basement and parts of the original sections of the building. That is one of the reasons why it did not completely burn down. However, the fire was not electrical," said Officer Reese.

"Okay, let's view the second video," said Agent Carson.

"And is this video of Church of the Living God?" asked Pastor Williams. He'd already knew the answer.

"Yes," said Agent Carson as he played another set of videos on the large monitor on the right.

As they watched the second set of videos, Pastor Williams and Bishop Hines saw someone walking into the church through the side exit visible by one of the videos. They remained silent as they waited for this person to come out of the church. The smoke rose from the church, and then flames appeared, but there was no visual of the person ever leaving. Unsure at first, Pastor Williams realized the identity of the individual.

"That person that went in, that was their trustee, John Copeland, correct?" asked Pastor Williams.

"Correct. Unfortunately, he never came out," said Agent Carson.

"His wife and their temporary pastor confirmed that he went there to do some church accounting stuff, like writing out checks and updating donation records," said Officer Reese.

"Temporary pastor, that's right, Pastor Harris recently quit the church. Any word from him?" asked Pastor Williams.

"We put out calls, but no one has heard from him. It looks like he left town and does not want to come back," said Officer Reese. He then had a thought. "You recently gave a sermon at their church, right?" asked Officer Reese.

"Yes. I did it as a favor to show support for their church's renovation dedication. But honestly, I don't know him that well. Oh, and just so you know, I did call his cell phone number after the fire, but it was disconnected," said Pastor Williams.

"We got that too. My team is working hard to find him. Now, we have no reason to believe he has anything to do with this, but it still would be good to get any information from him that we can," said Agent Carson.

"And what about a rear exit for this church?" asked Bishop Hines, still focused on the videos.

"There is one. It leads out to the back of the church's parking lot, along with the side door. But the elementary school is right behind it. So, without using a car, a person would have had to climb the retaining wall and avoid the parking lot in order not to be seen, and the school's cameras would have picked it up. But there was nothing on them as well," said Agent Carson.

"What about faulty building or electrical issues for this one?" asked Pastor Williams, feeling confused and desperate.

"None. My team and local code officials confirmed that the buildings were fine. Church of the Living God was recently renovated and had no issues," said Agent Carson. He continued explaining with more detail. "Now, this fire started in the main sanctuary. But, according to the construction drawings approved by the city, they installed higher-rated firewalls that buffered the side rooms and a new sprinkler system as part of their renovation that prevented the fire from spreading throughout the rest of the church."

"And luckily, our area's firehouse station is only a few blocks away from these churches. So, the firefighters' response was great on both fires, and they only sustained moderate damage. If not, the buildings could have gone up in full flames," said Officer Reese.

"They mentioned that on the news. But how did they actually start, then?" asked Pastor Williams.

"We believe that the fires were started with some type of accelerant," said Agent Carson.

"You mean like gasoline or another type of flammable liquid?" asked Pastor Williams.

"Correct," said Officer Reese.

"Well, accelerants just don't appear out of thin air and set fires themselves," said Bishop Hines.

"Exactly," said Officer Reese.

"And that's part of the reason why you are here. Something is going on that our cameras are not picking up. We need your help in listening to what people are saying around the blocks, keeping your eyes and ears open to anything suspicious, and reporting back to us if you hear anything," said Agent Carson.

"What's the other part?" said Bishop Hines.

Agent Carson and Officer Reese looked at each other, expressions grim. Then, Agent Carson pulled up an aerial map of the neighborhood on the computer.

"Well, again, the first church fire hit here on the Boulevard at old Ebenezer. Then the next fire hit here just a few blocks east, at Church of the Living God. If my assumptions are correct, and we do have a mysterious fire starter or arsonist, then I'm guessing they are going to hit the next church, just east again, and hit it tonight," said Agent Carson, emphasizing the dire situation.

"That's Mount Carmel. Did you let the pastor and congregation know?" asked Pastor Williams.

"Yes. Just as a precaution, I asked them to cancel any church activities planned for this evening and make sure no one is in or around the building. With what has been going on, the pastor said he was happy to do so," said Officer Reese.

Agent Carson interjected, "More concerning is that, two days from now is your—"

"Community revival," said Pastor Williams, completing Agent Carson's sentence.

"And you already know what the next church farther east after Mount Carmel is, right?" said Agent Carson. It was more of a statement than a question.

"My church," said Pastor Williams with his shoulders sagging.

"New Lighthouse Temple?" asked Bishop Hines, horrified.

"Yes," said Pastor Williams.

Pastor Williams thought about how the fires had just become more real and personal to him and his church. He thought, *Who could be doing this, and why? How are they doing it? Does my community revival have anything to do with this?* He cared about the safety of his members and others that would be attending the event. But, how could he let a *hunch* stop his community revival?

Agent Carson continued, "Yes. We think this may be a strategic and planned effort to destroy all of the churches in this neighborhood or to disrupt and cancel your community revival."

"You mean *my* community revival?" asked Pastor Williams, stressing the pride that he had for this event and all the work that he'd put into it over the years.

"Unfortunately, yes. First, it's interesting the church fires started right before your community revival. Second, your community revival is not exactly like other church revivals. You have outside vendors, activities for the kids, live music, and hundreds of people come out for this event," said Officer Reese.

"Your revivals are more like block parties, Pastor. And given the success that I heard you had last year, we assume the number of people may even increase by thirty percent or more, putting hundreds of people in unnecessary risk and danger," said Agent Carson.

"But it's an outside event," said Bishop Hines.

"Yes. But without us knowing what's going on and who's starting these fires, we have to assume everyone is in danger. Also, Pastor Williams always ends the night with a large neighborhood town hall meeting inside his church, right, Pastor?" asked Officer Reese.

Agent Carson interrupted the dialogue before Pastor Williams could respond. "Maybe it is a former church member that is angry, or maybe an inside job. We aren't sure. Are you willing to cancel or postpone this event, Pastor Williams?" asked Agent Carson.

"No way!" exclaimed Pastor Williams. "I'm sorry for yelling. Forgive me. But we just got done talking out front in this station about how the enemy never sleeps. And here he is at work again, to steal, kill, and destroy, including my church and others. I refuse to let him win and stop all the good that the community revival has done and will accomplish! You have any better ideas?"

"I told you," said Officer Reese as he looked at Agent Carson.

"What can we do?" asked a determined Bishop Hines.

"We are taking this one day at a time. Today, we are focusing on this evening. We will have a few plainclothes officers policing the area, but we want to make things seem as normal as possible. We are not even going to put surveillance into the church, as the arsonist might already be casing it. So, Officer Reese suggested that in addition to my team, we also have you walk around witnessing and talking to people on the streets like you normally do. You are such a familiar face on these streets, even at night. If something is going on, they will be more likely to talk to you instead of one of my guys. Maybe even bring Bishop Hines with you," said Agent Carson.

"Let's be clear. We do not want you or anyone else near the church, or to be some type of hero and cross paths with this person. We just need local and familiar eyes and ears way beyond the blocks of the church and our men," said Officer Reese.

"And we don't want to scare this person away. So, our guys will not even be in close proximity of the church, just in a clear distant view to see anything that our cameras do not pick up," said Agent Carson.

"If it is a person at all," said Bishop Hines.

"Excuse me. What could it be, then Mr. Hines?" asked an incredulous Agent Carson.

"It's Bishop Hines, and I said: If it is a person at all. The enemy can work in mysterious ways too, just like God," said Bishop Hines.

The three looked at Bishop Hines in confusion. Bishop Hines continued with his thought.

"From the videos, no suspects are walking in and out of these buildings. Something is used to spread the fires quickly, but there is no evidence of anyone in these buildings using them. Sounds more like a supernatural issue to me."

Pastor Williams ignored Bishop Hines' comment.

"I get it. I am fully aware that no one snitches in this city. I will make sure we stay away from the church; and I will let you know if we see or hear anything," said Pastor Williams.

"Thanks, Pastor. Let us get through the night and hope that we don't have to worry about your church and the revival," said Officer Reese.

"We will do all we can," said Pastor Williams.

"And we will too," said Agent Carson.

Pastor Williams and Bishop Hines nodded their goodbyes, left the room, and exited the police station.

Agent Carson closed the door behind them. He walked back to the computer monitors to talk privately with Officer Reese.

"That went as well as expected," said Agent Carson.

"Are you sure that we should not tell Pastor Williams about Trustee Copeland, how he was dead even before the fire started, or how his lifeless body was dragged from his office out to the main sanctuary then set on fire? Out of anyone I trust in this community, it's Pastor Williams," said Officer Reese.

"Look, I know it's frustrating not knowing how this arsonist and now murderer got in and out of these two churches. But, as I said before, it could be an inside job, and you don't get more inside than Pastor Williams within this community and its churches. Let's just focus on Mount Carmel right now. I have a feeling we will get a break with this one," said Agent Carson.

"Trust me. Pastor Williams has nothing to do with all of this. It's got to be Pastor Harris, especially with all the rumors we heard about him," said Officer Reese.

"That thought of yours, this early in the investigation, shows me that you are too close to all of this. So, just let me do my job," said Agent Carson.

"Speaking of that, how is your team's search going for Pastor Harris?" said Officer Reese.

"Don't worry. We will find him," said Agent Carson.

5

Promotion

Thursday morning—two days before the community revival.

Joshua woke up from Rocky's loud bark coming from downstairs. He did not get much sleep, as he had been thinking about Lauren all night. It was also most likely the reason why he did not have his terrifying re-occurring dream. He did not recall ever being so intrigued by anyone. Her presence felt like sunlight, warm and spiritual. Her words were like water, fluid and refreshing, compelling and captivating. Joshua leaned over to grab his cell phone off the nightstand. He unplugged the charger, fell back to his bed, and went through his phone comfortably. He'd missed a text from an unknown number.

[3:11 AM] Joshua? You up? – Lauren

Joshua thought, *Crap! I must have fallen asleep just before she texted me.* The last thing he remembered was staring at the ceiling and then looking at his cell phone with the clock reading 3:03 a.m. He thought, *Why couldn't I have stayed awake just eight more minutes?* He shook his head in disappointment and looked at the current time; it was 11:05 a.m. He wondered if it was too early to text her back. She had been up late, just like him. So maybe she was still sleeping. He closed his eyes, took a deep breath, and cleared his mind. At that moment, he envisioned her looking at her phone. He smiled and texted back:

[11:07 AM] Hey, Lauren. Looks like I fell asleep just before you texted me. How are you doing?

Lauren responded almost immediately.

[11:08 AM] Too late. I don't want to talk to you anymore.

Joshua's eyes widened a panic. He did not know how to respond. Lauren responded again before he had a chance.

[11:11 AM] Thinking what to say huh? lol

Joshua laughed and replied.

[11:11 AM] I'm still waking up.

[11:11 AM] Such a sleepy head. I am glad you finally responded. I thought I had the wrong number.

[11:12 AM] Ha! I guess I should have strung you along for the rest of the day. Maybe responded to your text with, Sorry. Who is Joshua?

[11:12 AM] LOL. Not unless you wanted a heel up your . . .!

[11:12 AM] Omg you and your heels again lol

[11:13 AM] I thought you liked my heels

[11:13 AM] I'm not answering that lol.

[11:14 AM] What are you doing today Joshua?

[11:14 AM] Nothing until 5. I have to work this evening.

Lauren did not immediately respond, so Joshua pressed.

[11:16 AM] Why?

[11:16 AM] Just wondering. Bishop called me about a half hour ago and asked that I meet him back at your house. Your uncle wants to talk about something.

Joshua lit up. He was excited about the chance to see her again today. He had to remind himself, Remain calm. Play it cool.

[11:17 AM] So you're coming back over?

[11:18 AM] Yes. Getting ready now.

[11:18 AM] Guess that means I gotta get up

[11:23 AM] And no doggy breath please lol.

Joshua laughed out loud. He thought about responding with, "Why, are you going to kiss me?" But he didn't have the courage. His response was conservative.

[11:23 AM] Haha I'm up already and yes I brushed my teeth thank you very much lol.

[11:24 AM] Sure right lol. See you soon Joshua

[11:24 AM] See you soon Lauren

Joshua realized that it would not be wise for him to do the quick wash, not today. He needed to get a real shower and wear something nice. So, he went into the closet to find something to wear. He picked one of the two pairs of designer jeans he owned. Dark blue with a thin white threaded swirl down both legs. He went through his closet for the shirt and picked a white button-down collared shirt with large end cuffs. When the cuffs were turned up, they showed a dark blue-and-white polka dot pattern. The waist of the shirt was slightly tapered, which gave Joshua an athletic look. He was satisfied with his selection. He quickly hopped in the shower to make sure he was clean, dressed, and downstairs before Lauren got there.

Fully dressed, Joshua grabbed the rail at the top of the stairs to skip down the steps, but then he realized that he'd forgotten to brush his teeth. He went back to the bathroom. While he brushed his teeth, Rocky was barking. The front door opened, and Joshua could hear his uncle and Bishop Hines talking. Joshua hoped Lauren was not already at the house with them. He skipped down the steps and was relieved when he did not see her.

"Good morning," said Joshua to everyone.

"You mean, good afternoon," said Angela. Bishop Hines laughed. Joshua had not seen his Aunt Angela sitting at the kitchen table.

"Oh, hey, Auntie," said Joshua.

"Wow. Don't you look all dapper today," said Angela.

Pastor Williams frowned, showing Angela that he was bothered by the thought of Joshua getting dressed up for the first time in months with the hope of seeing Lauren again.

"I wonder why?" asked Pastor Williams rhetorically.

Joshua just smiled.

"What did Officer Reese say?" asked Angela.

"Officer Reese?" asked Joshua, confused.

"Yes. We just came back from the station," said Pastor Williams.

"What? You were at the police station. What happened?" asked a now alarmed Joshua.

"Nothing happened. Well, not yet anyway. Officer Reese asked us to stop by the station to talk about the two church fires," said a tired-looking Pastor Williams.

Bishop Hines interjected. "I asked Lauren to stop by to hear this as well. Is it okay if we wait for her?"

"Sure," said Pastor Williams.

"Okay, good. She should be here any minute," said Bishop Hines.

Pastor Williams refrained from voicing his feelings about Lauren to Bishop Hines. He kept wondering who Lauren was and why the Bishop always wanted her around. He also felt slighted by the apparent late question of whether or not it was okay for Lauren to join them for this discussion. He thought, *What if I said no? She's already on her way. Would the Bishop call her and tell her to turn around and not come over? And why does he always want her around anyway?*

Angela looked at Joshua. He looked back at her and tried not to grin like a fool. She could still obviously tell that Joshua was excited.

"Any leftover food from yesterday?" asked Joshua.

"Yes. It's all in the refrigerator," said Angela.

Angela got up from the table and went into the living room to talk with her husband and Bishop Hines. Joshua made himself a plate of food and sat at the kitchen table to eat. He intentionally brought the fork up from the plate to his mouth slowly and carefully to not get any food on his shirt. He got up to pour himself a glass of 4C Iced Tea from the pitcher that his uncle had made yesterday. Pastor Williams did not like any kind of iced tea except the 4C brand. However, Angela did not care for any type of iced tea at all. She preferred water or an occasional glass of lemonade. So, Pastor Williams had always made it himself, for only himself. But Joshua was very fond of it as well. So, when Joshua started living with them, Pastor Williams had to make it more frequently and share with Joshua. The worst thing for Pastor Williams was to come home after a long day of service and preaching, open the refrigerator, and see just a little swig of the tea in the pitcher he had made the previous evening. He was not a cussing individual, but when that would happen, the urge to cuss would be at the tip of his tongue and in his heart. While Joshua was carefully drinking, the doorbell rang.

"Come in. It's open," yelled Angela.

The door opened. It was Lauren. She closed the door behind her as Rocky ran up to greet her. She smiled as she bent down to pet him for a few seconds. She then got back up and walked into the living room.

"Good afternoon, everyone," said Lauren.

"At least she knows what time it is," said Pastor Williams as he looked over at Joshua.

Angela and Bishop Hines laughed. Joshua shook his head.

"Hello, Lauren. You look lovely," said Angela.

"Thank you, Mrs. Williams. You look nice as well. I love your blouse," said Lauren, smiling.

"Interesting choice for a dress," said Angela as she looked over at

Joshua and noticed he'd had on the same colors.

Lauren had on another sundress, like yesterday. But today, she was wearing a white sundress with dark blue patterned flowers. It was as if Joshua and Lauren had planned to dress alike.

"Did you guys talk last night and decide to coordinate colors today?" asked Angela. She said it as a joke, but she also wanted to aggrandize the situation, knowing that it would further irritate her husband. He needed to be pushed out of his comfort zone a little more often. Also, she liked the idea of Joshua finding a girl that was smart and rooted in the church. Not to mention that hanging out with Lauren was way better, in her opinion, than Joshua hanging out with Monty all the time, who showed little to no ambition.

"Yes. Blue is our favorite color," said Joshua.

Lauren was surprised. She was not expecting Joshua to be so direct and engaging. She gladly replied in the same manner.

"Isn't it! I am so glad that you remembered, honey. Does this mean you are taking me on a date tonight?" asked Lauren.

Pastor Williams could not believe the directness of the conversation, especially in front of everyone.

"I would love to, my lady," said Joshua in an English accent. "But I have to work tonight. Maybe I can take off on—"

Pastor Williams interrupted Joshua.

"Okay, Prince Harry and Lady Markle. Before you two go on your royal date, we need to talk about what we just learned from Officer Reese," said Pastor Williams.

"Is this about the fires?" asked Joshua.

"Yes," said Pastor Williams.

"Did Joe say that they were intentional, and not just building issues?" asked Angela.

"Apparently so," said Pastor Williams.

"So, someone is setting the fires? Who?" asked Lauren.

"That's the question and mystery. The police and ATF have no clue," said Bishop Hines.

"ATF? Is it that serious?" asked Joshua.

"Yes. No witnesses, nothing on the street cams, and no signs of the churches being broken into," said Pastor Williams.

"How are they certain it's not building issues?" asked Angela.

"They had experts investigate the buildings. They completely ruled out faulty building issues," said Bishop Hines.

"The police were confused, just as we are. The ATF confirmed that the fires were started with some type of accelerant. They were able to pull videos from just about every angle of the buildings. No one went into or out of the buildings before or after the fires started," said Pastor Williams, obviously concerned.

"Except for that trustee," said Bishop Hines.

"Yes, except for Trustee Copeland of Church of the Living God, who went in and never came out," said Pastor Williams.

"My Lord," said Angela.

"Listen, it was pretty eerie watching the videos. It was like they were just started by themselves or by a ghost," said Bishop Hines.

Joshua and Lauren immediately looked at each other. They were thinking the same thing and knew it.

"That's interesting and all, but what did the police want from you two?" asked Angela.

"They wanted two things. One, they wanted to know if we knew anything or heard anything about the fires. Of course, that was a no. And two, and more importantly, they think this smart and mysterious arsonist may hit again tonight. This time at the Mount Carmel church," said Pastor Williams.

"Oh no! Mount Carmel?" exclaimed Angela.

"Yes, unfortunately," said Pastor Williams.

"They want us to be on the streets, but nowhere near the church. Just as additional eyes and ears for the talk of the neighborhood. They know most people are reluctant to talk to strangers, and especially the men in blue. But they will have undercover cops nearby to see what the cameras may not, and hopefully, catch this culprit," said Bishop Hines, revealing the magnitude of the threat.

"Does this mean you and the Bishop are going out there tonight?" asked Joshua as he looked at Pastor Williams.

"Yes." Pastor Williams nodded.

"Can we go too?" asked Joshua.

"That's a great idea! I knew I liked you," said Lauren.

"Absolutely not!" exclaimed Pastor Williams.

"I can't believe you asked your uncle that. You knew he was going to say no," said Angela.

"Joe specifically stated that he wanted the streets to look normal. I am out on these streets all the time, witnessing the gospel of Jesus Christ and also for the neighborhood watch group as well. So, everyone is used to seeing me on the streets during the day and late at night. For others to be out as well, that would look way too suspicious and is too dangerous. Plus, this ATF agent, working with Joe, looks like he does not play around," said Pastor Williams.

"Hmm . . . this ATF agent sounds just like you, Jerry," joked Angela. Everyone found it funny except, of course, Pastor Williams.

"This is a serious matter, Boobie," pleaded Pastor Williams.

"I know. I'm just joking, honey. Now, I do remember you and the deacons out witnessing pretty late before, but not too late, and definitely not after midnight. Just make sure you're aware of the time because that could look odd, too." Angela then turned to Joshua. "Josh and Lauren, how about you two hang out here until they get back?" she suggested. Pastor Williams turned to Angela with a fiery stare, as if she had just invited the devil to stay for dinner.

"Yes. I can come straight here after work," said Joshua without hesitation. Lauren smiled.

"Sounds like we get that royal date after all," said Lauren.

Pastor Williams was disturbed as he watched how the two flirted with each other. His suspicions about Lauren grew even more. He was still upset and felt disrespected that she'd challenged him, a pastor, in his own house, especially during the first time meeting him. He also thought about how she might continue to fill Joshua's head with nonsense about true realms and aliens instead of strong biblical foundations like the Ten Commandments or fruits of the spirit. In reality, Pastor Williams was just fearful of losing Joshua. He felt partially responsible for his mother's death, not being able to save her, and he always hoped Joshua would take over his church one day. It seemed that just within a day, Lauren could easily take Joshua away from him, and he would have no control over it. In any event, Pastor Williams decided not to hide his emotions any longer. "I don't know about that. You two barely know each other. We barely know her," said Pastor Williams.

"Excuse me, Pastor. Lauren is with me, and that's all you need to know. Respectfully, I suggest that you focus on the real problems, which are this arsonist and your community revival," said Bishop Hines with a loud and stern tone. Bishop Hines' voice then changed back to a softer tone to ease his message. "They are both adults. They are allowed to make their own choices now."

The excitement of spending time together caused Joshua and Lauren to be oblivious to Pastor Williams' statement and Bishop Hines' response. Joshua's eyes were wide open, and Lauren walked closer to Joshua, as she could feel that he was about to say something to her.

"So, you really okay with staying here?" asked Joshua.

"Of course," said Lauren.

"I might ask Monty to stop by as well," said Joshua as he turned to Angela. Pastor Williams glared at Angela again, letting her know that her suggestion just got even worse with Monty coming over.

"Well, if Monty shows up, then I may go out with your uncle and the Bishop," said Angela.

"Monty?" asked Lauren, wondering who he was.

"Oh, he's my best friend. He's harmless," said Joshua.

"Harmless, but annoying," said Angela as she patted Lauren on the shoulder. Pastor Williams interjected with his original point.

"Again, stay here and stay far away from Mount Carmel. We are not to be eyewitnesses, get on the news, or be superheroes. I am honored that Joe asked this of us, and I do not want to screw this up or his trust and our relationship with him in any way. Does everyone understand that?" asked Pastor Williams.

"We got it. I'm going to take Rocky out," said Joshua with a sigh.

Joshua went to the edge of the living room where Rocky was lying on the floor, quietly chewing on a bully stick. He grabbed Rocky's leash and led him out of the front door. He hoped that Lauren would follow him outside, and his hope was fulfilled. Lauren was right behind him before the door closed. Joshua smiled as they walked out the door.

"Isn't it interesting how no one saw anything and how the cameras didn't pick up anything either?" asked Lauren.

"Yeah. It sounds like we got a real mystery on our hands, here in my own community," said Joshua.

"Okay, Freddy," said Lauren, referencing Scooby-Doo. "I think we would be great at solving mysteries," said Lauren.

"You do?" asked Joshua.

Lauren walked closer to Joshua. He felt slightly uncomfortable. His instinct was to take a step back, but he held his ground. She looked up at him as she leaned in. Her eyes landed right on his lips, but she rolled up her eyes to look at him.

"Are you thinking of going near that church?" asked Lauren.

"Actually," Joshua said with a chuckle, "I am."

Lauren smiled. "Of course, I was thinking the same thing."

"Yes. I could tell. The excitement was all over your face when the Bishop mentioned ghosts," said Joshua.

"We spoke about a date earlier and look, the universe provided one," said Lauren.

"A date, huh? Looking for a pyromaniac or a ghost, or possibly getting into big trouble is a date to you?" asked Joshua.

"Yes. Sounds way better than a boring dinner date or bowling, right?" asked Lauren.

Joshua laughed. "You have a point." He paused for a few seconds. "You are quite different; you know that? I mean that in a good way. But like my uncle said, I barely know you," said Joshua.

Lauren turned around, facing the street, and leaned her back on his chest. Joshua was surprised.

"I barely know you too. But something about you just feels different and comfortable," said Lauren.

Joshua put his hands around her waist. "I'm going against every single guy code in the book by telling you this, but I was thinking about you all last night," said Joshua.

"Well, how come you didn't text me back?" asked Lauren.

Joshua shook his head. "I fell asleep right before you texted me, honest. Anyway, I really don't know you, but it just feels like I already do, you know?" Joshua paused again for a few seconds, thinking. He then vocalized his thought. "It's like my soul already knows your soul. Like I can feel it when it is near mine. I can't explain it," said Joshua, suddenly feeling nervous.

"Wow," said Lauren.

"I'm sorry. I'm saying way too much, aren't I? I sound like a bunch of mashed potatoes, I know." Joshua tripped over his words.

"No. You are saying exactly the right things, Joshua. I feel the same way. I just had no clue how to express or articulate it. But you said it exactly how I feel. Thank you," said Lauren.

Joshua looked down at Lauren with a smirk on his face, as if to say, "Really?"

"Seriously," said Lauren as she turned her head back to him and smiled. Joshua felt relieved. He felt even closer to her soul.

"I wish you didn't have to work," said Lauren.

"Me too. But I got to pay for shirts like this," said Joshua as he pinched up the collar of his shirt.

Lauren laughed. "At least I get to see you again sooner than I thought," she said.

"I get off work just a little after midnight. Can you be back here by then?" asked Joshua.

"Sure, works for me."

"Okay, I will have Monty meet us here too."

Lauren and Joshua smiled at each other like two little kids that just kissed at a water fountain.

They embraced each other with a long hug. Joshua could feel the energy between them. He felt her heart and the presence of her soul. She felt the same. Altogether, the outside background noises ceased. Joshua and Lauren heard nothing. It was like God Himself had hit the mute button on the world's remote control around them as they stared at one another.

6

A Royal Date

Thursday evening—two days before the community revival.

Joshua had been in his store for a little over two hours now. He was supposed to be there at 5:00 p.m., but he had arrived at 5:07. It was the first time Joshua had ever been late to work. The delay was from needing to change his clothes one more time after he'd got dressed up for Lauren. He was walking the perimeter of the inside of the store with Billy. They were checking dates on the refrigerated cases. Their store was due for a minor remodel, and any old or dated cases needed to get replaced regardless of their working condition. As they walked, Billy was venting about work, including how his schedule never made any sense, and he never got the number of hours he wanted. But Joshua's mind was on nothing but Lauren. He kept thinking about the feeling of their hug. The way her eyes had looked at him when they were talking.

"Wow. The date on this case goes back to 1999!" exclaimed Billy.

Joshua did not respond. He was supposed to write down the case information on the equipment inventory list that he had on a clipboard he was holding in his hand.

"Josh. Are you going to write that down? This one automatically

78

needs to be replaced, right? It's before the year 2000," said Billy.

"I'm sorry. I was in deep thought about the schedule since you mentioned it," said Joshua. Often, lies would flow easily off Joshua's tongue to avoid conflict or looking bad.

"Nineteen ninety-nine," said Joshua as he wrote it down on the inventory sheet. "What's the case number?"

Rick, the store manager, approached them.

"Hey, Josh. Oh, hey, Billy. Done with that list yet?" asked Rick.

"Almost. I thought you left a while ago," said Joshua.

"I had to finish up next week's schedule," said Rick.

Billy looked at Joshua out of the corner of his eye and smirked. Luckily, Rick could not see this, as Billy was slightly behind him. Joshua attempted to hide his smile.

"And I also need to talk to you about a few things. Can you come to my office for a few minutes?" asked Rick.

"No problem," said Joshua.

They walked together, eventually entering through the swing doors to the back-room area and into Rick's office.

"You know store seven eighty-one is under construction. I heard that it should be open in about three to four months," said Rick.

"That sounds extremely fast, at least compared to seven seventy-nine. That one seemed to take forever," said Joshua.

"Seven seventy-nine had a bunch of issues with the city's architectural review board. When they saw the building's accent colors in person, which they'd requested, they hated it. So, they asked us to redo the entire color scheme," said Rick.

"Really?" said Joshua.

"Yes. Nate said that hiccup, and a few other things, delayed the opening for another seven weeks."

"Since you brought up Nate, did everything go okay with his visit here?" asked Joshua.

"It did. And that's the reason why I wanted to talk to you," said Rick. "I am going to be the new manager for seven eighty-one."

"Wow. That is great! Isn't getting the opportunity to run a new store a big deal around here?" asked Joshua, genuinely happy for his longtime manager.

"Yes. It is one of the steps in eventually becoming a district manager, especially if the store does well."

"Well, congrats, you deserve it," said Joshua.

"Thanks, Josh," said Rick, smiling.

Joshua felt an even more positive shift in the atmosphere. He started to smile even before Rick made his next statement.

"Nate and I recommended to executive management and HR that you take over this store once I leave," said Rick.

"Really?" said Joshua, acting surprised.

"You are a hard worker, just like your mom was. You stay on top of everything without me even asking, and we know you have great potential," said Rick.

Joshua thought about how his mother would have been so proud of him. He worked hard, and it was paying off. He could almost hear her saying, "Boy, you really have to brush your teeth now!"

"Thanks, Rick. Do I need to interview or take a test or anything?" asked Joshua.

"No. You will meet with the HR director, Michelle, and Randy, our senior director of operations. They will come here and talk about the store and your thoughts on this new role. As long as they see you are confident about it, it's pretty much yours," said Rick.

"Okay, got it. I can do that," said Joshua.

"You also need to put together a fact sheet about the store: sales, gross margins, labor, store expenses, and net profit. Also, add anything else you think would be good talking points," Rick advised.

"Talking points?" asked Joshua.

"Like neighborhood demographics and competition. It will make it a more engaging and active conversation," said Rick.

"Got it," said Joshua. He started taking notes on the back of the inventory sheet with the clipboard.

"And make sure you use nothing but positive numbers. Show no declines and no losses," said Rick.

"How do I do that?" asked Joshua.

"Do it just like the politicians and news media outlets do. Pull the store sales and expense history book and select time frames that only show good results."

"You mean if last quarter to this quarter shows a growth, use that, but if it shows a negative, use the prior year instead, as long as it shows a positive growth?" asked Joshua.

"Yes, or two years or three years. Use a comparison time frame to tell the story you want them to know," said Rick.

"Interesting. Like, if I want to get elected as mayor. For a speech, I might select a specific time frame that shows the city's economy going down and then a different time frame that shows violence going up." Joshua began slurring his words to mimic how a politician would talk. "For the past two months, our city's economy has been starting to trend down, and since 2015 crime is up twenty-eight percent! Those are facts, and we need a change!" exclaimed Joshua.

"Exactly. Didn't I say you pick up things quickly? And if I was the mayor wanting to get reelected and wanted to counter your facts, I could say, 'Since I took office two years ago, the economy is up twenty-two percent, and compared to last year, crime is down five percent. Those are facts, voters; we are the change!" said Rick.

"So, they are both facts, but chosen periods to tell different stories," said Joshua.

"It's done all the time: to get elected, to sound like one point is valid while another is not. I could go on," said Rick.

"Man. I still have a lot to learn," said Joshua.

"But you're willing to learn it," Rick stressed.

"Yes. I am. When will HR and the senior director be here at the store?" asked Joshua.

"Sometime late Monday morning or in the early afternoon. I need you to come in early on that day just in case. But you can also leave early; I know you technically have that day off."

Monday! Joshua wondered, *Do I even have enough time to prepare?* But Joshua did not want to sound frantic, especially after getting this news. He told himself to calm down.

"No worries, Rick. I will start working on the store fact sheet later this evening," said Joshua.

"Good. I will stay late tomorrow to go through it with you to make sure it looks good. Then you can take the whole weekend to study and prepare," said Rick.

"So, you're not stopping by to check on the store at all this weekend?" asked Joshua.

"No. This weekend, I'm taking my family up to the Poconos. We need to make sure we are on the same page by tomorrow," said Rick.

"Sounds good," said Joshua, shaking his hand in gratitude.

Joshua walked out of the office back into the store. He paused to look at his cell phone and saw one missed call from Lauren and a few text messages. He felt frustrated with himself that he hadn't noticed them earlier.

[6:48 PM] Hey Joshua. Hope your day is going well
[6:49 PM] I can't stop thinking about that hug
[7:02 PM] Guess you're busy. Talk to you later

Josh quickly replied.

[7:41 PM] Was tied up talking to the store manager. Still thinking about that amazing hug.

Lauren immediately replied.

[7:42 PM] Thought you forgot about me again. But I get the feeling you just like to play it cool. Even though you're not lol

[7:42 PM] Only with you around lol

[7:43 PM] Smooth lol. It's a shame we won't be alone tonight.

Oh crap, Monty, thought Joshua. He'd forgotten that he was supposed to ask Monty to join them this evening.

[7:43 PM] Hold on one sec Lauren.

Joshua called Monty.

"Hello," said Monty, answering his phone.

"Yo, man," said Joshua.

"Yo, Josh," said Monty.

"What are you doing this evening?"

"Your uncle already called my dad. He told us the whole thing. I will be there tonight," said Monty.

"Your dad is going with them?" asked Joshua.

"Yeah. It sounds like I am hanging out with you and some girl named Lauren. Who's Lauren?" asked Monty.

"Yes. It's a long story. I will explain later. I must get back to work," said Joshua in a rush to get back to texting Lauren.

"Okay, man. Talk to you later," said Monty.

"Cool," said Joshua as they hung up.

Joshua received another notification. It was from Lauren again.

[7:44 PM] Is everything okay?

Joshua replied to Lauren's text.

[7:45 PM] Yes. Just had to take care of something. Maybe this weekend we can have a date by ourselves lol

[7:46 PM] Really Joshua. During your uncle's community revival? I think you need a dating for Christian dummies book lol.

[7:47 PM] Okay maybe Sunday evening. I may have something going on for us to celebrate. I can't wait to see you.

[7:47 PM] Same here.

[7:48 PM] Okay talk to you tonight.

[7:48 PM] Bye

[7:49 PM] See ya

Joshua went back to catch up with Billy to finish checking the cases. Billy was in the same spot where he and Joshua had left off. He had been on his cell phone the whole time.

"I'm back. You didn't continue without me?" asked Joshua.

"Umm, you have the clipboard and inventory sheet," said Billy.

Joshua looked at the clipboard still in his hand. "I guess I do," he said as he realized that he'd forgotten to leave the sheet with Billy.

They continued around the store, finishing the list. Through the remaining work hours, Joshua and Lauren continued to text each other. It did not matter that they'd texted their goodbyes. Anytime Joshua had a good break from the busyness of the store, he would text Lauren. Anytime there was a long pause in hearing from Joshua, Lauren would text him, both of them excited to see a message from the other, and both still thinking about how they felt with just a hug. Then when work was done, Joshua was excited to leave.

Joshua pulled his car up to his uncle's house. He parked on the street parallel to the sidewalk. It was 12:35 a.m., and Lauren and Monty were sitting on the porch waiting for Joshua. He got out of the car and walked up to greet them.

"Lauren, where's your car?" asked Joshua.

"I took a rideshare here from the Bishop's house," said Lauren.

"What about everyone else?" asked Joshua.

"They left an hour ago. Your aunt went with them. She said she'd make sure your uncle did not stay out too late," said Monty.

Lauren and Joshua looked at each other, remembering Angela's statement about going with them if Monty showed up.

"And I just got here right before you pulled up," said Lauren.

Joshua tried to introduce them to each other. "Lauren, Monty. Monty, Lauren," said Joshua.

Lauren laughed. "We've already been through that, Joshua."

"Your uncle wanted to get an early start," said Monty.

"You know my uncle. Are you two ready to go?" asked Joshua.

"Ready to go? What are you talking about?" asked Monty.

"Lauren and I already decided to drive by the church to see if we could see anything," said Joshua.

"Do you want your uncle to kill you, or better yet, get in trouble with the police?" asked an alarmed Monty. He continued, "Josh, you know I'm always down for a little bit of trouble, but that just sounds completely stupid."

Joshua and Lauren continued the conversation as if they had not heard anything Monty just said.

"Do you need to change?" asked Lauren.

"Yes. I'm going to run in the house and get a quick shower," said Joshua. "We might be out very late, and I want to make sure I am ready for work tomorrow, just in case."

"Nice to see you have your thinking cap on," said Lauren.

"I don't know how much of anything we're going to see now, especially if something has happened already," said Joshua.

"I can't believe this," said Monty.

Joshua and Lauren continued to ignore Monty.

"Maybe we should just park somewhere near Mount Carmel and sit in the car for a bit," said Joshua.

"Sounds good to me," said Lauren.

Joshua ran into the house, took a quick shower, and came back out within nine minutes.

"That was quick," said Monty.

"It doesn't take long when you stay clean," joked Joshua.

"You, clean? Really?" asked Monty. Monty and Lauren laughed.

They got into Joshua's car and drove over to Mount Carmel. Joshua was driving his black four-door Honda Accord. He used to have a sporty Toyota Supra that he'd bought online from a private seller in California. He'd gotten a great deal on it. It had low profile tires, expensive BBS rims, a rear spoiler, and a thunderous engine. It was used, and it had a lot of miles on it. But it was a cool type of car for a young kid like Joshua at the time. When he got the assistant manager position, he knew it was time to get a vehicle that appeared more mature and professional. So, he traded the Supra in for this new Accord. He drove fast but not reckless.

They approached Mount Carmel. Joshua drove by the church and circled the block. When he came back around, he parked just two blocks away. They still had a surprisingly good view of the building, but not of the front entrance or the street frontage. Joshua turned off the car and looked around.

"I don't think we are going to stay here long," said Joshua.

"Do you think we should be this close?" asked Monty.

"Technically, we were too close to the church as soon as we left Joshua's porch," said Lauren.

"And who are you again?" asked Monty.

"Lauren Alexander. We met on Joshua's front porch. Pleased to meet you again," said Lauren. Joshua laughed.

"Real funny," said Monty. "Earlier, Bishop Hines called you his daughter. Are you his daughter?" asked Monty.

Joshua sensed an odd accusation in Monty's question.

"No. I am not. But I'm like a daughter to him," said Lauren.

"Don't you mean almost a daughter-in-law?" asked Monty.

"What are you talking about?" asked Joshua.

Lauren shook her head and did not respond.

"The Bishop told us she was engaged to his son, Mike. But it was called off. From all the social media pics, it looks like they were very much in love too," said Monty.

"You're an anus, Monty!" exclaimed Lauren.

"Is that true?" asked Joshua, showing disappointment.

"Yes, I was engaged, but that was like a year ago; and I broke it off!" exclaimed Lauren.

Joshua felt his heart become heavy and sink into his stomach.

Monty continued, "Is it true what they say about preachers' daughters?" Monty paused. "Or future daughters-in-law?"

"Is it true what they say about annoying idiots getting kicked in the balls!" exclaimed Lauren.

Joshua intervened, despite the pit in his stomach.

"Dude. What is your problem? You just met her, and you barely know her," said Joshua.

"Didn't we all just meet her? I'm just saying," said Monty.

"Well, you can un-meet her and get out the car," said Joshua. "We're supposed to be here having fun, and you're in the back seat acting like an idgit!" exclaimed Joshua.

Lauren laughed. "What in the world is an idgit?" she said.

Monty laughed as well. "It's another word for idiot. He always calls me that when he gets mad." Monty paused and then sighed. "Josh is right. I'm sorry. Let's start over."

"Sure. Pleased to meet you, Mr. Idgit. My name is Lauren Alexander. We met on Joshua's front porch, then we met a few minutes ago in this car, and now again for the third time," said Lauren.

Joshua and Monty laughed.

"Wow. You are certainly some firecracker, I tell you. And I am *Sir* Idgit to you, Lauren Alexander," said Monty. They all laughed.

Joshua's mind quickly went back to Lauren being engaged.

"So, you are the one Mike was going to marry?" asked Joshua.

"Yes," said Lauren.

"My uncle and I were invited to the wedding, but we just had so much going on after my mom died. We sort of lost touch with the Bishop and Mike after that. Why did you two break it off? We know Mike. He's a good guy with some serious discipline," said Joshua.

Lauren hoped his questioning was just a little jealousy and not to start a list of reasons to back away from her and their connection.

Monty interjected. "Man, do we know Mike. Girls always loved him, and then when he started preaching, they were in his face trying to be the new First Lady for when he takes over the Bishop's church."

Joshua looked back over the seat at Monty. He glared at him as if to say, "You idgit!" again. Lauren tried to salvage the situation.

"Honestly. We did not connect. We had similar paths and loved learning, which is what brought us together. But Mike was way too orthodox for me; he could not look beyond what pages say to understand what they truly mean," said Lauren. She looked at Joshua. "It definitely was not love. I know for certain now that it was not love," she said firmly.

Joshua was relieved to hear that, but he still had an inexplicable feeling of hurt. He thought, *We aren't in any type of official relationship, so why am I so upset?* Monty continued the conversation.

"Okay, I'm intrigued. What do you mean by Mike not looking beyond the pages?" asked Monty.

"Looking for tips?" joked Joshua.

"Always!" said Monty.

"Okay. Do you believe in the Bible?" asked Lauren.

"Yes . . . well, no. Only some parts. I think a lot of it was written by man just to control this world and what we do. And it contradicts itself so many times," said Monty.

"Of course it was written by man," said Lauren. "Just like every other book, article, and cave wall before and after it. But not how you think. The Bible comprises massive amounts of literature works, historical accounts, stories, letters, and documents from different periods of time, by many different individuals, all with a common theme. But if it's all of that, wouldn't different viewpoints, cultural differences, and various times in history make it appear to be contradictory or even unbelievable?" asked Lauren.

"Maybe? Give me an example, and make it short, please! I can see you're a talker, and we could be here all night," said Monty.

Lauren gave him a look but continued. "If you read the book of Saint John, you would think Jesus was this powerful deity. He took no mess from anyone. Walked the earth with a massive presence and exerted his knowledge and power over everyone he encountered. But if you read the book of Saint Matthew, you would think Jesus was this meek, lowly man who walked slowly and was quiet and compassionate. Both Matthew and John walked with Jesus, and both saw him differently."

"Wow, kind of like facts," said Joshua.

Lauren and Monty looked at Joshua, confused.

"It's a long story. Never mind," said Joshua.

"So, you broke up over Saint Matthew and John?" joked Monty.

"No, stupid. Mike just cared more about bringing in membership numbers, money, and his godly image than he cared about the truth, or helping others find their true power in God," said Lauren. "That's acting fake to me. A true Christian would care more about a person's heart and soul than a mirror or a dollar."

Joshua loved hearing her talk. Her voice sounded so pure, yet the words that came out were forceful and captivating.

"And now I see what the Bishop meant. You got me rethinking some things," said Monty.

"What time is it? I don't think anything is happening tonight. I don't even see any undercover cops or anyone for that matter," said Lauren.

Joshua looked at his cell phone. He noticed that he received a text message from Pastor Williams.

"I got a text from my uncle," said Joshua as he looked at the message on his cell phone. "Looks like the police caught a suspect before we got here. That must be why everyone is gone."

"Did he say who?" asked Monty.

"Yup. He said, they caught Cliff behind the church," said Joshua.

"Cliff. Who is Cliff?" asked Lauren.

"He's a homeless drunk, but totally harmless," said Joshua.

"I agree. Cliff may be the most drunk person on this planet, but he is a nice guy and not the type to start any fires," said Monty.

"Agreed. There is no way Cliff started the fires," said Joshua.

Joshua looked over at the church. "Well, since the police are gone, do you mind if we get out to take a closer look before we leave?" asked Joshua as he was already getting out of the car, and not waiting for an official response.

"Oh my goodness, Joshua! I thought you'd never ask!" exclaimed Lauren. Lauren got out of the car as well.

"Hello! Where are you two going? We are supposed to stay away from the church! This is not a good idea!" said a worried Monty.

Joshua and Lauren were already out of the car and walking along the street's tree-and-bush line to the church, too far away to hear Monty's words. Monty's words continued anyway.

"Stay with the car," said Joshua.

"And here they call me the idgit," grumbled Monty.

Joshua grabbed Lauren's hand and led her to the church. As they got closer, they started to walk lower and lower, all the way to a full squat when they got to the cement blocks of the base of the building. They stopped, but Joshua was still holding Lauren's hand. Lauren kept looking at their locked hands in appreciation. Even though she knew she should not compare, her ex-fiancé Mike would never have done something like that. Lauren was excited. She felt less guilty as she thought to herself that it was Monty that had brought him up, and not her.

It was dark. Joshua and Lauren did not see any lights, so they walked through a few bushes around the back of the church. The back of the church was on a gradual incline. At the top of the grade, they could look closer at the top of the church. There were no windows or doors on the back of the building. Lauren sat down on the grass and wiped debris from the bushes off her legs.

"This building is a fortress. Not sure how anyone was getting in this place without doing some major damage. Well, at least it's a nice night," said Lauren.

"Yeah, not too cool, and not too hot," said Joshua.

Joshua grabbed his cell phone out of his pocket. He'd forgotten to take it off silent after he left work. His screen notifications showed two missed calls from his uncle and one text message from his Aunt Angela. The text message read:

[1:32 AM] We are back home. Where are you all?

"Looks like we should be getting back," said Joshua.

"Sure. But give me a few minutes just to enjoy this night. This is such a beautiful church," said Lauren.

Joshua looked at the church. He noticed a ground window on the side of the building. A ground window was usually in the basement and was required by code as an additional way of escape or air ventilation. Joshua went over to the window. He lay on the ground and wiggled up to look down into the basement through the window. Lauren was still slightly behind the building, but she could see Joshua from his hips down to his legs and feet. She noticed his functional all-black sneakers that he'd worn as part of his work uniform.

"Can you see anything?" asked Lauren.

Joshua didn't respond. He was too focused on looking through the dirty window long enough to make out anything worth seeing. Finally, his vision through the window started to focus. There was a little light on in the basement that helped improve his vision. Joshua thought it might be a night-light or an LED light from an exit sign. He could make out a few tables and some chairs. Some white squares and rectangles were hanging on the opposite wall. It was too dark to see the details, but from attending many churches and participating in a few vacation Bible schools, he already knew that they were most likely hand-drawn pictures or paintings. He attempted to look around for a few more seconds and then leaned up with his left elbow on the ground as he looked back at Lauren.

"I don't see anything," said Joshua.

As soon as he said that, he looked back down at the church's exterior wall to the right of the window. He felt something, almost like he could feel it through the church's cinder block walls. He lay back on the ground and looked through the window, but this time he looked to the right side of the basement. His breath hit the window with condensation as if the night had gotten a few degrees colder. His eyes focused on one spot, a spot just behind one of the tables. It was still too dark to make out anything fully.

Joshua leaned in more. He could feel a presence. It was negative, dark. His eyes were drawn to a spot behind the table. He thought he saw something jitter. He focused more on that spot, but then he thought his eyes were just playing tricks on him. He saw the jittering movement again. This time he was sure something was in there. Joshua's breathing intensified. He leaned in as close as he could to the window without touching the glass. And then, suddenly, the darkness behind the table moved.

Joshua immediately flinched back. He couldn't believe he just saw something. He leaned forward to the window again. The dark image was moving across the room. Right now, it only seemed to be a large shadow. All Joshua could feel was its horrible intentions. His intuition told him that it was some type of evil. Joshua's heart started racing. His breathing stuttered, almost uncontrollably.

From Joshua's silence, Lauren got up and walked toward Joshua. She was still unaware of what he was witnessing. Joshua saw her coming toward him. He got halfway up and violently waved her off.

"Get out of here! Go call the police!" he whisper-yelled to her.

"What?" said Lauren as she looked on, alarmed. She could tell something was very wrong.

He repeated it, but this time a lot louder. "Go call the police!"

She saw the fear in his face, and she heard the urgency in his voice. She assumed Joshua had caught the arsonist in action. She ran to the back of the church and then continued around the corner to go back to the car the same way they came.

Joshua looked back at the window. He leaned in again, this time even more slowly, to take another look. When he did, he saw a bright orange light near the table. It was causing a glare on the window. He looked closer and knew what it was. It was a small flame. *This shadow, it's the one starting the fires*, he thought. The flame got larger. Joshua could fully see the basement now. The flame increased and spread to a full blaze. The dark shadow remained behind the fire.

As the shadow moved, new fires started in front of it. Joshua could not believe what he was witnessing. The dark shadow stopped moving, and Joshua tried to rein in his panic. *What is it doing? Why did it stop moving?* He still could not tell what it truly was, or even what type of shape it had. And then, in an instant, the shadow rushed through the fire toward the window at lightning speed.

Joshua's eyes widened as he leaped back in fear. Joshua said to himself, *It sees me,* as he jumped up and ran around the corner of the church into the street. He was running in the opposite direction of his car and Lauren and Monty. If this thing followed him, Joshua did not want to lead it back to them. He got a block and a half away before he turned around to look back at the church.

As Joshua breathed heavily from his sprint, he stopped and stared at the church building. He saw smoke come from the basement through the sides of the church. He watched the flames grow to the church's main floor. He waited a little longer, but no one came out. Joshua wondered, *The presence I felt, the dark shadow I'd just seen, what was it? Was it still in there? Was it the same thing that I saw in my dreams? What do I do now?* He ran away.

The whole neighborhood was now watching the fire consume the Mount Carmel church building while the firefighters did their best to contain it. Pastor Williams, Angela, Bishop Hines, Lauren, Monty, and Monty's father all looked in disbelief. Officer Reese approached them. Pastor Williams could see Agent Carson and his men in the distance, talking to a few residents.

"Joe," said Pastor Williams.

"Pastor," said Officer Reese.

"Do you still have Cliff in custody and considering him as a suspect?" said Pastor Williams.

"No. Agent Carson's guys didn't know him, so they arrested him when he didn't come out from the back of the church. But it turns out, Cliff just went behind the church to drink. So, we let him go," said Officer Reese.

"When you called my cell phone and told me that they arrested Cliff, that made no sense to me," said Pastor Williams.

"It made no sense to us, except the ATF agents. But we did clip every entry point with security alarm triggers, including the windows," said Officer Reese. Pastor Williams responded impatiently.

"And?" asked Pastor Williams.

"And none of them were triggered," said Officer Reese.

"So, no one went into the church?" asked Pastor Williams.

"It may appear that way. However, Pastor, we do have two eyewitnesses, plus some of Agent Carson's men, who told us they saw your nephew running from the side of the building right before the fire started," said Officer Reese.

"You mean Josh?" asked Angela.

"Yes. Josh," said Officer Reese. "Our undercover officers saw him, but none of them knew who he was until they started asking the witnesses. They said he eventually disappeared in the streets."

"I told him and everyone to stay away from the church. That boy does not listen!" said Pastor Williams.

"I'm sorry, Pastor. We do need to speak to him. Where is he?" asked Officer Reese.

Lauren looked down with tears coming from her eyes.

"I don't know," said Pastor Williams as he stared down Lauren.

7

The Rehearsal

Lauren and Mike's Wedding Rehearsal

One year before the community revival.

The church, International Covenant Ministries, was almost ready for Lauren and Mike's wedding the next day. Large yellow and blue flowers filled the sanctuary. Small yellow corsages laced with light blue ribbons adorned the end caps of each pew.

The ceremonial wedding arch was being constructed by Sylvia, who was the wedding coordinator, and Lauren's Aunt Rita. The two had spent all day putting it together and decorating it from scratch. Sylvia had ordered the powder-white steel frame arch that was easy to assemble, while Rita had bought the green vine and yellow silk flowers as garland to attach to the vine. Upon completion, they thought it was still missing something, so they went back to the craft store and bought a few rolls of four-inch sheer wired tissue ribbon as an added accent. Sylvia added it to the left side, while Rita watched and mimicked the same to the right.

"It is finished," said Sylvia. Rita and Sylvia looked at each other and smiled in accomplishment. At that very moment, there was a loud bang. A few kids had been running around the church playing tag when one of them hit the scaffolding that was along the right wall in the back of the church. It had been used by painters earlier that day, providing touch-up paint to the walls and ceiling before Lauren and Mike's big day. The scaffolding was secure, but it was rocking with the appearance of possibly falling. It was enough to push Rita over the edge.

"How many times do I have to tell you kids, stop running! No running in the church! Go outside and play," yelled Rita. The kids laughed and chuckled while they all walked quickly down the church's side aisle to go back out to the vestibule, where they stayed and continued to play their game of tag.

"I'm going to have a heart attack before this wedding is over. When are the workers coming back to get that thing?" asked Rita.

"I texted the painter about an hour ago. He said they would be back before we leave tonight," said Sylvia.

"They better. If not, the groomsmen or deacons will be taking it down in the morning," said Rita.

"Either way, I will make sure it gets removed. I'm only glad they were able to come on such short notice," said Sylvia.

"How much money are Bishop Hines and Lauren's parents spending on this wedding?" asked Rita.

"Way more than enough. If I had to guess, Mike and his mother, Sarah, account for eighty percent of the overages of the wedding's budgeted amount," said Sylvia.

"Let me guess. The other twenty percent is related to anything that has to do with the colors yellow and blue, right?" asked Rita. Sylvia laughed, confirming Rita's thought.

"Sweet Lauren. Ever since that girl was little, the only three colors she ever wore were yellow, blue, or both," said Rita.

"Hey, I am not complaining about the work. Getting selected to be *the* wedding coordinator for the Bishop's son's wedding is great and will look amazing in my website's recent projects section. But what is up with Lauren? She's not acting like your typical bride-to-be, at least not any that I've ever dealt with before," said Sylvia.

"Let me guess. She's not interested in the details of the wedding, right?" asked Rita.

"Yes. Most brides have magazine cutouts or internet photos of exactly how they want their bouquet, dress, jewelry, hair, makeup, and all the other little things. But Lauren, her only words of contribution for anything have been basically, 'Can we get those in yellow or blue?'" said Sylvia.

"Lauren and Mike look like the perfect couple. But when you hear them arguing, you realize they are vastly different," said Rita.

"I'm a witness to that," said Sylvia. "They could not even agree on what scriptures they wanted to be read during the ceremony. If you can't agree on something as simple as that, how do you expect to agree on anything?" said Sylvia.

"That doesn't surprise me. Lauren always walked around quoting scriptures in the Bible that you never knew were in there," said Rita.

"Really?" said Sylvia.

"One time, the Bishop put Lauren on the program of one of our youth services to read the scripture. But he forgot to dictate which scripture she should read," said Rita. "She took it upon herself to come up with a scripture on her own." Rita paused. "Exodus 23:19."

"Exodus 23:19?" asked Sylvia.

"It says something like thou shalt not seethe or boil a kid in his mother's milk," said Rita, as she laughed.

"Wait, what? I'm not sure what I should ask first. Did she really say that during service, and is that really in the Bible?" asked Sylvia.

"I know, right. It sure made everyone in that church grab their Bible and look it up, including me!" exclaimed Rita.

"Lauren is something else. Was Mike there? How did he feel about it?" asked Sylvia.

"You mean, Minister Perfection Mike?" said Rita. "After service, you could hear them arguing in the car while leaving the parking lot. I'm surprised we even made it to this rehearsal night."

Rita and Sylvia turned their heads as they heard loud stomping coming from the wooden basement steps from the rear of the church. It was the wedding party. The empty sanctuary amplified the sound of their footsteps, making it sound and feel like an army brigade storming the building. They had been in the basement eating hors d'oeuvres, just talking and waiting for the wedding rehearsal to start. Bishop Hines' wife and Mike's mother, Sarah, was still downstairs with Lauren's mother and father, Marion and Fred Alexander. A few others were down there, including the church's kitchen staff preparing for the rehearsal dinner. Bishop Hines was running unusually late, as he'd found out at the last minute that the guest soloist needed a ride to the church. Therefore, Bishop Hines had the dilemma of being on time or doing the right thing. He chose the latter. He had to send a text to Mike and Lauren, stating that he would be about five to ten minutes late. Nonetheless, no one wanted to be late or not ready in front of Bishop Hines, even if Bishop Hines was late himself.

When they approached the front of the church, Rita yelled back to them, "You all sound worse than them kids, running up the steps!"

They laughed as they walked along the right-side aisle wall to take their seats. The women sat on the first pew, while the men took seats sporadically behind them on the third- and fourth-row pews. Lauren followed behind them, leading her husband-to-be, Mike, Bishop Hines' son. Mike appeared happy.

The couple continued to the very front of the church and greeted Rita and Sylvia with hugs. After the greetings and small talk, Lauren walked over to the church's left side and sat on the first pew. Mike followed and sat next to her.

Lauren's side of the party included Jessica, who was her closest friend and maid of honor. Lauren had never had any other close girlfriends, as her views and free speech hindered her in making lasting relationships. She was never good at just lending an ear to a situation. More often than not, Lauren would speak her mind, and what she thought was typically the opposite of what the other person wanted to hear. However, Jessica thought Lauren's honesty and "weird" thoughts, as she called them, were refreshing and entertaining. There were three other bridesmaids. The first was Nina, who was Lauren's older cousin. The second was Lindsay, Lauren's friend from high school. Now, Lauren and Lindsay were close but would periodically go for a few months without any contact. Last was Jewel, who was Mike's younger sister. She was just old enough to be considered a junior bridesmaid.

Mike's groomsmen included Sean, who was his best man and his best friend since the fifth grade. Next was Christian, who was part of their high school trio, and could have easily been the best man as well. Another groomsman was James, who was Mike's close friend from Dartmouth College. Mike graduated with an economics degree with a minor in finance, while James majored in finance with a minor in economics. It played very well for studying together and making sure the other received good grades and stayed out of trouble. And last was Xavier, Mike's nephew, who was the junior groomsman. Jewel and Xavier were about the same age, but Jewel had about two inches of height on him, without heels.

Sylvia started the rehearsal. "Hello, everyone. While we are waiting for the Bishop, let's get started with how we will perform the bridal party processional into the church. I'd also like to determine the exact positions on where and how you will stand up here during the ceremony. But first, can everyone come up here, form a circle, and join hands?" asked Sylvia. She directed them, almost like an aircraft marshaller, waving her arms and hands, bringing them up to the gate.

Everyone got up from their seats and strolled up to the altar, forming a circle and joining hands.

"Mike, can you open us up in prayer?" asked Sylvia.

"Certainly, Sylvia," said Mike. "Dear Gracious and Heavenly Father, we thank you for this wonderful day and for waking us up this morning, having movement in our limbs, and allowing traveling mercies for all of us to be here to prepare for the great union of marriage. We just ask that your Spirit—"

Mike's prayer was interrupted by another loud bang. Someone had just hit the scaffolding again. Sylvia assumed it was the kids. But before she could re-scold them, she saw that it was a man that had just walked into the church. Everyone stared at the man, wondering what he was doing there. His appearance did not help. His clothes looked worn, he was in dire need of a shave and haircut, and his movements were slow. However, Mike, Lauren, and Rita were familiar with him. His name was Marcus. He'd attended the church a few times before, but he was a known drug addict. He would generally come to a Sunday service and go up to the altar to give his life to Christ and ask for forgiveness. Then the following week, he would have a relapse and disappear for another couple of weeks. Mike decided to finish up his prayer quickly; he cleared his throat and continued.

"We ask that your Spirit be among us and guide us this evening to glorify your holy name. In the name of Jesus, we all pray and believe. Amen," said Mike.

Without his notice, Lauren decided to add to Mike's prayer. "And thank you, angels of protection, angels of ministry, and angels of support for all that you do. All your efforts for us are greatly appreciated. Amen," said Lauren.

"Did you just say angels and their efforts are greatly appreciated? Why are you thanking them?" asked Sean.

Lauren walked closer to Sean. "When you go to Burger King after church every Sunday, do you call that Burger King's franchise owner or the president of the Burger King corporation and thank him for your food? Or do you thank the workers?" asked Lauren.

Sean looked confused for a second, then realized her point.

"Angels do a lot of God's work. We should always thank them as well," said Lauren.

"And that's why I love her," said Jessica as she chuckled.

Marcus was now seated on the second-to-the-last pew in the back, just in front of the scaffolding. Sylvia started to facilitate the rehearsal.

"Since Lauren had no preference on how she wanted her bridal party to march into the church, Rita and I looked up a few wedding videos online to get caught up on new trends of wedding processionals. We came up with a combination that we think would look good," said Sylvia. As she continued to explain the processional, it was apparent that Mike was distracted by Marcus' presence. Mike walked halfway toward the back.

"Hello. Marcus, right? Can I help you?" asked Mike.

Lauren looked on, confused as to why Mike would leave the group to go talk to this man.

"Hello, Minister. From the looks of things, I guess there's no Friday night service?" asked Marcus.

"No, sir. It was canceled. We have the wedding rehearsal for Lauren and me," said Mike.

"Congratulations. The Bishop must be very proud," said Marcus.

"Thanks," said Mike.

Sylvia stopped talking, and the church was quiet now. Everyone could hear the conversation.

"Do you mind if I stay and watch?" asked Marcus.

"Unfortunately, I do mind. No offense. This is a private event, and no one can be here but the wedding party," said Mike.

Lauren was furious as she heard Mike's statement. "Excuse me, honey! Can we get back to preparing, and please let him stay?" asked Lauren in a very forceful tone.

Rita and Sylvia looked at each other. Others looked either down or up as if it distanced them from the situation. Mike walked back to the front of the church to Lauren.

"Can I talk to you for a second?" asked Mike.

"Sure," said Lauren.

"Excuse us for a second," said Mike to the wedding group. He proceeded out the church's side door to the parking lot. Lauren followed. Mike waited for the door to fully close.

"What are you doing?" Mike demanded.

"The question is, what are *you* doing?" asked Lauren.

"He can't stay here," said Mike.

"Why not?" said Lauren with her hands on her hips.

"Number one, he is not supposed to be here; number two, he will be a distraction; and number three, we have the rehearsal dinner downstairs in the cafeteria right after this. He is most likely going to want to stay once he knows there is food, and maybe that's why he wants to stay here in the first place," said Mike.

Lauren quickly responded, "Well, number one, everything happens for a reason, so maybe he is supposed to be here; number two, let's be crystal clear: he is only a distraction to you, not me; number three, if he is hungry, why shouldn't we feed him? We have more than enough food and more than enough room. And number four, you are smart. Do you think he drove here? You already know he either walks or gets a ride home with the church van. This is still a church, which is for the needs of the people, regardless of our wedding rehearsal," said Lauren. Mike gave up the battle.

"Fine. He is your guest. *You* take care of him," said Mike.

Lauren and Mike continued to debate so intensely that they did not even realize that Bishop Hines had pulled into the parking lot, gotten out of his car, and approached them with Evangelist Marie Lewis, the wedding soloist. In addition to being one of the church's evangelists, she'd also released a quasi-popular gospel album a few years ago.

"I am so sorry for my tardiness," said Bishop Hines, as he looked guilty of committing a major sin. "Is everything okay?" He could tell they were arguing.

"Yes, Dad. Everything is fine. Hello, Evangelist Lewis. Thank you for coming this evening," said Mike.

"Hello, Minister Hines. Hello, Sister Lauren," said Marie.

"Hello," said Lauren.

"And, no problem. I am glad to support you two," said Marie.

"We were just going back in," said Mike.

Mike opened the door, and the four walked into the church.

As Mike introduced everyone to Evangelist Lewis, Bishop Hines greeted everyone, but he noticed Marcus was situated in the back. He immediately walked back to him.

Marcus stood up to greet Bishop Hines.

"Hello, Bishop Hines," said Marcus.

"God bless you, Brother Marcus!" exclaimed Bishop Hines. "I'm so glad to see you this evening. Albeit, sorry you came all this way for nothing," said Bishop Hines.

"No problem, Bishop. I walked here, and I usually take the van back.

I was just resting my legs before I walked home," said Marcus.

"Listen, Brother. Please stay. I will take you home, and I would love for you to join us downstairs for dinner after all of this is done," said Bishop Hines.

"Bishop, you are too kind. I don't want to interrupt what's going on here," said Marcus.

"Nonsense. You are part of the church family, and that makes you part of my family," said Bishop Hines.

"Thanks, Bishop. I could use a good meal," said Marcus.

Bishop Hines walked back to the front of the church.

"Do we need to get him a rideshare home?" asked Mike.

"No. I am going to take him. I will drop him off before I take Evangelist Marie home. You don't mind if he stays for the rehearsal dinner, do you?" asked Bishop Hines.

"Really?" asked Mike, exasperated.

"Not at all!" exclaimed Lauren.

Bishop Hines saw Lauren's enthusiasm. He responded.

"Marcus being here is nothing but God's work. I was just talking with the deacons earlier about how we have all these partnerships with so many different organizations. However, we have no partnerships with any drug rehabilitation centers to help our members and visitors with their addictions," said Bishop Hines.

"That sounds amazing, Bishop," said Lauren.

"How can we let them come into our church and not have something to meet their needs? Everyone jumps and shouts for them if they give their life to Christ. But once church service is over, we send them back out into the world to the same atmosphere and environment that promotes their problem. And then we look down on them when they fail. They should be looking down on us for not acting Christlike and doing more to show them the way," said Bishop Hines.

Mike remained quiet as his thoughts were indirectly thrown back in his face. He hoped Lauren would not bring up their recent argument and his position of being opposed to Marcus staying.

Lauren could not contain her excitement. "Bishop, can you imagine how much more successful they would be, if in rehab, they knew that a whole church was supporting them, encouraging them, even visiting them just like we do with the sick?" asked Lauren.

Bishop Hines smiled and said, "Speak the truth, my daughter. That's the true ministry of Jesus Christ. God is so good."

This moment was like many Lauren had with Bishop Hines while dating his son, Mike. Bishop Hines was not only a mentor to her but also a father figure. Bishop Hines never had a daughter, and Lauren's father, Fred Alexander, was busy most days and nights working as a mechanic at his self-owned car repair shop. Fred would always say, if he's not working on a car, then they're not eating or paying bills. Therefore, he spent most of his time, even late nights, at the shop. Unlike Lauren, he was more concerned about daily living and supporting his family than becoming great or changing the world. Lauren appreciated her dad's hard work, but for her, she believed God had put her on the earth to do more than just work and live.

Hanging around Bishop Hines gave Lauren a sense of purpose. She was able to express her thoughts around him freely. If Bishop Hines disagreed, he still encouraged her to speak her thoughts and diligently research them to confirm or deny their truth.

The first time she'd expressed her views around him was when she brought up a common Christianity debate on all the different Bible versions, especially newer versions. Bishop Hines had said to her, "Lauren, there is nothing new under the sun. The King James version was compiled from many different Bible versions to get all Christians on the same page with God's Word. Even that did not work, as many different Bibles still existed, with different books in each. But for your-self, Lauren, study to show thyself approved. Take your thoughts and try to think even deeper, not as man would think with all his cultural and present-day biases. But as God would think. So, question every-thing you hear, even from me. And question everything you read. The true spiritual warriors of God are always led back to the truth, while the glorious light is hidden to them that are lost." To this day, she still considered those words the best that had ever been spoken to her.

"To help welcome the Spirit of God into this rehearsal, Marie, would you do us the pleasure of blessing us in a song, just like you will do at the ceremony tomorrow?" asked Bishop Hines.

"Yes. Of course," said Marie.

Other than the yellow-and-blue theme and lots of flowers, the only other thing that Lauren cared about making sure was part of her wed-ding was that the ceremony began with a soloist singing the Chris-tian worship song, "*I Exalt Thee*" written by Pete Sanchez. Lauren had heard this popular song many times over the years. But, it was one specific day when she heard this song that she credited for changing her spiritual life completely.

* * *

It was approximately one year before this rehearsal dinner that she attended a funeral at New Lighthouse Temple, with Bishop Hines and Mike. Mike and Lauren had just started dating, and Bishop Hines asked her to come with them to the funeral. He thought it was an ex-cellent way to get to know Lauren during the drive. When they entered the church for the funeral, Lauren sat closer to the back of the church. Bishop Hines and Mike sat in the pulpit with all the other ministers. Pastor Williams and his wife, Angela, were situated on the front pew with a few other family members.

Lauren didn't know anyone, but she knew Mike and Bishop Hines were extremely close to this family, and she wanted to support them. During the funeral, she read the program, including the obituary for Denise Williams, the mother of Joshua Williams, who'd died in the church from a heart attack. The picture on the front of the program and photo collage inside it showed a vibrant, beautiful woman full of life. Lauren thought, *This woman was so young, so beautiful, and for her to die so young is a tragedy.* Lauren glanced from the obituary to the program itinerary list. She noticed that Denise Williams' son, Joshua Williams, was on the program to sing the song *"Goin' Up Yonder."* She was now more saddened to know that this beautiful lady left behind a son, who had to be very young. But the courage of this young man to sing at his own mother's funeral must be great. She patiently waited for that part of the program.

Finally, the guest emcee for the funeral held the microphone and said, "And now, we will have the singing of 'Goin' Up Yonder' by our very own Josh Williams."

The church was silent as Joshua appeared from the door behind the pulpit. All the ministers stood to greet and hug him, one by one. The last and most sincere hug was from Bishop Hines. Everyone in the church could feel it. Joshua held on to Bishop Hines longer than the other ministers. Even though you could not see their faces, they all knew that they were both in tears. So, tears began to fall from the eyes of most of the congregation, including Lauren's.

Joshua went to the full-sized electronic piano that was situated next to the organ. He sat down on the long seat and grabbed the tilted microphone stand and adjusted the distance and height so he could sing. He began on the piano with a D-flat chord and started playing the introduction melody to "Goin' Up Yonder." The church was silent, listening to him play. He played the introduction melody one more time and then stopped playing. The church remained silent. Everyone, including

Lauren, was wondering why he'd stopped. Was he too emotional to sing? She observed him closely. She looked deep into his eyes and at his face. He still looked calm, not emotional at all. She saw him take a deep breath, exhale, part his lips, and forcefully say,

"Church. Please help me sing this song."

He paused, then played a G chord, and began to sing and play the song, "*I Exalt Thee*" by Pete Sanchez. The entire church stood up and joined Joshua in singing. After they sang the chorus a few more times, Joshua raised his hand and closed his fist. The congregation stopped singing while Joshua continued to masterfully play the music's chords, including some of his own creative and extemporaneous combinations. This was when the Spirit of God fell on the church like never before in the history of New Lighthouse Temple. People were standing, waving their hands, crying, and speaking in tongues.

But Lauren saw more than this; she knew Joshua had communicated with the Spirit of God to sing what needed to be sung at that exact moment, and it was not what the funeral program had written. She had always opened her mind to wisdom and knowledge, but this Joshua, this young man, had just opened himself up to the Spirit of God. She wondered, *Was it because of his intuition, or had angels whispered to him to change the song? What had happened in the true realm that changed, or was Joshua himself the one that changed it?* Either way, Lauren realized that with all her search for knowledge and the truth, it meant nothing if she did not have faith in herself and the Spirit of God to change the world. She believed in what she could research, what she could get her hands on, and debate and dissect. Things like faith and trust without evidence were emotions and constructs that she intentionally avoided. However, on this day and in this moment, she cried with Joshua. She asked God to take full control of her life, to create in her a clean heart and renew God's Spirit in her so that one day she would be able to let go and trust what she did not see, but what she knew was true.

* * *

Lauren sat quietly and remembered this moment of Joshua singing at his mother's funeral, as Evangelist Marie sang the same song now during her wedding rehearsal. She remembered how her life had been changed just by that one action of Joshua. She wondered, *Am I playing it safe by marrying Mike? Is there more to marriage than just being the Bishop's daughter-in-law or being the future First Lady of International Covenant Ministries? Do I even really want to be a minister's wife? What if tomorrow is a big mistake?*

8

Late-Night Delivery

Friday early morning (2:30 a.m.)—one day before the community revival.

Even though the firefighters had extinguished the flames consuming Mount Carmel, most of the neighborhood residents were still outside, amazed that another church fire had occurred, and only a few blocks away from the last one. In addition, the fire trucks, police, and emergency vehicles' flashing red-and-blue lights did not help get the residents back inside their homes.

Officer Reese concluded his conversation with Pastor Williams. "So, Pastor, if you see Josh or hear from him, even a text message, you let me know," said Officer Reese.

"I hear you, Joe," said Pastor Williams, as he gave Officer Reese a half wave goodbye.

Pastor Williams walked back to the group.

"What else did he say?" asked Angela.

"Joe said the street cam confirmed the neighbors' account that Josh was standing not too far from the church when the fire started," said Pastor Williams. He turned to Lauren and Monty. "What in God's name were you doing near the church? I told you all specifically to stay

111

away!" exclaimed Pastor Williams.

Lauren and Monty looked at each other and did not say a word.

"Does any of the street cameras show Joshua or anyone else starting the fire?" asked Bishop Hines.

"No. It only picked up Josh when he came out running from the side of the building. And without any other leads, I have a feeling that Officer Reese and the ATF will focus on him as the primary and maybe only suspect," said Pastor Williams.

"You know he didn't do anything," protested Lauren.

"Joe also said there were no signs of forced entry, and you two were the only ones near the building. So, it appears to them that he could have done something to start the fire," said Pastor Williams.

"Perception is always reality," said Bishop Hines dispiritedly.

"He also wants you and Monty to go to the police station in the morning to give a statement, hopefully with Josh," said Pastor Williams. "You would have been considered a suspect too if you had run off just like Josh and not called 911. But my assumption is that, even though you were the one that called 911, they think that you are still protecting him in some way."

"This is crazy!" said Angela.

"Bishop, I told Joe you would probably want to accompany Lauren tomorrow," said Pastor Williams.

"Of course," said Bishop Hines.

Angela walked closer to Lauren and put her hands on Lauren's shoulders. "Why did Josh run off? Where did he go?" asked Angela.

"I don't know. Joshua was looking in the basement window, and he saw something. I don't know what it was, but I am positive he saw something," said Lauren, visibly shaken.

Monty added to the conversation, "Lauren came back to the car running, and then we saw Josh running from the church. Then suddenly, we saw smoke and then the fire. If that looked weird to me, I could only imagine what it looked like to anyone else who saw him running from the church," said Monty.

"I am certain that Joshua saw something. I don't know what it was, but I am certain something was happening in that basement, and Joshua saw it," said Lauren.

"What was Joshua doing?" asked Bishop Hines to Lauren.

"He was just on the ground looking through the basement window, and then it was like he saw a ghost. I started going toward him, but he frantically waved me off and told me to get away and call the cops. You do not tell someone to call the cops if you are the one guilty of something!" exclaimed Lauren.

Pastor Williams' anger intensified as Lauren was speaking. "I knew it was a bad idea for you two to be together," he said.

"Honey, now is not the time for that. Maybe he is already back at the house," said Angela.

"Maybe. Let's all head back there just in case," said Bishop Hines.

"Fine," said Pastor Williams.

Everyone left, except Lauren and Monty. It was assumed the two would drive Joshua's car back to the house.

Lauren and Monty walked back to Joshua's car.

"Luckily, he left the keys in the ignition when you two ran off like two idgits," said Monty. Lauren did not respond. "Hello!" exclaimed Monty, trying to get her attention.

Lauren continued to ignore Monty and was thinking, *No way Joshua is back at the house. But where could he be?* She remembered how Joshua had taken a deep breath before he sang at his mother's funeral. She thought this was how he'd gotten in touch with the Spirit of God. So, she closed her eyes, took a deep breath, and slowly exhaled. A thought popped into her head.

"You know where Joshua works, right?" asked Lauren.

"Of course," said Monty.

"Take me there," said Lauren.

"He actually may be back at the house, you know," said Monty.

"If he is, I am sure his uncle or the Bishop will call one of us to let us know," said Lauren.

Monty started the car and drove to Joshua's grocery store with Lauren. He drove up to the crosswalk at the store's front entrance.

The parking lot was dark, except for some luminance from the wall pack lights on the store building's exterior.

"Looks pretty dark in there. As I said before, I think Joshua's back at the house," said Monty.

Lauren got out of the car.

"Thanks, Monty," said Lauren.

"Umm, Lauren. Where are you going? The store is closed and locked," said Monty.

"I'm just going to look around. I will be fine," said Lauren.

"Now, what kind of guy would I be to leave you here all by yourself?" asked Monty.

"I'm a big girl, Monty. I can handle myself. You should get this car back to the house. If not, *all* of us will look suspicious," said Lauren.

"But . . ."

"Bye, Monty!" Lauren said in a singsong voice as she shut the car door. Monty waited for a few seconds, but then he saw a text notification from his dad.

[2:45 AM] Where are you?

From spending just those few hours with Lauren, Monty knew that any effort to stop her or change her mind would be pointless.

He texted back:

[2:46 AM] On my way

Monty drove off back to Pastor Williams' house.

Lauren walked along the front perimeter of the grocery store building, looking through glass windows to see if she could see anything inside. When she stopped, she put her face as close to the window as possible. Lauren covered the sides of her face with her hands to see more clearly into the building. From what she could tell, no lights were on except for the exit signs. Suddenly, a loud horn honked from a car going down the street. Lauren jumped and lost her breath.

As she turned toward the car horn, she saw a man walking across the street. It was not Joshua. The man had been crossing the street as the car was coming. He continued down the sidewalk, not noticing Lauren, nor the vehicle that almost ran him over.

Lauren edged away quietly to not draw his attention, continuing to the corner of the building. She carefully turned down the building's side, still confident she'd find Joshua.

It was very dark, as this side of the tall building had no lights or windows. The grass was moistened and muddy from the previous days' rainfall. Lauren's sneakers were getting dirty. She continued resolutely along, touching the building's wall for a sense of security. Her right hand skirted along one of the horizontal lines of bricks. She grasped each pilaster she encountered protruding from the building.

Around this side, she could see bright lights emitting from behind the building. She knew she would feel safer once she got there. As Lauren made it to the back of the building, the ground turned back to asphalt. She looked at her shoes and couldn't believe how muddy they were. She stomped her feet repeatedly on the ground to shake the mud and dirt off.

"Hello? Who's there!" yelled a voice.

Lauren stopped stomping and walked around the trash compactor that was blocking her view of the speaker. The voice was coming from the loading dock area.

"I know that idgit voice anywhere," said Lauren as she finally appeared in Joshua's view. Joshua was sitting on the loading dock with his legs hanging over the edge, right next to the dock's rubber bumpers, which prevented a truck from damaging the dock's concrete wall. The wall pack lights on the back of the building were even brighter than those on the front.

"Lauren? How? How did you find me?" asked Joshua.

"I may only have known you for a short time, but I've already figured out that the only places you go to are work and home. So, I figured it had to be either one; and there is no way I saw you going right home. Plus, I had a little help from the universe," said Lauren. She intentionally omitted the breathing technique she'd copied from Joshua. Joshua smiled.

"Man, why is it so bright back here?" asked Lauren.

"Sometimes we get late-night deliveries, especially during snow emergencies. Where's Monty?" asked Joshua.

"He drove me here and then went back to your uncle's house, I guess," said Lauren.

"He left you?" exclaimed Joshua.

"You mean, just like how you left me back at the church? What are you doing out here, Joshua? Everyone wondered what happened and why you ran off, including the police!" Lauren's concern translated to anger in her voice at how he'd made her worry.

"The police?" asked Joshua.

"Yes. You were seen running from the church, and then the fire started. You know that makes you look guilty," said Lauren.

"I'm sorry, Lauren. When I ran into the street, I saw you were already back near the car. And then when the fire started burning the rest of the church, I . . . I just panicked," said Joshua, still startled.

"You are still not telling me what happened," said Lauren.

Joshua looked down to the ground past the loading dock.

"What did you see in the window?" asked a calmer Lauren.

Joshua looked at Lauren and looked as if he was going to tell her, but he stopped himself and turned his head back to the ground.

"Are you serious, Joshua? You don't trust me now?" asked a frustrated Lauren.

"I barely know you, and you barely know me," said Joshua.

"Wait. You were the one that said, 'It's like our souls already know each other.' Or maybe that was just a smooth Christian pickup line you use all the time with all the church girls," said Lauren.

Joshua sighed, frustrated. "I'm sorry. You're right. I don't know you, but it feels like I've known you my entire life. I have never been this comfortable around anyone, ever. I just don't know what I saw or how even to explain it," said Joshua.

"But you can try. I've seen many things in my life. You'd be surprised," said Lauren.

Joshua did not respond.

"If we are being honest, I know more about you than you think I do," said Lauren.

"What do you mean? You've been stalking my social media before you showed up at my house with the Bishop?" asked Joshua.

"No. Well, not this week anyway," joked Lauren. "Two years ago, I attended your mother's funeral," said Lauren quietly.

"What? You were at the funeral?" asked Joshua.

"Yes. Mike and I had just started dating, and we had a trip planned to the Jersey shore the same weekend of your mother's funeral. When they got word that your mom passed away, the Bishop asked Mike to cancel our trip. He then he asked me to go to the funeral with them," Lauren explained.

117

"What did Mike say?" asked Joshua.

"He immediately cried. He told me that the lady that passed away and her son were close to their family. She was like an aunt to him. I see now that the tenderheartedness he showed that day was only a reflection of how he felt about your family and not necessarily a consistent personality trait," said Lauren warily.

"And so, you came to my mother's funeral?" asked Joshua.

"Yes. I could tell showing support was important to them. So, I made it important to me," said Lauren.

Joshua sighed. "I relive that day in my mind every day," he said.

"I can't imagine how you feel, even until today. But, I think about that funeral just about every day as well," said Lauren.

"You do? Why?" asked Joshua.

"It was the day that changed my whole outlook on life, God, and myself, really," said Lauren.

"My mother's funeral did that for you?" asked Joshua.

"No. You did that, Joshua," said Lauren. She continued, "When you were walking across the pulpit, and you and the Bishop hugged, I felt just a glimpse of your pain. I think everyone did. And at the time, I'd never had anyone close to me die. It was the worst feeling I'd ever had. So, I can't even imagine how you felt. But then, despite that feeling and all that you were going through, you reached down into your soul. You were such a blessing to everyone in that church, all those who were not mourning the death of their mother. Those who were not going through what you were going through. You did not follow the program of what you were supposed to sing. You decided to sing and play exactly what everyone needed at that moment. The Spirit of God fell on you and everyone in that building, especially me. I've never felt God's presence on me, in me, like I did that day. With your music, you, Joshua, brought everyone in that church closer to God," said Lauren.

"I never looked at it like that. Sometimes I can just feel what needs to be done or said," said Joshua.

"That is called the spirit of discernment, one of the gifts of God. And your use and control of it are remarkable, Joshua," said Lauren.

"Well, I am not sure about that. I do not live a wholly righteous life for God to be giving me gifts," said Joshua.

"You've got it all wrong, Joshua. The Bible says, 'The gifts of God are without repentance.' And no, you are not perfect, but I think you have been doing your best up until now. And any gift you can practice, you can get better at, just like you have done with your music. There are no limitations and no boundaries to what God can do through you, Joshua, especially if you fully submit your life and soul over to him," said Lauren.

"I hear you," said Joshua as he looked away.

"I know you hear me, but are you listening?" prodded Lauren. Joshua turned back to look at her.

She continued, "Ever since I was young, I knew all the scriptures. I always had a lot of biblical and historical knowledge, even debated many ministers to the ground with their false teachings. But that day, you made me realize I was missing something. Something big and imperative," said Lauren.

"What was that?" asked Joshua.

"Faith," said Lauren.

"Ha! Really Lauren. I find it hard to believe that you didn't have any faith," said Joshua.

"Look. I believe in God and the power of God. And I know He can do anything at any time. I just did not have faith in myself or faith that God had a plan and purpose for my life other than just learning and education. And I did not have faith that I could be someone that made a significant difference in this world. For a while, I didn't even have faith that someone other than Mike would ever want me, like me, or even love me," said Lauren.

"Wait, what? You seriously doubted if someone would ever want you other than Mike? You must be joking, right? You are extraordinary, inside and out. The light you have inside of you, Lauren, shines brighter than any lighthouse ever made. And I feel that light every time I see you, every time I think of you," said Joshua.

"Wow, Joshua, You really know how to make a girl feel uncomfortable," said Lauren, loudly.

"I'm sorry. I didn't mean—"

Lauren immediately interrupted, "I meant that in a good way. A really good way, Joshua."

Joshua was relieved.

"It didn't happen overnight. But slowly, over time, I gained more confidence, more insight, and more faith in myself and God. All thanks to you," said Lauren.

"I am sure many others had a lot to do with it," said Joshua.

"Obviously, hanging with the Bishop Hines helped cultivate it. But even if others watered it later on, at your mother's funeral, you were the one that planted that seed in me," said Lauren.

"Thank you for that, Lauren. I guess I needed to hear that. I doubt myself a lot right now," said Joshua.

"Doubting what—what you saw earlier, in the church? You told me to call the police. Did you see someone in the window, was it the arsonist?" asked Lauren.

"Yes, well, sort of. Maybe. I really don't know," said Joshua.

"Either you saw someone, or you didn't," said Lauren.

"I did see someone." Joshua paused. "Or something."

"Something?" asked Lauren.

"Listen, I don't know exactly what I saw. It was something down there before the fire started. This thing was moving around, and then I saw flames," said Joshua.

"Maybe it was a person, the one who has been setting all these fires," said Lauren.

"Maybe. But when it saw me looking at it through the window, it moved closer to the window to look at me. But it went directly into the fire to get to the window. It was in the fire, but it didn't get burned. It seemed like, it wasn't even bothered by it. Then it just quickly shot from the fire toward me, and that's when I ran," said Joshua.

"Wow. Are you sure—"

Joshua cut off Lauren before she could finish her sentence. "I know it sounds crazy. Even hearing myself say it sounds unbelievable to *me*. But that's why I didn't want to say anything."

"How can you be sure? It could have looked like this person was in the fire, but maybe he or she was actually in front of it," asked Lauren. "It was dark."

"And yes, I was on the ground, and the windows were dirty. I know. I know," said Joshua. "It's just that . . ." Joshua trailed off.

"It's just that, what?" asked Lauren.

"I think that I've seen this thing before, many times before actually," said Joshua.

"I am not following you," said Lauren.

"I have this reoccurring dream. There is this shadow. A dark presence or something evil that is after me," said Joshua.

"A shadow?" asked Lauren.

"That's the only way I can describe it. When it is around me in my dreams, it feels heavy, dark, and definitely evil," said Joshua. "That thing I saw in Mount Carmel resembled it, and I got the same feeling," said Joshua.

Lauren did not say a word.

"Hello!" exclaimed Joshua. "After that speech you gave me, I tell you all of that, and you have nothing to say?"

"Just give me a moment, Joshua. I'm processing all of this information," said Lauren.

"Okay, process away," said Joshua.

Joshua quietly sat as Lauren thought about what he'd said. After a minute, Lauren closed her eyes, took a deep breath, and slowly exhaled. She looked up at Joshua and smiled.

"I got it. Let's think of all the possibilities of what it could be?" suggested Lauren.

"Okay," Joshua agreed.

"Remember, the police said that with the previous church fires, there were no signs of breaking and entering, and no one was seen entering or leaving the churches, right?" asked Lauren.

"Right. Well, except for Trustee Copeland, who died in the second fire at Church of the Living God. But the cameras only saw him and no one else entering, and no one left after he entered," said Joshua.

"And no broken-into doors or windows, right?" asked Lauren.

"Right. And there were no signs of faulty electrical or building issues," said Joshua.

"Yes. And if that's true, then the arsonist is the smartest and most sophisticated intruder ever known, or we are dealing with something supernatural?" said Lauren.

"Supernatural. You mean like a demon?" asked Joshua.

"Yes, or it could be a ghost, like we talked about earlier in the Book of Samuel. But, it could also be a ghost that is a vengeful spirit. I'm just guessing right now," said Lauren.

"But why? Let's just say it is supernatural. Why would something supernatural be burning churches to the ground?" asked Joshua.

"I don't know, Joshua. Maybe there's a connection between your dream, these fires, and what you saw tonight?"

Joshua nodded; these were the same questions he'd been having.

"Let's go do some research!" exclaimed Lauren.

"You are strangely excited about all of this," said Joshua.

"I am," said Lauren.

"Wow," said Joshua.

"Maybe the arsonist is just a man or woman playing dangerous fire pranks. But what if it is something unexplained, something supernatural? You have to admit, Joshua, that would be pretty cool for us to uncover."

Joshua laughed. "Yes, I guess it would be. But it also sounds dangerous too."

"What's a mystery without a little danger? And the way you wanted to get a closer look inside the church tonight showed me you feel the same as I do," said Lauren.

Joshua laughed again. "Touché," he said.

It was daybreak, and the sky was getting brighter. The lights no longer lit the loading dock.

"I can't believe how late—I mean how early it is. We should get home," said Joshua.

"I don't think that is a good idea," said Lauren. "Remember, the police want to talk to you."

"After talking to you, I am calm now. I didn't start the fire, and I have nothing to hide," said Joshua.

"Joshua. Are you going to tell them exactly what you saw and why you ran, and, oh yeah, why don't you throw your dreams in there while you're at it?" asked Lauren.

Joshua sighed. "I guess not. Good point."

"I assume they have no evidence to arrest you, but you can be absolutely certain you will be there all day, and maybe all night getting interrogated," said Lauren.

"Yes. You're right. We better get going before the opening shift gets here, or a delivery truck shows up." Joshua stood up to leave.

Lauren looked around the loading area and noticed all the trash on the ground and a few broken shopping carts against the building.

"You certainly take me to the most interesting places for our dates, Joshua. I tell you," said Lauren.

Joshua laughed.

"Hey. Can you text Monty to come pick us up?" asked Lauren.

"I guess. Where could we go? I don't feel like dealing with my uncle right now," said Joshua.

"We can go to the Bishop's house. It's so big you can have a party on one side of the home, and anyone on the other side would never know," said Lauren.

"Ain't that the truth. I remember the first time I went there as a kid. It felt like I was walking into a castle," said Joshua.

"I have a key to the side door, and we can go down to the guest basement. When I'm not at the library, I sleep and work on my thesis there. It's so large, and no one ever bothers me," said Lauren.

"What about the Bishop?" asked Joshua.

"I'll tell him that I'm at the library. I'm positive he will not come down there. And even if he is home, he is usually up in his study reading the Bible or writing sermons. Trust me. He won't know we are there," said Lauren.

"What about Mike?" asked Joshua hesitantly.

"Mike doesn't live there anymore, Joshua. He's all grown up with a totally separate life," said Lauren.

Joshua took this comment as a slight insult since he still lived with his uncle. "Are you trying to say something?" said Joshua.

"Don't get all insecure on me now. Mike moved a long time ago. And he travels so much, he is never around," said Lauren.

"Okay. Let me text Monty," said Joshua.

"Wow. Another date!" exclaimed Lauren.

Joshua smiled as he grabbed his cell phone to text Monty.

9

Soul Much

Friday morning—the day before the community revival.

Monty pulled Joshua's car up to Bishop Hines' house. Joshua and Lauren were in the back seat together. Bishop Hines' home was situated on four acres of green, freshly cross-hatched cut lawn bordered by tall evergreen trees. The landscaping bed lined the entire front of the house. It only broke at the front step entrance. It was full of low bushes, various plants, and an assortment of purple and yellow perennials that skirted the brick pavers that led to the front steps. It was a 7,981-square-foot redbrick house, with stone wainscoting on the bottom of the front façade. From looking at the front of the house, the home appeared to have three separate sections, as both the right and left wings were relatively large and protruded out farther than the middle part of the house. It had six bedrooms, four full bathrooms, and three half baths. And the one main benefit of the home for Joshua and Lauren was that the house possessed two separate finished basements. The main basement encompassed the lower level of just the main section and right wing of the house, while the left wing had a separate side entrance with its own smaller finished basement. The main basement was used for entertainment purposes, while the separate left wing basement was used for extended stay guests. For the moment, it was occupied by Lauren.

"Is this the Bishop's house?" asked Monty in awe.

"Yup," said Joshua.

"Oh man, his house is huge!" exclaimed Monty.

"I told you to come with me every time I visited. We always had so much fun coming here," said Joshua.

"You could have a party on just the one side of the house, and no one on the other side would even know it," said Monty.

Lauren laughed. "I said the same thing." She pointed. "Keep going, Monty. Pull a little farther up so we can walk back without being seen," said Lauren.

"Doesn't the Bishop get any flak from having such a big house and then preaching to people that don't have anything? A lot of broke church members might find this offensive," said Monty.

"It's funny that you say that. I was just watching this video the other day on how this pastor was getting audited and was trying to justify his high lifestyle and shopping habits funded by the members of his church," said Joshua.

"And what's the difference here?" asked Monty.

"In the video that I was watching, the pastor used church funds to pay for most of his personal expenses. All his expensive clothes, his cars, his vacations, his home. And he didn't report any of it as income," said Joshua.

"I'm pretty sure I saw that video too," said Lauren.

"But Bishop Hines was a millionaire way before he became a bishop," said Joshua.

"A millionaire?" asked Monty.

"He grew up broke. But, he loved saving money and hated spending it. He would always say, 'The key to living is to pray, save, and invest.' So, he invested in commercial real estate and made a lot of money. He's such a great role model," said Joshua.

"How do you invest in commercial real estate?" asked Monty.

"The Bishop calls it being an equity investor?" said Lauren. "Real estate developers need to raise money for projects, and the Bishop is one of the investors they call. He gets a return for each project, collecting money each month for doing nothing," said Lauren.

"So, he told you all about his businesses too?" asked Joshua.

"You know the Bishop loves to talk. If you spend enough time around him, you will hear everything. He owns a few shopping centers and gets a portion of their rental income every year," said Lauren. Monty looked at Lauren, confused.

"But if he doesn't like spending money, why all this?" asked Monty as he pointed back at the house.

"He got this property as part of one of his investment deals. I don't know how exactly, but it was part of a portfolio deal that he and some other investors acquired from a business that went bankrupt. The portfolio included residential, commercial properties, and some other types of investments," said Joshua.

"That was before he got heavy into the ministry. But after he became a bishop, he completed a significant amount of renovations on this house. That must have cost a fortune," said Lauren.

"I see. It has been a while since I have been here," said Joshua.

"I can see how he has garnered a lot of respect compared to other ministers," said Monty.

"Exactly. If you ever fell on hard financial times and needed a breakthrough, who would you ask to pray for you—Bishop Hines, whom God favored with all of this?" said Joshua as he pointed back at Bishop Hines' house. "Or Pastor Jeffries from Grace Temple, whose hooptie car never starts after church?" asked Joshua.

"Truth, and point taken. It's so embarrassing driving by that church and always seeing somebody grabbing jumper cables for that junk car of his," said Monty.

"Joshua. We need to go," said Lauren.

"You two better give me a good rideshare rating," joked Monty.

"Five stars, buddy, but no extra tip," said Joshua.

"So, what do I tell everyone again when they ask if I saw you two? You want me to lie?" asked Monty.

"You're smart. You'll figure something out," said Lauren.

"We won't be here long. I'll be home in no time," said Joshua.

"Yeah right," said Monty sarcastically.

"Seriously. Plus, I *have* to be at work this evening. I definitely cannot stay late," said Joshua.

At that moment, Joshua stopped in his tracks for a moment before he got out of the car. He remembered that he was supposed to work on the store fact sheet and review it this evening with Rick before their meeting with HR and the head of operations on Monday.

Lauren attempted to get Joshua's attention. "Joshua? Is everything okay?" asked Lauren.

"Yes. I just forgot that I need to do something," said Joshua, shaking his head.

"Do you want to forget about this?" asked Lauren.

"No. Not at all. Let's just not take too long," said Joshua.

Joshua and Lauren got out of the car and quickly walked to the left wing's side door. Lauren had a key. They walked through the door and then down a narrow hallway with a ten-foot-high ceiling and simple white patterned 12 x 12" tile on the floor. It led to a door and another hallway right next to it. The entry went down to the basement, while the adjacent hall went to the rest of the house. Lauren opened the door and walked down the steps. Joshua followed.

"Shut the door," said Lauren.

Joshua went back up a few steps and shut the door behind him. He walked down to the bottom of the steps. Joshua looked around and was still amazed at how beautiful even the home's small basement was compared to an apartment or small house.

"No matter how many times I come here, it always blows my mind how amazing this place is," said Joshua.

"I can't believe it either. The guest basement is bigger than any apartment that I've lived in," said Lauren.

"It's definitely bigger than my bedroom at my uncle's house, maybe even larger than our whole first floor," said Joshua.

"Definitely," said Lauren. They both laughed.

Joshua looked around. He saw Lauren's stuff was everywhere: books, papers, a few clothes.

"You sure made yourself at home," said Joshua.

"Hilarious Joshua," said Lauren.

"Where is Mike again? Does he still hang around here?" asked Joshua, pretending to be nonchalant.

"Now you're just being an idgit," said Lauren.

Joshua laughed. "If you can't handle the heat, don't walk in the fire," said Joshua.

"Now is not the time for fire jokes, Joshua," said Lauren.

"You're right. That was such an idgit joke," said Joshua.

"Not impressive at all," joked Lauren.

Joshua remembered that he had not looked at his cell phone for a long time. He had twelve missed calls and five unread text messages. He read the last two texts, both from his uncle.

[6:12 AM] Don't be irresponsible. Call me!

[8:47 AM] Joe said ATF confirmed this morning that there were no

signs of anyone breaking in or out of the church again. Eyewitnesses and undercover police only saw you leaving the scene.

"I got a few messages from my uncle and a few others. But my uncle says it's just like the other fires. No signs of anyone entering or leaving the building. Oh, just me leaving the scene. How come they didn't see you?" asked Joshua.

"Because I am not as clumsy as you. But seriously, are you absolutely sure you saw someone in that church?" asked Lauren.

"I am one thousand percent sure, someone or something," responded Joshua immediately.

"Guess that confirms we are dealing with something either supernatural or incredibly unique. Let's get started," said Lauren.

Lauren sat down at the table in the mini kitchen. It was a round wooden table with four matching chairs. She had a stack of four books on the table near the seat that she took, and three other books were spaced out on the remaining area of the table. Joshua picked up one of the books and read the title.

"Interesting. *Constantine: Creator of a Religion or Killer of a Society?*" said Joshua. "I heard a little about Constantine, but I'm confused. Didn't he help define Christianity as we know it? So how could he be a killer of a society?" asked Joshua.

"It's unclear what Constantine did. According to some books, he helped make Christianity an official religion. But with Christianity, it meant that other societies and cultures would be equal to the Romans, and they would no longer be the elite society. So many Romans hated and rejected this movement. In response, many people wrote stories and books that contradicted this and his legacy. Then later, people who supported Constantine wrote books against those people and back and forth for many decades. So, it is unclear what the real historical truth is about Constantine," said Lauren.

"So basically, everyone wanted their own historical facts or truth remembered in history," said Joshua.

"Yes, absolutely. It was important back then to be remembered in history forever and make sure your enemies were forgotten. That is why you need to read as much as you can, but you cannot believe everything you read either. Some written history was falsely written to discredit an event or an entire culture, like which side really won a battle, or what society dominated an era," said Lauren.

"Manipulating facts," said Joshua.

Lauren chuckled. "Yes. Manipulating facts."

"Nice history lesson. But what about this arsonist or dark being, or fire-starter entity?" asked Joshua.

"Entity. Nice word, Joshua," said Lauren.

Lauren rummaged through the stack of books. She picked one and handed it to Joshua. "You can go through this one while I look at some old text," said Lauren.

"Old text in the Bible?" asked Joshua.

"No. Actual text that didn't make it into the King James Version of the Bible. For my thesis research, the Bishop had one of his contacts at the Vatican get me scans of some rare unpublished translated scripts from some sacred manuscripts. I asked the Bishop if they were parts of the unpublished Dead Sea Scrolls, but he would neither confirm nor deny it," said Lauren.

"Bishop Hines is something else," said Joshua.

"He generated so many contacts from his investments and charity and mission work overseas, I wouldn't be surprised if he met the Pope himself," said Lauren.

Lauren continued to talk while Joshua stared, admiring her beauty. He loved the fact that she had so much spiritual insight and knowledge. She was challenging everything he thought about God, religion, and spirituality. He felt it was drawing him closer to her and God. *Everything happens for a reason. Maybe she was meant to come into my life at this very moment. The situation with these fires, my job, my dreams— how could I have gone through all of this without her?* He began to pray to himself. *Lord, I thank you for my life and strength. I thank you for putting Lauren in my life right now. God knows . . . I mean, you know I need someone like her to help me figure all of this out. I open my heart to your will. In the name of Jesus, I pray. Amen.*

"Joshua! Are you even listening to me?" asked Lauren.

"Yes. Of course, I am," said Joshua.

"You were looking down, but your lips were moving. Like you were talking to yourself," said Lauren.

"I was—" Joshua started, but Lauren interrupted him.

"Joshua. I can already feel you are about to tell me a little white lie. I'm not sure why, though. There's no reason to. You should know by now we can tell each other anything," said Lauren.

"Man. You know me like the back of your heels," said Joshua. Lauren smiled. "I was just praying for this situation. I mean for us in this situation," said Joshua.

"Are you serious? That is wonderful. Next time, please let me know. I would love to hear you pray," said Lauren.

"Got it," said Joshua.

"I've been in these clothes all night and day. I'm going to get a shower and change," said Lauren.

"What about the research?" asked Joshua.

"I've been reading for weeks. I think you can take the lead for now. I will be right in there," said Lauren as she pointed to the guest bedroom on the other side of the room.

The guest bedroom had a full bath and shower. She walked to the bedroom door and turned back to look at Joshua and smile. Joshua smiled back, but he was unsure if this was an invitation to join her or just confirmation that things were going exceptionally well. He thought it was too much of a risk to assume the former and decided just to be happy with the latter.

Joshua grabbed two books and one of Lauren's Bibles and placed them in front of him. He opened one and started speed-reading, looking for keywords about anything supernatural.

Not used to researching, Joshua felt reading the books page by page was very tedious and took too long. To speed up the process, he took out his phone and downloaded a Bible concordance application.

He remembered seeing it on one of the ads in his Bible app when he was looking up a scripture during a church service one Sunday. Pastor Williams had asked him to come up to the altar and read that week's scripture, already placed on the program. Joshua walked up to the podium and pulled out his phone instead of an actual hard-copy Bible. When he opened the Bible app on his phone, an ad for a Bible concordance application popped up on his screen. Joshua's repeated efforts to close the ad and return to the Bible did not work.

To make the matter worse, he could not even get his phone back to the main screen. He had to completely shut off his phone and wait for it to turn on again. Pastor Williams could not wait any longer and walked up to Joshua and handed him a Bible while the congregation patiently waited for them to find the scripture. When Joshua finally began reading, Pastor Williams walked back to his original position with displeasure still shown on his face.

Joshua looked around Bishop Hines' basement with the feeling of guilt for using the app instead of reading as Lauren had suggested. The concordance app was downloaded, and Joshua opened it up and typed in the word *angel* in the search box. A full list of all the scriptures that included the word angel appeared. He read through a few of them in detail. He then typed in the words *evil spirit*. This made his research go so much quicker. He loved what he was reading; there was so much he didn't know! These things were never taught to him in Sunday school, vacation Bible school, or even Bible study. He whispered, *How could I attend so many Bible studies and never really know the Bible?* He wanted to know more. He continued his search with a few more keywords. Then, he noticed one of Lauren's notebooks sticking out of her book bag. He grabbed it, found a pen, and began taking notes on a blank page.

- *Genesis 1:26 – God says let "us" make man in "our" image. Who is "us" and "our" in this scripture?*

- *Old Testament – There is "the angel of the Lord" and "the angel of God" and just "angels." Is there a difference? It says, God used them for "good" and for "evil." If God is all good, why did he "repent of his evil"?*

- *I Samuel 16:23 – God sends an "evil spirit" upon Saul*

- *I Samuel 28 – Psychic witnesses "gods ascending from the earth" and brings up Samuel's ghost to talk to Saul. Who are these other gods? Are they the "us" when God says let "us" make man? Or they the other gods that different cultures worship, such as Horus, Osiris, Ganesh, or Krishna? Or are they angels?*

- *Mark 5 – Man possessed with "many devils." Are these devils fallen angels?*

- *John 14:12 – Jesus said, 'He that believeth on me, shall do also greater works than these.'*

- *So many scriptures about dreams. How is my dream related to all of this?*

Joshua put the pen down and put his hands on his head and sighed. The shower stopped. He stared at the bedroom door, imagining Lauren coming out. He heard the bathroom door open. He could tell she was drying herself off and opening and closing some dresser drawers.

Then, suddenly, the noises in the bedroom stopped. Joshua listened for a few more minutes and still did not hear anything.

"Lauren. Are you okay?" Joshua said toward the bedroom. He heard no response and got up from his chair. He then ripped the page of his notes out of Lauren's notebook. He folded the piece of paper with his notes and carried it in his right hand as he approached the bedroom door and lightly knocked.

"Hello. Lauren." He'd said again, but this time with more concern in his voice. He opened the door a crack. He saw Lauren, who was not dressed but wrapped in a bath towel. She was putting on lotion. Joshua's eyes brightened up like light bulbs that had just received a massive burst of energy.

Lauren saw his face and started laughing. "You never saw a girl in a towel before?" asked Lauren.

Joshua was speechless. Even if he knew what to say, which he didn't, he was sure that his mouth could not form the words to speak it correctly or without sounding like he had a speech impediment.

"What do you have in your hand?" asked Lauren.

"Notes," said Joshua. He was relieved that he only had to respond with one word.

"Let me see," said Lauren.

Joshua walked over to Lauren and handed her the piece of paper. She unfolded it and saw all the notes Joshua had taken.

"You were really busy out there. You know you can sit down, right?" said Lauren as she folded the paper up and gave it back to Joshua.

Joshua sat down on the bed next to Lauren on her left side. He put the notes in his back pocket. His posture was straight and stiff.

"Relax, Joshua. Are you worried about the Bishop or someone else coming down here?" asked Lauren.

"Neither. Honestly, I just don't want to do anything that you may regret in the future," said Joshua.

"Now, why would I regret anything?" asked Lauren, giving him a sidelong glance.

"Things didn't work out with you and Mike. That must have been really tough. I don't want you going through anything like that again," said Joshua.

"Does that mean you're planning to hurt me?" asked Lauren.

"Never. I could never hurt you. My soul . . ." Joshua paused for a moment. He took a deep breath, exhaled, and then said, "My soul loves your soul way too much, Lauren."

Lauren was speechless. Not only was that the best thing that any guy could ever say to her, but she also could feel it was true. She felt that truth in her heart and could see that truth in his eyes. But more importantly, her soul could feel the truth of his acknowledgment. It was as if his soul had spoken directly to her soul. Her eyes watered. Joshua leaned over to embrace Lauren, and both her arms reached over his shoulders and pulled him into her. He immediately wrapped his arms around her waist and held her tightly. She placed her face in his neck and began to cry. As she wept, Joshua leaned back, put his face in front of her face, leaned in slowly, and kissed the center of her forehead. Lauren stopped crying, but her face was still wet from tears and her nose slightly leaking. Joshua wiped her face, including her nose, with his right hand.

Lauren laughed. "Is that payback from earlier?"

"No. But I have no tissues," said Joshua.

"There is a box in the bathroom," said Lauren.

"It's fine," said Joshua as he wiped his hand on his jeans.

"My soul loves your soul too, Joshua," said Lauren.

Joshua kissed her forehead one more time. He then lowered his face and kissed her on her nose, then down to her lips. They looked at each other for a brief moment and then kissed again. Lauren leaned down and put her forehead onto Joshua's chest. She sighed. She felt the resonance of love between them.

"I think that's how a kiss is supposed to feel," said Lauren.

"You mean like this?" asked Joshua as he leaned in to kiss her again, this time longer and more passionately.

If emotions ever had electricity, it was with them at this very moment. Neither of them had ever connected so much with anyone. Even their lips and tongues appeared to be synchronized perfectly together. Not too deep and not weak. While they continued to kiss, Joshua's left hand grabbed Lauren's right leg and pulled her on top of him, so that she was straddling him while they kissed. The top part of her towel fell below her chest. Joshua departed from her lips to kiss her neck, down to her collarbone, slightly above her chest. He grabbed her waist with his right arm and held her up as he turned around and laid her on her back.

She slid up to the head of the bed while Joshua continued to kiss her body. He crawled the remainder of the way up to meet her face-to-face. Joshua slid his arms under her back, and she raised herself to allow them to get fully under her. He embraced her tightly with his arms, connecting their bodies together like a lock and key. Lauren was like a waterfall, saturating him. Her arms locked even tighter around Joshua's back like he was a tree breathing new life into her. Time passed, but to them, it stood still. They felt and heard nothing outside of each other, only each other's soul. The world was silent before them as they experienced the oneness of true love. It was absolute. It was unconditional.

10

Light and Darkness

Friday evening—the day before the community revival.

Joshua looked toward the altar. He saw two men fighting, but it was more like wrestling around on the ground. A few ministers tried to break it up. The screams of the congregation filled the air, joining the dark smoke clouding the cathedral ceiling. The fire was spreading. Flames skirted the wooden ceiling support beams and smoke filled the top of the church. Parts of the ceiling and other objects, like the large hanging speakers, the lights, the large spinning fans, and the chandelier, crashed to the floor one by one. Joshua looked back in front of him and saw the flames were now on top of the organ. Then the organ keys burnt hot, forcing Joshua to immediately remove his hands from the organ.

He jumped off the seat to help the ministers break up the two men fighting. He felt something behind him and saw the dark being just a few feet away, staring at him. It was too fast, and within a second, it hovered over him. Joshua could not get away. He barely made it off the altar steps before the presence closed in on him. It jumped on top of Joshua, forcing him to the ground. Its weight was heavy. Despite

Joshua's attempts, he could not move the dark being off of him. It felt like a large burning log was on top of him. Joshua could feel his skin burning. He tried to push it off of him, but his hands burned red from touching it. The dark being stared Joshua in the face as it wrapped its hands around Joshua's neck and, with a forceful hold, began choking him. He could not breathe. Joshua tried to remove its hands from his neck, but it was too strong. He gasped for air, but there was none. Joshua tried to move again, but his body was paralyzed. He opened his mouth to yell for help, but the grip was too tight, and he could force no sound out of his mouth. He felt death approaching and tried to yell one more time.

"Jesus!" yelled Joshua. He finally got it out, as it awakened him on the bed with Lauren lying on his chest. With the loud outburst, he jumped straight up, automatically pushing Lauren off him and grabbing his neck with both his hands. Barely focused, his eyes looked up and saw a group of small spheres of light sparkling and hovering over top of them. Lauren rolled hard to the side from Joshua's push and awoke, startled and confused.

"Joshua!" yelled Lauren.

As Joshua sat straight up, he quickly closed his eyes and reopened them, refocusing in the same area. The mysterious spherical lights were gone.

"What in God's name, Joshua!" exclaimed Lauren.

Joshua continued to look around, confused about what he thought he just saw.

"What just happened?" asked Lauren.

"Oh my goodness, Lauren. I'm so sorry. I think I saw something, and it startled me," said Joshua.

Lauren looked at the bedroom door, then at the bathroom door. "Did you see someone? Someone peeking in?" asked Lauren.

"No. There were some things over the top of us," said Joshua.

"What do you mean by some things?" asked Lauren.

"It was like small circles of light or something. I don't know. But they were over top of us," said Joshua.

"You were dreaming, silly. Images from your dreams can remain in your vision even after you open up your eyes," said Lauren.

"What are you talking about?" asked Joshua.

"You know, when you blink your eyes a whole bunch of times, then close them real tightly and see all different shapes and colors. But when you open your eyes, you can still see them for a few seconds," said Lauren. Lauren demonstrated by blinking her eyes multiple times, then looking around the room.

"You are crazy," said Joshua as he laughed.

"Yes, but you like it," said Lauren.

"I do," said Joshua.

"Okay. Now think about what you just saw again. What do you remember seeing?" asked Lauren.

"Just like I said, when I woke up, there were little circles of light over the top of us. But when I jumped up, they were gone. Maybe it was just a carryover image from my dream, as you just wonderfully demonstrated," said Joshua.

"You mean you had that dream again? The same one you talked about earlier at the loading dock?" asked Lauren.

"Yes," said Joshua.

"Was there something after you?" asked Lauren.

"Yes. Definitely. And I am certain now that it has something to do with the fires. When this dark being was over me, it was extremely heavy, and it felt like it was on fire, burning me. Then it was choking me, trying to kill me," said Joshua.

"Wow! I don't even know what to say," said Lauren.

"I know it sounds ludicrous. I feel stupid just hearing myself talking about it," said Joshua.

"Maybe you were able to tap into the spirit world so many times with your music ministry and daily life, that you opened a spiritual door that is either warning or helping you. And God has communicated to many people in their dreams," said Lauren.

"I don't know. It sounds too farfetched to me. Do you know how that sounds?" asked Joshua.

"Well, you're the one that said you saw something in the basement of that completely locked church, not me," said Lauren.

"Point taken," said Joshua.

"Remember, in the Book of Job? God let Satan tap into Job's world. He allowed it for a purpose. And what was the one command that God gave the devil? Do you remember?" asked Lauren.

"Yes. To do Job no harm," said Joshua.

"Yes. So, I believe God has you protected as well," said Lauren.

"Yes. But that did not stop Satan from harming the people that Job loved," said Joshua.

Lauren now regretted bringing up that scripture. "Stop thinking like that, Joshua," said Lauren.

"It's facts. I am now more worried about everyone than ever before, especially you," said Joshua.

"God will protect us all, Joshua. We will pray and believe that he will. While we are at it, we might as well pray to the sons of God as well. I think we need all the help we can get," said Lauren.

"The sons of God?" asked Joshua.

"Just like we were talking about, in the Book of Job. Didn't you ever read it?" asked Lauren.

"Of course. It's about God talking to Satan about how great his servant Job is. It is a common scripture that preachers use all the time to talk about how what you might be going through is not that bad, and Job had it so much worse, and in the end, God blessed him more abundantly than before because of his faith," said Joshua.

"Nice, Mr. Biblical Scholar. You are correct. But no one ever mentions that it was not just Satan and God in that discussion. Others were there too," said Lauren.

"Really?" asked Joshua.

Lauren grabbed her phone from the nightstand and pulled up her Bible app. She read, "Job, chapter one, verse six:

"'Now there was a day when the sons of God came to present themselves before the Lord, and Satan came also among them.'

"So, Joshua, who are the sons of God? Are they just angels? And why are they going to God? And, why is Satan following or hanging out with them? I never heard anyone ask those questions, and I am not sure why," said Lauren.

"By now, I should not be surprised with you," said Joshua.

Lauren smiled at her success.

Joshua looked out the window and finally noticed how dark it was compared to earlier. He realized that they had been asleep for an awfully long time.

"Crap! What time is it?" asked Joshua.

Lauren looked at her watch. "It's six thirty," said Lauren.

"No! No! No! I was supposed to be at work at five o'clock! I have to go," said Joshua.

"Joshua. Are you really considering leaving me here by myself after all of this? After what we've just done? Why don't you just call off from work?" asked Lauren.

"Trust me. Any other time, I would undoubtedly call off. I was supposed to put this report sheet thing together and review it with my boss this evening. We've got this big event on Monday, and he is not around this weekend," said Joshua.

"If it's that important, then you should just go," said Lauren as she backed away from Joshua.

Joshua could hear the disheartened tone in her voice.

"Look, it's not like that," said Joshua.

"Whatever. Just go!" exclaimed Lauren.

Joshua worked to comfort Lauren. "I don't want to leave you. Not right now. Not ever. But I already promised to do this thing, and today my boss was staying later than he normally does to help me. He is probably waiting right now, upset, wondering where I am. I just hope he hasn't left already."

"I understand, Joshua. You can go," said Lauren, this time more calmly. But Joshua knew she was not happy.

Joshua took a deep breath, cleared his mind, and slowly exhaled.

"Look. How about you take me to the store? I need a ride anyway. I can introduce you to him, and we can talk about the fire last night as some type of excuse for why I am running late," said Joshua.

Lauren was pleased and smiled. "That sounds good!"

"Okay, but let's hurry up and get dressed," said Joshua.

They scrambled to get on their clothes. Joshua looked for the clothing articles he'd had on earlier as Lauren looked for something clean in one of her travel bags. She grabbed some undergarments, a pair of jeans, a blue blouse, and a yellow t-shirt to go underneath the blouse.

They walked out of the bedroom. Lauren grabbed her car keys, then put her notebook and a few other books in her book bag. Joshua and Lauren went up the steps, out the basement door, and into the left-wing hallway. They heard a voice from the central part of the house. It was coming from the living room just on the other side of the hall.

"Hello! Who's there?" said a heavy male voice.

"Oh no!" whispered Lauren to herself.

"Is that . . .?" asked Joshua. His question was incomplete because he already knew the answer.

"Yes. It's Mike," said Lauren.

"Just great," said Joshua as he looked at Lauren in grief, remembering how she'd convinced him that no one would be in the house, especially Mike, Bishop Hines' son, Lauren's ex-fiancé.

Lauren walked down the adjacent hallway, and Joshua followed. She walked confidently into the room first.

"Lauren," said Mike.

He'd known that she was most likely there from seeing her car in the driveway. However, Lauren gave a half smile as Joshua then entered the room, coming up from behind her.

"Josh?" said Mike, now with a confused look on his face.

Joshua gave him a quick hand-chop wave hello.

"What are you doing here?" asked Mike as he looked at Joshua.

"Uh, just helping out Lauren on a project," said Joshua as he put his head down. Joshua thought, *Out of all the people to see right now, it had to be Mike. I should not be surprised. He did grow up in this house. But, it would have been better to run into the Bishop.*

"*You,* Josh, you're helping *Lauren* on a project?" asked Mike with distrust. He thought, *Lauren never needed help on anything.* He knew it was a lie and could tell that they were more than just friends by the look of guilt on their faces.

"Look, Mike. Please don't make this more awkward than it already is," said Lauren.

"Are you serious? You think *I'm* the one making this awkward? You're the one in my house with this kid," said Mike.

"So, I'm just a kid to you now?" asked Joshua with a temper.

"Am I talking to you, Josh?" exclaimed Mike.

"No, but I am talking to you!" exclaimed Joshua.

"Really? I could kick your ass back then, and I can still kick your ass now," said Mike.

"I'm not a little kid anymore, Mike. You don't know me like you think you do," said Joshua with confidence.

"Minister Mike. You always like to lose that title and start cussing when somebody makes you mad," said Lauren.

"I knew my dad keeping you around was eventually going to be a big problem," said Mike.

"I am not the Bishop's little pet, and him wanting me to hang around him and participate in his church affairs was his choice," said Lauren.

"Let's see what he thinks about that choice now, especially when he finds out that you were hiding out in our house with this guy. I also heard that he might be the one causing the church fires," said Mike.

"I had nothing to do with them," said Joshua.

"Well, I wouldn't know because, according to you, I don't know you anymore," said Mike.

"Don't push me!" yelled Joshua as he stood tall, looking at Mike in a furious rage.

"What are you going to do; hit me? Or better yet, you going to set our house on fire?" responded Mike, mocking Joshua.

Suddenly, Joshua balled up his fist and gave Mike a right hook directly to his jaw. Mike fell to the ground.

"Joshua!" yelled Lauren.

Mike got halfway up from the floor to a sitting position, holding his jaw. "You really hit me, in my own house!" exclaimed Mike.

"What is wrong with you, Joshua?" yelled Lauren.

Joshua's anger subsided. Reality and logic sank back into his brain. He realized that he'd just made a bad situation even worse. He tried to rectify it.

"Mike. I'm sorry," said Joshua with guilt in his voice as he looked at

Mike, still on the floor.

"Save it for the police. Just get out of here before I call them right now!" yelled Mike.

Lauren grabbed Joshua's arm.

"We have to go. Right now, Joshua!" urged Lauren.

Lauren led Joshua out of the front door. After walking about twenty feet, Lauren stopped, then grabbed Joshua's face to look down at her.

"What was your problem back there?" she yelled.

"My problem? What about Mike?" said Joshua.

"You have way more to lose right now. This situation is already not looking good for you. Then, you get into a fight with Mike in the Bishop's house! How is that going to look? You are throwing all of your credibility out the window," said Lauren.

With Lauren's statement, Joshua realized that if he were in the same position as Mike, he probably would have felt and reacted the same way. He thought, *If your ex-fiancée shows up in your house with one of your old friends, that should make anyone mad.* But then he also thought, *How does it look for Lauren to get caught in the Bishop's house making love to someone other than Mike? That would not look good for her, either.* He pondered on this for a few more seconds but didn't mention it.

"You're right. I was not thinking. I'm sorry," said Joshua.

They got into Lauren's car, and Lauren sped out of the driveway. She drove toward Joshua's store.

"I am so late," groaned Joshua.

"You really should call off from work now. And we barely got any sleep," said Lauren.

"I can't. I told you that I have this big thing on Monday. Some corporate managers are coming to our store, and I have to review a few things with my boss tonight in preparation," said Joshua. For a few moments, they were silent. Lauren continued to drive, remembering the way back to Joshua's work.

"Did you bring those notes you wrote down?" asked Lauren.

Joshua pushed his body up with his feet on the car floor to reach into his back pocket. He grabbed the piece of paper and unfolded it as he sat back down in the seat.

"So, what do you think about what you read?" asked Lauren.

"One of your books focused on a lot of the supernatural entities mentioned in the Bible," said Joshua. Joshua did not have the courage to tell her that he'd only read the table of contents of her books and then did the real research with his concordance phone app.

"For example, for instance, such as?" asked Lauren.

"For example, the Bible talks about 'other gods' a lot. But in church, they do not talk about them," said Joshua.

"Just like the scripture about Saul and Samuel and how other gods were coming up from the earth," said Lauren.

"Yes. But then I started thinking. If I assume the fires are supernatural, then why? Maybe God is not pleased with these churches, and they have more to hide than we know, or maybe it is the devil because he is mad at the work these churches are doing, and he's looking to cause harm or to 'steal, and to kill, and to destroy,' as it says in the Book of John. But . . ." Joshua paused.

"But," prompted Lauren.

"But I did read a few times how God sent evil spirits to coerce people to do what He wants," said Joshua.

"That's always been an interesting and confusing part of the Bible for me. God used evil spirits against his enemies," said Lauren.

"But God also sent *angels of God*, and *angels of the Lord* to people as well. But again, I am not sure if they are the same thing," said Joshua.

"Interesting thought, Joshua. God uses both angels and evil spirits.

That would show that he has full control over all things supernatural, good and evil, right?" asked Lauren.

"I guess. Can you imagine how Satan would feel with God taking one of his evil spirits away from him to do something good?" Joshua chuckled.

Lauren laughed. It helped to hear her laughter. The tension of his encounter with Mike was starting to melt away.

"You mean like, evil spirits are in hell praising Satan, and then God shows up, breaks up the party, and says, 'Oh sorry to interrupt your fun and bother y'all. But, I'm just going to borrow this one evil spirit right here for a second,'" said Lauren.

Joshua laughed as well and continued the joke.

"And that evil spirit is looking at Satan like, 'Dude, I was just worshipping you, your evilness! Do something!'"

Lauren followed up, "And Satan is like, 'Uh, sorry, bro. He's God. You're on your own.'" They laughed hysterically together. Lauren had tears coming out of her eyes.

"You're hilarious." Lauren sighed after she got control of her laughter. Then she had a thought.

"Wait. So does the entire Bible show that God only used angels when He wanted to influence the people called to a great mission; and only used evil spirits when He wanted to influence his enemies?" asked Joshua.

"Wow, Joshua. I never thought about that. If that is the case, then why? I would love to research that theory," said Lauren.

"Listen, Lauren. Regardless of what I saw and felt at that church, I am still not convinced that these church fires are because of something supernatural. It was dark, and the windows were dirty. Maybe my mind was playing tricks on me. It could be a logical explanation for all of this," said Joshua.

"Well, whatever is going on, it still does not make any sense," said Lauren. She turned into the parking lot to Joshua's store.

"Stop!" yelled Joshua.

Lauren braked so hard that they fell forward toward the dashboard from the car's forward momentum. "What!" yelled Lauren.

"Don't stop here, not in the middle of the drive aisle!" exclaimed Joshua. "Pull over into one of these spots." Joshua pointed to the parking spots in the back of the parking lot. Lauren turned left toward the back of the parking lot to park the car.

"Do not ever yell like that while I am driving. You made me think I was going to hit something," said a shaken Lauren.

"Look," said Joshua as he nodded his head up toward the direction of the store's entrance.

Lauren's eyes followed his direction and saw a gray unmarked police car sitting in front of the store. "The police?" asked Lauren.

"Yes. And when the officers park over the crosswalk like that, you know it is not just to go in for coffee and donuts. And that's Officer Joe's car, my uncle's friend," said Joshua.

"You mean Officer Reese?" asked Lauren.

"Yes. Officer Joe Reese. You already know him?" asked Joshua.

"Oh, yes. I met him last night. He and this other guy were super serious about finding you. They wanted to ask you questions about the fire and why you ran away," said Lauren.

Joshua looked over to the other side of the parking lot. He saw Rick's car was still there. Joshua could only imagine what they were saying to Rick right now. He thought, *Did they pull the store's camera footage and see Lauren and me on the loading dock last night? Maybe I shouldn't be seen with her anymore. She could get wrapped up in this mess with me.*

Officer Reese and Agent Carson walked out of the front entrance of the store with Rick. Joshua and Lauren watched as Agent Carson gave

Rick his business card. Officer Reese and Agent Carson got into the unmarked police car and drove out the parking lot, passing Lauren's car on the way. Lauren and Joshua squatted down in the seats until they could no longer see them.

"It's a good thing we drove my car. I assume they have no clue what it looks like," said Lauren.

Joshua did not respond to her comment.

"Stay here. I have to go into the store," said Joshua.

"Are you crazy? Any of the store workers may call the police as soon as you walk in that door," said Lauren.

"Good point. I will go in the back," said Joshua.

"For what?" asked Lauren.

"I need to talk to my boss, but he has to see my face. With the police speaking to him, he must hear directly from me that I had nothing to do with that fire. If not, he will believe the police or anyone else for that matter. This job and his trust are way too important to me. I have to do this," said Joshua.

"I can respect that, Joshua. I will keep a lookout and call you if I see them coming back. Make sure your phone is on loud and vibrate," said Lauren.

Joshua checked to make sure they were both on. He then got out of the car and ran through the lot. Joshua got to the back of the store and hopped up onto the loading dock. He went to the vendor door but couldn't open it since it had no outside handle. It could only open from the inside. He pulled out his cell phone from his pocket. He had multiple messages and missed phone calls from his uncle, aunt, Monty, and one unknown number.

He saw one from Lauren that she'd sent after he got out of the car.

[7:02 PM] Idgit!

Joshua laughed. He responded:

[7:04 PM] Mrs. Idgit!

He again noticed all the other unread messages but ignored them. He sent Billy a text message, hoping he was in the store.

[7:04 PM] Hey Billy. I'm at the back door. Can you let me in?

Joshua waited for two minutes. Then, as he pulled out his phone to text Billy again, the door partially opened.

"Do I get anything for assisting a suspect?" joked Billy.

"You get a sucker punch in the face if you don't. And I am not a real suspect. I did nothing at all," said Joshua.

"That's what they all say," said Billy. He smiled as he fully opened the door, letting Joshua into the back room of the store.

"Can you get Rick and tell him to meet me up on the mezzanine?" asked Joshua. Billy nodded his head and started walking away. "And please don't let anyone else know I am here," said Joshua.

"I'll always have your back, Josh," said Billy.

Joshua walked up the metal steps that led to the mezzanine level of the building.

The mezzanine area was a large platform above the ground floor but also below the high ceiling. It was only used for the building's electrical panels, refrigeration, and HVAC equipment.

This equipment was extremely loud. Therefore, if employees did not want to be seen or heard, this was the perfect place to hide or even have a private conversation.

Rick walked up the steps to the mezzanine to meet Joshua.

"I can't believe you are showing up here right now," said Rick.

"Just give me two minutes, Rick," said Joshua.

"You have thirty seconds, and then I have to call the cops and tell them you were here. If not, I could get fired, and I am sure you are already heading down that path, too," said Rick.

Joshua took a deep breath, cleared his mind, then exhaled, and said,

"You remember the first time I met you?"

Rick shook his head. "Josh, don't go there," he said.

"You remember, don't you? I got in a fight in school right before graduation. I was just trying to help a special needs girl who was getting bullied by a group of students. Even though they kept pushing me back and forth, I got suspended because I threw the first punch. My mother was so upset and scared for me; she made me come with her to work here the very next day. I spent the whole day in this grocery store, most of it on this very mezzanine. You told me what I did was wrong according to the rules and regulations of the school. But it was honorable, and I should be proud of myself for standing up for someone that could not stand up for themselves. Nothing has changed. I'm that same kid. I am my mother's son, and you know me," said Joshua.

"Man, Josh. You always know how to win someone over. So, you were near the church, like the police said?" asked Rick.

"Yes. I should not have been anywhere near that church, but I did not start that fire. I had nothing to do with any of them," said Joshua.

Rick sighed. "I believe you."

"I will talk to the police. I promise. I just need to figure a few things out first. If not, this will all go the wrong way, implicating me in something that I had nothing to do with," said Joshua.

"Well, you better hurry up. They are fast on your trail," said Rick.

"What about Monday and corporate?" asked Joshua.

"I'm not sure. I will figure something out. But even if you do resolve all of this, I cannot guarantee that the offer for my current position will still stand," said Rick.

"Understood. I just wanted to make sure you knew I had nothing to do with all of these fires, regardless of what happens in the end," said Joshua.

"And that's why you will always have my respect and support, Josh," said Rick. "Your mom would be immensely proud. Just make her even prouder and fix this," said Rick.

"I will, and thank you," said Joshua.

Joshua walked down the steps and out the back of the store to get back to Lauren's car.

Lauren had been patiently waiting, looking around for Officer Reese's car or another police car that might pull into the lot. She looked over on Joshua's seat and noticed the piece of paper with Joshua's notes. It had fallen out of his pocket when he got out of the car. She unfolded the paper and quickly glanced down the bullet point list. She paid close attention to his last note:

- *John 14:12 – Jesus said, 'He that believeth on me, shall do also greater works than these.'*

Lauren wondered and thought, *So if a person has absolute true faith in God, then one should be able to do even greater works than Jesus. Greater power, greater works, and greater miracles. Whatever we are facing, with these fires, and with Joshua's dreams, I must be greater.*

Joshua opened the car door, got in, and slammed the door shut. Lauren looked at him and smiled.

"Did everything go okay?" asked Lauren.

"It did. I am starting to believe in this greater power stuff. I knew what needed to be said to Rick, my boss," said Joshua.

Lauren could not believe the coincidence. She had just been thinking to herself about being greater. Before she could speak a word, Joshua continued.

"I have a feeling that I need to get to my uncle's house right away," said Joshua.

"Well, let's go," said Lauren.

11

The Rehearsal Dinner

Lauren and Mike's Rehearsal Dinner

One year before the community revival.

The wedding party, family, and close friends sat around the long table, eating at Lauren and Mike's rehearsal dinner. With wedding coordinator Sylvia's direction, and the presence of Bishop Hines, things went smoothly and without a hitch. In the basement, the church's kitchen staff had combined two long tables and just enough chairs for the entire group. Another separate table was for the junior bridesmaid and junior groomsman, and the other kids who'd just finished playing outside, which included the flower girl and ring bearer. Bishop Hines was at the head of the wedding party table, while his son, Mike, was sitting at the head of the opposite end. Lauren was in the seat closest to Mike on his right side. The bridesmaids were side by side next to Lauren going down the table, and all the groomsmen followed the same next to Mike, but along the left side of the table. Bishop Hines' wife, Sarah, the wedding coordinator, Sylvia, Lauren's mother and father, Marion and Fred Alexander, Aunt Rita, and Deacon Lukens sat down

155

at the end of the table closest to Bishop Hines. There could have been one empty space on the groomsmen's side of the table closest to Bishop Hines. However, that seat was now taken by Marcus, the drug addict, who had been unexpectedly invited to the dinner by Bishop Hines. The kitchen staff prepared a homestyle-cooked meal of ham, fried chicken, sweet potatoes, scalloped potatoes, potato salad, mashed potatoes, string beans, corn on the cob, cranberry sauce, and macaroni salad.

"Are you sure we all won't turn into a bunch of potatoes before the wedding tomorrow?" said Sean, Mike's best man.

Everyone laughed, except Mike. He was too distracted from the thought of his father inviting Marcus to their dinner. Mike angrily wondered, *Why is Marcus sitting in that seat, like he is the center of attention? Couldn't he sit in the kitchen or at the kids' table? He would still be getting something to eat.*

Sylvia interrupted the laughter. "We all know that marriage is not easy. Amen. So, as we sit here in fellowship and celebrate the union of this beautiful couple, can we all show additional support tonight by providing them with some advice from the group?" asked Sylvia.

"Amen!" said most of the group in response. Sylvia continued.

"Whether you are young and think you have some great advice, or you've been married with years of experience, let's all go around the table and give this wonderful couple something that they can take with them into their marriage tomorrow to help them along with this forever journey of love. Amen," said Sylvia.

"Amen!" responded the group again.

"Bishop, can we start with you?" asked Sylvia.

"Praise the Lord, everybody," said Bishop Hines.

"Praise the Lord," said everyone in response.

"Of course, I must first say to the future husband and wife, always put God first. Seek ye first the kingdom of God and his righteousness,

156

and all other things shall be added unto you. Second, Mike, Lauren will always be right. Get that in your head now. And the sooner you do, the better off you two will be," said Bishop Hines.

Everyone laughed.

"Why don't we have the father of the bride go next. Could you, Fred?" asked Sylvia. Fred perked up in his seat.

"Sure. In a marriage, nothing ever stays the same. Life always changes with time, and so will the both of you. Love and accept each other's changes. For that is true love," said Fred. Everyone responded with smiles and sounds of approval.

"Dad, that was so sweet! Thank you," said Lauren.

"Yes. Thank you," said Mike.

"Deacon Lukens, how about you?" asked Sylvia. He leaned back in his chair and grabbed his suspenders.

"Well, let me tell you, the good book says that he that findeth a wife findeth a good thing. After tomorrow, stop trying to findeth!" exclaimed Deacon Lukens. Everyone laughed. As usual, Deacon Lukens laughed harder at his own joke than everyone else. From all the laughs, Deacon Lukens decided to continue the joke. "Your searching days are officially over, young man!"

Sylvia gave a look of apathy and pressed on. "Brother . . .?" said Sylvia, pausing, as she was unsure of Marcus' name.

"Marcus. That is Brother Marcus," said Bishop Hines.

"Brother Marcus. Would you like to give the couple any advice?" asked Sylvia.

"I do have one thing to say, and it goes back to what the Bishop was saying. From experience with my late wife, always let her decorate the Christmas tree and pick out all the decorations," said Marcus as everyone chuckled. "I can't tell you how, all throughout the year, we were like lovebirds on fantasy island, but when we started decorating that tree, we just never saw eye to eye on the decorations, the colors, and whether the lights should blink or not. One year, I finally got smart and just let her handle everything, and it made for more peaceful Christmases year after year," said Marcus.

"That's really good advice," said Christian, Mike's friend since high school.

"Well, we won't have to worry about that. There will be no Christmas tree in our house," said Mike.

"What do you mean, no Christmas tree?" asked Lauren.

"We stopped having a Christmas tree a long time ago. And from hearing Brother Marcus' story, it sounds like it is a great idea not ever to have one," said Mike. His last sentence was an attempt at a joke. But only a few people chuckled.

"Are you going to blame a Christmas tree for them arguing? I guess the last time you and I argued was because I didn't wear a skirt that was four inches below my knees, right?" asked Lauren.

"That is not it, Lauren," said Mike.

"And please don't try to tell me again that the Bible forbids women wearing pants because pantaloons were not even invented until the nineteenth century," said Lauren.

"Lauren!" exclaimed Marion, Lauren's mother.

No one else said a word. After a few moments, Mike decided to defend his statement.

"Lauren, I think you are overreacting. All I am saying is that a Christmas tree is part of a pagan tradition, from ones who did not believe in our God. A Christmas tree promotes many false gods, including Santa Claus, who has now taken the place of Jesus Christ's holiday or holy day celebrations. What kind of Christian would I be to allow that in my own house?" asked Mike.

Lauren responded, "You would be a Christian that loves God's nature and uses one of His most adored creations since the beginning of time to celebrate His life on earth and how he dwelt among us," said Lauren. She waited for a counter to her response.

"You must not understand what I am saying," said Mike.

"No, Mike. I understand very well. I've heard this argument so many times. Why do some Christians forget that it is a tree that creates and breathes oxygen and life into all of us every day, just like God breathed life into Adam? It is a tree that provides fruit and other meals to the world. It is a tree that held our Lord and Savior up when He died so that we might be saved today. Can you come up with a better symbol from nature than a wonderful tree to celebrate His birth and gift to us on that day?" asked Lauren.

Bishop Hines interjected before Mike could respond.

"Interesting thoughts, Lauren. And what about the pagans?" asked Bishop Hines, intrigued.

"Bishop, doesn't the Bible say that 'the earth is the Lords, the fullness thereof, the world and they that dwell therein'? Therefore, everything on this earth belongs to God. Nothing belongs to the devil or any pagans. But the church of God keeps giving over God's creations to the secular world. And if this continues, we will not have anything left to call our own, let alone God's. If pagans did use a tree for their rituals to their gods, I say, so what? We should take it back, for goodness' sake, because it belongs to God, not them," said Lauren.

Everyone looked at Bishop Hines, waiting for his response.

"Girl, I truly need you in my Bible classes challenging the ministers on their teachings," said Bishop Hines. Everyone chuckled.

He continued, "The most interesting thing that you said was what the tree means to you. Decades from now, even centuries from now, people and the history books will not talk about how Christians used a pagan tree. They will talk about how we used it to celebrate the life of our Lord and Savior. How we blessed others with it, and how it brought families and friends together year after year. In the future, the Christmas tree will be viewed differently based on how it is used now, and not how it was used centuries ago before us. Great words, Lauren," said Bishop Hines.

Christian looked at Mike and said, "Looks like you're gonna have a Christmas tree this year, bro!" Everyone laughed.

They continued to eat and talk. Mike and Lauren did not say much other than occasional responses to questions from others.

"Okay. Is everyone sure what they need to do tomorrow?" asked Sylvia. Only a few people said yes, but no one said no.

"Good," said Sylvia.

"Behave tonight, boys," said Sarah.

"Of course, Mother. We are a bunch of angels," said Mike in jest.

"So that means Fred and I can come with you gentlemen too, right?" teased Bishop Hines.

All the groomsmen looked at Mike in panic. Mike attempted to respond. "Well . . ."

"I'm just joking. I trust that you all will behave and make it on time tomorrow," said Bishop Hines. The groomsmen were relieved.

"Mike. Can you lead us out in prayer?" asked Sylvia.

"Yes, of course. Can we all stand?" asked Mike. As they stood and held hands, Mike closed out the evening with, "Now unto Him who is able to keep you from falling, and to present you faultless before the presence of His glory with exceeding joy. To the only wise God our Savior, be glory and majesty, and dominion and power, both now and ever. Amen," said Mike.

The young ring bearer, Travis, loudly interjected, "That's not how we close out!" followed by a few giggles.

"How are we supposed to close out, young man?" asked Sylvia.

"We close out with, 'Let the words of my mouth,'" said Travis in a high-pitched voice.

"Well then, you can close us out the right way," said Sylvia.

Travis took a deep breath and shouted, "Okay, everybody! Psalm nineteen and fourteen: Let the words of my mouth, and the meditation of my heart, be acceptable in thy sight. Oh, Lord. My strength and *my* redeemer. Amen!"

"Amen!" said the group collectively.

Brother Marcus turned to Bishop Hines and said, "That is another reason why I love this church, Bishop. You train the youth to have no fear and to speak up," said Marcus.

"Yes. We must. They will be our church one day. I assume you still need a ride, right?" asked Bishop Hines.

"If it's not too much of a bother, Bishop," said Marcus.

Lauren approached Marcus. "Thank you for joining us, Brother Marcus," said Lauren.

"No. Thank you for allowing me to fellowship with you and your family. It was terrific to be around other people tonight. It took my mind off some things and made me forget about the places I would typically go on a night like tonight," said Marcus.

"I understand. I am so glad that we could help," said Lauren.

A few others were speaking to Mike. Though he tried to appear attentive, 95 percent of his attention was on Lauren. He was closely watching her in his periphery vision.

"Well, is that okay? Mike?" asked Sylvia as she waited for a response and trying to regain his attention.

Mike realized Sylvia had asked him a direct question, and he had no clue what she'd just said. It did not matter, though. He said, "Excuse me," and turned from her to walk over to Lauren and Marcus.

"Excuse me, Brother Marcus. Lauren, can I talk to you for a second?"

asked Mike.

"Good seeing you again, Brother Marcus," said Lauren.

"Good seeing you too. And thank you again. Take care," said Marcus. Marcus walked away toward Bishop Hines.

"Follow me," said Mike as he led Lauren down the side hallway into one of the small classrooms used for children's church. Lauren walked in, and Mike shut the door behind her.

"I don't appreciate how you talk to me in front of everyone," said Mike. Lauren did not respond. "If you disagree with me, you don't have to go on some rant. These are things we can talk about after everyone leaves or another time." Lauren still did not respond. Mike became more frustrated. "Hello! Am I talking to myself? Say something!" exclaimed Mike.

"At first, you don't want me to say anything at all. Now you want me to talk. Can you make up your mind? How about I just give you a remote control so you can mute me, turn my volume down, or just change my thoughts when you do not like what you hear," said Lauren as she turned to the side to avoid eye contact.

"Why do you have to be so extra? I'm just asking you to put yourself in my position," said Mike.

Lauren faced back to him. "Mike, do you really think that conversation would have gone any differently if we were alone?" asked Lauren. Mike looked away.

"I used to think that you and me being opposites, with different thoughts, was a benefit to our relationship. You'd help me grow and see things differently, and I'd do the same for you. But I'm beginning to think that being different just means we are going to argue all the time," said Lauren.

"Opposites always attract," said Mike.

"But that doesn't mean that they stay together," said Lauren.

"Again, I'm just asking that you give me the respect of being your future husband and let me lead," said Mike.

There was a knock at the door. It was Sean. He was looking at Lauren and Mike through the upper part of the door, which was a glass pane. Lauren and Mike could hear him.

"C'mon, Mike. We need to go!" said Sean as he repeatedly pointed to his smartwatch.

"All right. Give me two minutes," said Mike.

Sean gave the door two hard pounds with the side of his closed fist, stressing the urgency of leaving right away. Mike mouthed the word, "Okay." Then Sean walked away.

"I have to go," said Mike.

"Well, go then. Can't have the Bishop's son late for his own bachelor party," said Lauren.

"It's not a bachelor party. Sean and Christian said we were just going to watch the fight," said Mike.

"And you expect me to believe that?" asked Lauren.

"Everyone knows that these nights aren't for the bachelor anyway. It is just an excuse for the other fellas to hang out and do whatever they want for a night. It will be about me for the first thirty minutes, and then they won't even miss me if I slip away," said Mike.

"Isn't that the truth," muttered Lauren.

"I love you," said Mike.

Mike lowered his head to kiss Lauren. But she turned away. However, that didn't stop her from saying, "I love you too."

Mike left the room. Then, Lauren walked out, slightly behind him. Mike ran out the side door that led to the stairs up to the church's parking lot. The basement was empty except for Sylvia, Rita, and Lauren's mom, Marion. Deacon Lukens was in the kitchen, patiently waiting for everyone to leave so that he could lock up the church.

"I'm going to head out," said Rita.

"Me too. It's getting late," said Sylvia.

"Thank you. You two have done a great job so far and have made things so much easier on all of us," said Marion.

"Yes. Thank you," said Lauren.

"No problem," said Sylvia.

"No problem at all," said Rita.

"We will see you bright and early. Good night," said Sylvia. "Call or text me if you need anything, Lauren."

"Will do," said Lauren.

"Take care," said Marion.

Sylvia and Rita also exited the side door out to the parking lot.

"Dad is gone already?" asked Lauren.

"Yes. He left with the Bishop," said Marion.

"Now that you mention it, I just realized that Evangelist Marie was not eating dinner with us. Where did she go?" asked Lauren.

"She took a rideshare home. I think she had to be back home by a certain time because of her babysitter," said Marion.

"*She* must have been the reason why the Bishop was late this evening," said Lauren.

"Right. When you were in the back with Mike, everyone was teasing the Bishop for being late," said Marion as she laughed.

"This has got to be the first time that he was ever late to anything!" exclaimed Lauren.

"Deacon Lukens said he was going to bring it up at the next church officials' meeting. The Bishop did not know how to respond. That was the first time I ever saw him speechless," said Marion as she smiled.

Lauren's attention was already gone. Marion tried to reel Lauren back into the conversation.

"Evangelist Lewis sang so well tonight, didn't she?" asked Marion.

"She did okay, I guess," said Lauren.

"You guess? She has an amazing voice," said Marion.

"Yes. She does. But, the way she sung it is not what I had envisioned in my head," said Lauren.

"Really? Maybe tomorrow will be different. This was just practice, remember," said Marion.

"Yes. But sometimes it is more about the spirit and the emotion than just the voice," said Lauren.

"It feels to me, a lot of this ceremony is not what you have envisioned," said Marion.

Lauren's eyes began to water. She tried to hold them back from becoming actual tears. Marion got up and walked over to the large rectangular opening in the wall into the kitchen. She grabbed a few paper towels from a roll sitting on the long shelf connected to the lower part of the opening. Marion saw Deacon Lukens sitting at one of the tables in the kitchen on his phone. She remembered that he was waiting for everyone to leave.

"Deacon, I know you must be ready to leave, but can you give us a few more minutes?" asked Marion.

Deacon Lukens got up out of his chair and peeked through the opening to see who she meant by the word "us." He saw Lauren sitting at the table on the verge of tears.

"Sure, I'm in no rush. I'll go upstairs and begin shutting everything down before I come back down here. Plus, Bishop Hines always leaves something on, like his computer," said Deacon Lukens.

Marion laughed. "That sounds like the Bishop. Never a person that takes care of the details," said Marion.

"Exactly. Just let me know when you are ready to leave, no rush at all," said Deacon Lukens.

"Thank you," said Marion.

Deacon Lukens walked out of the kitchen and up the steps to the sanctuary. Marion walked back over to Lauren and sat in the chair next to her. Lauren kept her head down, looking at the floor. Marion attempted to comfort her daughter.

"When your father and I got married, we were going through so much at the time. We didn't have a lot of money. And at the time, your father was not a dedicated Christian, so many people, including your Aunt Rita, would tell me that he would not be faithful. They would always say, 'You two are not equally yoked; it's not going to work out.' I was so young and confused. But I knew he was the one for me, even though at times it did not look like it or even feel like it," said Marion.

"So did Dad ever cheat on you?" asked Lauren.

"No. Well, at least I don't think so. Your dad feels so guilty about the littlest things. So, I always assumed that if he made it home from being out late at night, that he did not cheat. He would be more likely to drive off a bridge than deal with the guilt of facing me," said Marion.

Lauren started to brighten up. "I remember when I was twelve, he felt bad about taking ten dollars from my savings jar without telling me. He put back thirty dollars even though he only took ten," said Lauren, smiling from the memory.

"I do remember that. Money was tight, and your father needed lunch money for work," said Marion. "He felt so bad and thought you would never trust him again." Lauren chuckled.

"The point is, I didn't listen to anyone but myself. And everything worked out. And look at this amazing, beautiful daughter we have together. You are so intelligent and independent, and Mike is the luckiest guy on Earth to be marrying you," said Marion.

"Thanks, Mom. But what if we are not equally yoked? I mean . . ." Lauren paused. "Even more now than ever, I feel that we are not equally yoked," she said.

"What do you mean? You two are Christians. You two are both strong and smart. And you both love God," said Marion.

"It's complicated."

"Well, I'm listening."

"Mike is a good man. He is honest, and he loves God and loves to learn. His love for God and his intelligence are what captivated me when we first started dating. But . . ." said Lauren.

"But what?" asked Marion.

"But most of the time we spend together is either in church, or a seminar, or just watching a movie. It is never us talking alone with each other or having conversations about things in life other than church. And when we do talk, we usually argue because he says I question too many things. I am also starting to realize that he is not as godly as I thought he was," said Lauren.

"Mike, ungodly? He appears very Christlike and dedicated to me, isn't he," asked Marion.

"In that sense, Mom, yes, he is. But for me, righteousness and Christianity go beyond the four walls of this church. He only wants to preach to those who attend service, and just with a message from the pulpit or laying hands on them in prayer after preaching. He doesn't seem to show real compassion for people, especially those who are not in church. Brother Marcus' presence here tonight showed me that. Also, could you see him working at a homeless shelter? Could you see him working on missions in Africa, feeding the hungry? Could you even see him talking to the teens on this very street who never come to church? These are the people who need his ministry the most," said Lauren, frustrated.

"I hear you, Lauren. But everyone is not like you," said Marion.

"You're right. And knowing that, do you see me sitting under Mike week after week here at this church? Do you see me as the future First

Lady of this church? If I am not out getting my hands dirty to change the system, a life, or a soul, then it is not for me," said Lauren.

"Wow. My little girl is not so little anymore. Have you spoken to him about this?" asked Marion.

"Yes. But Mike responds like he doesn't care or isn't listening. It's like our souls just don't communicate with each other," said Lauren.

"You two have been dating for quite some time. You mean to tell me you are just now feeling this?" asked Marion.

"Honestly, everyone kept telling me that arguing was normal. So, I couldn't tell if our arguments were normal relationship issues or if we were not compatible. It's not until now, spending so much time together these past few months and for the wedding, that I realize how vastly different we are," said Lauren.

"Listen, Lauren. I cannot make any decisions for you. But please know that your soul will always be correct about who you are and who God wants you to be. Your soul will especially be correct with who needs to be in and out your life. Always listen to it. God orders your steps, and whatever decisions you make, as long as you ask God to take full control of your life and direct your paths, he will do it. I love you so much, my baby. I'm always here for you," said Marion.

"I love you too, Mom. Thank you," said Lauren. They hugged each other as Marion wiped Lauren's tears away from her eyes. They heard Deacon Lukens walking down the steps into the café area.

"All the lights are off upstairs. And, of course, I had to turn off the Bishop's computer. Are you two ready to leave now? If not, I can wait longer," asked Deacon Lukens.

"Yes, we are," said Marion.

Deacon Lukens looked at Lauren. "You are going to be a beautiful bride tomorrow. I will be praying for you," he said.

"Thank you," said Lauren.

12

Fall from Grace

Friday evening—the day before the community revival.

Joshua and Lauren walked into Pastor Williams' house. Joshua felt
unprepared for how he was going to respond to his uncle's expected
anger and rage, since Joshua had not returned any of his calls and had
been out all night and most of the day with Lauren.

"Where have you been!" yelled Pastor Williams. He gave Joshua no
time to respond before he continued.

"You don't answer your phone. You don't respond to any of my text
messages. Do you know how many people are out there looking for
you? Not to mention how many people are calling Angela and me
wondering if we heard from you or asking if you are the one setting
the fires!"

"Uncle, I can explain," said Joshua.

"Can you explain why you disobeyed me and went to the church last
night?" asked Pastor Williams.

"It was my fault," said Lauren attempting to take some of the pressure
off Joshua.

Pastor Williams turned to look at Lauren. "I knew it! Now you finally said something we agree on." Pastor Williams turned back to Joshua. "Please tell me why she is here!" exclaimed Pastor Williams.

"I gave Joshua a ride home," said Lauren.

"Excuse me, young lady. I was talking to Josh, not you," said a furious Pastor Williams.

"Excuse me," said Lauren right back.

"Lauren, thank you for bringing him home. Now please leave," said Pastor Williams in a softer tone.

"Really?" asked an incredulous Lauren.

"Yes, really. This is my house, and I am telling you to get out. And remember, I don't know you. For all I know, you are the one that has been setting the fires the whole time. And maybe even now, brought my nephew into all of this," said Pastor Williams.

"You think I am the one setting these fires?" asked Lauren. Her face became stoic.

"Well, it's funny how *you* just magically appeared the same time the fires started happening. You're a smart girl. Maybe you found a way to set them without getting caught. And now my nephew is acting like someone I don't even know," said Pastor Williams.

Even though Joshua felt Lauren had nothing to do with the fires, his uncle had just put a thought in his head. Joshua thought, *The timing of Lauren arriving during all of this is strange.*

"Hello!" exclaimed Lauren as she looked at Joshua. "Are you just going to stand there and not say anything and let him talk to me like that?" she asked.

"Lauren, will you wait in the car, please? I will be out there in a second," said Joshua.

"No way," said Pastor Williams. He ranted on, "You need to get in the car with me and go to the police station so you can give your statement about what happened last night."

"I'm not going there. Not right now," said Joshua. He turned back to Lauren. "Lauren, I got this. Trust me. Please, for me, go outside and wait in the car," said Joshua.

Lauren rushed out of the living room into the foyer and slammed the door hard as she walked out of the house.

"Look at that. She is nothing but trouble. You need to stay away from her," said Pastor Williams.

"Just a few minutes ago, you were saying that you didn't know her. Now you do?" asked Joshua.

"I know that right now, she is preventing you from doing the one thing that you should be doing to make this right, and that is going down to the station to give your statement," said Pastor Williams.

"If I go there now, I have a feeling I won't be leaving for a very long time. Plus, if I gave a statement on what I really saw, they may lock me away in a mental institution just for that alone," said Joshua.

"Boy, you are not making any sense. Be responsible for your own actions," said Pastor Williams as he ignored Joshua's comment about what he saw in Mount Carmel's basement window the night of the fire. Joshua angrily interrupted.

"I've done nothing wrong!" yelled Joshua. "I have always been responsible for my actions! I've had to be the man of the house ever since I was a kid. It was just mom and me, and I always had to be responsible. I had no choice. I took care of things and stayed out of trouble so that she had one less thing to worry about! And when she died . . ." Joshua paused to hold back tears. "When she died, I didn't let it stop me from doing what I needed to do. I have been working hard at the store, maybe even getting a promotion that could be gone now because of these fires and a misunderstanding. But I always helped you out around this house and at the church. And to add on to all of that, do I have any real friends other than Monty? No. Because my whole life, I have been too busy being responsible. Lauren is the first person that I have felt connected to in an awfully long time," said Joshua as his voice trembled.

The look on Pastor Williams' face showed that he finally respected Joshua's comments, especially after he brought his sister Denise into the conversation.

"Listen, Josh. All I am saying is this does not look good, and it will only worsen. You are not thinking clearly, and I think that girl out there has a lot to do with it," said Pastor Williams.

"Well, since you mentioned things getting worse. I guess it is best if you hear it from me first. I got into a fight earlier today," said Joshua.

"A fight!" yelled Pastor Williams.

"Yes," said Joshua.

"With whom?" asked Pastor Williams.

"Mike," said Joshua.

"Mike who?" asked Pastor Williams, bewildered.

"Mike Hines," said Joshua reluctantly.

"The Bishop's son, Mike!" exclaimed Pastor Williams. Joshua nodded yes as he looked down to the ground.

Pastor Williams threw up his arms and hands and quickly flung them back down in frustration. "What is wrong with you? You two always got along," said Pastor Williams.

"Well. Mike was engaged to Lauren," said Joshua.

"So, she was the one that Mike was marrying about a year ago? Now, why doesn't that surprise me? I bet he broke it off for the same reason I'm telling you to," said Pastor Williams.

"It's not like that. Lauren is truly helping me. Seriously. I have it all under control, and I am going to fix it," said Joshua.

"You honestly think you have this all under control. You are more clueless than I thought," said Pastor Williams.

Pastor Williams and Joshua quieted their debate as they heard the television news break.

Live News 10 reporter Talia Jones was speaking. "In addition to this breaking news, police are looking for this man, Joshua Alexander Williams, of the seven hundred block of Prout Drive, for questioning regarding the recent church fires and the recent death of Trustee John Copeland of Church of the Living God." The news showed a picture of Joshua, obtained from one of his social media accounts. Talia Jones continued, "He was purportedly seen leaving the scene of the Mount Carmel church right before the start of its fire. He is believed to be the nephew of Jerry Williams, community activist and pastor of New Lighthouse Temple, also along the Boulevard. We will report more as this situation develops."

Pastor Williams sat down on the couch. He put his right hand over his face and put his head down.

"Jesus," said Pastor Williams.

Joshua realized the situation had gotten out of control, way out of his control.

"I'm sorry, Uncle. It was not my intention to bring you into all of this," said Joshua.

"Well, now you did," said Pastor Williams, not looking back up.

"I had nothing to do with any of those fires. And I am one hundred percent certain that Lauren did not either," said Joshua.

Pastor Williams finally looked up. "Either you leave with me now to go to the police station, or I have no choice but to call Joe and let him know you are here," said Pastor Williams.

"I will leave, and you can tell him that you tried to stop me, but I didn't listen. I don't want you to get into any trouble or be associated with this, more than you already are," Joshua added with a wince.

"You have three minutes before I make the call to Officer Reese," said Pastor Williams.

"Understood. Where is Auntie?" asked Joshua.

"I don't know. She is probably out looking for you. You didn't answer any of her calls either," said a sullen Pastor Williams.

"Please tell her that I had nothing to do with the fire last night, or any of them, for that matter," said Joshua.

"I don't know, Josh," said Pastor Williams.

"Uncle, if there are any two people on this planet that need to believe me, it is you and Auntie. You may not know Lauren. But you do know me," said Joshua. Pastor Williams did not respond.

"Please, Uncle," said Joshua.

Pastor Williams sighed. "I will pray on it, Josh. Just hurry up and get out of here," he said.

"Thank you. I love you," said Joshua. Joshua knew his uncle had to respond to those three words. It was embedded in Pastor Williams' Christian DNA.

"I love you too, Josh. Just be careful, especially around Lauren. I will pray to God to help work all of this out. We need God to be in control of this situation, not you, not the police, and not anyone else," said Pastor Williams.

"I hear you. And I agree," said Joshua.

"Two minutes and thirty-three seconds," said Pastor Williams, to signify that he had been counting down to call Officer Reese. Joshua ran into the foyer and out the front door. He got into the car with Lauren, and she sped off.

Pastor Williams waited another minute and then picked up the phone to make a call.

"Hello, Joe. Josh was just here," said Pastor Williams.

"Keep him there. We will be right over," said Officer Reese.

"I just said he was here, but not anymore. I tried to get him to stay, but he drove off," said Pastor Williams.

Officer Reese squeezed his cell phone tightly and cursed under his breath. "I am sorry, Pastor. It is apparent that he is intentionally evading us. And for someone that is supposedly innocent, he is acting mighty guilty. I will have to put out an APB on him and his car."

Pastor Williams did not respond. He realized that he was in a real dilemma. Since Joshua had left with Lauren, Pastor Williams had to tell Officer Reese that Joshua's car was still out in front of the house. And that meant that he would also have to say that Joshua had left with Lauren, and in Lauren's car. But he could not mislead the police in any way; it would only make matters worse.

"His car is still here. But, he left with that girl, Lauren," said Pastor Williams.

"The Bishop's daughter? She was there last night, right?" asked Officer Reese.

"No. I mean yes," said Pastor Williams. "That's her, but she's not the Bishop's daughter."

"Then who is she?" asked Officer Reese.

Pastor Williams spoke slowly, even confusing himself with his next statement. "She's the Bishop's former future daughter-in-law, if that makes any sense," said Pastor Williams.

"That sounds too confusing. But the reason Lauren is here is that she is with the Bishop, correct?" asked Officer Reese.

"Correct," said Pastor Williams.

"Can you give me a description of her car?" asked Officer Reese.

"I never paid any attention to it. I just know it's black," said Pastor Williams. Angela walked in the door. She could tell from her husband's face he was on an intense phone call. Angela figured it was regarding Joshua and the fire last night. She quickly glanced around the house and saw no signs of Joshua.

"Four-door or two doors?" asked Officer Reese.

"Four doors?" said Pastor Williams.

"You sure you can't remember a make or model? Could it have been a Nissan, Volkswagen, Honda?" asked Officer Reese.

"Look, Joe, I couldn't tell you the difference among any of them. The only two cars I know are mine and Angela's. That is the best you're going to get from me," said Pastor Williams.

"Okay, I get it. But one more thing: Can you text me the Bishop's cell phone number?" said Officer Reese.

"I guess. Sure," said Pastor Williams.

"Pastor, I know this is an uncomfortable situation for all of us. I am sorry you and I are in this position. But if you can get Josh to cooperate with us, at least give us a statement, then I will do whatever I can to help him out," said Officer Reese.

"I hear you, Joe. You just make sure you and your officers are doing your job properly and not just focusing on Josh. Remember, these fires started way before yesterday," said Pastor Williams.

"Point taken, Pastor. I will be in touch," said Officer Reese. They hung up. Angela walked closer to her husband.

"I assume you were talking to Joe again," said Angela.

"Yes. I didn't want to, but I had to call him to let him know that Josh was here," said Pastor Williams.

"Josh was here?" asked Angela, surprised but also disappointed that he'd left.

"Yes. He came in here with Lauren," said Pastor Williams.

"Lauren. How did she find him?" asked Angela.

"I don't know. We didn't get into that," said Pastor Williams.

"What did he say? Where did they go?" asked Angela.

"He said that he had nothing to do with the fire. And he did not say where he was going. I tried to get him to go with me to the police station, but he was adamant about not going."

"Why wouldn't he go to the police station?"

"Technically, he said, 'Just not right now.'"

"This is getting out of hand. Just yesterday, everything was fine. And now, all of this," said Angela.

"Well, it has gotten even worse," said Pastor Williams.

"Worse than this! How?" asked Angela.

"Josh told me that he got into a fight with Mike, the Bishop's son," said Pastor Williams.

"A fight with Mike? You must be joking! How did that even happen, and where?" exclaimed Angela.

"I'm not sure," said Pastor Williams.

Angela opened her eyes wide and raised her eyebrows from a thought that had just popped into her head. "Now it makes sense. You have to call the Bishop right away. He called me right before I walked in the door, saying he could not reach you. But I guess you were on the phone with Joe. He said he needed to speak to you right away. He sounded pretty upset. Mike must have told him that he got into it with Josh," said Angela.

"I didn't even think about that. Now that's a call I don't want to make. Oh, and one more thing," said Pastor Williams.

"There's more?" asked Angela in disbelief.

"Yes. While Josh was here, the news was on. They flashed a photo of him, saying that police wanted him for questioning. They even mentioned that he was my nephew," said Pastor Williams.

"Lord Jesus," said Angela.

"That's what I said. I know it all has to do with that girl, Lauren. Ever since she came around, things have been going from bad to worse, especially with Josh," said Pastor Williams.

"Honey, you don't know that," said Angela.

"He was in here defending her over me," said Pastor Williams.

"What do you mean defending her? Please do not tell me you got into it with her again," said Angela.

"She was in my house talking to me like we were on some type of reality show, trying to get Josh to vote me off the island in my own house. She gave me no respect," said Pastor Williams.

"Really, Jerry. Lauren appears highly intelligent, and she is working on getting a master's degree. Also, Josh has done quite well for himself at the store. He works hard and is dedicated. But they are still just two young kids with a lot of growing up and learning to do. They do not have years of experience on this planet, as you and I do. You, out of all people, know that you have to communicate with them differently," said Angela.

"I'm going to ignore the indirect 'you're old' comment that you just made. But Josh and Lauren are old enough to know better. Josh knows he should be at the police station right now. If not, it makes him look guilty, even if he isn't. And Lauren may be very smart, but so were Jim Jones and many other false prophets and preachers. Godly people don't talk about the universe, and true realms and aliens. You may see her as a sheep, but to me, she looks more like a wolf in sheep's clothing," said Pastor Williams, holding firmly on to his opinion.

"Jerry, you have a big heart, but sometimes you can be very blind. Did your parents like me at first? Do you remember things they said about me when you and I were dating? Also, did you and I make all the right choices when we were their age?" asked Angela.

Pastor Williams did not respond. He already knew that she was not done with her point.

"Since when do any of us have it all together and get everything right, especially at their age? Just a few Sundays ago, you were preaching a sermon about how life is a 'make-it-up-as-you-go' journey, that we all make mistakes and bad decisions, but if God called us, and according to His purpose, things will work out in the end. Maybe in Josh's mind, he is trying. Just not the way you would like," said Angela.

"I hate that you remember every word I say. But no matter what you say, it's still something about that girl," said Pastor Williams.

"Maybe. Maybe not. But that is for Josh to figure out. Not you. I was happy that he finally had someone else to hang around besides annoying Monty," joked Angela.

Pastor Williams chuckled. "That boy is pretty annoying. Nothing like his parents at all," said Pastor Williams.

"Do you see him close with anyone else?" asked Angela. Pastor Williams' silence was confirmation of his agreement. "After all he's been through from his childhood and dealing with Denise's death, we are very blessed that we haven't seen Satan trying to steal, kill, and destroy him like this even sooner. He is so talented and such a hard worker. He is a miracle," said Angela.

"As usual, you are right. But I was just hoping that he wasn't changing. He's always been like a son to me, and if I let evil or disaster come near him and destroy his life, how could I ever live with myself?" said Pastor Williams.

"Everything you just said is out of love and concern, and I love that about you. But you are not God, and you are not his God. You did what you could while he was growing up. But if you are always there to tell him what decisions to make or to pick up all the pieces when he fails, how will he ever learn to trust God on his own? When will he ever cry out to God for help and have God and God alone show him how He can provide? How will Josh ever grow his faith and be a God-fearing man if he's told to only put his trust in you?" asked Angela.

"What about Lauren?" asked Pastor Williams, starting to concede.

"Time will tell. But have faith that God is in control. He is always in control," said Angela.

The television was still on, and a segment promotion about an up-coming news story came across the screen.

"News tonight at eleven. It was just a few years ago that astrono-mers found a potential super-Earth orbiting the nearest star from our sun, four point two light-years away. Now researchers may have traced a signal coming from this planet. Could this be a sign of life on this planet, similar to Earth? More news on this at eleven," said the news anchor. Angela laughed.

"Well, look at that. There go your aliens Lauren was talking about earlier," said Angela.

"Maybe," said Pastor Williams. Pastor Williams smiled and grabbed Angela by her hips so that they were face-to-face. "And that is why you are my helpmate, my soulmate. How could I have ever pastored a church without you?" asked Pastor Williams.

"What are you going to do now?" said Angela.

Pastor Williams took a deep breath and released it. "I'm going to call the Bishop. But before I do, let's pray for Josh and Lauren," said Pastor Williams.

"Now that's the husband I know," said Angela.

Pastor Williams grabbed Angela's hands and closed his eyes. "Dear most holy and magnificent God, I ask that you reach out to Josh and Lauren wherever they are right now and guide them to make the right decisions. Honestly, Lord, I don't trust this girl, Lauren. But as my wife just reminded me, you, Lord, are in control . . ." Pastor Williams con-tinued his prayer for Josh and Lauren. Angela was pleased.

13

Revelations

Friday late evening—the day before the community revival.

Lauren was driving, with Joshua in the passenger seat, slightly above the speed limit.

"How could you not defend me in there?" yelled Lauren.

"It would have been pointless. You don't know my uncle like I do," said Joshua.

"According to him, he doesn't know me either. And for some reason, no one does. I'm getting sick of everyone saying that they don't know me!" exclaimed Lauren.

"Calm down. Once my uncle gets something in his head, there is no talking him out of his train of thought," said Joshua.

"Don't tell me to calm down! I only left out of respect for you and his house," said Lauren forcefully.

"He only changes his mind by seeing and experiencing something himself. You would have only made things worse. And remember, I did stand up for you at the Bishop's house against Mike, and you yelled at me for that," said Joshua.

"Don't remind me. And you did that for yourself, not me," said a still-miffed Lauren.

"Hey, we don't need any cops pulling us over. Please slow down?" asked Joshua. Lauren looked down at the car's speedometer and eased up the pressure of her foot on the gas pedal.

"Where are we going now?" asked Lauren.

"I don't know. I need somewhere to think," said Joshua.

"How about that new coffee shop on Castor? I heard it has two levels. We could sit upstairs," suggested Lauren.

"No. We might see somebody there I know. We need somewhere private," said Joshua.

"You mean like the library?" asked Lauren.

"Yes! But let's go across the bridge into New Jersey. There will be fewer familiar faces over there," said Joshua.

Lauren drove south down I-95 across the Walt Whitman Bridge into New Jersey. They arrived at the T.B. Johnson Memorial Library just outside of Camden. They walked in the front entrance and had to walk through the metal detector. Joshua was apprehensive, hoping that no one recognized him from the Live News 10 story. They got through with no problems, though.

It was a massive library with three floors. While Joshua took his time grabbing all his personal items from the small dish container at the metal detector, Lauren walked over to the tall electronic kiosk pad. It had a library map, a reference catalog of the books, and other library resources. She quickly scrolled through the screens with her index finger and found what she needed.

Lauren whispered to herself, "Second floor, east side of the building." Joshua finally approached her after obtaining all his items.

"How much stuff did you have in your pockets?" asked Lauren.

"Apparently, more than I thought," said Joshua.

Lauren grabbed Joshua's hand and pulled him up the escalator to the second floor. They looked around and saw the massive book collection. There were also reading sections filled with sofas and low cushioned chairs spread throughout the level.

"Over here," said Lauren as she turned right and then walked through a few bookcase rows. Joshua followed. They stopped at the religious books section.

"You know your way around a library," said Joshua.

"Hello. I've practically lived in a library and read books for the past year, remember?" said Lauren.

Joshua sat down at a wooden four-chair table against the wall in the very back of the section.

"This looks like a pretty private area," said Joshua. Lauren looked around, and the only person visible was a male librarian walking the end of the rows with a book cart, returning books to their proper locations. Lauren sat down next to Joshua.

"Where's my bag?" asked Lauren quietly.

"You left it in the car," said Joshua.

"Shoot! You should have reminded me, you idgit!" exclaimed Lauren with a much louder voice.

"Shh! Keep your voice down," said the librarian.

They turned their heads to him, both with looks of guilt.

"Sorry," whispered Lauren to the man.

"Do you want me to go back and get it?" asked Joshua.

"No. There are plenty of books here, and you will just take another hour going through that detector again," said Lauren.

Joshua chuckled. The librarian shot them another dirty look.

This time Joshua whispered to him, "Sorry."

Lauren pulled out Joshua's notes that he took from his readings at Bishop Hines' house.

"Hey. Where did you get that?" asked Joshua as he frantically checked his pockets, wondering how she swiped it away from him.

"I could have taken your wallet too if I wanted," said Lauren.

"All forty-seven dollars, huh," said Joshua.

"It's a start for all the trouble you got me in now," said Lauren.

"Me? You are the one that wanted to go on a church date at night. Next time, I will just take you bowling or out to dinner. It may be boring, but at least we will stay out of trouble," said Joshua.

"According to the police, there is no trouble until you show up," joked Lauren. Joshua did not laugh or respond. Lauren could tell that he was offended.

"I'm sorry," she quickly said. "I didn't mean it like that."

"Remember when you stormed out of my uncle's house like a bull out of a gate?" asked Joshua.

"Yes," said Lauren, her eyes narrowing.

"When you left, the news came on the TV, and I was on it as a person of interest wanted for questioning by the police regarding last night's fire," said Joshua.

"Seriously? This has gotten way out of control," said Lauren.

"I know. I said the same thing," said Joshua.

"You had nothing to do with any of this," insisted Lauren.

"Well, now I have to show up at that police station at some point. I was hoping they would have caught the person by now and not have to worry about me," said Joshua.

"What about what you saw in the window?" asked Lauren.

"I don't know what I saw," said Joshua. He turned to the side and quietly laughed.

"What's so funny?" asked Lauren.

"I never thought about it until now. But, when I was a little kid, maybe seven or eight years old, we stayed at my uncle's house for a while. My mom left for a few weeks, and I thought my uncle left the house to go to church to practice his sermons. I was playing outside, and for some reason, maybe boredom, I decided to look into his neighbor's window," said Joshua.

"You heinous little boy!" exclaimed Lauren.

"Just listen. While I was peeking in this house, my uncle came home and must have seen me. He came out of nowhere and yelled, 'Boy! Get away from that house!' I jumped back so quickly, and my heart must have fallen to the bottom of my pants. I was so scared. When we got back into his house, he said to me, 'Don't ever be a peeping Tom!' Then his voice got low and very creepy and said, 'One day, you're going to look into a window and see something you wished you never saw!' I was scared to look into any window ever since," said Joshua.

"I never thought about peeping like that," said Lauren.

"I listened to that advice for so many years until now, and look what happened," said Joshua.

"Funny. But not funny. I wonder if that was the universe giving you advanced warning of what was to come in your future, or if your uncle's words spoke this moment into existence," said Lauren.

"Or maybe, it was just a crazy coincidence," said Joshua.

"Maybe. Maybe not," said Lauren.

"Maybe, maybe not?" questioned Joshua.

"It's like when you were a kid jumping on the bed. And one of your parents said, 'Stop jumping! You're going to get hurt.' But you keep jumping and then fall off and bump your head. And then, they say, 'See. I told you that you were going to get hurt!'" said Lauren.

"Yes. Stuff like that happened all the time as a kid. One time I was jumping on the bed, and my mom told me to stop or I would get hurt, and I fell off and hit my head on our metal space heater. I had the biggest lump on my head for days. But what does that have to do with anything?" asked Joshua.

185

"Let me ask you this. Did you fall off the bed because you accidentally did something wrong to make yourself fall, or did you fall off the bed because your mom told you it was going to happen?" asked Lauren.

"Are you saying that fell because my mom spoke it into existence, and not because I was being careless by jumping on the bed?"

"Possibly, or because you heard your mom say that it would happen, and then you subconsciously made it happen," said Lauren.

"I don't know about that," said Joshua.

"It is no different with positive or negative reinforcement. Just like saying to a kid, 'You are so smart and will grow up to be a successful person,' compared to saying, 'You are so stupid and will never amount to anything.' The kid usually believes the words spoken and makes them a reality," said Lauren.

"Well, whether spoken into existence or not, I wish I never went to that church last night, looked into that window, and saw what I saw. Is there any way to unsee anything?" asked Joshua.

"Hmm. Let's find out," said Lauren. She got up and searched for books. She grabbed two books and placed them on their table. Then she noticed that the librarian was closer to them. She got his attention.

"Excuse me. I'm looking for books on religion and—"

The librarian interrupted Lauren before she finished her sentence. "You're in the right section."

"I am looking for a book on spirits and ghosts, or even dreams, perhaps one that is biblically based. Can you think of any books like that here?" asked Lauren.

"Look in row 2R-AG. You can also look over in the sci-fi section," said the librarian.

"The sci-fi section?" asked Lauren.

"Yes. Many books about religious based spirits, dreams, and the underworld are deemed sci-fi here in this library. I personally call them the 'too hot to handle' books for the traditional and even contemporary religious reader. But, they are closely related, hence being located in sections right near each other."

Joshua chuckled. "Too hot to handle, huh," he said.

"Over in row 2SF-CB, there is one book that is specifically about people who had spiritual dreams or prophecies that would come true, including biblical characters—like Daniel, who was able to interpret dreams that were messages from God," said the librarian.

"Is that deemed fiction or nonfiction?" asked Joshua.

"You decide. With every myth, there was always some foundation of historical truth to it," said the librarian.

"Okay. You seem somewhat knowledgeable in this area. Give me an example," said Lauren, excited to test this man's knowledge.

"I should. I spend most of my time in these two sections of this library. But okay. Let me give you an example," he said. The librarian rolled up his eyes as if he were looking up into his brain for an example. He was successful.

"I have a good one. Vampires," said the librarian.

"Vampires? Are you saying some of these books here say vampires are real?" asked Lauren. She already knew where he was going with this, but she played along.

"It's more complicated than that. Think of all these books like a bunch of puzzle pieces. Each is its separate piece, but the right ones together tell a complete story. For example, if you look at some old historical medical books, you will see that certain people have a skin condition called photosensitivity."

Joshua jumped into the conversation. "Those are people whose skin is super sensitive to the sun, right?"

"Yes," said the librarian.

"My cousin had it when we were growing up. If the sun were too bright, he couldn't play with us outside," said Joshua.

"Yes. In severe cases, some could only come out at night. If they came out in the day, especially with a hot sun in the sky, their skin would break out into hives, rashes, or even feel like it was burning. They would sleep all day and only come out of the house at night," said the librarian. Lauren interrupted.

"And bite people and drink their blood?" she asked sarcastically.

"That is not as farfetched as you may think. For centuries, people have used human blood as an ingredient in many different medicines or remedies. If these people thought that healthy blood helped their condition, they might try to obtain it at all costs. Even go crazy trying to obtain it directly from other humans. And with all the folklore and other random stories passed down from generation to generation of possible bad encounters with these people that had this true medical condition, one may view them as a bloodthirsty human, aka—a vampire," said the librarian.

Lauren smiled and said, "I love it. You confirmed my theory that we mistakenly judge historical and religious events based on our own current cultural and historical time biases."

"I totally agree," said the librarian.

"Very insightful. What is your name?" asked Lauren.

"Brian," said the librarian.

"Thanks, Brian," said Lauren. Joshua just smiled.

"You said you wanted a biblical book on spirits and ghosts, correct?" asked Brian.

"Yes." Lauren nodded.

"I may just have the thing for you. I will also get you that book on dreams and prophecies," said Brian. He walked around the two sections for a minute or two and came back with the two books. He handed one book to Lauren and the other to Joshua.

"Great! Thanks so much!" said Lauren.

"My pleasure. Let me know if you need anything else. I will be here for a while," said Brian.

"Will do," said Joshua.

Brian went back to reshelving the books.

"Looks like we have some reading to do," said Lauren.

"Looks like it," said Joshua.

They read their respective books. Lauren read quickly, flipping page to page, while Joshua took his time and writing more notes on the same paper he had from Bishop Hines' house.

"Look at you, still writing notes. I'm impressed," said Lauren.

"I have to. If I don't write it down, I will forget it. I have a terrible memory. What's your name again?" Joshua joked as he gave Lauren a confused look.

Lauren laughed. "My name is: you-better-not-forget-my-name-or-you're-going-to-get-a-foot-up-your . . ."

Joshua raised his eyebrows, wondering if she was going to curse.

". . . alley . . . a foot up your alley," said Lauren.

"Nice save. So, what have you read so far?" asked Joshua.

Lauren and Joshua continued to read for a while longer. Lauren broke their reading with a statement.

"Brian was right. This book *is* fascinating. It is talking about the parallels of good and evil. How they mimic each other even in the church of today," said Lauren.

"Mimic, how?" asked Joshua.

"It starts off talking about how if demons were once angels and demons can possess humans, then is it not a possibility that angels can possess humans as well? It then compares how rituals and practices of the church are similar to Satanic rituals. For example, evil cults use upside-down crosses and read scriptures backward. Also, during church, people filled with the Holy Spirit or speaking in tongues could be viewed the same as someone possessed by a demon. How we ask God's spirit to fill us and take control, and how that is the same with Satan worshippers asking Satan or demonic spirits to take control of them. How we act like we are drinking blood when we take communion, but they will drink actual blood as part of their rituals. The list goes on and on." said Lauren.

"Just so I am clear, is it saying those Christian church rituals are bad?" asked Joshua.

"No. It says since these spirits were all part of God's kingdom at one point in time, it would only make sense that good and evil practices would be either very similar or the exact opposite to each other. It's interesting," said Lauren.

"Yes, interesting. Once, someone in our church shouted wildly and speaking in tongues louder than normal. It sounded so eerie, even scary. Everyone looked around like, 'Wait a minute. Is that person filled with the Holy Spirit, or are they possessed?' Sometimes you could not tell the difference," said Joshua.

"Oh my goodness, same here. And when you are a kid, it can be terrifying," said Lauren.

"Yes! When I was younger, that was the worst!" exclaimed Joshua. They laughed.

"Now I'm thinking, whatever's causing the church fires, maybe started with some type of ritual. Possibly a ritual to call upon an evil spirit to cause all of this to happen. I don't know," said Lauren.

"But why? I'm not convinced. I always learned the most important thing in life is not the what, but the why. Why do people act the way they do? Why did some event occur? And for these fires, why is this happening to these churches, and why now? It all has to be for some reason," said Joshua.

"Interesting. I like to think about *the what*, and it appears that you like to think about *the why*. Sounds like together, we could solve anything," said Lauren.

"I hope. Because we better solve something soon; I can't do much solving while I am in jail," said Joshua.

"Don't even think like that, Joshua. We will figure this out, and God is in control," said Lauren.

"You're right. And I do," said Joshua.

"Now, you give me the details of your book," demanded Lauren.

"I didn't read much, but this book is focused more on people's dreams about the spiritual world and angels," said Joshua.

"That's different," said Lauren.

"Yeah, it's crazy. It's all speculative, with accounts of people who had dreams about an event. Then later, had a déjà vu moment and did something extraordinary or supernatural, like lift a car off someone after an accident, or jump from a three-story building and not get hurt. They all say it felt as if it was not them. Something positive and peaceful took control, and they just watched it happen from inside their body. But the most interesting thing is how it talks about how angels are in daily life, protecting us, preaching to us, shifting the world around us to make sure we walk on the right paths. And they are constantly battling evil spirits on our behalf. Some people even talk about seeing small circles or spheres of lights as ghosts or angels. Similar to what I saw when I woke up with you," said Joshua.

"Sounds like it really relates to what you saw in the church window and what you see in your dreams?" asked Lauren.

"Well, just that last part about angels battling spirits on our behalf. If this thing is some type of spirit, then this book talks about how something would have had to happen that was so devastating or so horrific that it would have impacted the natural and spiritual realm at the same time," said Joshua.

"You mean like a gruesome death or horrible event that leaves its mark in that specific place," said Lauren.

"Yes. Like a haunted house that was the location of a past murder, or an old psychiatric hospital whose staff tortured people and did unthinkable types of experiments on the patients," said Joshua.

"Something terrible may have happened in this neighborhood, or maybe even in one of these churches, to break the plane or blanket between the natural and spiritual realms, that is now causing all of this, maybe even an evil spirit," said Lauren.

"Maybe," said Joshua.

"If so, what do we do now?" asked Lauren.

Joshua paused in thought. He closed his eyes, took a deep breath, and slowly exhaled. He reopened his eyes with a thought.

"You know what? I think we need to visit where all of this may have started," said Joshua.

"You mean the first church fire?" asked Lauren.

"Yes. Ebenezer AME," said Joshua.

"Right now?"

"Why not?" asked Joshua.

"Okay. Let's go," said Lauren.

"Let's go, but please don't call this another date." Joshua chuckled, and Lauren made a face of disappointment.

14

Poor Ebenezer

Friday late evening—the day before the community revival.

Back at the house, Pastor Williams grabbed his phone to call Bishop Hines. He gave a loud sigh as he looked at his cell phone. He knew this was not going to be an easy conversation.

"You know, the sooner you call, the sooner you get it over with," said Angela as she witnessed his reluctance.

Pastor Williams sighed again. He knew his wife was right, so he made the call. Bishop Hines answered his phone immediately.

"Hello, Pastor," said Bishop Hines.

Pastor Williams noticed Bishop Hines' voice lacked its usual buoyant tone. He responded.

"Hello, Bishop," said Pastor Williams.

"I assume you are calling me because Joshua and Lauren are over there," said Bishop Hines.

"They were here. But not anymore," said Pastor Williams. Bishop Hines did not immediately respond.

The pause was uncomfortable. But Pastor Williams remained quiet, fearful of saying the wrong thing. He could not remember the last time that there had been a silence between the two.

Bishop Hines finally spoke. "Did Joshua tell you that he and Lauren were over here and that he hit Mike? What in the world is—"

Pastor Williams interrupted before Bishop Hines' anger peaked. "Yes, he did. I am so sorry that happened, Bishop. I had a long talk with him, and this is not like him. Honestly, I think Lauren has a lot to do with all this," said Pastor Williams.

Bishop Hines did not respond to Pastor Williams' indictment of Lauren. Pastor Williams continued, "Respectfully, Bishop, it is just so ironic how when she comes around, all these fires start happening, and Josh is now getting into trouble with the police and getting into fights. This is not like Josh. Either Lauren is trouble or trouble knows how to follow her around," said Pastor Williams.

"Respectfully, Pastor, I truly doubt that Lauren has anything to do with any of this," said Bishop Hines.

"Respectfully, Bishop, are you sure? How long was Mike dating her before they got engaged? Do you really know her that well?" asked Pastor Williams.

"Way better than you think, Pastor. Out of anyone, you should know my judge of character. And right now, the character in question is Joshua's, not Lauren's," said Bishop Hines.

"I am not sure, Bishop," said Pastor Williams, shaking his head, though Bishop Hines could not see it.

Bishop Hines took control of the conversation. "There are two things that you seem to be oblivious to right now. Number one, Joshua is grown and no longer a kid. Therefore, no matter who you think is around him or influencing him, he is still responsible for his actions. Number two, we wrestle not against flesh and blood, but against principalities and spiritual wickedness. You have a great mission with this community revival. I remember how many souls and lives were changed in your community last year because of it. Did you think Satan was going to sit idle another year without trying to steal, kill, and destroy the victory of this event?"

Pastor Williams' heart stilled, as he knew Bishop Hines was right. "So, instead of playing the blame game, step up and be a leader in all of this, not only for your family, but for this community as well. I saw the news earlier implicating Joshua in these fires. How do you think the community will respond with thinking Joshua is involved? Have you thought about that?" asked Bishop Hines.

"I have not," said a regretful Pastor Williams.

"Before the wrong narrative and story spreads to every ear and mind in your neighborhood, get ahead of it. It could not only destroy the upcoming community revival, but it could also destroy your very church and reputation in the community as well," said Bishop Hines.

"What do you suggest I do?" asked Pastor Williams.

"No. You tell me what you think you should do. Or better yet, what do you think God needs you to do?" asked Bishop Hines.

Pastor Williams took a moment to carefully think before he spoke. "I should make a few calls to the other churches and talk to their pastors about the fires and how we can make sure it doesn't happen again. And to let them know the community revival is still on, and I need their support to make sure it will be more of a success than last year," said Pastor Williams.

"Amen, brother. Now you sound like a true leader—a true pastor," said Bishop Hines.

"What about Josh and Lauren? I don't want them out there making this situation even worse," said Pastor Williams.

"Let me handle those two. You have other things on your plate to worry about," said Bishop Hines.

"Okay, thanks again, Bishop," said Pastor Williams.

"No problem, Pastor. We will talk later," said Bishop Hines.

"Goodbye, Bishop," said Pastor Williams.

"Take care," said Bishop Hines.

* * *

Lauren's cell phone rang. She looked to see who was calling. She was on the passenger side of her car with Joshua driving as they headed out to Ebenezer AME, the first church that had caught fire.

"Don't answer that," said Joshua.

"Hello?" said Lauren, answering her cell phone and disregarding Joshua's request.

"Why did you answer?" whispered Joshua.

Lauren covered her cell phone. "I had to, it's the Bishop," said Lauren, bewildered. Bishop Hines continued.

"Lauren. Is Joshua with you?" asked Bishop Hines.

Lauren uncovered her phone and responded, "Yes, Bishop."

"I need you to take him to the police station right now to give his statement on what happened. You two are only making things worse and creating the appearance of guilt," said Bishop Hines.

"You are absolutely correct, Bishop. But you already know how this goes. Once Joshua walks into that station and gives his statement, he will be primary suspect number one. especially if they have no other leads right now," said Lauren.

"That may be true, Lauren. However, if he has done nothing wrong, then he needs to trust God and respect the process and follow the law of the land," said Bishop Hines.

"He will, Bishop. I will take him to the station myself. I promise. There is just one thing we need to do first," said Lauren.

"And what is that?" asked Bishop Hines.

"I can't say right now. But after this, we will be on our way to the station for sure," said Lauren.

"Do I have your word?" asked Bishop Hines.

"Yes, Bishop. You have my absolute word," said Lauren.

"Why do I have a feeling that whatever you are about to do may cause even more trouble?" said a weary Bishop Hines.

"Please do not worry, Bishop. We can't possibly get into any more trouble," said Lauren.

"Now, you know what happens when people say that, especially on television or in a movie. But call me when you head to the station," said Bishop Hines.

"Will do," said Lauren. She hung up.

Joshua parked the car. They were just a block and a half away from Ebenezer AME, but they still had a clear view of it. They got out of their car and walked toward the church.

"Really, Lauren? 'We can't possibly get into any more trouble'? I'm not superstitious, but even I know that you are never supposed to say stuff like that," said Joshua.

"The Bishop said the same thing. But, it won't matter because we are going to the police station right after this, right?" asked Lauren.

"I guess I have no choice," said Joshua.

"So, this is Ebenezer AME?" asked Lauren as they arrived at the partially burned-down building.

"Yes," said Joshua.

"And it was the first church that caught fire?" asked Lauren.

"Yes," said Joshua.

Ebenezer AME's church building had been closed and abandoned for many years. Before the fire, the property had been unkempt with overgrown weeds on the ground and vines covering the exterior walls. It was an eyesore in the community. But the fire had made this eyesore even worse.

Historically, it was a small church that used to be an old schoolhouse, built in 1850 and deemed an official historic building by the City of Philadelphia. It was initially built as a brick-and-stone building, with one set of stairs that led to an upper platform in only the front part of the church, originally used as the office for the schoolmaster.

When the Boulevard Street School opened in 1897, the schoolhouse was renovated and became a town hall building. In 1968, it was restored again as a Catholic church and included the addition of exterior wood panels installed on top of the old brick. It remained such until 1982. Then, the property transferred ownership and became the Ebenezer AME church.

"Did anyone die in this one?" asked Lauren.

"No. This church has been vacant for a long time. That's why everyone assumed it was just an electrical fire or something building-related," said Joshua.

"Are we going inside?" asked Lauren.

"Of course. We didn't drive all the way back across the bridge for nothing," said Joshua.

"Guess not. I'm really surprised they haven't demoed the building yet," said Lauren.

"I heard it was scheduled to be knocked down this week, primarily for safety reasons. But I guess it was put on hold when the other fires started happening. The former pastor moved down south somewhere when this church failed."

"Failed?" asked Lauren.

"It's not like we have a shortage of churches around here. Way too many if you ask me. But this pastor came from another local church to start his own, and their attendance was not stellar," said Joshua.

"And low attendance means low offerings that can't pay for the bills and expenses of the church," said Lauren.

"I guess it's the mortgage company's problem now," said Joshua.

"It's a shame that it is partially destroyed. This would have made a good building for our first church," joked Lauren.

"Our church? What makes you think I would want to start a church, and with you?" teased Joshua.

"You don't think you and I would make a good pastor and co-pastor?" asked Lauren.

Joshua laughed. "I don't think either one of us is pastor material. From our connection, I get the feeling that we would be too busy making out at home ever to make it to church on time," said Joshua.

Lauren laughed. She grabbed Joshua by his waist with her arms and looked directly up at his face.

"You might be right. Once I start kissing these lips, it is so hard for me to stop," said Lauren. They kissed in the middle of the sidewalk, right in front of the church.

After a few more kisses, they tightly held hands as they walked to the church.

"If we did start a church, what would we call it?" asked Joshua.

"I grew up Baptist," said Lauren.

"Well, I grew up Pentecostal," said Joshua.

"But I always wanted to go to a nondenominational church growing up," said Lauren.

"And I always wanted to go to a church where they didn't start shouting, and I felt obligated to get up on an organ or piano and start playing," said Joshua.

"Really? I thought you loved to play," asked Lauren.

"I do. I just hate not having a choice. Even when visiting another church and they don't have anyone to play, it is just expected of me to get up and play the organ or piano. Sometimes I just want to sit there and do nothing and listen like everyone else," said Joshua.

"Guess we have to call our church, The Church of the Delivered Baptist and Non-Piano-or-Organ-Playing Pentecostal Faith Sanctuary," said Lauren.

Joshua laughed. "That's not long enough. It should be, The Church of the Delivered Baptist and Non-Piano-or-Organ-Playing Pentecostal Faith Sanctuary Set on Holy Ghost Fire Community Nondenominational Church on the Corner."

"Set on fire. Really, Joshua? That was not funny," said Lauren.

"It's funny to me," said Joshua while laughing.

"Sorry, I am not laughing at that corny joke," said Lauren.

"How should we get in this church?" asked Joshua.

"We can climb through one of those broken windows," said Lauren as she pointed.

They were on the west side of the church, which was to the left when facing the front of the church. Three of the four windows were broken, most likely by the firefighters to help put out the fire. But the fire had left its mark. Those windows and the high roofline were imprinted with dark black soot, reminders of the intense flames that had poured out of the windows. Joshua looked on the ground and found a large rock. He used it to break off the rest of the sharp glass that bordered one of the window frames' edges. Joshua climbed in the window headfirst. Regrettably, he landed extremely hard and awkwardly on the floor. Joshua looked around and saw that he had just broken into the pastor's office. As he was getting up, he saw Lauren calmly coming through the window, legs first. Her feet landed softly on the ground. Joshua thought, *Why didn't I do that?*

Lauren looked down and saw Joshua getting up from the ground. She looked at him in confusion, wondering why he was on the floor. Joshua grimaced. Lauren shook her head but did not say a word. Joshua wiped off his jeans from the dust- and ash-covered floor.

They walked out of the office into the pulpit area in the front of the sanctuary, where they looked around in horror. They had never seen the full destruction of a fire up close. The sanctuary was gray, blankets of ash covering the floor and furniture of the entire church. The majority of the pews and sections of the walls were now just broken-up fragments of wooden debris, either damaged by the fire or axed by the firefighters in their attempts to contain the flames. The walls were fully exposed to the stud frames and old bricks. The smell of the fire remained heavy in the air.

"Oh my god. This is so horrific," said Lauren. Her eyes watered, looking around at the aftermath caused by the fire.

"I can't believe this used to be Ebenezer. My mom and I used to visit this church all the time when I was a child," said Joshua. "It still smells like the church is burning."

The smell was bad, but not unbearable. It had been a few days since the church was set on fire, and all of the broken windows provided a fair amount of air circulation. Joshua was in the middle of the church. He picked up one of the burnt Bibles. Part of it crumbled into ash. The lower portion of the Bible cover remained. He wiped it off. The first exposed page was 347. Joshua focused his eyes on Psalm 14:1:

To the chief Musician. A Psalm of David. The fool hath said in his heart, There is no God. They are corrupt, they have done abominable works, there is none that doeth good.

While Joshua continued reading, Lauren was making her way to the back of the church, carefully stepping over debris.

"Lauren, be careful. The fire started in the basement, and parts of this floor may be very weak and unstable," warned Joshua.

"Got it," said Lauren. She got to the back of the church and noticed a set of steps. They went up a level and down a level. Joshua put the Bible on one of the remaining pews. He quickly traversed through the debris to try to meet her.

"Hey, look. Going up must lead to the balcony," said Lauren as she immediately ran up the steps.

"Hey, I said, be careful!" yelled Joshua. He followed Lauren up the steps but went far more cautiously than her.

At the top was a landing that had a large window overlooking the central part of the church, and another small window on the back wall that viewed the front grounds of the church, out to the street. It was the upper level used by the headmaster when the building had been just a schoolhouse. The headmaster was able to look down into the classroom to check on the students without being seen. Now, it was only used to store random church items.

"How cool is this?" asked Lauren as she fully opened the small window to bring fresh air into the area from outside.

"This is pretty cool," admitted Joshua.

Lauren sat on the floor. "It's been a long, crazy day," she said.

"You mean days," said Joshua. He sat down next to her, and she laid her head on his shoulder.

"Joshua, I can't believe you socked Mike in the face like that. You got a nice punch," said Lauren.

"Don't remind me," said Joshua.

"Trust me. I'm sure Mike had it coming for some reason or another," said Lauren.

"Did you love him?" asked Joshua.

"At the time, I thought I did. But each day, I realized I did less and less. It wasn't until the day of our wedding that it was completely obvious to me. After that, I had to get away and did a short mission trip in Africa. I have been focusing on my studies ever since. What about you, Sir Joshua? Any former loves in your life?" asked a curious Lauren.

"No, none at all. I had a few girlfriends, but nothing serious. I guess I've just been focusing on surviving day by day," said Joshua.

Lauren lifted her head from his shoulder and smiled. As she put her head back on his shoulder, Joshua kissed her forehead. She lifted her head back up, and they looked into each other's eyes. The connection between their two souls grew even more. They slowly leaned into each other and then kissed while embracing. Joshua got up and found a large drop cloth to lie out on the floor. Lauren got up to meet Joshua as he stood.

Lauren smiled as a thank-you as she drew closer to his lips. They kissed again and then lay on top of the fabric, kissing more passionately. At that moment, Lauren felt their emotions and desire to make love again become uncontrollable. She turned over with her back against Joshua, deciding to resist this temptation. Joshua looked at Lauren, confused, wondering why she'd stopped.

"Is everything okay?" asked Joshua.

"Yes. I would love to continue, but remember where we are, Joshua," said Lauren.

"Right," said Joshua, in evident disappointment.

"We don't want to find out if us being intimate in a church is another reason why God would send out an evil spirit," said Lauren.

"Right!" exclaimed Joshua in agreement. "No worries."

Joshua kissed Lauren on her cheek. He put his head down on the ground and wrapped his arm around her, pulling her close against him. He held her tightly as they fell asleep.

15

A Darkness Uncovered

Saturday afternoon—the day of the community revival.

Joshua and Lauren woke up and separated from their sleeping hug cradle. They got up from the ground and held each other for a moment more, sharing a kiss. Lauren began folding the drop cloth while Joshua looked outside through the small window. They held hands as they walked back down the steps to the main floor. Lauren noticed how the steps continued further down.

"This must lead to the basement level. Do you want to go down and take a look?" asked Lauren.

"Does it look clear and safe?" asked Joshua.

"Most likely. The steps are made from some type of cement," said Lauren, as she tested the solidity of the stairs by tapping her foot on them and confirmed it.

"It looks pretty dark down there," asked Joshua.

Lauren grabbed her phone and turned on her light. Joshua decided to do the same. They walked down the set of steps to a flat four-by-four landing; then they turned right to go down four more steps into the low-ceilinged basement. Due to the stone walls and the polished concrete floor, the fire damage was not as bad as in the sanctuary above their heads. They both scanned the area with their lights while they walked closer to the middle of the basement. There were a few tables and chairs that had been consumed by the fire.

"Good gracious, it is so cold down here!" exclaimed Lauren.

"Looks like this basement hasn't been used in a very long time, not even when it was occupied," said Joshua.

Joshua walked to the left side of the basement. He saw a short stack of white boxes burned from the fire. With a closer look, he saw that they were VCT flooring tiles. Joshua picked up a box and inspected the tiles, which had no fire damage.

"Looks like they were supposed to put new flooring down at some point, but these tiles are very old," said Joshua.

"Didn't you say this church was abandoned for quite some time?" asked Lauren.

"Yeah. Maybe they ran out of money before they could start the work," said Joshua. "One time, Monty and I went to this revival service in Delaware with my uncle. He was the guest preacher for that night. Honestly, eighty percent of the service was talking about giving and offerings. Monty and I counted a total of six different offerings," said Joshua. Joshua then started laughing from a thought.

"What is so funny?" asked Lauren.

"After service, Monty said that they took up so many offerings, it felt like they just kept picking him up and turning him upside down by his ankles to shake all remaining money out of his pockets," said Joshua. Lauren laughed.

"I can't stand a service where they are up near the altar begging for money. If I weren't obligated to play music, I would get up and leave," said Joshua.

"I do believe in giving, and there is a tremendous blessing in it. But a church should not take advantage of people's faith," said Lauren.

"Yes. I agree," said Joshua.

"Honestly, that is one of the main reasons why Mike and I didn't work out," said Lauren.

"What do you mean?" asked Joshua.

"Even if Mike started his sermons talking about God's love, forgiveness, or even the salvation of Jesus Christ, he would always end up whooping and hollering about giving, so that God can bless you with either great finances or some type of success," said Lauren.

"Did you ever point that out to him?" asked Joshua.

"All the time. But, since the altar was always full of people, what I said didn't matter. It only started arguments," said Lauren.

Joshua got distracted by something beneath Lauren's feet.

"Hey. Shine your light on the ground," said Joshua. Lauren looked down as she shone her light where Joshua directed. They noticed a symbol burned into the middle of the concrete floor.

"Is that a star burned onto the floor?" asked Joshua.

Lauren backed up to get a better view of the entire symbol.

"No. It's a rough drawing of a pentagram. The Sigil of Baphomet, to be exact," said Lauren.

"As in, the devil's symbol?" asked Joshua.

"Yes. The Church of Satan uses this symbol to represent their beliefs," said Lauren.

"It had to have been burned with some type of flammable liquid, right?" asked Joshua.

Lauren looked closer. "I think so," she said.

"My uncle said the police were certain that some type of accelerant started the fires. I guess this is what they saw. No one mentioned this symbol, though," said Joshua.

"This is getting interesting. Why this symbol, and why this church?"

asked Lauren, intrigued.

"I don't know. But I do know I have to pee, and I can't hold it any longer," said Joshua. He shone the light on the men's restroom door located in the back of the basement.

"You are silly," said Lauren.

"Are you going to be okay by yourself?" asked Joshua.

"Are you?" asked Lauren.

Joshua remembered that she was more than capable of handling herself in any situation. He still liked to check, though. "Well, yell if you see anything," said Joshua.

He went to the back of the basement and opened the door to the bathroom. It was a large bathroom that was partitioned off from the rest of the basement. Just like the central part of the basement, it had a concrete floor and stone walls. It was dark and even colder than just outside the door.

Joshua intensely focused on his walk along the floor to avoid tripping over anything. He saw one of the white urinals and approached it. Joshua realized that he should not hold his cell phone and use the urinal at the same time. So, he put his phone in his pocket and relieved himself. He sighed in relief.

Lauren yelled, "Are you okay in there?"

Joshua yelled back, "No talking while I'm going!"

He then looked closer at the wall directly in front of him. Just above the urinal, he noticed some type of red marking. He moved his head closer to get a better look. He squinted his eyes to try to see it clearer. He wondered, *Is that paint or blood?* He took his hand and wiped the marking on the wall with his finger. It was somewhat fresh. He was more convinced now that it was blood. Joshua zipped up his pants and grabbed his cell phone out of his pocket. He turned on the flashlight and shone it on the marking. It was another symbol, but this one was written in blood.

"Lauren! Come in here now!" exclaimed Joshua. Lauren came running into the bathroom.

"What is it?" asked Lauren as she shone her phone light in on his pants and the urinal.

"No! Not down there, you idgit! Put your light on the wall," pointed Joshua, confounded.

"Oh, sorry," said Lauren as she flipped her phone up to the wall.

They saw numerous symbols written in blood. Lauren then used her cell phone to scan the rest of the bathroom. Their eyes widened as they saw similar multiple symbols on each wall.

"My god," breathed Joshua.

"Is that blood?" whispered Lauren.

"Yes, I think so," said Joshua.

"Whose blood? Who did all of this?" asked Lauren.

"I wiped some of it with my finger. It's not completely fresh, but it sure hasn't been sitting on these walls for a long time," said Joshua.

"Do you think the cops saw all of this?" asked Lauren.

"Maybe not. I think it was done sometime after the fire. Maybe even yesterday," said Joshua.

"This is crazy," said Lauren.

"What kind of symbols are these? They remind me of fraternity and sorority letters," said Joshua.

"I think they are Enochian," said Lauren.

"Enochian? What is that?" asked Joshua.

"From my recollection, it's supposed to be some type of lost language of angels. But they are not exactly what I have seen before. They are slightly different," said Lauren.

"If demons were once angels, does this mean Enochian is their language as well?" asked Joshua.

"Not sure. I only read a little bit about it in my studies. However, I have read that the Enochian language may have been used to conjure spells or ward off spiritual entities," said Lauren.

"You mean the symbols would prevent spirits from finding this bathroom?" asked Joshua.

"Maybe," said Lauren.

"Well, somebody or something did this, and they did it recently, and for some reason," said Joshua.

"What if this bathroom is a doorway?" asked Lauren.

"You mean to the spiritual world?" said Joshua.

"Joshua, this is real blood. Unless they have special powers, whoever did this had to get in and out of here somehow. And since there are no signs of blood outside of the bathroom, I highly doubt they climbed through the windows upstairs like us," said Lauren.

Joshua and Lauren scoured the bathroom, looking and feeling along the sections of the stone walls. At first, they did not notice anything unusual about the structure of the stones.

"It doesn't look like there's any way out. Everything feels pretty solid," said Lauren.

"It appears so," said Joshua, disappointed.

"But there has to be a way. It doesn't make sense," said Lauren.

Joshua thought for a moment. "Let me try something," he said.

He closed his eyes, took a deep breath, and slowly exhaled. He envisioned the bathroom and stone walls in his mind. He imagined the blood symbol markings. He took another deep breath and slowly exhaled again. Joshua moved his head toward the direction of the lower left corner of the bathroom. He opened his eyes and went to squat down in front of the stones in the corner. He waved his hands over a larger stone near the bottom of the wall. His hand stopped.

"I feel a draft!" shouted Joshua.

"Seriously, Joshua? Like we are in some movie?" asked Lauren.

"Yes. Don't you believe me? Come here and feel," said Joshua. Lauren walked over and shone her cell phone light on the stone. She bent down and put her hand near the stone.

"Wow. I feel cold air!" exclaimed Lauren.

"See, I told you," said Joshua.

"No. I am the one that told you that your gift is remarkable, and you just did it again. Now imagine if you practiced it, had faith in it," said Lauren. Joshua smiled.

Lauren refocused back on the stone. "Do you think we can remove it? It's so large."

"It looks large enough that we should be able to fit through it. But the confusing thing is that, like you already said, it *is* so large. How could anyone remove it or even put it back in place from the other side?" wondered Joshua.

"Well, let's figure out how to remove it first," said Lauren.

"Good idea, Lauren. Look around for something we can use as a wedge, preferably thin and made of metal. Wait. It just hit me that I saw a large putty knife out there near the floor tile boxes," said Joshua. He ran out of the bathroom to get the putty knife.

As the bathroom door shut behind Joshua, Lauren saw a metal coat hanger hanging on a hook on the back of the door. She jumped toward the door and grabbed it. She started untwisting and unbending it while Joshua walked back in with the putty knife.

"I got it. But I think we are going to need something else," said Joshua, as he looked around.

"You mean like this?" asked Lauren as she showed him the fully straightened-out metal hanger. She kept working on adjusting the hook at the end of it.

"Where did you get that?" asked Joshua.

"I am very resourceful," said Lauren, confident.

"Yes. I have seen it again and again." Joshua grinned.

Joshua and Lauren worked together with the putty knife and hanger to remove the stone. It was taking longer than they expected. All their efforts had only moved the stone out about half an inch from the rest of the wall.

"The stone is too heavy and too thick. How far do you think it goes back?" asked Lauren.

"Not sure," huffed Joshua, worn out.

"I am now going back to your thought on how in the world this stone could have been removed and put back so easily," said Lauren.

"Right? But we are moving it. So there has to be a way. We don't know what we don't know," said Joshua.

"Can't you just take a few more deep breaths and levitate the rock? Just float it out of its place," joked Lauren.

"Very funny, Miss Resourceful. Maybe whoever made these markings was able to do that to remove this rock," said Joshua.

"Ha ha ha," said Lauren sarcastically.

"I got an idea. The bottom of the stone is too coarse. That is why we can't budge it much. But if we slide both the hanger and the knife under the stone, we may be able to move it side to side while pushing it out of place, kind of like moving heavy furniture," said Joshua.

"Okay, let's try it," said Lauren. They slid the hanger and knife under the stone and began working the stone side to side in unison.

"It's working," said Lauren.

They pushed the stone halfway out the other side.

"I think we can just push it completely out now," said Joshua. They each put one hand on the stone and pushed it completely out. It fell on the ground on the other side of the wall. Joshua shone his cell phone light into the space behind the wall.

211

"What do you see?" asked Lauren.

"It looks like a small cave area. The walls are dirt. It's not tall enough to fully stand in there," said Joshua.

"Do you see a way out?" asked Lauren.

"No. But, I may need to climb all the way inside to see the whole area," said Joshua.

"Well, are you going to or what?" asked an impatient Lauren, peering around him.

"Are you?" asked Joshua.

"After all of that, don't tell me you're scared now?" said Lauren.

"I am not scared. I just don't want anything happening to you," said Joshua. Before Lauren could even respond, Joshua continued, "And yes, I know. You can take care of yourself. But that still doesn't change the fact that sometimes things happen that we can't control. And I don't know how I would be able to handle it if something happened to you."

Lauren smiled. "I appreciate your concern, Joshua. I don't think I've ever had anyone so deeply concerned about my safety and well-being as much as you. Let's just peek in there together and then get right back out," said Lauren.

"Let me go first," said Joshua. He turned around, lying on the ground, and then started sliding his feet and legs into the space first.

"Why are you climbing in backward?" asked Lauren.

"I learned from you earlier. Plus, if something is going to fall on me while I am climbing in there, what do I want it to hit first, my legs or my head?" said Joshua.

"Good point," said Lauren.

Joshua managed to get his entire body fully into the small area. Joshua had been correct. It was just high enough for him to squat without his head touching the dirt ceiling.

Lauren followed Joshua in the same manner, legs first. She got fully through the opening. The area was tight. They were face-to-face, just inches from each other.

"Very intimate, Joshua," said Lauren.

"Don't ever say I don't take you anywhere," said Joshua.

Lauren looked down at the removed stone and saw that it had an old iron handle and plate secured to the opposite end. "Look at that," said Lauren. Joshua shone his light on it. He slowly read the barely legible engraving on the plate.

"Shields Iron 1850," said Joshua.

"So that's how they were able to remove that heavy stone so easily," said Lauren.

"Must be. But it's more likely used to pull it out. If someone were inside this wall like we are, one could easily push the stone back in place. And to anyone in the bathroom, it would look and feel no different than the rest of the wall. I could see how the police may have missed this," said Joshua.

"Look!" said Lauren. She shone her light on a wooden trap door flush with the ground. There was a handle on the door with the same plate that was on the stone.

"You have to be joking! I think I know what this place is. I bet you if we open this wooden door, it will lead to a tunnel underneath this church," said Joshua.

"A tunnel?" asked Lauren.

Joshua grabbed the handle and pulled up the door. Below the trap door was an iron ladder that led down to a tunnel under the church.

"I knew it," said Joshua.

"So, this is how someone was able to start the fire and get away without being seen?" asked Lauren.

"I believe so. This church is a historic building and used to be an old school. But guess what I learned in high school," said Joshua.

"What?" said Lauren, intrigued.

"I learned that certain parts of the city were part of the Underground Railroad," said Joshua.

"You mean the Harriet Tubman Underground Railroad? Helping slaves escape their masters?" asked Lauren.

"Yes! Even after they escaped, many slave owners would hire people to find their slaves and bring them back. Sometimes the owners even went looking for them on their own, including way up here in the North, to get them back," said Joshua.

"Yes, Unfortunately, the financial impact of losing a slave was just that great," said Lauren.

"So, look here," said Joshua as he pointed his light back on the two separate handles. "These plates read 'Shields Iron 1850.' That is the local iron manufacturing company in our neighborhood that shut down a long time ago. During Black History Month, we learned about one of the sons of Charles Shields, founder of the Shields Iron Factory right here in Philadelphia. I forget his name, but he was a secret abolitionist. He was eventually caught in the South, helping to free some slaves. He was then burned alive with a few other secret abolitionists and some runaway slaves. He must have helped set up and construct these underground tunnels without his father or family knowing," said Joshua.

"Maybe they did know, but were intentionally kept uninformed of everything he did," said Lauren.

"But, why?" asked Joshua.

"That way, they still supported him, but had plausible deniability in the event they were ever confronted about it," said Lauren.

"You could be right," said Joshua.

"There are many unnamed African Americans that we don't know about who sacrificed their lives for our freedom. I am sure there are many unnamed Caucasians or whites and others that stood up and sacrificed themselves as well," said Lauren.

"But these fires can't be about that," said Joshua.

"No. Not with that symbol out there in the middle of the basement floor, and those Enochian writings in blood on the wall. It must be about hatred for God and the Christian church. Whoever or whatever is doing this is true evil," said Lauren.

"But again, why here and why now? It still does not make any sense, so I am not convinced on that," said Joshua.

"I think now would be a good time to go to the police, Joshua. We now know something they do not. Hopefully, that should get you off the hook, at least for now," said Lauren.

"I concur. I just want to take a quick look," said Joshua.

"You just went from silly to stupid," said Lauren.

"Come on. How cool would it be to say you saw an actual tunnel from the Underground Railroad?" asked Joshua.

"Very cool if you live to talk about it. You know I love a great date, but our last one did not end too well. With fires and symbols, this is getting way too dangerous," said Lauren.

"Okay. How about I go down the ladder only halfway to take a picture with my phone? It is extremely dark down there. So, unless this person has night vision, I should be able to see them coming with a flashlight or something," said Joshua. Lauren looked at him in doubt.

"Just halfway down. It will take me just thirty-three seconds. I promise," said Joshua.

"How far do you think it goes down?" asked Lauren.

"From the looks of it, I'd say about twenty feet," said Joshua.

"Alright. Go down five to ten feet and hurry back up," said Lauren, feeling anxious.

Joshua grinned and started to climb down the ladder. He went halfway down and pulled out his cell phone. He leaned down to take a picture, but the flash wasn't on.

"Vite, vite!" said Lauren as she looked down at Joshua.

"What do you mean, vite?" Joshua yelled back up to her.

"It means hurry in French," said Lauren.

"This is not French class, Lauren. I have to turn on the flash on my phone and adjust the night settings," he explained.

Joshua took both hands off the ladder and leaned forward against it to balance himself. He attempted to push the flash icon on his phone, but he lost his balance. He quickly grabbed the ladder, but his cell phone slipped from his hand, and it fell to the ground.

"Crap! I dropped my phone!" yelled Joshua.

"You idgit! Forget about it! Just leave it," said a frantic Lauren.

"I can't!" yelled Joshua. "If the police find my cell phone in this tunnel, it really won't look good for me."

Lauren put her head down with her hand over her face. She knew he was right. His cell phone in the tunnel would be hard evidence for the police to convict Joshua of the fires, including the murder of Trustee John Copeland. Joshua yelled back up to Lauren.

"It's still hard for me to see. Can you shine your light a little lower into the tunnel?" asked Joshua.

Lauren lowered her arm, holding her cell phone deeper into the tunnel as far as she could without losing her balance on the edge.

"Does that help?" asked Lauren.

"Yes. Well, a little," said Joshua.

Her light still did not shine all the way to the ground. Joshua leaned down as far as he could while holding onto the ladder. He could barely see the ground, but he finally saw the glimmer of his cell phone.

"I see it!" yelled Joshua.

"Can you get it?" asked Lauren.

"It looks like I have to climb all the way down, but yes, I think so," said Joshua. But, he was less confident than he communicated.

"Watch yourself!" exclaimed Lauren.

Joshua noticed that the ladder did not reach all the way to the ground. The bottom of it stopped about five feet above the ground.

He thought, *No problem. That's an easy jump from there.* He continued down the ladder. The next rung of the ladder squeaked as he stepped on it. It was not as sturdy as the others. He cautiously bounced a little weight on it with his foot to test it before completely stepping on it. It held. With confidence and without delay, Joshua went down to the next rung, but it broke off. He fell hard to the ground. Lauren heard the loud thump of Joshua's body hitting the ground.

"Joshua!" yelled Lauren. He did not respond. "Joshua! Are you okay?" repeated Lauren.

Joshua landed on his back. He slowly leaned up off the ground to sit up. He was dazed, and his body ached from the fall.

"Joshua! Answer me!" screamed Lauren.

Joshua was getting ready to yell up to Lauren that he was okay. However, he felt something behind him. It had the same dark presence that Joshua had felt before. He knew that it had evil intentions. As Joshua sat on the ground, he slowly turned his head to look behind him. He saw a large image with an unclear form standing approximately five feet behind him. It was too dark for him to tell what or who it was. But he had feared that it was the same thing that he'd seen through the window of the basement of Mount Carmel.

Joshua strained his eyes in its direction, trying to see clearer. He blinked his eyes a few times and refocused. This time Joshua saw its fiery eyes looking at him. The mysterious being ran at Joshua. Before Joshua could get up or even yell for Lauren, he was hit in the head with a hard metal object similar to a short pipe. The blow knocked Joshua out cold. Joshua fell back to the ground. The dark being grabbed him and easily dragged him away down the dark tunnel.

Lauren yelled, one more time, "Joshua!"

She received no response and knew something was terribly wrong. She took a deep breath and climbed down the ladder.

16

The Wedding Ceremony

Lauren and Mike's Wedding Day

One year before the community revival.

Half of Lauren's dark hair was folded up in clips, partially done. She was sitting in a chair in front of the vanity mirror with her eyes closed. Katherine, the hired makeup artist, put on Lauren's eye shadow. Lauren was covered by the thin white silk robe given to her by her maid of honor, Jessica. Jessica had given it to Lauren as a gift during the bridal shower a few weeks ago. It was personalized and embroidered with Lauren's name on the front.

Jessica and the other bridesmaids were in the room as well. They were getting dressed and putting on their makeup. Soft music was playing in the background. The music had been Jessica's idea. She figured it might help keep Lauren calm in the event she became ill-tempered with any unpredicted mishaps that always occur on a wedding day. Lauren and the bridesmaids were in Bishop Hines' overnight study at his church, International Covenant Ministries. Since Bishop Hines spent so much time at the church, especially Saturday nights preparing for Sunday morning sermons, he'd decided to convert one of the church's offices into an overnight room. It possessed a private bathroom, a large flat-screen television on the wall, two sofas, and a few mismatched chairs. Also in the room was the hired photographer's wife, periodically taking memorable snapshots of the bridal party getting ready. She took one of Lauren with her eyes closed. After hearing the camera shutter, Lauren opened her eyes and smiled.

Katherine looked in the mirror at Lauren. "You are such a beautiful bride," she said. Lauren looked up and continued to smile.

"Yes. And thanks to Miss Beautiful, soon to be Mrs. Beautiful, we are running so behind," said Jessica, referring to how late they'd arrived at the church because of Lauren's rare procrastination.

"Isn't it bad luck if the bride is on time? I am supposed to have everyone waiting on me, right?" asked Lauren.

"And if you are late, where are they all going to go? This is your day, sweetie," said Katherine.

"Exactly. Mike and his boys can wait," said Lauren.

"Okay, you're right. This is your day," said Jessica, holding her hands up in a placating gesture.

"Jessica only wants us to hurry up so she can get out there and take a look at all of the eligible bachelors," said Lauren's cousin, Nina. The group laughed.

"Love is always in the air at weddings," said Katherine.

"Well, I'm sure I won't be the only one trying to breathe in a little of that air today!" exclaimed Jessica. They all laughed again.

The door opened. It was Lauren's mom, Marion.

"Hello, ladies," said Marion. She was fully dressed for the wedding, wearing a raisin-colored gown with lace sleeves.

"Mrs. Alexander, you look amazing," said Jessica.

"Thank you. All of you girls look beautiful," said Marion.

She walked over to Lauren and kissed her on the cheek. "My goodness! Especially my little girl," Marion added.

"Mom! You're messing up my makeup!" squealed Lauren.

"It's okay. I can easily fix it," said Katherine.

The door opened again. This time it was the wedding coordinator, Sylvia. Unlike her typical vibrant smile and semblance, she walked into the room with a concerned look on her face.

Jessica assumed Sylvia was upset because they were running late. "It's Lauren's fault. We will be ready in no time." Jessica pleaded.

"You're fine, ladies, and you all look beautiful. Lauren, I need to talk to you for a brief minute," said Sylvia.

"Can it wait until she's done with my makeup?" asked Lauren.

"I will be done in about ten more minutes," said Katherine.

"You were going to say your own vows, correct?" asked Sylvia.

"Yes. Why?" asked Lauren.

"Did you write them down?" asked Sylvia.

"No. I have them all in my head. Well, for the most part, I do. I did not want to write them down and then have them sound so generic or robotic. Why?" asked Lauren.

Sylvia did not immediately respond. She hesitated as she knew that once she told Lauren why, it would create a big problem.

"Mike . . ." Sylvia paused, then continued, "Mike wants to see them before the wedding."

"He wants to what!" exclaimed Marion. Jessica and the other bridesmaids also looked on with surprise.

"Isn't that bad luck, kind of like seeing her in person before the wedding?" asked Jessica.

Lauren and Sylvia looked at Jessica, confused. Lauren focused back on the request.

"Why would he want to see my vows, especially before the ceremony?" asked Lauren.

Sylvia reluctantly answered the question. "I did ask him why," said Sylvia, avoiding eye contact.

"And . . .?" asked Lauren.

"He wants to make sure your vows are appropriate," said Sylvia.

"Appropriate! What the heck does Mike mean by that?" yelled Marion in a rage.

"Oh my goodness, Mom!" exclaimed Lauren, surprised but not offended by her outburst.

"I'm sorry. But Mike needs checking," said Marion.

Lauren grabbed her cell phone off the vanity and scrolled down through it to her recent calls and selected "Mike's Cell." She put the cell phone to her ear and abruptly walked into the bathroom, and slammed the door shut behind her.

Mike answered his phone on the third ring. "Hey, my future Mrs.," he said. Lauren wasted no time in getting to the point.

"Can you explain to me why you want to see my vows?" asked Lauren. Mike could hear the displeasure in her voice.

"Before you get your dress all wrinkled, this day is about our union and us. I just wanted to make sure that what we say is appropriate, especially with the number of people that will be here. Not to mention all the dignitaries here to support my father and us," said Mike.

"Don't you mean, make sure what *I* say is appropriate, right, Mike?" asked Lauren.

"Listen, I am going to be very honest with you. You tend to speak without thinking and—"

Lauren interrupted Mike. "I don't have to think. I already know what I need to say," said Lauren.

"That's what I am talking about, Lauren. You don't even listen. You just say whatever comes to your head; and most of the time, it's not appropriate or even respectful," said Mike.

Lauren's frustration completely took over. "I am going to be honest as well. The only reason why you think what I say is inappropriate is because it differs from your thoughts, and you just want me to keep my mouth shut. And if I ever do open it, you just want me to agree with everything you say. For the record, I am not like you. In fact, I would never want to be like you!" exclaimed Lauren.

"Oh my god!" yelled Mike. "You are such a . . ." He stopped himself before allowing the last word to proceed out of his mouth.

"Come on, Minister Mike Hines! Say it! Go ahead and say that word. Don't chicken out now!" exclaimed Lauren.

"If you don't like me or ever want to be like me, as you said, then why would you want to marry me?" asked Mike.

"Well, if you think you need to change me, then why would you want to marry me?" asked Lauren.

"Maybe I don't anymore. Look, you are beautiful, and I respected your love for God and knowledge. But you cannot always say what you think. You cannot always do what you want. I have a role that I have to play for this church and this community. Now we both have that same role with this marriage. We don't always get to choose, Lauren. Do you understand that?" asked Mike.

"No. You're wrong, Mike. I always have a choice, married or not," said Lauren.

"Listen Lauren, either you choose to be with me, or you choose to be against me," said Mike.

Lauren put her cell phone down to her neck as she unsuccessfully tried to hold back the tears. She picked it back up to her face.

"You're a real piece of work. I was so blind. But today, you have spat on the ground and made mud, and then put it on my eyes for me to see clearly," said Lauren.

"Really, Lauren," said Mike, while shaking his head with his eyes closed, as he understood Lauren's Biblical reference.

"I will never fit into your world. And nor do I want to. The wedding is off!" exclaimed Lauren. Mike did not respond.

"Goodbye," said Lauren.

She hung up the phone, fell to the ground against the bathroom door, and quietly wept. She'd never felt so much pain. She thought, *Maybe Mike was right.* Lauren was unique and had never really fit in with any group. Perhaps she wasn't ever meant to get married. Perhaps she wasn't ever meant to be happy. Then, Lauren put her head down and cried hysterically.

Everyone on the other side of the door could hear her. They felt her pain and were saddened. Marion, Jessica, and Sylvia banged on the door, asking Lauren to open it up. Lauren ignored them.

"You ladies continue to get dressed. I am going to get the Bishop," said Sylvia as she ran out of the room. The photographer's wife followed after her.

"Lauren. My sweet, sweet daughter. I am not going anywhere. I am right here for you," said Marion as her eyes teared up for her daughter. Jessica embraced Marion from behind.

"None of us are going anywhere, Lauren," said Jessica. Lauren leaned her head back against the door as she sat on the floor, wiping her eyes with the back of her hands.

"Mike is such a jackass! He doesn't deserve Lauren," said Nina.

"Shh!" said Jessica as she walked away from the door up to Nina. "She can hear you, and we don't need to make her more upset."

Even though the wedding seemed to be off, the bridesmaids continued to get fully dressed, as Sylvia instructed. Marion grabbed one of the chairs and sat patiently by the bathroom door with the hope of Lauren coming out. Lauren was now standing up, looking in the bathroom mirror, attempting to fix her makeup, which had been weathered by the tears. There was a knock on the door out in the main room. It was Sylvia, who poked her head in the room and looked around.

"Is everyone dressed?" asked Sylvia.

"Yes," said Jessica.

Sylvia walked into the room, with Bishop Hines following. Everyone felt his towering presence. They were comforted, as they knew that he had always treated Lauren like a daughter of his. During the last few months before this wedding day, anywhere you saw Bishop Hines, you also saw Lauren, even if Mike was not around. As Bishop Hines walked into the room, he greeted each of the ladies separately with a nod and a smile.

He was wearing a special custom-made robe, also known as a cassock, to perform the ceremony. It was a full-length black robe with a minister's collar, and it had light blue and silver brocade details on the center front area, cuffs, and lower trim, with two silver crosses adorning the left and right upper chest area.

"I love your robe, Bishop Hines," said Jessica.

"Thank you so much. You all look just lovely, especially you, Mother Alexander," said Bishop Hines as he embraced Marion.

"Thank you, Bishop," said Marion.

"Is Lauren in there?" asked Bishop Hines as he pointed to the bathroom door.

"Yes," said Marion.

"Ladies, would you please give us some time? You can go to my library, which is down the hall. I believe the second door on the right. It has a pretty big sitting area with two large sofas and a few chairs." The ladies started leaving the room.

"Please stay here with me, Mother," said Bishop Hines as he put his hand on Marion's shoulder. Marion sat back down in the chair. "Sylvia.

Can you have the caterer bring some refreshments to my library for the bridesmaids?" asked Bishop Hines.

"Absolutely," said Sylvia.

"Thank you," said Bishop Hines. The bridesmaids left the room, including Sylvia.

Bishop Hines walked up to the bathroom door and knocked on it three times. "Lauren, my daughter, it's me, Bishop Hines."

Lauren thought, *Why did he just introduce himself? I obviously know it's him.*

"Hear me out. I do not need you to open the door or even say a word. I just want to say a few things to you." He took a deep breath and whispered to himself, "Lord, speak through me." He continued.

"These last few months with you becoming part of my family have been one of the most wonderful and cherished experiences of my life. Over the years, I have been around so many people, from the homeless to prominent ministers to celebrities and politicians. And no one has ever had more of a positive influence on my character and my ministry than you, Lauren," said Bishop Hines.

Marion's eyes began to water again. Bishop Hines continued.

"Everyone usually agrees with everything I say, but you challenge me when you know I could do better, especially in showing and replicating the love of God to others. More importantly, you reminded me that this building is not my church, but the church is the people of God. There is no one that I know that has more compassion for others than you. And no one I know has more true godly love or agape love than you. No one searches for the truth more than you. And because of this, you will always be different. You will rarely fit in, and times like this will hurt and be more painful than those who experience the same. But that is why God gave you favor over others, and the angels and all the heavenly hosts look down on you and smile. I apologize for the ignorance and lack of respect that my son has shown you on this day. Out of all days, for him to act like this is a disgrace. I take full responsibility for his words and actions.

But it is not about him or me. It's about God's plan for your life. And this pain will pass, because your love is greater than any pain or situation you will ever encounter. And I do not doubt that you will find an equal or even greater love that you surely deserve. I love you so much, just like you are my own, and nothing will ever change that," said Bishop Hines.

Lauren opened the bathroom door with tears flowing down her face and immediately hugged Bishop Hines. She put her wet face directly on Bishop Hines' robe. Marion looked at him, smiling gratefully for getting her out of the bathroom and knowing that his robe may be ruined. Bishop Hines smiled back at her, acknowledging the same, but he did not care. He gently pulled away from Lauren.

"Now, I would not be a good bishop, or even a good father for that matter, if I did not provide consultation with you two to make sure this is what you want to do," said Bishop Hines.

"Okay, Bishop. But I am pretty certain Mike and I will not be getting married today," said Lauren.

"Understood. Let's make it official. You can go to my office, and I will go get Mike," said Bishop Hines.

"Thank you, Bishop. I will walk with her," said Marion.

"Mike and I will see you there in a few minutes," said Bishop Hines.

Bishop Hines walked out the door and went to the other side of the sanctuary to get Mike.

"You should put something on to cover yourself," said Marion. Lauren was still in the robe that Jessica had bought her.

"I have a sweatshirt and a pair of pantaloons on that chair," said Lauren as she pointed across the room.

227

"Pantaloons, Lauren?" asked Marion. Lauren smiled.

Marion walked across the room and grabbed Lauren's gray sweatshirt and light blue jeans off the chair. Lauren quickly changed and put on her sneakers. They walked out of the room and turned left toward Bishop Hines' office. As they walked to the office, they passed a few church workers along the way. All were astonished to see Lauren dressed down, and it was very apparent that she had been crying. They entered Bishop's Hines office. Even though it was a church office, the design and layout were more like that of a large conference room that you would find in a corporate building. There was a thin gray, basic carpet with industrial padding, eggshell paint on the walls, a ten-foot-high ceiling, and full-length windows to give Bishop Hines a good view of the city. His excuse for the large windows was that the view reminded him every Sunday that his church's purpose was for the community. However, it was also a good view of the main parking lot, so that he could tell which of his church officials made it to service on time or not.

Bishop Hines' desk was the most remarkable thing in the office, maybe even the whole church. It resembled the Resolute desk found in the White House's Oval Office, made from English oak, and weighed approximately 820 pounds. It was hand-carved with biblical images of angels, olive branches, and the official church crest of International Covenant Ministries. It had been a gift from Archbishop Bennett of the Catholic Church.

The Archbishop had traveled with Bishop Hines many times to Vatican City and many underdeveloped countries. They collectively worked on interdenominational missions. With his wealth of knowledge and his charming personality, Bishop Hines had managed to successfully navigate through the most politically hardened, war-torn regions of Africa and the Middle East, including many areas previously restricted from the Archbishop and his missionaries. Among other things, they provided fresh drinking water, schools, and improved housing in those areas. Even though they disagreed on the specifics of religion, the desk was a sign of respect the entire Catholic Church and other denominations had for Bishop Hines and his ministry.

During a trip to Africa, one of the region's ministers brought up, in front of the Archbishop, how some Christians in America had criticized Bishop Hines on social media for working with other religions. Bishop Hines stated that he had never let it bother him. In his Swahili accent, the minister told the Bishop that, "Unless they are willing to come out the four walls of their church to help the poor, let alone the poor in their neighborhood, tell them to shut their mouths!" Bishop Hines just smiled. At that moment, Archbishop Bennett realized not only was Bishop Hines fighting the culture and politics of these international regions, but Bishop Hines was also fighting Christians back home, even in his religious denomination.

That's when he had the idea for the desk as a gift to Bishop Hines. Lauren had first seen the desk when it was being constructed. Bishop Hines had a meeting in Washington, D.C., with a few state representatives and asked Mike and Lauren to join him. While he was there, Archbishop Bennett gave Bishop Hines an address to a lumber company in Leesburg, Virginia, just outside of Washington, D.C. By saying it was imperative for their future missions, the Archbishop convinced Bishop Hines to visit it before he left to go back up to Philadelphia. Even though he had no idea what for, Bishop Hines took Mike and Lauren out to the lumber company. The owner of the lumber company and its workers already knew of Bishop Hines. But Bishop Hines did not know of them or why he was there. They led him to a section in the warehouse, where they took off the plastic covering the desk. "A gift from Archbishop Bennett," said the owner, revealing the desk that was approximately eighty percent complete. It brought Bishop Hines to tears. "We should have it completed in about one or two more months, and we will deliver it directly to your church," said the owner.

Remembering that event, Lauren walked back and forth in front of this desk, dragging her index finger along the front carvings.

Marion was sitting in one of the three chairs situated in front of the desk. They waited quietly in the office for Bishop Hines and Mike to enter the room. After a few minutes, Bishop Hines walked into the room with Mike following behind him. Bishop Hines sat down at his desk. Mike sat down on the chair on the left, closest to the door, while Lauren took one last finger trace along the desk before she sat down between Mike and her mother.

"Ladies, thank you for your patience," said Bishop Hines.

"Of course, Bishop," said Marion.

"In my experience, conversations like this need to be face-to-face, not through a phone call, and definitely not through text messages. However, I am not here to control this conversation. I just want to make sure that you two saw each other's face when discussing what happens next. Hiding behind a phone is easy. But people who care about one another discuss their issues in person, and not with third parties or phone applications.

You know that I love you both, and if you want Lauren's mother and me to leave, we will. But if you want us to stay, that is fine too. It is totally up to you," said Bishop Hines.

"Dad, I am fine either way," said Mike with a stoic face, portraying that he no longer cared.

"I would prefer you both to stay," said Lauren as her eyes began to water again.

"Son. You go first. What's this all about?" asked Bishop Hines.

"No offense, but she needs to think before she speaks," said Mike.

"I do think before I speak. It's not my fault some people's thoughts take longer to catch up to mine," said Lauren.

"Are you talking about me? Remember, I'm the one with the doctorate," said Mike.

"And that degree still doesn't change the fact that you have no logic or common sense. I can insult you today, and you won't even realize it until next week," said Lauren.

"Look how you insult me by talking about how you can insult me. Man, I can't wait to post that on social media for our first anniversary and say, 'A year since I married this beautiful woman, and she is so smart that all of her insults go over my head. She is just so thoughtful!'" said Mike. He then looked at his father with the expectation that his point was just made.

"And my anniversary post would read, 'A year later and he still has that doctorate! I'm such a lucky girl!'" exclaimed Lauren. Marion attempted to contain her laughter, albeit unsuccessful.

"See. Right there is why I wanted to see your vows before the wedding. I should have known you were not going to write them down," said Mike. Bishop Hines became even more disappointed.

"Wait a minute. Sylvia only told me that you said something ignorant and belittling to Lauren that pushed her over the edge to call off the wedding. In a rush, I guess I mistakenly did not stop to ask about the full details. Mike, you wanted to see or hear her vows in advance of the ceremony?" asked Bishop Hines.

"Dad, you know more than anyone that she does not always say the most appropriate things at the appropriate time," said Mike.

"I could say the same things about your sermons," said Lauren.

"That's really funny because you do! You're always criticizing my messages or the scriptures I use," said Mike.

"Those are not criticisms, but suggestions. Do you ever listen to what I say and process it to determine whether it makes sense or not? You criticize everything I say. In fact, you probably would criticize me opening up my mouth just to breathe if it didn't keep me alive," said Lauren.

"You always make things up in your head," said Mike.

"I do? A perfect example was last night. You wanted to kick Marcus out of the church during our rehearsal. You did not even think that he might have needed the fellowship or even a meal. But when I tried to convince you otherwise, you just blew me off because you were set in your thoughts and your ways. No one could be one with you in marriage. Not how you are today," said Lauren.

"You ungrateful, unprofessional little brat!" exclaimed Mike. Bishop Hines jumped in before Marion, visibly angry, responded.

"Hey! We are not here to do that," said Bishop Hines strenuously as he looked at Mike.

"It's okay, Bishop. He always wanted to call it quits anyway. In his mind, it's Proverbs chapter twenty-one, verse nine," said Lauren.

"And what is Proverbs twenty-one and nine, Oh Mighty Smart One?" asked Mike, rolling his eyes.

Bishop Hines interjected. "This scripture says it's better to live in the corner of a rooftop than with a quarrelsome woman.

But I know your mother and I raised you way better than what I see from you today. You are not only disappointing me but embarrassing me as well. Now, in retrospect, I should have started us off in prayer before anyone said anything. So, everyone, please bow your heads and close your eyes." Bishop Hines stared them down until they complied.

"Oh Lord of mercy and truth, the alpha and omega, the great I am, we ask that if there is anything that is not of you that it be removed from us, this room, and this church, right now. Fill this temple and this office with your love and your wisdom to control our words all for the glory and edification of the kingdom of God. In the name of Jesus, we pray and believe done right now. Amen and Amen."

Bishop Hines looked up to see the prayer had worked. Mike's and Lauren's faces were more relaxed, even apologetic.

"Now, Michael. Can you act like you are a child of God and show Lauren respect? You must have cared about her if you were willing to marry her," said Bishop Hines.

"I'm sorry, Dad. I get it. Lauren and I have been—" Bishop Hines interrupted Mike.

"Son, don't talk to me. Talk to Lauren."

"Okay." Mike sighed. He turned to face Lauren. "Lauren, I'm sorry. When I first met you, I thought you were an angel. You are beautiful, smart, and your compassion for others is second to none. You appeared to have everything I ever wanted in a woman, a wife. You also seemed to just fit in with our family so easily. But honestly, when we are alone, we just cannot get along. We are never on the same page. And no matter how hard we try to make it work, it just doesn't. This day was about us becoming one, and whether the problem is me, or you, or the both of us, it doesn't seem like we will ever be one. I love you with all my heart, but I do not feel that I am in love with you. I will always have the utmost respect for you and will continue to appreciate our friendship," said Mike.

Lauren still had tears in her eyes, but she matched his respectful tone with confidence. "I guess that's the difference between you and me, and probably me and everyone else for that matter. For the love and husband that God has planned for me, I do not believe that I will have to try to make it work. Will there be problems? Yes. Will we need to work together to resolve issues? Yes. But all of that is external. My mom and dad taught me that God is love; and that God is not the author of confusion or even contention. If it is truly God's love in a marriage, why would it be confusing or destructive?

You may love me, and I may love you. But I am not in love with you or your soul. Most times, I do not even feel your soul. When you're angry, I am afraid to speak my mind or share my thoughts. And God has not given us the spirit of fear, but of love, power, and a sound mind. Around you, I do not have a sound mind.

I realize that my words and actions have not helped our relationship in any way, and I have not acted like a true friend to you, maybe because of what I was feeling. I am sorry," said Lauren.

"Mike," Bishop Hines said. "What you may not understand is that, from what I can tell, Lauren is what some other cultures call an alpha submissive female. It means she is strong, confident, and an independent thinker and problem solver. But she will be submissive for her true soulmate, or twin flame, as they call it, who is also an alpha submissive male. He will, in turn, do the exact same for her. Her soul feels that you are not this person," said Bishop Hines.

He then turned to Lauren. "And for you, Lauren, what you may not understand is that Mike has a specific direction in life and his ministry. Ever since he was a little boy, Mike knew what he wanted to do and where he wanted to go. Maybe his frustration is that he hoped you were the one that would walk with him in this endeavor. However, this vision of you and him together, and the hope of you being that person with him, died daily. You have love and respect for each other. Let us at least keep that alive," said Bishop Hines.

"So, I guess there will be no wedding today," said Mike as he half smiled at Lauren.

"I guess not," said Lauren as she slightly smiled back. Lauren and Mike felt a little relieved.

Bishop Hines turned to Marion. "I am sorry, Mother. It looks like you got all dressed up for nothing," said Bishop Hines.

"No, it was worth it. I'd rather Lauren and Mike go through this to-day as opposed to a year from now, and all of us seeing those insulting social media posts they just talked about," said Marion. They all laughed. "Thank you, Bishop," said Marion.

"Looks like we have an announcement to make," said Mike.

"Can you give us two a moment, Bishop? We will be out there in a second," said Lauren, referring to her and her mom.

"Of course. Take as much time as you need," said Bishop Hines.

"Thank you," said Lauren. Bishop Hines and Mike walked out of the room. In full tears, Lauren immediately hugged her mother. After a few seconds of their embrace, Marion leaned back to get a good look at Lauren.

"Everything is going to be okay, lovely. After our talk last night, I really couldn't see you in church every Sunday wearing one of those large fancy First Lady hats anyway," joked Marion. Lauren smiled. Marion continued, "Now me, on the other hand, I would just *love* to be a First Lady. You know I would look good in them hats," said Marion. They laughed while Lauren wiped the rest of her tears from her eyes.

"I am disappointed. But I guess deep down inside, my soul always knew he was not the one," said Lauren.

"Always trust your soul and the Spirit of God, Lauren. They will never lie to you," said Marion.

"Always," said Lauren as she embraced her mother one more time. Then, they left the room and met up with Bishop Hines and Mike to collectively announce that the wedding was off.

17

The True Realm

Saturday late afternoon—the day of the community revival.

Lauren climbed down the ladder, skipping the broken rung, made her way to the bottom, and easily jumped to the ground. She grabbed her phone out of her pocket and shone the light around the tunnel.

"Joshua!" yelled Lauren.

She heard nothing in return. No talking. No footsteps. If it were not for her cell phone, she would be in complete darkness. She saw Joshua's phone on the ground, not too far from the ladder. She picked it up and put it into her pocket. It confirmed that something terrible had happened. Her breathing intensified. Lauren slowly walked forward, step by step, about twenty-five feet, only to reach a dead-end dirt wall. She had no idea what had happened to Joshua and was unaware that she was in the very spot where the dark being had waited to ambush him. She turned around and went back to the ladder

She yelled, "Joshua! Joshua!"

It was even colder in the tunnel than it was in the church basement. Her panicked breathing now turned to a stutter, as fear for Joshua started to overwhelm her. She cautiously walked past the ladder until she noticed a fork that split into two separate tunnels. This split had been dug intentionally as part of the Underground Railroad to confuse would-be pursuers wanting to capture slaves. This fork could buy the slaves a few moments of additional time, increasing their chance of escape. Now, over a hundred years later, Lauren was frustrated that she must make the same choice. She thought, *Do I take the tunnel to the left or to the right?* She hesitantly took the tunnel to the left and continued down its shaft at a slow pace.

"Joshua!" yelled Lauren. There was still no response, and she no longer expected one, which frightened her even more.

The dirt walls were moist. The ground was uneven and rocky. Approximately every five feet, wood framing shored up the tunnel's dirt walls and ceiling. Wooden slats had been placed on the ground where it was slippery from either water filtration or any significant grade incline. After a few minutes into the tunnel from the split, Lauren began to think she'd taken the wrong path. But as she went a few more paces, she saw an object farther down the tunnel. She went closer. It was another ladder, which led up to the surface. She jumped up to grab the first rung and quickly climbed up the ladder. She reached the top, which was a trap door. She used her body to push up on the door and peeked around the area. It was slightly lit. She saw an old iron furnace and a couple of large water pipes with old wheel shut-off valves. Lauren inferred that this must be another church along the Boulevard. She was correct. The tunnel and ladder had taken her to Church of the Living God, the location of the second church fire. The trap door was in the basement of the church's former furnace and utility room, which was closed off from public access and the rest of the church. When the church had been renovated not too long ago, it included a new HVAC and piping system on the other side of the church. It was also one of the church sections that had been, fortunately, spared from the fire's destruction with the recent building code upgrades.

Lauren got up and walked around. The same Enochian markings covered the walls, just like in the bathroom at Ebenezer AME. Lauren paid attention to a light coming from an aluminum soffit air vent close to one of the walls' bottom edge. The wall had been installed to enclose the area. Lauren walked over to the vent and bent down to look through it. On the other side was one of the church offices. She could see a large desk, a few chairs, a tall filing cabinet, and a safe. It was where the church's trustees came back to count the offerings and pay bills, and most likely where Trustee John Copeland, who died in the second fire, spent most of his time.

Lauren grabbed the vent, which was loose. She realized that she could easily take it off, and it was wide enough for her or anyone else to fit through. She was about to take the vent off the wall when she paused and thought, *Wait. This vent is still in place. Did Joshua come this way?* She decided to try Joshua's spiritual connection technique again. She closed her eyes, took a deep breath, and exhaled. A vision of Joshua going through the tunnel on the right of the fork, and not the left, appeared in her mind. Lauren gasped and opened her eyes. She was confident that she'd taken the wrong tunnel. She immediately ran back to the trap door to go back down the ladder.

* * *

Lauren's vision had been correct. The dark being did take the unconscious Joshua down the tunnel to the right. However, the dark being was already at work on Joshua. At the split, it picked Joshua up and carried him on its shoulder down the second tunnel to a large enclosed cave. This cave had been used for secret meetings and a temporary habitat for slaves if bounty hunters were in the neighborhood.

The dark being brought Joshua into the cave. He laid him upon a large flat stone that appeared to balance on smaller rocks between it and the ground. It was theorized that balanced rocks produced higher-than-normal electromagnetic energy. Some cultures even believed that balanced rocks were portals to other worlds or the spiritual realm. Joshua's hands and feet were bound. They were tied down by a solid braided black nylon rope typically used to secure boats and cargo. The ropes were secured from underneath the stone table. The dark being placed a piece of black electrical tape over Joshua's mouth and walked away from him to another large stone table just behind Joshua's head. At that moment, Joshua awoke in confusion. He shook his head as he attempted to get his wits about him. He realized he was bound in every way and could not yell for help. The tape contained his voice and turned it into a murmur. He fearfully looked around the cave. The dirt walls and cold temperature confirmed that he was still somewhere in the tunnel. The cave's primary light was created by two oversized industrial flashlights hanging on metal hooks on opposite sides of the cave, placed facing up. Joshua looked over and saw the back of the dark being at the other stone table. On the table were many small lit candles and a few objects that Joshua could not decipher. Joshua looked down toward his feet and saw the opening of the cave. To the left of the cave's entrance were two red containers used to store gasoline, and what appeared to be a metal backpack with a long nozzle, most likely a flamethrower. Joshua struggled to break free while grunting under the mask of the tape. He was unsuccessful.

The dark being continued to work at the stone table, seemingly unbothered by Joshua's attempts. The dark being turned around and approached Joshua. Joshua saw the dark being clearly for the first time. It seemed to be a human wearing a wool coat, a leather aviator helmet cap, and goggles, similar to what an old fighter pilot would wear in World War II, except with no lower face covering and no oxygen hose or mask. Therefore, Joshua could only see its mouth, lower cheeks, and jawline, and not the dark being's entire face. The exposed mouth, cheeks, and chin showed many fresh and old cuts, most likely from a knife, maybe even self-inflicted.

The dark being smiled at Joshua with an evil grin. Joshua's eyes opened even wider with surprise as he noticed a few of the dark being's teeth were filed down and resembled razor-sharp, thin vampire teeth. Joshua attempted to struggle out of the ropes again, but to no avail. The dark being grabbed Joshua's arm with one hand and revealed a hypodermic needle with the other. Joshua screamed in excruciating pain under the electrical tape, as the dark being had a forceful grip on his arm, more powerful than anything Joshua had ever felt in his whole life. The radius and ulna bones of Joshua's forearm felt like they were being crushed together by a set of oversized vice grip mechanical pliers. Joshua had thought this dark being was human, but he reconsidered now after feeling this superhuman grip. It injected Joshua's arm with the needle and then walked back to the table. After a few seconds, Joshua became drowsy, and his vision blurred. He no longer felt any pain in his forearm. He laid his head back on the stone and looked up. He was disoriented. The cave began to spin slowly, counterclockwise. The dark being walked back to Joshua with a dirty rag. It took the rag and wiped Joshua's face with it. Joshua could feel the cold, wet rag, almost as if the dark being was cleaning Joshua's face with it. It then tilted Joshua's head back to raise his jawbone and continued to wipe Joshua's neck.

It walked down to the opposite end of the stone and took off Joshua's socks and shoes. It adjusted Joshua's legs to be more in line with the entry into the cave. It then went back to the table, grabbed two gold coins, and slowly placed them over Joshua's eyes. It then took some type of putty or clay and pushed it into Joshua's ears.

It went to the table again and grabbed a black five-gallon bucket. It was filled with mud. The mud mix was approximately one part dirt and two parts water. It then took the mud in the bucket and covered Joshua's face with it, including his eyes and ears, just enough to keep the coins and clay in his ears in place and still allow Joshua to breathe. Then, the dark being took more mud and covered Joshua's hands and feet, and any other parts of Joshua's exposed skin.

It then took a pocketknife out of its coat pocket, most likely the same old dull knife it had used to mutilate itself. The dark being stood over Joshua's body and raised its left hand, cutting it with its right. Joshua was semiconscious from the injection. However, he could now hear the dark being speaking words like in a prayer or a chant. But Joshua couldn't understand the words.

"Ad mortem te . . . ad mortem te . . . ad mortem te . . ." said the dark being. It repeated the phrase again and again.

As time went on, the dark being's voice became fainter to Joshua. "Ad mortem te . . . ad mortem te . . . ad mortem te . . ." repeated the dark being again and again without end.

Joshua's body began to tremble and then shake violently. Then his body stopped moving. He relaxed his hands, and his head tilted to the side. He fell into a deeper unconscious state.

After what felt like just a few moments, Joshua opened his eyes. The cave no longer had any walls. He was there all by himself, lying on the same stone, but no longer bound. He got up and looked around. The air was cold, but the ground was warm beneath his bare feet. There was a thick blanket of dark fog everywhere. Joshua looked around as he walked away from the stone. There were no walls, no boundaries of any sort in this place. It was dark, but he saw hundreds, maybe thousands of small spheres of sparkling light coming up from the ground and floating up to the heavens, scorching the dark sky, like comets moving in slow motion.

Joshua thought, *Are those gods ascending from the earth, just like in the Bible? Am I dead?* He continued to walk along the ground away from the stone, searching for a sign that someone else is there, or a clue to help determine his whereabouts.

Joshua tried to yell, "Lauren! Lauren!"

He stopped. He had spoken, and he could hear what he had said, but no words had come out of his mouth. He tried again, but this time with his mouth closed. "Lauren! Lauren!" He could hear it again, as loud as could be, but his mouth was shut. He wondered, *How could this be?* For some reason, in this place, he could hear his thoughts without any actual sound. He was confused and tried to listen for any type of noise with his ears. It was complete silence. No one was talking. There was no background noise, not even any wind. Joshua snapped his fingers and then clapped his hands and heard nothing. This place was soundless. But then he spoke, "Hello!" He heard it, but again, not from his mouth. At that moment, a group of the small spheres formed a tornado pattern and slowly circled Joshua, with Joshua being the eye. Their lights sparkled even brighter as they circled Joshua. One of the spheres broke formation and descended to him. It hovered in front of Joshua for a few seconds and spoke.

"The mighty and great Joshua. Why do you look for the living among the dead?" asked the sphere of light.

"What did you say?" asked Joshua, astounded.

"Lauren is not here. You are a long way from home, where she remains," said the sphere of light.

"How come there is no sound here, and how come I can hear you in my mind, but we are not actually speaking?" asked Joshua.

"Mouths and ears are not needed in this realm, not even your eyes, mighty Joshua. This is not your world," said the sphere of light.

"What are you, and where am I? Am I dead?" asked Joshua.

"That is not my place to say," said the sphere of light. Suddenly, the other spheres in the sky scattered. A separate, more distinct sphere appeared from a distance and descended through the scattered lights toward Joshua. The first sphere flew away as this new sphere floated in front of him. Joshua felt its presence. This time, he knew what and who it was.

"Joshua," said the sphere of light in a pleasant, calming voice. The voice confirmed Joshua's thought.

"Mom?" asked Joshua as he trembled, waiting for confirmation.

"My son. My son, Joshua," said the sphere of light.

Joshua thought, *This must be a dream.* He scanned his surroundings again in an attempt to find some clue or sign that he was dreaming. He was unsuccessful. He looked back at the sphere with apprehension.

"Mom? Is that really you? I must be dreaming. This can't be real," said Joshua in disbelief.

"I felt your presence when you broke through the Celeste. We all did. I knew it was you. I traveled a long way to come here and see you," said the sphere of light.

"What am I doing here? I have so many questions to ask you," said Joshua. The sphere did not answer his question.

"I am so proud of the man you have become. My soul is joyful in your presence. But my fears are finally coming true, and now I cannot protect you anymore," said the sphere of light.

"What does that mean?" said Joshua, growing more desperate.

"Things are not what they seem, Joshua. *Be ye not deceived,*" exclaimed the sphere of light. Joshua could feel the intensity of the warning. "Good bringeth forth good, and evil bringeth forth evil," said the sphere of light.

"What is going on?" asked Joshua.

"My son. My strong and mighty son, Joshua. I must go now. We all must go," said the sphere of light.

"Mom! I don't understand," said Joshua.

"Continue to trust your soul. It communes with the Father daily. Remember, be strong and of a good courage, only be thou strong and very courageous, Joshua," said the sphere of light.

The familiar sphere flew back in line with the other spheres of light. Then all the spheres of light flew away in a synchronized collective pattern and disappeared into the upper sky. Without their light, the area was now pitch black. Joshua couldn't see a thing, not even the hand in front of his face when he tried. The air turned much colder. He started to shiver.

"Mom! Mom!" thought Joshua. He felt something behind him. He looked back, but he couldn't see anything through the dark void and emptiness. He knew something was there, though. It was the same feeling he got during his reoccurring dream, and the same feeling he'd had when he saw the dark being setting fire to the basement of Mount Carmel. The same feeling he'd had in the tunnel before he was hit over the head by the dark being. Joshua began to walk forward, away from this evil presence. He held his arms and hands in front of his face while he moved forward, hoping it would prevent him from running into something.

Joshua thought, *First, I was dealing without any sound. Now, I have to deal with absolute darkness.*

He stopped as he felt the dark presence directly behind him, at his back. It was a gray smoke, now circling Joshua like an enormous tornado. Joshua lost the air in his lungs. He couldn't breathe. He fell to the ground on his knees, grabbing his throat and gasping for air. Air that was no longer present.

* * *

Lauren slowly walked back down the tunnel and turned the correct way to catch up to Joshua. She was purposefully quiet, as she felt certain something else other than Joshua was down there. Lauren saw light coming from the opposite end of the tunnel, far away. She no longer needed her cell phone's light and put her phone in her pocket. She cautiously moved forward. The cave's opening was now brightly visible to her.

Lauren heard a voice speaking. She couldn't make out who it was or what it was saying. However, she knew the voice was not Joshua's. Lauren got to the opening of the cave. She swiftly slid into a nook just in front of the left side of the cave to avoid being seen. Lauren peeked in and saw Joshua lying on the stone covered in mud. She opened her mouth to speak his name, but then she quickly covered it with her hands and fell back into the nook when she saw the dark being standing over him. She listened carefully, still with her hand over her mouth.

". . . ad mortem te . . . ad mortem te . . . ad mortem te . . ." chanted the dark being repeatedly.

Lauren thought furiously, *It's Latin. Mortem? To death and you?* Lauren turned back to look again. This time she saw the dark being in more detail. She could tell it was tall, maybe just above six feet. She noticed the pilot's helmet covering its upper face and the lower face with its blooded self-inflicted cuts. Lauren recoiled at its altered sharp teeth. She looked around the cave and saw the table behind it with all types of different objects. She then looked down near her feet and saw a large can of blood and a dead goat next to it. Lauren assumed that was how this dark being made the markings on the wall. She looked to the opposite side of the cave's entrance and saw a gasoline container and a flamethrower. Lauren realized this dark being must be human.

She closely looked at him again. He was still chanting, but his head was tilted, looking up at the ceiling. She looked at Joshua. His body was trembling; he seemed semiconscious.

Joshua's body shook more violently. She knew something terrible was happening to him, and she must do something quickly.

Lauren closed her eyes, took a deep breath, exhaled, and then opened her eyes. She saw the flamethrower again. She also saw a lighter hooked onto the flamethrower that was most likely used to ignite its flame. She eyed the gasoline containers right next to the flamethrower. An idea popped in her head as the dark being continued its chant while Joshua's body shook on the table.

Lauren squatted down and quickly ran over to the other side of the entrance near the flamethrower. She leaned down and unhooked the lighter from it, then fell back in front of the cave, out of sight. The dark being looked down at the entrance but did not see anything. It looked back up to the top of the cave, closed its eyes, and continued its chant, ". . . ad mortem te . . . ad mortem te . . . ad mortem te . . ."

Lauren reached back into the cave and grabbed one of the gasoline containers. She thought, *What do I do now?* She looked back into the cave and noticed that the cave's floor grade sloped down from the entrance to the table, where the dark being was standing over Joshua. She twisted off the container cap and slowly poured the gasoline into the cave. The gasoline quietly flowed along the ground like a newly created river from a dam being broken. The stream circulated its way around the rocks of the table down to the boots of the dark being.

* * *

In Joshua's vision, he had his hands flat on the ground, struggling to find at least one molecule of air. His heart was pounding faster and harder. The pain was incredible. It was as if his heart and blood vessels were going to explode from the increased pressure of not having any oxygen.

He fell prostrate onto the ground, body flinching with just a little life, and his soul almost gone. The reality of death felt certain.

* * *

Lauren struck the lighter and lit the tail of the gasoline stream. The gasoline lit up, and a tall flame burst along the trail, setting fire to the dark being's feet and legs. Lauren jumped and threw the gasoline container at the dark being, catching the rest of him on fire. He violently turned and twisted in attempts to brush the flames off him. His pocketknife fell on the ground. Lauren ran to pick up the knife. She quickly opened it and began cutting the ropes, freeing Joshua, first his hands and then his legs. She wiped the mud off his eyes and removed the two coins.

"Joshua! Wake Up! Joshua!" As she pulled him up off the stone, Joshua awoke from his vision, choking and gasping for air.

"We need to get out of here!" yelled Lauren. The knife fell to the ground as she put his arm over her shoulders and helped carry him out of the cave. The dark being had put most of the fire out, except a flame on his back. He started to walk toward them.

"He must be wearing flame-resistant material," said Joshua in a feeble voice. Lauren continued moving forward

"C'mon!" said Lauren as she pulled Joshua along.

Joshua regained his wits and strength as they got farther away from the cave. After a few yards, he could carry himself fully again. They ran at a full stride back down the tunnel.

They ran, eventually reaching the fork and the ladder that took them back up to Ebenezer AME. Lauren jumped to the first rung and pulled herself up, climbing as fast as she could up the ladder. Joshua followed right behind her. She got to the top of the ladder and pushed up the trap door. It flipped hard to the ground.

Lauren saw the large stone was still removed from the wall. Joshua made it to the top as Lauren helped him up. They quickly closed the lid of the trap door, and they sat on it just in case. Joshua was still covered in mud. Lauren attempted to wipe him off.

"I'm fine," said Joshua as he took off his long-sleeve shirt, revealing his white T-shirt underneath. He used it to wipe off his face and the rest of his body. He removed the wax from his ears with a pained face, but it was more of disgust. Lauren looked at Joshua in disbelief.

"Well, it looks like I left my shoes and socks back at the ranch," said Joshua as he looked down at his feet. Lauren shook her head but smiled at him, allowing a bit of relief to wash over her.

"On our way back here, I saw a fork. Are there two sets of tunnels?" asked Joshua.

"Yes. I believe the one on the left leads to all the other churches down the Boulevard, at least to Church of the Living God. The one on the right takes you to the cave you were just in," said Lauren.

"Looks like we found the real arsonist," said Joshua.

"Yes, definitely. And he appears to be human. Not a ghost or a spirit," said Lauren.

"No. But he did have some superhuman strength. The way he gripped my arm felt like a giant crab claw crushing my arm. He also injected me with something; I don't know what. It must have knocked me out," said Joshua as he continued to rub his forearm.

"I was so confused. He was chanting some type of Latin phrase about death, and he put coins over your eyes just like in old burial rituals," said Lauren.

"I could hear him, but I couldn't understand what he was saying," said Joshua.

"Yeah. He also had you on a large rock and covered you in mud. It was like he was trying a ritual to commune with the dead or the spiritual world with you. It does not make any sense," said Lauren.

"Is that what he was doing?" asked Joshua.

"I guess," said Lauren.

"It's interesting that you say that, because I thought I was just dreaming or having a vision, but it felt so real. And I heard no sounds. If I did hear anything, it was only in my mind," said Joshua.

"Some people who have had near-death experiences claim that there is no sound in the spiritual world, only what you can hear in your mind. What were you dreaming? Your body was shaking so violently. I was so scared," said Lauren.

"Scared? You seemed pretty brave to me. Well, I saw my mom. She was there. She spoke to me," said Joshua.

"Your mother? Are you sure?" asked Lauren.

"I can't recall everything, but she was like a small sphere of light, just like the ones I saw at the Bishop's house. But I could feel it was her. I just knew it was her. There were many other spheres of light there as well, all sparkling. Most of them were moving together in the same pattern," said Joshua.

"Wow!" said Lauren.

"Yes. They were coming up from the ground, going up to the sky. I really have no clue, but it felt like some were ghosts or some other spiritual-type entities, like angels, little gods, or something, just like mentioned in the first book of Samuel," said Joshua.

"Okay, I got a million questions now. But first, what was it like seeing your mother? Did she say anything?" asked Lauren.

"She said something about not being deceived, and things are not as they appear," said Joshua.

"Really. Is that all?" asked Lauren.

"She told me to remember that good bringeth forth good, and evil bringeth forth evil. She also said that I should be strong and courageous," said Joshua.

"Like in the Book of Joshua? Like what God told Joshua? And your name is Joshua," said Lauren, stressing the coincidence.

"I guess," said Joshua.

"Wow. I cannot believe all of this. But we can talk more in the car. We need to get out of here," said Lauren.

"You're right. You go first while I hold this door down just in case it tries to come up the ladder," said Joshua.

Lauren grabbed Joshua's cell phone out of her pocket and gave it back to him. She climbed through the large hole in the wall back into the bathroom in Ebenezer AME's basement. Joshua was about to climb through the wall to follow her, but then he stopped. He heard his mom's words in his head again: "Be strong and of a good courage, only be thou strong and very courageous."

Lauren noticed Joshua was not moving.

"What are you doing? Come on!" said Lauren as she lay on the ground, looking at him through the hole.

Joshua took a deep breath, exhaled, waited a moment, and then said, "You go. Go tell the police. I have to stay here."

"Are you crazy? That thing will kill you!" yelled Lauren.

"If he gets away, then I am still the main suspect, and now you are too. And everything we saw down there would mean nothing and still fall on us. The fires, the markings, the blood, they will all think it was us. I can't let that happen," said Joshua.

"Well, I am going back with you!" said Lauren as she started to climb back through the hole. Joshua put his hand in her way.

"No! I will not let anything happen to you. We have to work together on this. Hey, there is nothing I would rather do more than be with you in every single moment and every single situation. But right now, we have to split up. You must get the police, and I must go back and find that arsonist before he gets away. I will not do anything idgit-like, I promise. I will just find him, and then I will call you and let you know so you can tell the police," said Joshua.

"No way, Joshua. I am not letting you go down there again by yourself," said Lauren.

"You have no choice. I love you, Lauren," said Joshua as he quickly grabbed the stone by its handle, picked it up, and pushed it back into the hole. Lauren tried to stop it with her hand, but it was too late. Joshua pushed it fully in place. He looked around and found another large rock, and placed it in front of the stone, making sure Lauren could not move it out again.

"Joshua! No!" Lauren screamed as she beat her hand against the stone. She attempted to push it back out a few more times.

Joshua put his hand on the wall and said quietly, "My soul loves your soul. My soul loves your soul, Lauren." He lifted the trap door and climbed back down the ladder.

18

The Revival

The community revival.

Hundreds of people filled the street. Police cars and wooden A-frame barricades blocked off three street blocks along the Boulevard. Pre-registered vendors lined up along the Boulevard sidewalks, selling everything from clothing articles and jewelry to food, profiting from all the traffic generated by the community revival. Large ten-foot-tall speakers with wires along the road amplified the sounds coming from Manor Park, located between the two blocks. A gospel jazz band was playing on the constructed stage. Approximately a hundred chairs were in front of the stage, most of them filled. Children were either running around playing tag, throwing footballs, getting their faces painted, or waiting in line for custom-made animal balloons. The cool temperature made the atmosphere enjoyable for all. Many people stood by themselves or gathered in a spot, and either swayed or stomped their feet to the music's beat. Others walked up and down the street profiling, either to see who was there or just to be seen. In the back of the park, there was a small line of people looking at valuable items on tables for the community revival's silent auction; there were signed sports jerseys, event tickets, rare books, and paintings. As opposed to taking up an offering during the community revival, Pastor Williams had decided to use a silent auction to raise money. One side of the block closest to his church was reserved for charitable gifts that could be taken freely by anyone in need. It contained racks of donated clothing, but there were also a few tables with household appliances and electronics, such as microwaves and small flat-screen TVs. The electronics items were taken very quickly. However, just as fast as they were removed, they were immediately replaced with other similar items from more generous people.

One thing new this year for the community revival was the praying booth. It was a tall kiosk, roughly made from a combination of wood and cardboard, just like an old town fair's kissing booth. The volunteer workers had put it at the end of the block, right next to Pastor Williams' New Lighthouse Temple church. A minister staffed it at all times to immediately pray for someone upon their request or to help someone fill out a prayer request card. If someone filled out a card, it was placed in the prayer box that would be read in prayer to God at the end of the night by Pastor Williams. Pastor Williams and Bishop Hines stood at the front of the church, looking down the street at all the people. Pastor Williams noticed the line at the praying booth.

"The praying booth was a great idea," said Pastor Williams.

"Thanks, Pastor," said Bishop Hines. Bishop Hines did not tell Pastor Williams that the praying booth idea had actually come from Lauren. "Taking time out to pray for someone not only helps get a person's prayers answered, but it also shows that person that you truly care," said Bishop Hines.

"Yes, Bishop. Seeing the smiles and gratitude of the people leaving that booth are absolutely amazing. I guess hearing someone spontaneously praying for you means so much more than just saying the words, 'I will keep you in prayer,'" said Pastor Williams.

"Exactly, Pastor. But I have heard a few parents yell at their kids and say, 'Boy! You need prayer!' and then take them over to the booth," said Bishop Hines as he chuckled.

Pastor Williams laughed. "I've seen that a few times myself. The look on the minister's face when they bring kids up to the booth is priceless," said Pastor Williams.

"Oh, Lord. Here come your new best friends," said Bishop Hines. Pastor Williams turned his head and saw Officer Reese and Agent Carson approaching them.

"Lord Jesus," said Pastor Williams as he shook his head.

"Good day, Bishop Hines. Good day, Pastor," said Officer Reese.

"Good day," said Pastor Williams. Bishop Hines nodded.

"I gotta say, Pastor. This year's event seems even better than last year," said Officer Reese.

"Thanks, Joe. We appreciate you providing a few more officers for additional security. We know their time is valuable and expensive," said Pastor Williams.

"No worries. I was glad you called the churches of this neighborhood and me to help organize this event, considering the fires. We have some plainclothes officers in the crowd as well, including heavy surveillance on your church," said Officer Reese as he pointed to New Lighthouse Temple.

"Speaking of which, have you heard from your nephew, Pastor?" asked Agent Carson. He then turned to Bishop Hines and said, "Or maybe your almost-daughter-in-law, Bishop Hines? How's she coming along with her master's degree studies with all of this happening?" asked Agent Carson.

It was now apparent to Pastor Williams and Bishop Hines that Agent Carson had been doing some research; and, more importantly, no suspect had been identified other than Joshua. If so, they would have mentioned it by now.

Bishop Hines took offense. He responded, "Instead of wasting your time, shouldn't you be more concerned with the real person or persons who are starting these fires?"

"Maybe we are. Should we consider more?" asked Agent Carson as he stepped in front of Bishop Hines' face.

"Now hold on. What is that supposed to mean? Joe!" exclaimed Pastor Williams.

"Nothing, nothing at all," said Officer Reese as he took the back of his hand and pushed Agent Carson away from Bishop Hines.

"Looks like you haven't done all your research, Agent. There are some lines you better not cross," said Bishop Hines as he puffed out his chest and broad shoulders.

"We'll see about that," said Agent Carson.

"We won't see about anything," said Officer Reese as he pulled Agent Carson away by the arm. "But if you see or hear from either of them, you contact me immediately, Pastor," said Officer Reese.

The event's background noise got even louder as the New Jerusalem Mass Choir from Trenton, New Jersey, took the stage and started to sing. The choir's volume got louder, and the crowd around them grew as people rushed to get a seat.

Pastor Williams put his hand up by his ear and mouthed the words, "What? I can't hear you?" Officer Reese and Agent Carson looked at the two as they walked away. Bishop Hines sarcastically gave them a wave goodbye.

Officer Reese looked at Agent Carson and said, "You better not mess with Bishop Hines. He has friends in very high places. Trust me." Agent Carson looked back at Bishop Hines one more time.

"Lord, if I wasn't a man of God," said Bishop Hines.

"I think you might need to go over to the prayer booth with some of those bad kids and calm down," said Pastor Williams.

Bishop Hines laughed harder than usual from the rarity of a joke coming from Pastor Williams. Pastor William ignored the laughter.

"It's like you told me the other day, Bishop. We can't have an event like this without Satan trying to steal, kill, and destroy it," said Pastor Williams. "I'm beginning to see how I have been looking at this situation all wrong, with Josh and maybe even with Lauren as well. Have you heard from either of them?" asked Pastor Williams.

"No. Have you?" asked Bishop Hines.

"No. Angela said she'd try reaching out to him throughout the day so that I can focus on the community revival," said Pastor Williams.

"Well, that's good to know. Joshua and Lauren are both adults. I know they can handle themselves. And after just seeing Detective Burnett and Agent Lowrey over there, I'm not certain that Josh and Lauren missing in action is a bad thing," said Bishop Hines.

"Maybe not," said Pastor Williams.

"God is in control, Pastor, not us. Let us go over and listen to New Jerusalem and show our faces to the crowd," said Bishop Hines.

"Sounds good," said Pastor Williams.

* * *

Back in the tunnel, Joshua hesitantly continued down the ladder, now doubting whether he was making the right decision to leave Lauren. He jumped to the ground, wiped himself off, and pulled out his cell phone, turning on the light. His battery was low. He had to hurry. He quickly walked down the tunnel path toward the cave.

After Joshua was out of sight, the dark being came out from the back of the tunnel, from behind the ladder. He had been hiding there again, all this time. The dark being climbed up to the top of the ladder. He heard Lauren still yelling for Joshua. He reached into his coat pocket and pulled out a large padlock that had an extra-long shackle. He hooked and latched it underneath the bottom of the trap door. The trap door was now securely locked by the oversized padlock. He climbed back down the ladder and briefly looked down the tunnel that Joshua had taken toward the cave. Unlike Joshua, he continued down the opposite tunnel, heading toward the churches.

Joshua was out of breath. Even though the distance was not that long to the cave, the uneven and treacherous terrain and walking fast had worn him out. *I need to start running regularly again*, he thought. He could see the opening of the cave, but it was dark, no longer lit from the hanging flashlights. He slowed down his approach, stopping at the entryway and peeking into the cave. Using his cell phone for light, he scanned from one side of the cave to the other. The only thing he could see were the remnants of the small fire set by Lauren and a few objects still on the stone table in the back of the cave, but no dark being.

He did see his socks and shoes still on the table. He went over to grab them and put them on. He scanned the cave again, but this time from the opposite side. He gasped with surprise as he saw that the flamethrower was gone. Suddenly, Joshua's phone beeped with a low battery notification. Joshua looked at his phone and noticed the time. He remembered the urgency.

"Oh no! The community revival!" he said. Joshua ran back down the tunnel toward the fork. As he reached the tunnel split and turned the corner, without hesitation, he made the 90-degree turn into the opposite tunnel toward the other churches.

* * *

Lauren attempted to push the stone out of place, but with no success. She realized Joshua must have used the other rock to block the stone from being moved. Lauren then remembered the sealed-off room and vent opening she'd seen at Church of the Living God. If she could make it there, she could back down the tunnel that way.

Lauren ran out of the bathroom, through the basement, and then back upstairs through the ruined church. She climbed out the pastor's office window that she and Joshua had climbed through earlier to get in the church. She ran to her car, got in, and sped off out the parking lot down the Boulevard to Church of the Living God in attempt to catch up to Joshua.

After a few minutes of driving, Lauren was stopped by flooded traffic as she reached Olive Street, which was just two blocks away from Church of the Living God. The detours and blocked-off streets had created a traffic standstill. Police were directing traffic, forcing cars eastbound on the Boulevard to make a right onto Olive Street. Lauren saw traffic was backed up on Olive Street as well. She backed up a little and swung her car to the left side of the street, up against the sidewalk. With the positioning of other parked vehicles, her car did not fully fit into the parking space. The tail of her car protruded out into the street. But she threw the gear into park anyway and quickly got out of her car.

"Hey! You can't leave your car there with its rear end sticking out like that!" yelled the police officer who was directing traffic.

"I'll be right back!" yelled Lauren. Without even pausing, she ran away down the sidewalk of the Boulevard.

"You'll get towed!" yelled the police officer. Lauren did not turn around. She kept running as the police officer grabbed his radio off his jacket strap.

"Jenkins Ten to Dispatch," he said into the radio.

"Dispatch to Jenkins Ten. Go ahead."

"Code nine at corner of Boulevard and Olive. Need additional assistance. Over."

"Code nine at corner of Boulevard and Olive. Sending additional assistance. Over." Officer Jenkins walked over to Lauren's car.

"Walking over to vehicle to obtain and provide license number for plate check. Over."

"Waiting for license number for plate check. Over."

* * *

In the tunnel, Joshua saw a ladder ahead of him. He walked past it and looked down at the rest of the tunnel. Joshua walked back to the ladder. He thought this ladder must be for Church of the Living God, but he would have to check to make sure. He looked around one more time before he climbed the ladder.

* * *

Lauren ran down the sidewalk at full speed until she arrived at a white church building that she thought was the church. As she got closer, she saw it was boarded off with caution tape and orange cones surrounding the building. Then she saw a four-foot-high monument sign on the small section of grass in front of the building. It read, "Church of the Living God." Lauren ran up the short set of steps to the front door. It was locked. She raised her head as she looked over the front of the church. She noticed that it was hardly damaged. However, she then ran to the side of the building, looking for another entryway, and that was where she saw the fire damage, mostly to the center section of the sanctuary building.

Lauren saw a side door that was slightly damaged by the fire. It was locked, but she thought the damage from the fire or actions of the firefighters might have loosened the frame or hinges. Lauren took a few steps back and ran directly into the door with her right shoulder. She was either right or stronger than she thought. The door broke open into a hallway. She turned right and ran down the hallway to the end. She only saw two restrooms. She then ran back down the hallway toward the opposite end. She saw a door with two small plate signs on it that read, "Treasurer" and "Authorized Personnel Only." She knew this door must be the one that led to the room with the vent she saw earlier.

But, right before she opened the door, she saw a light trail of blood on the floor. As she looked down, she noticed the trail of blood led out to the sanctuary. She slowly opened the door. The line of blood led just two feet past the doorway into the room. She assumed this was the blood of Trustee John Copeland. She looked over at the back wall and saw the same air vent that she'd seen earlier when searching for Joshua. But this time, she was on the opposite side of the wall. From looking at the trail of blood that led out to the sanctuary and the vent that led to the tunnels, she realized that this church fire had not killed Trustee Copeland, and most likely, the dark being did. *Did the police know he was not killed by the fire but by something else? Have they been keeping that a secret this whole time?* She wondered in horror.

* * *

Joshua reached the top of the ladder of the sealed-off room at Church of the Living God. He pushed up the trap door, but it only raised about an inch and then fell back down. Joshua pushed it up again but got the same unsuccessful result. He shone his light on the bottom of the trap door and saw a padlock latched on a hook. Joshua realized that the dark being must have put the lock on the door to prevent anyone from getting in or out. He climbed as high as he could and attempted to push it open with his shoulder. It did not work. Out of frustration, he banged on it and yelped in surprise. Lauren ran over to the air vent. She grabbed the edges of the vent with her hands and was able to pull it off the wall. Lauren climbed through the vent space. She couldn't suppress a yelp when she heard someone banging on it. Lauren assumed the pounding was the dark being attempting to come up through the trap door. She looked around for a weapon and found a sizeable 18-inch cast iron pipe wrench used to adjust the older water valves. She leaned over the trap door and waited. Joshua pounded on the door a few more times and then sighed. Lauren heard him sigh, and then she dropped her body to the ground, with the pipe still in her hand.

"Joshua!" exclaimed Lauren at the trap door.

"Lauren!" Joshua said, as surprised as she was.

"Joshua! You are okay!" yelled Lauren.

"What are you doing here?" Joshua hollered back.

"I couldn't leave you," said Lauren.

She stood up and grabbed onto the handle of the trap door and attempted to pull it up. It raised about an inch and then fell back down with a loud bang. "I can't open it. It must be locked from your side," said Lauren.

"Yes. That thing must have put this large padlock on it. Without the key, I can't open it," said Joshua.

Lauren held up her weapon. "I have a wrench?" she offered.

"What good is that going to do me?" said Joshua.

"Guess not," said Lauren as she put the pipe down.

"The tunnel must go down to the next church. Maybe I can get out from there," said Joshua.

"And what if you can't?" asked Lauren.

"Then I guess I will be stuck down here. Or maybe, it continues down the Boulevard to my uncle's church. But if it does go down that far, that is bad, really bad," said Joshua.

"Do not think like that or speak something like that into existence. You are going to be okay. Now, what's the next church along this Boulevard?" asked Lauren.

"Mount Carmel," said Joshua.

"You mean the church where you saw this thing from the window that started the fire?" asked Lauren.

"Yes. That is the one," said Joshua.

"Oh, God. How far away is it?" asked Lauren.

"Four blocks," said Joshua.

"Okay. I will meet you there. Vite! Vite!" exclaimed Lauren.

"Okay!" said Joshua as he climbed back down the ladder.

"Be careful!" said Lauren. She got up and ran back to the wall and through the vent space, exiting the church. She ran as fast as she could, east to Mount Carmel.

* * *

Outside on the Boulevard, Officer Jenkins, the police officer working traffic duty, got communication back from Dispatch about Lauren's car.

"Dispatch to Jenkins Ten."

"Jenkins Ten to Dispatch. Go ahead."

"Possible code five with plate check. Repeat. Possible code five with plate check. Backup en route. Repeat. Backup en route. Over."

Officer Jenkins started running east on the Boulevard in pursuit of Lauren.

"Copy that, Dispatch. Vehicle is stationary. In pursuit of possible code five heading on foot eastbound on Boulevard from Olive. Over."

"Copy that, Jenkins Ten. In pursuit of code five, heading on foot eastbound on Boulevard from Olive. Backup en route and will update location. Over."

"Copy that, Dispatch. Over and out."

Officer Jenkins put his radio back on his jacket and continued running down the Boulevard.

* * *

Joshua and Lauren were running in parallel together down the Boulevard, Lauren on the street, Joshua in the Underground Railroad tunnel. Lauren was running as fast as she could, bobbing and weaving on the sidewalk through the event's crowd and hurdling over trash bags, kids, and other objects. Joshua was running as fast as he could directly underneath her in the tunnel, avoiding and hurdling over rocks and water-filled divots in the ground.

* * *

Officer Reese got a call on his cell phone. "Copy that," he said, hanging up. Officer Reese looked at Agent Carson.

"That was dispatch. We have a code five, a possible sighting of Lauren," said Officer Reese.

"Where at?" asked Agent Carson.

"Boulevard and Olive," said Officer Reese.

"Let's go!" said Agent Carson. Agent Carson then waved to his team of plain-clothed men. Pastor Williams and Bishop Hines witnessed the active dialogue of Officer Reese and Agent Carson from across the street. They saw them take off running up the Boulevard with a few other people in the crowd, who now revealed themselves as other officers working with Officer Reese.

"Looks like they found something," said Pastor Williams.

"Or someone," said Bishop Hines.

The sky started to drizzle with rain, and with perfect timing, the New Jerusalem choir finished their last song selection. Pastor Williams reluctantly ran up on stage and grabbed the microphone.

"Praise the Lord, everybody!" yelled Pastor Williams.

"Praise the Lord!" replied the crowd.

"God is good!" yelled Pastor Williams.

"All the time!" replied the crowd.

Pastor Williams continued. "First of all, I want to thank everyone for helping, participating, and attending this wonderful event. However, I am certain that all of you can feel the mist of the rain beginning to fall. This rain is no surprise. We did watch the news forecast this week, and only by the grace of God, they were correct in their prediction." The crowd laughed.

"Secondly, before this drizzle turns into a full downpour, I would like to invite everyone into the beautiful sanctuary of New Lighthouse Temple, where we plan to continue this community revival with the results of our silent auction, followed by an open and truthful discussion regarding neighborhood concerns, and then, last, a prayer for the community led by the well-known and respected Bishop Hines of International Covenant Ministries. Drinks and refreshments are provided inside as well."

Pastor Williams changed his tone and began to semi-preach charismatically in a musical key. "Let us not waste time. Haste makes waste! Let us enter into the house of God with praise! Let's enter his courts with thanksgiving! There is room at the cross for you! And there is room in the sanctuary for everyone! Can I get an Amen!" shouted Pastor Williams.

"Amen!" the crowd replied.

"Amen and Amen!" yelled Pastor Williams.

A third of the crowd began walking over to New Lighthouse Temple. Another third decided to go home, while the last third remained in the street to hang out and continue to talk. Pastor Williams and Bishop Hines walked up to the New Lighthouse Temple front door entrance to greet people as they entered the building.

"Good word," approved Bishop Hines.

"Thanks, Bishop. Everything is in God's hand now, right? There is nothing we can do," said Pastor Williams.

"Just pray for Joshua and Lauren. Pray that this all works out for everyone. Are you sure you are ready for this neighborhood meeting in your church? You know they will bring up the fires, and most likely Joshua's potential involvement," said Bishop Hines.

"Ready as I will ever be," said Pastor Williams.

* * *

Lauren made it to Mount Carmel just as the rain started. She ran around the church to the very same basement window where Joshua had seen the dark being before the building was set ablaze. Lauren kicked in the window with her foot, breaking the glass. She continued to kick and break off the sharp fragments that remained, then she lay on the ground and slid in backward, feetfirst, into the basement window of the church.

Just as her body and head went entirely through the window, Officer Reese, Agent Carson, and the other officers ran right past the church, completely missing her as they continued to Olive Street.

Lauren's legs dangled in the air, her body against the basement wall, as she firmly held onto the window's bottom exterior sill, preparing to let go. She looked down and realized that her feet were not too far from the ground. She released her grip and landed safely in a squat. When she raised herself back up, she looked at her hands, feeling the minor cuts acquired from the sharp fragments of glass that remained on the window. The cuts were minor and had a few traces of blood in them. But Lauren was more concerned with the dark ash that covered her hands, forearms, and clothes, which she'd obtained from the window apron and wall. She wiped herself off as best as she could.

At the same time, Joshua reached the next iron ladder of the tunnel. He started to climb.

Lauren ran around the basement from area to area while skirting all the fire damage and debris, looking for some type of secret wall or any sign where a trap door might be located. The windows on the opposite wall provided a fair bit of sunlight into the basement. She found a storage closet in the very back of the basement. The door was blackened from the fire and partially hanging off its frame. She opened the door to a dim room, as sunlight did not reach this area of the basement. She saw a light switch and flicked it to the on position. It did not work. She looked up at the light fixture on the ceiling in disappointment, but she also realized that this should have been expected with the fire.

Examining the poorly lit room, Lauren saw boxes of papers and old music equipment, such as bongos, broken tambourines, a few microphone stands, and a small amplifier, all mostly burned and damaged from the fire. Lauren walked farther into the room, moving everything out the way. She made her way to the back of the room, reaching a dead end. There was no sign of a trap door. She looked around one more time and then started to walk out of the closet. Right before she flicked the nonfunctional light switch off, she heard a banging noise. It was Joshua! He had reached the top of the ladder and was now banging on the trap door. Lauren ran to the back of the room and removed a shelving rack from along the right wall. She saw a small latch built into the faux-wood slat paneling. She clicked down the latch, and a cut of the wall opened, just large enough for a person to bend down and enter into the secret closed-off room. Joshua banged on the trap door again. Lauren bent down and crept into the room. She paid no attention to the Enochian symbols on the floor and the walls. She saw the wooden trap door with the same iron handle and felt relieved that she found it.

"Joshua!" yelled Lauren as she fell on the ground just in front of the trap door.

"Lauren! It's locked!" yelled Joshua.

The dark being had placed the same type of large padlock on the trap door. Joshua attempted to break the lock by ramming his shoulder up against the door. Lauren grabbed onto the handle with repeated attempts to pull open the door. She continued to yell. "Joshua! Joshua!" But Joshua was out of breath. He gave up and wrapped his arm around the top rung to rest. Lauren was banging on the top of the trap door with her open hand and eyes full of tears.

"It's no use, Lauren," said Joshua.

"There has to be a way to get you out," said Lauren.

"The tunnel continues farther down. It looks like I am correct that it goes to at least one more church," said Joshua.

"Your uncle's church," said Lauren.

"Yes. It's another four or five blocks. And it's in the heart of the community revival. That thing is probably on its way there now, if not already. And to start one more fire. This time, many people could die. My uncle's church will be filled with people from the community revival," said Joshua.

"You have to wait here. It's too dangerous for you to go. That door may be locked too!" exclaimed Lauren.

"Not if he already went through it. I have to get there right away to stop him. No one has a clue that he is going there or what he is about to do, not even the police. If I wait, it may be too late, and I can't take that risk," said Joshua.

"There has to be another way," said Lauren.

"The only way is for the police or me to catch this thing. And I cannot rely on them right now. They are probably still running around up there like a bunch of idgits looking for only us," said Joshua. He was correct.

"There still has to be another way. Maybe, I should just let the police find me if they're looking for us," said Lauren.

"No Lauren. Not right now. Remember, if that thing or person gets away, we still have no proof that it was him or who he is. And if they find me down here without him, who do you think will get all of the blame? It's not like he had pictures of himself or his family hanging on the wall of that cave, right?" asked Joshua.

"Right," said Lauren.

"And if that happens, this thing could make a getaway, and we both will be locked up with just a story about a dark being and satanic rituals," said Joshua.

"Okay. I get it," said a frustrated Lauren.

"I know, and I'm sorry. Back at the last church, I did not get to tell you," said Joshua.

"Tell me what?" asked Lauren.

Joshua put his hand on the bottom of the trap door. "No matter what happens, Lauren, my soul loves your soul," he said.

Lauren, still in tears, put her hand on the top of the trap door. "No matter what happens, Joshua, my soul loves your soul," Lauren said back to him.

Joshua climbed back down the ladder, jumped to the ground, and sprinted toward New Lighthouse Temple. Lauren got out of the secret room, then ran out of the basement and church, making her way out toward New Lighthouse Temple as well.

Officer Reese, Agent Carson, and the other police officers ran into the policeman, Officer Jenkins, who had reported seeing Lauren. Officer Jenkins had just finished speaking to a few people in front of Church of the Living God.

"You're the one that alerted the code five?" asked Officer Reese.

"Yes. It was the girl," said Officer Jenkins.

"Dispatch said she was running this way. But we didn't see her on our way up to you," said Officer Reese.

"Those people over there just told me they saw a girl that fit her same description run into this church," said Officer Jenkins.

"You mean this church, Church of the Living God?" asked Officer Reese. They were still unaware that Lauren had already left that church and was just at Mount Carmel, making her way farther down to New Lighthouse Temple.

"Are they trying to start another fire?" asked Agent Carson.

"Doesn't matter," said Officer Reese. Officer Reese pointed and gave directions to all the officers. "Okay, I need you, two men, to cover the back. You, Officer, cover the east of the building, and you cover the west. The agent and I will take everyone else through the front. One will remain covering, while everyone else searches the place. Oh yeah, be careful! With the fire damage, assume nothing is stable in there, not the floors, not the walls, and not the ceiling," said Officer Reese. They stormed the church, searching for Lauren. They did not find her. However, Officer Jenkins uncovered the secret.

"Sir, you better come look at this," said Officer Jenkins to Officer Reese. They walked back to the treasurer's office. Officer Reese was familiar with the office, as it had been part of the crime scene for the death of Trustee John Copeland.

"We've been here before," said Officer Reese. It looked to him like nothing had changed.

"Well, apparently, you must have done a sloppy investigation," said Officer Jenkins. Officer Jenkins pointed his flashlight to the removed air vent on the wall.

"Crap!" said Officer Reese. He ran over to the hole and grabbed his flashlight. He got on his knees and shone his light, looking through the space. Agent Carson stood behind him.

"What is it?" asked Agent Carson.

"Looks like an old furnace and utility room that was closed off during the renovation. Easy enough for someone to hide back here," said Officer Reese.

"So no one knew about this space?" asked Agent Carson in distrust.

"Since the body was dragged from this office to the center of the church, and then set on fire near the altar, our initial focus had been on the murder and any potential evidence on or around the victim's body. We got sloppy," said Officer Reese.

"Don't be too hard on yourself, Reese. These fires happened back-to-back so fast, none of us had the time to complete the investigation on any of them fully. While we were investigating the first one, then another happened, then another," said Agent Carson.

"Wow, I did not know all of this. Did the public or anyone else know about the body being burned or that it was an actual murder and not the fire that killed the trustee?" asked Officer Jenkins.

"No. We kept all of that a secret. We haven't even let the family see the body yet. They are throwing lawsuits at us as we speak. Again, it all happened so fast," said Officer Reese.

"Let me ask this again. Was *anyone* aware of this space?" asked Agent Carson.

"Sorry, I forgot you asked that question. I don't know," said Officer Reese. He continued. "We interviewed a few of the members, but they only talked about the recent rumored scandal with their leader of this church, Pastor Harris. Pastor Harris would have been the only one to know about this space, but he is still MIA, right?" asked Officer Reese, reminding Agent Carson that his team was supposed to find him for questioning.

Officer Jenkins forcefully interjected. "Yes. I heard about that. The rumor was Pastor Harris was messing around with a bunch of girls, maybe even raped one. Everyone thought it was true. But he quit and left town before any exact details became public. But sorry, sir. You are still not looking hard enough. Please look again."

Officer Reese took his flashlight and shone it back into the room through the air vent hole. This time his eyes focused on the walls.

"What in the world is that?" asked Officer Reese. He finally saw the Enochian symbols on the wall and floor.

"What is it?" asked Agent Carson.

"You better get in there and check it out as well," said Officer Jenkins to Agent Carson. They all climbed into the space.

"They are markings made in blood," said Officer Reese.

"They look like some type of hieroglyphics," said Agent Carson.

"Or maybe some type of satanic lettering, since it's in blood," said Officer Reese.

"Would Josh be into something like this?" asked Agent Carson.

"No. Not at all. Maybe some stupid pranks with his idiot friend Monty. I caught them getting high now and then, but nothing ever like this," said Officer Reese. He continued to shine his flashlight around until he shone it on the trap door with the handle.

"What the—" said Officer Reese. They all looked in amazement.

"That handle looks very antiquated," said Agent Carson as he attempted to lift the door, but it was still locked from the other side.

"Oh my goodness! This church and that door. Is this part of the city's old Underground Railroad system?" asked Officer Jenkins.

"Are you saying that there's a tunnel underneath this church?" asked Agent Carson.

"Yes, and most likely underneath all the ones that were set on fire," said Officer Jenkins.

"So, that's how the arsonist was able to set the fires without being seen! I can't believe it," said Agent Carson.

"The Underground Railroad underneath the Boulevard all this time, and leading to all these churches, including . . ." Officer Reese trailed off as he realized. "Oh no!" he said, looking horrified.

"Including what?" asked Agent Carson.

"We need to get back to New Lighthouse Temple ASAP!" exclaimed Officer Reese, scrambling to go back through the vent space and out the door.

"Pastor Williams' church?" asked Agent Carson.

"Yes. And radio for more backup there now!" yelled Officer Reese at Officer Jenkins. The officers ran out of the church back down the Boulevard toward New Lighthouse Temple.

19

Renovated Destruction

Sunday morning—one month before the community revival.

Church of the Living God's attendance was at maximum capacity. There was little to no elbow room among the congregation that sat in the pews. The choir box possessed all of its listed members for the first time in months. One reason why church attendance was higher than usual this day was that today's church service included a baby christening. Therefore, additional family members and friends were in attendance for this ceremony. Another reason for the increased attendance was that Pastor Harris, the pastor of Church of the Living God, was performing a consecration and dedication ceremony for the church. It was a celebration of Pastor Harris' recent completion of a full renovation on the building.

When the renovation had initially started, a good portion of the community was upset that Pastor Harris selected a general construction contractor from New Jersey instead of a local one. However, this contractor met two of his primary qualifications: (1) They were cheap; and (2) They were a verified and registered minority-owned business. And not just any minority-owned company; the owner was Dominique

Moreau, a prominent black woman from Camden, New Jersey. Her construction company was Moreau Construction. Dominique Moreau also owned a consulting business. But the construction company had been started and run by her husband before he died.

Along with other assets, she'd taken over as head of the company. Pastor Harris thought everyone would be glad to hear about it, especially since it was *thee* highly respected Moreau Construction. But things did not go as planned. Even though Moreau Construction was a registered minority-owned business, most laborers and subcontractors employed by the company were actually non-minority or white. When the company's masons and painters showed up on-site to start the work on the church's exterior, it took everyone by surprise that there were hardly any minority workers. A few residents started picketing the site, claiming that Pastor Harris had lied to the whole community and did not actually hire a minority-owned construction company. It took Pastor Harris a few weeks of damage control and acknowledgment on both sides of unwitting prejudice before the whole confusion was put to rest. But for those who knew that history, it was very amusing to see Dominque Moreau among the ministers in the pulpit, waiting to be acknowledged for her outstanding work on the church, while many of her laborers—again, mostly Caucasian—were in the audience. All her workers were casually dressed in jeans, light sweatshirts, and steel-toe boots, taking up two full pews in the middle of the sanctuary.

During the church's renovation, two of the plumbing subcontractors had stumbled across the trap door in the old furnace room that led to the tunnel system under the church. It was locked from underneath, so they were unable to open it. They just assumed it was an old bomb safety bunker used in the early 1950s during the Cold War, and this church had conducted many "duck and cover" drills during that time. In any event, they reported it during one of the weekly construction meetings. As a result, it was also recorded in the official construction notes for that week. Among many others, these notes were sent via email to Dominque Moreau, Pastor Harris, the church's bank lender, and the church's head trustee, John Copeland. Since the contract company was from New Jersey and not local, the construction manager assumed that the church and members were aware of the trap door.

Simultaneously, the company had many other projects going on at the same time. So, Dominique's email inbox was inundated with weekly construction notes. So, unless there was a problem that needed an executive decision, there was no point for her and her office staff to review them all. Since Pastor Harris and Trustee John Copeland had little construction knowledge, they stayed out of the way of the workers, and did not attend any construction meetings unless a major change order was required. Things went smoothly; they were under budget, and that was all that mattered.

In addition, Pastor Harris had other problems to worry about, such as rumors flying around that he was having affairs with a few women. For fear of being asked about it, he kept his interaction with his church members to a minimum. But his best friend, Trustee John Copeland, would always cover for him if anyone ever brought it up. One of the rumored women left the church and moved away so quickly that no one confirmed the infidelity.

But today was a new day. A new building, the potential new members in the large crowd, and a brand-new message by guest minister Pastor Williams of New Lighthouse Temple were going to bring a fresh start to this church. Since Pastor Williams had done such a great job lobbying community support and membership when he built his church many years ago, Pastor Harris figured that he needed Pastor Williams' public stamp of approval to help validate his own church's ministry. Pastor Harris thought the support of Pastor Williams was imperative for the success of Church of the Living God within the neighborhood and had invited him to be their guest speaker for the dedication service.

The service went smoothly. After being introduced as the guest speaker, Pastor Williams walked up to the podium in his long black robe with his Bible in his hand. To the congregation, he looked calm and confident. However, Pastor Williams was extremely nervous. No matter how many times he gave a sermon, he was always nervous with anxiety in the pit of his stomach before uttering his sermon's first words. He was always nervous until he would grab the microphone and say,

"Praise the Lord, everybody!" exclaimed Pastor Williams.

"Praise the Lord," said the congregation.

"Come on, church! I know you can do better than that. I said, Praise the Lord, everybody!" yelled Pastor Williams.

"Praise the Lord!" yelled the congregation.

"I'm going to get to my message in a second. But I hear the voice of God crying out to the church right now, saying, if my people, which are called by my name, shall humble themselves, and pray, and seek my face, and turn from their wicked ways, then will I hear from heaven, and will forgive their sin, and will heal their land! Can I get an Amen?" yelled Pastor Williams.

"Amen!" yelled the congregation as most of them stood to their feet in excitement.

"You haven't sought His face! You haven't cried out His name! You haven't turned from your wicked ways! He's waiting for you to call out His name! He's waiting to heal your land! Who will answer the call of the Almighty? Who will stand up in the midst of their problems and in the midst of their enemies and trust God? Who will be that great person that God created you to be, walking divinely in your purpose?" yelled Pastor Williams.

"Amen!" shouted the congregation.

Pastor Williams looked over at the organist playing concurrently with him. For that brief moment, he reminisced, wishing his nephew, Joshua, was backing him up on the organ with his creative music chords. He'd been reminded that Joshua had not stepped into a church since Denise's funeral.

He continued the inspiring message until he got to the end of his written notes. The one person in the audience that was most inspired by the message was the homeless man Ezekiel "Zeke" Wilson. Pastor Williams always spoke to him in the street late at night, while Pastor Williams was either witnessing or on duty for the neighborhood watch group. They would talk about how Ezekiel had become homeless, God, and even sports—football mostly.

Before Ezekiel was homeless, he'd worked at the Shields Iron Factory. He started working there right out of high school at the age of eighteen. A few years ago, the factory shut down, and Ezekiel and many others lost their job. They did not even receive a severance package as anticipated. Ezekiel and many other employees officially appealed to the company, but before a decision was made, the bankruptcy court took over handling the remaining assets of the company, and subsequently denied their claim. Ezekiel's mortgage company eventually foreclosed on his home, and one year after that, his son died in a car accident. The losses were just too great, and Ezekiel's wife left him and moved to Buckeye, Arizona. Ezekiel found an apartment that he could barely afford. But after a few months, that caught up to him as well. He could not hold down a job and then was evicted from his apartment. His lack of skills and a lack of a registered address prevented him from getting any real job opportunities.

A few days before this building dedication service, things had become worse. Ezekiel was kicked out of the homeless shelter for the last time. He'd gotten into an argument with another homeless man in the shelter. When the police arrived, Ezekiel was noticeably high from some type of narcotic drug. He'd injected himself with heroin earlier that day while hanging out around the city's Thornton Park. The park was so well-known for drug users, especially at night, that groups of cleanup crews would gather each morning to go around the park, picking up all the dangerous and possibly infected hypodermic needles sporadically lying around. This offense was Ezekiel's third and final strike of being in the shelter while under the influence of narcotics. Strict shelter rules forbade it. He was no longer allowed to stay there.

Late last night, Pastor Williams, Pastor Harris, and a few others had been out witnessing, passing out gospel tracts and promotional flyers for the building dedication ceremony. After many years of pastoring, Pastor Williams' passion was still reaching out to people on the streets in the hope of bringing them into the church to change their lives.

When Pastor Williams saw Ezekiel lying on a street bench in front of a bus stop, he stopped to talk to him. Ezekiel looked worse than usual. He had no shoes on his feet, two sweaters layered on top of each other that were worn and torn, and a long old jacket that he'd gotten from Pastor Williams' church during a clothing drive.

"Zeke, my friend. God bless you," said Pastor Williams.

"Hi, Pastor Williams," said Ezekiel in a raspy voice while adding a few coughs at the end.

"We are almost done for the evening. Would you like to come with us to get some coffee?" asked Pastor Williams.

"No sir. I'm fine right here on the Boulevard," said Ezekiel.

"Okay. But you know where to find us if you change your mind," said Pastor Williams.

"Yes, sir," said Ezekiel. Pastor Williams knew from his dilated eyes that he was under the influence of some drug.

"Before we go, let me pray for you right here, right now. Is that okay?" asked Pastor Williams.

"Yes, sir," said Ezekiel. Pastor Williams prayed for Ezekiel and then invited him to church in the morning.

"If you are up to it, I'm going to put this flyer in your pocket," said Pastor Williams as he folded up a flyer and placed it in Ezekiel's jacket pocket. "I am speaking tomorrow at Church of the Living God, and all are welcome, including you. God may have a word just for you, Zeke," said Pastor Williams. Pastor Harris felt the need to chime into the conversation.

"We just renovated our church, and a lot of great things will be going on there. Maybe we can do something special for you, help you out in any way we can," said Pastor Harris.

Ezekiel's face lit up with a glimmer of hope. He had not felt the feeling of hope in an exceptionally long time, years. "I will try," said Ezekiel as he smiled and placed his hand over the pocket.

"Please do," said Pastor Williams.

"Thank you so much, Pastors," said Ezekiel.

"No worries at all. If the Lord wills, we will see you tomorrow, brother Zeke," said Pastor Williams.

Ezekiel did not go to Thornton Park that night. He woke up early and used the coins in his panhandling box to get a cup of coffee from one of the Boulevard's newsstands. Ezekiel went into his duffel bag and found the cleanest shirt that he had. He ran into a gas station bathroom, washed himself up, and put on the shirt. Ezekiel was off walking down the Boulevard to Church of the Living God to hear Pastor Williams' message and talk to Pastor Harris about what help they could provide him. Upon reaching the church's block, he assimilated into the crowd proudly walking into the newly renovated church building.

Ezekiel was touched by Pastor Williams' sermon so much that he was the first to come up to the altar for prayer. Pastor Williams leaped down from the pulpit and embraced Ezekiel in joy. This inspiration brought many to tears and inspired others to come to the altar as well. Pastor Williams grabbed Ezekiel by the hands and looked him directly in the face and said, "Once you give your life to God, you are asking God to come into your heart and into your life, so that He can change it for His will and His purpose. And if you truly mean it, thou shalt be saved. And from that point on, it is God's job to direct and guide your paths. You may fall and stumble, but you will be a new creature. You will be forgiven and washed in the blood of the Lamb. Is that what you want today?" asked Pastor Williams.

Ezekiel gave a direct reply to Pastor Williams. "Just being honest, Pastor. I really don't understand everything you said. But I want to learn. I need to change my life," said Ezekiel.

"Well, that is the first step, my brother! Right now, I will just pray for you, and we can talk with Pastor Harris about getting you in some classes and possibly working in this church in the future just like he said," said Pastor Williams.

"Sounds good, Pastor," said Ezekiel.

Pastor Williams placed his hands on Ezekiel and prayed for him. Ezekiel could feel the love and care from Pastor Williams so much that it brought him to tears. As he walked away from the altar back to his seat, many people also greeted him with hugs, even those who had not previously spoken to him or even looked at him on the street. All of the workers from Moreau Construction stood in a line to hug him as well. Not one of them was without a tear. Ezekiel felt so much love and so much joy. He was glad that he'd decided to come to the service.

After the long service, Ezekiel waited patiently in his seat for Pastor Williams and Pastor Harris to finish all their goodbye discussions with the congregation. He felt this took longer than the service itself. With so many people around trying to talk to him, Pastor Williams almost forgot about Ezekiel, until he saw him sitting in the pew all by himself. Pastor Williams walked over to Pastor Harris, said a few words, and then walked over to Ezekiel.

"Zeke, I am so glad that you came!" exclaimed Pastor Williams.

"I'm glad that you invited me," said Ezekiel.

"I know you have been staying at the shelter. Therefore, I thought this church might work out better for you since it is a lot closer to the shelter than my church. Plus, it sounds like Pastor Harris could use some additional help. Either way, I will always be available to you if needed. Pastor Harris is going to talk to you after he is done. I must hurry up and get out of here. I'm going out to eat with my nephew today," said Pastor Williams.

"You mean Josh?" asked Ezekiel.

"Yes," said Pastor Williams.

"Tell him I said hello," said Ezekiel.

"I will," said Pastor Williams, smiling.

"Ever since he was just a young boy, he was always so nice to me. Even when my situation got worse, and I started looking really bad, Josh would still look at me and talk to me the same. Like I was still a human being. You both did," said Ezekiel.

"He's a good kid," said Pastor Williams.

"Yes, he is. Hey, listen. I know it has been a while, but I am sorry about Denise. That must have been a tough time for you and Joshua," said Ezekiel.

"It's okay. And thank you for that, Zeke. That means a lot to me," said Pastor Williams.

Pastor Harris finally made his way over to them. Pastor Williams took his cue to leave once Pastor Harris approached them.

"Okay, I must go. Great dedication ceremony, Pastor Harris. I will talk to you later. I am running so late," said Pastor Williams.

"Thanks again for your support and for that awesome message. Tell your wife, I said hello," said Pastor Harris.

"No problem. And take care, Zeke," said Pastor Williams as he walked away.

Pastor Harris turned to Ezekiel once Pastor Williams was gone. "Hey, listen, Zeke. Service ran so late, and I still have so many things to do. Can you come back next Sunday when I have more time?"

At this moment, Ezekiel realized that he had no money for the day, let alone to last a whole week. He would have to go back to his same life at least until next Sunday. Even worse, he'd been banned from the shelter and had no place to stay.

Ezekiel hesitantly made a request. "Well, Pastor Harris. I am in a bind today. Is there anything you or the church could do to help me out?" asked Ezekiel.

"You mean, like money? Right now?" asked Pastor Harris. Ezekiel could tell that his request had irritated him.

"I guess," said Ezekiel. "I was under the impression from you and Pastor Williams that—"

Pastor Harris shook his head and interrupted Ezekiel. "Fine. Go see my treasurer. Tell him that I said to give you thirty dollars. But, not more than that," said Pastor Harris.

"Who?" said Ezekiel.

"Trustee Copeland. Go out to that hall, and you will see his office at the end of the hallway," said Pastor Harris.

"And he will just give it to me?" asked Ezekiel.

"Oh, right. Tell Trustee Copeland, 'Code 291.' That is today's money code, and he will give you the money without needing to confirm with me," said Pastor Harris.

"Okay, thank you very much," said Ezekiel. Pastor Harris was already walking away from the pew without giving Ezekiel an official goodbye. He acted like he was too busy from saying goodbye to other people.

That was not how Ezekiel had envisioned the rest of the day going. Ezekiel made his way out of the sanctuary into the hallway. He looked down at one end and saw the restrooms. He looked down at the other and saw two signs on a closed door. The signs read, "Treasurer" and "Authorized Personnel Only." Ezekiel knocked on the door. There was no answer. He knocked again.

"Come in," said Trustee Copeland.

Ezekiel walked into the room.

"Hello. Are you Trustee Copeland?" asked Ezekiel.

"Yes. What do you want?" asked Trustee Copeland. Trustee Copeland remembered seeing Ezekiel on the Boulevard a few times searching through a few street corner trash cans.

"Oh, yes. Pastor Harris told me to tell you to give me thirty dollars," said Ezekiel.

"Thirty dollars! For what?" said Trustee Copeland.

"Just because, I guess," said Ezekiel.

"Just because huh. Well, I need to talk to him first. Come back next Sunday," said Trustee Copeland.

"He said to tell you 'Code 291,'" said Ezekiel.

"You got to be joking," said Trustee Copeland, as the code confirmed the authorization to give Ezekiel the money. "Are you going to use this money just to buy drugs or cigarettes? Because the church is not in the business of supporting your habits!" exclaimed Trustee Copeland.

Ezekiel did not respond. Trustee Copeland grabbed the large checkbook binder from the edge of his desk.

"That's really not going to help me. I don't have a bank account. Well, not anymore," said Ezekiel.

"Guess not," said Trustee Copeland. He opened the lower side drawer of his desk and pulled out a rectangular tin box with the words "Petty Cash" written on it in red marker. He opened it up and counted three ten-dollar bills. Ezekiel walked the rest of the way to the desk and put his hand out to receive the money. However, Trustee Copeland flung the money at the edge of the desk and immediately put the box back in the drawer.

As Ezekiel picked up the money off the desk, he said, "Thank you," but one of the ten-dollar bills fell on the floor. Trustee Copeland ignored the bill that fell and returned to inputting the tithes and offerings information into the computer from the collected envelopes. Ezekiel bent down to pick up the money, but it slightly moved as if a gust of wind blew on it. Ezekiel looked around and noticed a soffit air vent in the wall behind Trustee Copeland. He picked up the ten-dollar bill and walked out of the office and the church. Despite the wonderful service, he was now feeling even worse than he had last night, before he saw Pastor Williams. Ezekiel tried to justify it all in his mind. He thought, *It was a busy service. Maybe the renovation was more expensive than anticipated. Maybe the pastor and trustee were upset they didn't bring in more money today than they hoped. He also thought, But, Pastor Williams would have never acted like that. They just don't know me, yet.*

Ezekiel took the thirty dollars to the Raceway Diner for a full breakfast meal. He then went over to the gas station across the street and bought a pack of cigarettes, a lighter, and some snacks for future meals. Ezekiel felt it was worth a shot to make one more attempt to get back into the homeless shelter. To no surprise, the admissions guard rejected his entry.

Ezekiel walked the Boulevard aimlessly with his duffel bag. It was getting dark, but he saw Ebenezer AME's building. It had been vacant for quite some time and was still boarded up. He thought it would be a great place to stay, at least for a few nights. He walked to the side of the church and saw a door. He took a small hammer out of his duffel bag that he used as protection. With it, he broke off the doorknob and lock, allowing access into the church. He said to himself, *I will just stay here until I figure things out with Pastor Harris' church.*

One month later, Ebenezer AME is the first church set on fire along the Boulevard, others followed.

20

The Battle Is Not Yours

The community revival.

Officer Reese and Agent Carson rushed out of Church of the Living God. Officer Jenkins attempted to get into another police officer's cruiser on the street, but Officer Reese yelled to him.

"No, Jenkins. All the streets are backed up from the revival! You will just sit in traffic!"

Officer Jenkins looked down the Boulevard and realized the same. The sidewalks were not any better. From Olive Street to Prince Street, the Boulevard had a typical pedestrian count of over 2,000 walkers a day. During the community revival, the pedestrian count along the Boulevard had increased to approximately 4,000. Attempting to capitalize on the halo effect of the event, vendors from all over the city had set up shop along the sidewalks. Remarkably similar to the city's parades, residents came out in masses to find good deals on products, food, and other items along the sidewalk, even if they were not interested in attending the revival. It made rushing back to the corner of the Boulevard and Prince Street challenging for the police officers.

They were many blocks away, and Lauren was already out of Mount

Carmel running toward New Lighthouse Temple.

* * *

Joshua was running through the tunnel, making his way to what he hoped was the underground of New Lighthouse Temple. However, he had grown up in that church, been through every inch of it, and had never seen any part of the church that could possess a passageway that would connect to this section of the Underground Railroad. As Joshua traversed the tunnel, he feared that his mad dash might come to a complete halt if he came face-to-face with the dark being. He had no choice but to continue, though, knowing fire may already be consuming New Lighthouse Temple.

He saw the tunnel was coming to an end. Thankfully, there was another iron ladder just as he'd suspected. He looked up and saw this ladder was much taller than the others. He did not see the top, but the ladder appeared to continue way above ground level.

Joshua grabbed the first rung, and his heart started pumping to an intense beat. He hesitated in pulling himself up to make the climb. Joshua took a deep breath, exhaled, waited a moment, and then climbed the ladder. He climbed up approximately fifteen feet and looked down. From climbing the other ladders, Joshua knew this spot should be at ground level. However, as he looked up with his cell phone light, he saw he had a lot farther to go. He took another deep breath, released it, and continued up the ladder.

* * *

In New Lighthouse Temple, the church was extremely loud. In addition to the low-level background music playing from the sound system, a gospel CD selected by Pastor Williams, the crowd in the church was in an uproar. Many people were talking and yelling all at the same time. Pastor Williams, his church officials, and Bishop Hines were at the front of the church at a folding table with microphones attempting

286

to quiet the crowd. It was supposed to be a panel forum discussion about community issues. However, it had turned into a shouting match of blame regarding the recent church fires.

The two police officers that had not gone with Officer Reese and Agent Carson up the Boulevard were now targets of blame as well, people angrily accusing them of not doing their job regarding the fires. A few residents came there intentionally to raise the fact that Joshua, Pastor Williams' nephew, was on the news as a person of interest regarding the fires. At this moment, they focused on Joshua with their comments and attacks.

"Yes. My nephew, Josh, was mentioned by the police and the news media as just a person of interest and not a suspect! Did everyone hear me? He is not a suspect!" exclaimed Pastor Williams.

"Then, where is he?" yelled Jason Copeland, the brother of Trustee John Copeland, who'd died in Church of the Living God during its fire.

Jason Copeland was still furious over the sudden death of his brother. He had been initially seated in the middle of a pew halfway back from the front of the church. But, to be clearly heard and seen, he stood up and walked into the middle aisle. The crowd's uproar grew even louder.

"Now, Brother Jason. We all have concerns and have a little fear right now. And I fully understand that you probably have more than all of us. But let's not jump to conclusions," said Pastor Williams.

"From what I hear, he has been staying with you. But he still has not stepped foot in this church in over a year! Maybe he hates churches ever since his mother died right here in this very church, and you did nothing about it but watch.

Maybe that is why he wants to burn them all down, and that's why you are protecting him!" yelled Jason Copeland.

Pastor Williams could not hold back his temper any longer. He jumped up from the table, aggressively pushing it farther away from the group panel.

"You are talking about my sister and my nephew! Did you watch your brother die right in front of you like I watched my sister? Did you hear the screams of your nephew asking you to save her, and there was nothing you could do? I hear those same screams every time I look at him, and there is still nothing I can do to bring her back!" exclaimed Pastor Williams.

Mrs. Tucker, who lived across the street, yelled, "Maybe that is exactly why you are protecting him!" Mrs. Tucker was a longtime resident who opposed Pastor Williams taking over the property for New Lighthouse Temple during entitlements. She was the one most vocal during his neighborhood meetings about his vision for the church. Mrs. Tucker was not a churchgoer, nor did she want to deal with the noise and double-parked cars during services. Even though she would give Pastor Williams an evil look, he would still greet her and say hello. But she would never speak back to him, until now.

"I always knew something bad would happen from this church, and you being here! I felt it in my bones!" screamed Mrs. Tucker.

Bishop Hines took over the conversation. "Now wait a minute. I have known Pastor Williams for years, and many of you have too. You know he is a true man of God that has always been here for you and this community," said Bishop Hines.

"You mean just like some of those faith televangelist scam artists, either living a secret alternate life or swindling money from the poor?" yelled one person. More people commented on many other recent scandals of churches in the news. Some of New Lighthouse Temple's official members started yelling back at the disrupters in defense of Pastor Williams and Joshua. It only made things worse.

* * *

Joshua finally made it to the top of the ladder. He'd had to climb another twenty or thirty feet. He saw a latch on the bottom of the trap door, but thankfully there was no padlock on it like the others. As he lifted the door, he heard a bunch of noise. It was a lot of yelling and screaming, and he feared the worst. He quickly climbed out the trap door onto a platform, looking at the wall in front of him. He had seen this wall before. It displayed a mural of clouds and three female angels facing two male angels reaching out to each other with a dove above them. It was the same mural located high in the ceiling above the chandelier lights and support framing at the highest point of the cathedral ceiling of New Lighthouse Temple. It was situated in the very back of the ceiling, so high in a built-in concave opening that you must be standing in the very front of the church to see it. Joshua realized the tall wall behind the pulpit possessed a way down to the underground tunnel this whole time. Since Pastor Williams wanted to keep the integrity of the sanctuary and ceiling, this part of the church had not been improved during construction. And since the ceilings were so high, it would have easily remained hidden from anyone, until now.

Joshua looked around. Due to a lower second platform with a parapet that extended pretty far out, he was unable to see down to the church. Joshua could only see straight across to the balcony over the front entrance that was slightly lower than his current position. Not knowing the platform's stability, Joshua took one step at a time as he made his way to the edge. He took a while to get there, as he was also focused on the yelling and arguing that he could barely understand. The music coming from the three hanging speakers evenly spaced out just below him further muffled the sounds below. He peeked over the edge and saw only a few pews near the church's front entrance, and then his vision was cut off by the second extended platform. He looked down at this platform, and his eyes widened as he saw the dark being just below his feet in the same coat, leather helmet cap, and goggles.

But this time, the dark being had the flamethrower on his back. Joshua jumped back out of sight. He squatted down even more and lost control of his breathing.

Joshua knew he had to hurry; he could feel time running out. He inched his way forward again to the edge. He saw the dark being, looking more and more like a man now, had a large gasoline container in his left hand, and a long hose connected to it in his right. He was walking along the second level platform below, spraying gasoline on the upper part of the walls, the wood frame support beams near the platform, and the chandelier.

Joshua yelled, "Stop!"

The dark being turned around and looked up to the upper platform and saw Joshua. It immediately dropped the gasoline container and hose and reached around its back and grabbed the flamethrower's long nozzle. It sprayed the platform at Joshua's feet, which was immediately engulfed in flames, causing Joshua to jump back as far as he could up against the back ceiling.

The dark being continued to spray, making Joshua see nothing but flames in front of him. More from feeling the extreme heat from the fire than courage, Joshua ran through the flames and jumped down onto the second platform with the dark being. But it was too late. The dark being had already used that brief moment to turn around and set his trails of gasoline ablaze. Joshua looked through the sporadic fire on the platform and looked down at the church.

He had seen this exact scene before. It was the same scene in his reoccurring dream, but instead of sitting on the organ seat, he was up high on a platform looking down on the church.

***

It was chaos. The church's large beautiful cathedral ceiling and the colorful pane glass windows along the high walls only amplified the sounds of the screams, the yelling, and the noise of objects falling and breaking. The dark smoke was fully visible in the air. Everyone was pushed frantically to get out to the closest exit. The sanctuary was too small for the crowded church, way above capacity.

Joshua looked down toward the pulpit. Two men were fighting just in front of the altar. These two men were Jason Copeland, and Deacon Wade from New Lighthouse Temple, who stopped Jason Copeland from attacking Pastor Williams. Pastor Williams, Bishop Hines, and the two police officers were trying to break them apart. They were the only ones now oblivious to the imminent danger of the fire quickly spreading above them. Joshua yelled again, "Get out of here!" But there was too much commotion and noise for anyone to hear him, as they ran and pushed to get out.

The dark being pointed his flamethrower at Joshua. With limited space around him, Joshua didn't know what to do. The dark being ignited the flamethrower, and the flames fell just a few feet in front of Joshua. He did not get burned, but he could feel its intense heat on his skin. The dark being ignited the flamethrower again, this time running at Joshua. Joshua had no choice but to jump off the platform. As he fell, he grabbed onto one of the enormous speakers, luckily just below him. It was suspended by three bolted hanging wires, two of which broke from the ceiling. Plaster fell.

Joshua was now hanging and swaying. He knew the last wire was not going to hold him long. The speaker, barely holding Joshua, swung to the right just over the musician area and broke from the ceiling. Joshua fell hard to the ground on the floor behind the organ while the speaker crashed directly onto the organ, breaking apart into many pieces. Wood from the organ cover broke into pieces as well. More of the ceiling broke apart and crashed down to the floor, including parts that were on fire.

Pastor Williams, Bishop Hines, and everyone at the pulpit ran down the church's central aisle without looking back, as they assumed the whole ceiling was coming down on them in flames.

They ran out of the church, unaware that Joshua was one of the fallen objects, and that the real arsonist was in the building with him. The people that remained in the streets looked on in horror as they saw the rampaging crowd rushing out of the church, screaming with fear. They saw the flames within the church lighting up and flickering against the pane glass windows.

The rooftop and exterior sides pushed out dark smoke that was quickly filling up the top of the sanctuary, so fast it was flowing just like water percolating through the building's holes, cracks, and airways to escape into the night sky.

Pastor Williams, Bishop Hines, Jason Copeland, and Deacon Wade were the closest to the church. The two police officers stood at guard with them, more concerned about them continuing their fight. Jason Copeland and Deacon Wade looked at each other in disbelief and realized that their quarrel had almost cost them their lives.

Suddenly, Lauren quickly approached the church, dashing through the onlooking crowd. She ran up to the concrete curb directly in front of the church. She attempted to run up the church steps, But Pastor Williams quickly grabbed her in a bear clinch from behind.

"No, Lauren! You can't go in there!" yelled Pastor Williams as he struggled to keep her in his grasp. Bishop Hines stood in front of them both to add another blockade between her and the church.

"Joshua! Joshua!" yelled Lauren directly into the front door of the church from her distant location.

"What is wrong with you? Josh is not in there!" huffed Pastor Williams, struggling to keep his grip on the frantic young woman.

"Joshua *is* in there! He *is* in there! Get off me!" yelled Lauren as she violently broke the hold of Pastor Williams.

She immediately shoved Bishop Hines aside and did a full break toward the church's entrance. She stopped when she saw the two police officers in front of her. She knew it would be difficult, almost impossible to get into the church now. But she knew she could not give up. She said to herself, *Joshua needs me. I can be greater. Help me, God to be greater. I am greater.*

Lauren closed her eyes, took a deep breath, exhaled, and then reopened her eyes, giving the officers a forceful stare. The two police officers looked at her and could see her apparent determination. Then, Lauren ran full speed at them. The officers immediately attempted to close the gap of her lane into the church from opposite sides.

Still, she was too fast, too strong, and too determined as she lowered her body and broke through them both like a football linebacker, causing them to fall to the ground. Without hesitation, she ran into the church through a set of flames just beyond the entrance into the sanctuary.

The two police officers got up and, with Bishop Hines, tried to run in after her. But then the two tall support columns just inside of the church ominously collapsed, causing the church's entire balcony to fall to the ground, blocking the entrance. The loud crash caused Lauren to flinch and turn around only to see her way out was now blocked. She turned back toward the front of the church and continued down the church's central aisle.

"Joshua! Joshua!" yelled Lauren again.

She started to cough as the smoke hindered her visibility and breathing. Lauren squatted down as low as she could and waggled all the way to the pulpit, avoiding some of the burning and destroyed pews. She heard some rumbling near the musicians' platform and saw some debris moving. She stopped in fear, wary that it could be the dark being.

Then she heard a faint voice that came from it.

"Lauren," said Joshua, coughing.

"Joshua!" said Lauren as she got up and ran over to him. He was covered in wall plaster and fragments from the organ.

"Oh my god, Joshua! There is no time. We have to get out of here," said Lauren as she removed the debris from him. "Come on. Get up!" Lauren attempted to pull Joshua up from the ground and on his feet, but he floundered.

"I fell from the top. I think I broke my ankle," said Joshua in pain. Lauren saw spots of blood on his pants, his shirt, and a blotch of it on his face. "I will help you walk," said Lauren.

She looked around and attempted to support Joshua on her shoulder while covering her mouth with her shirt. They made it to the middle of the church before more ceiling parts and debris fell to the ground around them. The flames all around them had grown and intensified. They heard fire trucks, but the sirens did not sound like they were just outside the church. The closed-off blocks and double-parked cars from the community revival made it impossible for the two local fire trucks and an ambulance to take a direct route to get there quickly. Lauren tried to walk forward some more with Joshua, but then she had a thought.

"Wait. Where's that thing?" asked Lauren.

"It tried to set me on fire, and I fell from the ceiling. After that, I don't know," said Joshua.

While they were facing the church's front door, searching for a clear way out, the dark being ran from behind the musicians' stage toward them. Before Joshua noticed, it had already reached a pew and stepped up on its seat to get a leaping attack on them. Joshua turned around toward it when he saw it in his periphery. But it was too late. The dark being was already in the air, coming down on Joshua with a knife in its hand. Joshua forcefully pushed Lauren forward and out of the way. She fell hard, face forward to the ground. The dark being landed on top of Joshua. In one motion, it stabbed Joshua in the upper inside of his shoulder with the large pocketknife. Joshua screamed out in pain.

Lauren got up and saw the dark being over top of Joshua. She swiftly got into a runner's starting block position and bolted toward the two. She pulled her leg back as far as she could and then swung it forward, kicking the dark being directly in the face and causing it to flip back hard onto the floor, off Joshua. Lauren helped Joshua up, and as they started to move forward again, the dark being stood up. It flung something at them. Lauren immediately jumped in front of Joshua and pushed him out of the way. He fell to the ground from the push and his weak ankle, and she flinched, bracing for an impact. But instead of getting hit as she'd anticipated, she felt some type of liquid being sprayed on her. The dark being had pulled out a small bottle of lighter fluid from its coat pocket and doused Lauren with it. Lauren's eyes were blinded and burned from the liquid sprayed on her face. The rest of her body was now wet from the flammable liquid. She yelled out in pain, covering her eyes. The dark being then kicked Lauren to the ground. She fell backward and hit the back of her head on the end of a pew, knocked unconscious right in front of Joshua.

The dark being looked around and grabbed a fragment of a wooden pew that was on fire. He was deliberately walking slowly, strolling, over to set Lauren on fire, ready to enjoy what was about to happen. Joshua wasted no time and immediately got up; he ran, limping, over to the dark being and tackled it to the ground. The wood fragment in the dark being's hand fell and set another trail of fire on the floor from the remnants of the lighter fluid. Suddenly, one of the giant ceiling fans fell to the ground, on fire. Joshua got on top of the dark being and began punching it in the face repeatedly in anger. He could not control himself; his rage was too intense. Joshua's hands and knuckles were bloody from punch after punch given to the dark being.

He pulled off its goggles and leather helmet cap, and Joshua looked at him in horror. He knew this person, not a dark being at all. It was Ezekiel "Zeke" Wilson. His homeless friend. Joshua shook his head in disbelief. He then looked over at Lauren, blinded and unconscious.

His anger returned, this time with even greater rage. Joshua grabbed Ezekiel's neck with his hands. He began choking him. The adrenaline rushed through Joshua's body and gave him even more power than ever. Joshua's grip strangled Ezekiel with twice as much force compared to what Ezekiel had used when he'd grabbed Joshua's arm in the cave. The vice grip around Ezekiel's neck caused his eyes to open wide in surprise. No air could either enter or exit Ezekiel's lungs at this point. He tried to pull Joshua's hands off his neck, but with no success. Joshua was too strong, his grip too tight. Ezekiel's lower body moved frantically with the fear of his imminent death.

Flashes of recent memories only fueled Joshua's rage and strength. His mother's death in the very same church, where no one was able to help her; the news and police thinking he was a suspect; his fight with Mike; his battle with his uncle thinking Lauren was the problem. And now, his love, his soul, Lauren, the only person that had been fighting for and with him through all of this, even risking her life for him, was knocked out on the ground because of Ezekiel. Joshua's rage turned from anger to hate, and then from hate to satisfaction, with the thought of taking Ezekiel's life. Joshua grinned in the enjoyment of his chokehold. But at that moment, a part of a large wooden support beam that was on fire fell from the ceiling. Half of it landed hard on the ground with a loud crash. The other half landed slanted on the pew right over Lauren's head and body as she still lay unconscious. Its flames were just a few inches away from Lauren's face, still covered in lighter fluid.

Joshua looked on in fear, and stopped choking Ezekiel. He looked at his hands and remembered his mother's words, "Good bringeth forth good, evil bringeth forth evil." He was suddenly consumed with guilt and shame. But he knew he had to save Lauren.

However, once he did, Ezekiel, the arsonist, the murder of Trustee Copeland, would be able to either get away or attack him. He had no choice, though, as the flames grew along the beam. All it would take would be one little flame or one little spark to fall on her, and she would be burned alive. He abruptly got off of Ezekiel and ran over to Lauren. He knelt on the floor in front of the beam over her, not sure yet what to do.

At this moment, Pastor Williams, Bishop Hines, and the police officers were now working to remove the rubble and debris from the fallen balcony to get to Lauren. But it was too much. It would take them a few more minutes to clear a path.

They could barely see into the church, except for through a few small openings among the debris. They peeked into the church in amazement that Lauren had been right. Joshua was in the building, along with someone else lying on the ground behind them.

"Josh! Lauren! Get out of there!" yelled Pastor Williams. The firefighters were much closer, but still a few blocks away.

Joshua looked down at his hands again. They were covered with lighter fluid from his struggle with Ezekiel. He thought, *I can't possibly lift the heavy beam off Lauren now. Not only is it too heavy, but the entire wood is on fire, and my hands are greased with lighter fluid and would immediately burn with just one touch.* He needed more time to think.

The center chandelier fell to the ground in flames. The loud crash caused Joshua to flinch. The smoke in the church was getting too thick. Joshua knew he had to do something this very moment.

So, he took a deep breath, exhaled, waited a moment, and then he heard his mother's voice saying, "Be strong and of a good courage, my son, my mighty Joshua. Only be thou strong and very courageous."

Another large ceiling fan fell to the ground. This time, Joshua did not flinch. He took another deep breath, and with the exhale, he let go of his anger, his hate, his emotions, his pain, his mother's death, and his desire to kill Ezekiel. He closed his eyes and said out loud, "I speak peace in my mind. I speak strength in my body. I speak greatness in my actions, and I speak your purpose in my life, in the name of Jesus," said Joshua.

With his eyes still closed, he placed his hands on the flaming crossbeam over Lauren. He squatted to get leverage with his legs, and he began to push the beam up a few inches. The flames on the wood where his hand grasped it turned from a fiery orange to a fiery blue. The more he pushed up on the wooden beam, the more intense the flames of blue on his hands became. His hands burned, but they were not consumed. He lifted the beam high enough to the point where he thought he could safely pull Lauren away. He took his left hand off the beam while still holding it up with his right. Unfortunately, as he tried to reach down to Lauren, the beam started to fall; it was too heavy for just his one hand. He grabbed on to her shoulder and shirt, but then the beam fell even lower. He put his hands back on the beam. His hands were still miraculously not burning from the contact. But he started to have doubts. He could not do both, hold the beam up and pull Lauren out from under it at the same time.

Joshua closed his eyes and yelled, "Please help! Help me, please!" He travailed out again, "Please, God. Help me!"

Pastor Williams could barely see through the fire and smoke, but he heard Joshua's screams. He'd heard them before, and again he could do nothing to help Joshua. Pastor Williams started to cry with regret at how he had last treated Joshua at his house, how he wanted to embrace Joshua one more time. He attempted to go through the church and get to him, but the police held him back.

Joshua opened his eyes. Then, suddenly, he saw the same small spheres of light that he had seen before, first when he was with Lauren, and then in his vision in the cave. Joshua looked around in amazement. He could not believe this was real, and he was not dreaming. The spheres of light were both ascending from the ground and descending from the ceiling. They surrounded Joshua, circling him slowly in a tornado-like formation. Joshua looked at them, and tears fell down his face. He felt their energy, and it revived him.

He tried one more time. He grunted with this last effort. This time, he lifted the beam back up with his one hand and pulled Lauren completely out from under it with his other. He dropped the beam, and it broke on the pews and fell to the ground. He looked at his hands and was amazed to find they were not burned; they did not even have a mark. He looked back at the beam as the spheres of light flew up into the air, disappearing one by one.

He looked over and saw Ezekiel still on the floor. His eyes were wide open, looking on in amazement. Joshua stood up, and then firefighters in full gear broke through the flames, rushing toward them. Suddenly, the second platform area exploded from the flamethrower left up there by Ezekiel. They flinched and jumped back from the blast.

Joshua looked back at the pulpit. He felt something different, almost as if there was another dark presence, other than Ezekiel's, and much stronger. But Joshua's vision in that direction was blurred by the flames and smoke. Joshua turned back toward the front of the church. The firefighters re-engaged after the blast and reached all three of them. They rushed Joshua out of the church, while one firefighter carried Lauren over his shoulder.

Pastor Williams, Bishop Hines, Officer Reese, and Agent Carson were amazed to see Joshua come out with Lauren. They were even more surprised to see the last firefighter bringing out Ezekiel Wilson, cloaked in dark attire with his mutilated face. After what he'd just seen Joshua do, Ezekiel had given up his fight and went freely to the police.

Lauren was put on a stretcher, and her mouth was covered with a CPR oxygen mask in an attempt to fully recover her while they placed her in the ambulance. Bishop Hines jumped in the emergency vehicle with her. Unfortunately, she was still unresponsive. While the rear ambulance door closed, Pastor Williams got a glimpse of them administering CPR and wrapping bandaged around her head and eyes.

Joshua was placed on a stretcher as well, but they put him in a separate ambulance. Pastor Williams got in with him.

"Where's Lauren?" asked Joshua.

"She's in the other ambulance," said Pastor Williams.

"I need to make sure she's okay," said Joshua.

"They will make sure she is fine, Joshua," said Pastor Williams, trying to reassure him.

"You don't know that. Were her eyes open?" asked Joshua.

"I don't know," said Pastor Williams.

"Was she awake? Was she alive when they put her in the ambulance?" asked Joshua.

"Joshua, I'm not sure." Pastor Williams hesitated.

"Was she?" yelled Joshua.

"I don't know. I don't know," whispered Pastor Williams as he looked at Joshua, hopeless. He remembered feeling the same when Joshua's mother died.

21

A Visitor Unknown

After the community revival.

It was overcast. A large group of people crowded the burial site, much larger than the white tent could cover. The chairs lined up, row to row all filled, and many other people were standing. Blue and yellow flowers covered the pillar stands at each corner of the tent. A large blue-and-yellow flower spray covered the casket, based on Lauren's favorite colors. Mostly everyone was wearing black, but some were wearing gray. An empty seat was in the middle of the front row, situated next to Jessica and Lauren's mom. The chair was reserved for Joshua. However, he was not there. He looked from afar in sunglasses, sitting in his car farther down the road at the edge of the cemetery. He waited for the burial ceremony to end. When it did end, and everyone departed, Joshua drove up closer to the plot. He got out of his car and walked over toward the tent. Joshua took off his sunglasses and sat on the ground next to someone else's beveled grave marker, about forty feet away from Lauren's grave. He patiently waited as the cemetery crew backfilled Lauren's grave, wanting to beat the anticipated downpour.

When they were done, Joshua walked the rest of the way to Lauren's grave. He lost control and fell to his knees in front of her upright headstone with tears in his eyes. It read, "Lauren Ann Alexander—A Gift to this World and Now A Gift to Heaven." After reading, Joshua began banging on the fresh earth with his fists above her grave. He cried out like a little boy. "No! No! No! No!" yelled Joshua.

He fell hard to the ground, laying his whole body flat on the dirt with the side of his face on the ground as if to feel her soul one more time. But he couldn't. She was gone. Joshua continued to weep in a softer tone, and then said quietly, "My soul loves your soul. My soul loves your soul, Lauren, always." He wiped away his tears.

At that moment, a man came up behind Joshua and stood without saying a word. Joshua got up and wiped the dirt off his face and hands. Joshua looked up at him, thinking he was part of the cemetery crew and said, "I will be out of here in a second," said Joshua.

The man responded, "Take as much time as you like, Joshua. But why do you look for the living among the dead?"

Joshua's eyes shot open, and he looked back at the man. At that moment, there was a loud clap of thunder from the sky, and the earth began to shake violently. Many chairs from the burial ceremony fell over, and a few tombstones in the cemetery broke apart and fell to the ground. Joshua tried to hold firmly to the ground as it shook underneath him. He looked around in fear, as he assumed it was a terrible earthquake.

Joshua then heard a loud clap, and someone yelled his name, "Josh! Josh! Wake up!"

Joshua woke up. He was in a hospital room in its bed. Pastor Williams and a doctor were directly over him, trying to wake him up. Joshua looked around in confusion. He realized he'd just had another dream. He looked at Pastor Williams, and the first thing he said was,

"Lauren!" as he tried to jump up from the bed.

Pastor Williams and the doctor successfully restrained him.

"Don't worry, she is fine. She is in another room down the hall, getting rest," said Pastor Williams.

"We almost lost her, but she is a fighter. She is going to be okay, just like you," said the doctor.

"So, she is completely fine?" demanded Joshua.

"Well, there is one thing. Her eyes were injured pretty badly. It is uncertain how much vision she will retain. She could be partially blind or completely blind, or her eyes may make a full recovery. We have to do some more tests, and only time will tell," said the doctor.

The doctor turned to Pastor Williams and said, "He seems to be fine. I have some rounds to do, but I will be back to check on him."

"Thank you, Doctor," said Pastor Williams.

"Uncle Jerry, I will not be able to live with myself if she cannot see again," said Joshua.

"Hey, let's not worry ourselves by jumping to conclusions. I am certain her eyesight will be okay," said Pastor Williams.

Joshua relaxed back into the bed.

"What happened?" asked Joshua.

Pastor Williams laughed. "You happened, my extraordinary nephew," said Pastor Williams.

"Is it over?" asked Joshua.

"It seems that way," said Pastor Williams.

"Listen, Uncle. Lauren and I made some stupid mistakes this past week, and I know how you feel about her. But she has helped me through all of this," said Joshua.

Pastor Williams smiled. "You know, I never really talked to you about this, but the story about Adam and Eve is one of the most interesting stories in the Bible," he said.

Joshua looked confused. He thought, *Is Uncle really going to give me a sermon right now?* Despite his thought, he attentively listened.

Pastor Williams continued, "First, the story of Adam and Eve must be significant, or why else would it be in the very beginning of the Bible? Second, most ministers in their sermons only focus on the sin of Eve eating the apple, and then the sin of Adam. But the reality is, it was the first love story. The first true twin souls, or twin flames as you young people call it. But, their sin just showed how an imperfect woman and an imperfect man were perfect for each other. If you ask me, I think God allowed them to sin to make sure that they learned how to work together to find their way back to the garden or back to God. Who knows what abilities and powers they had together before they sinned? Both men and women can do great things. But imagine two people, a man and a woman, who absolutely and unconditionally love each other with God's true love, and who are truly meant to be together in the purpose and destiny of God. When they come together, they have no choice but to do remarkable and extraordinary things. Nothing shall be impossible to them, especially with the Spirit of God operating within them."

Joshua looked on in amazement; he had never heard his uncle speak this way. Pastor Williams continued with a more personal message.

"The way Lauren fought to get into our church to find you showed me just how great her love is for you. There is no greater love than one willing to lay down their life for another. She is definitely extraordinary, just like you."

"Thank you, Uncle. And while we are being completely open, I do need to say something to you. When my mom died, it was the hardest thing I ever had to deal with. In fact, I am still dealing with it. But you were always there for me before and after she died. Yes, she was my mom, and I miss her so much. But she was also your sister. And I never really told you that I am so sorry for your loss too. I know how much she meant to you as well," said Joshua.

Pastor Williams started to tear up. "Thank you, Josh. She raised a wonderful boy, who is now turning out to be a great man. And you know what she would say to you right now if she were here?" asked Pastor Williams.

Joshua did not have an answer.

"She would say, 'Boy, you better brush them teeth!'" joked Pastor Williams. Joshua grinned.

Officer Reese walked into the room. "Hello, fellas," he said.

"Hello Joe," said Pastor Williams.

"Hey," said Joshua.

"Man, aren't you and your girl the heroes of the neighborhood, Josh. I want to say thank you. I appreciate everything you did; and honestly, I am sorry for focusing on you as a suspect. That stupid ATF agent got in my ear and head, and I guess I never really stopped to listen to my heart and instincts. Once again, I am sorry, Joshua," said Officer Reese.

"No problem. We all did some stupid things during this past week," said Joshua.

"So, it was Zeke the whole time? He started all of the fires?" asked Pastor Williams.

"Yes. Josh beat him up pretty severely, but he was still willing to talk in holding. He said a lot of stuff about Josh and Lauren in your church. It didn't make any sense. But, he gave us all the details about the previous fires.

"He used his panhandling money to get a hold of that cheap old flamethrower and a few other things, including his flame-retardant coat, from the military store," said Officer Reese.

"And he was using the tunnels under the Boulevard to get back and forth from the churches without being seen," said Joshua.

"Yes. The Underground Railroad, part of our very own neighborhood. No one knew. I certainly didn't," said Officer Reese.

"So, your guys and the ATF didn't uncover that during your investigations of the building?" asked Pastor Williams.

"Don't remind me. Yes, we got sloppy and did a shoddy investigation. But the fires happened so closely together, and with the gruesome death of Trustee Copeland, we stopped focusing on the buildings and started focusing on suspects. Again, sorry, Josh," said Officer Reese with a saddened face.

"The important thing is it all worked out, and you caught the real arsonist and murderer, right?" asked Pastor Williams.

"Yes. Zeke confessed to the murder of Trustee Copeland as well. The way he died was something we could not initially tell you. We didn't know who killed him, but we knew he didn't die from the fire," said Officer Reese.

"But why kill him? Why the fires? Why now? It doesn't make any sense," said Pastor Williams.

"See, now you're asking the right questions," said Joshua.

"Apparently, when Zeke started going to Church of the Living God, they didn't help him out like they said they would. They pretty much made him feel worse and treated him like he was trash, especially Trustee Copeland. He got kicked out of the shelter and started staying in the old abandoned Ebenezer AME building," said Officer Reese.

"So that's how he found out about the tunnel," said Joshua.

"Yes and no. Zeke heard about the rumored tunnels in this area from working at the factory a long time ago, but he didn't know they connected all four churches, including Church of the Living God.

Eventually, Zeke realized that he could get to Trustee Copeland's office through the tunnel, and he would see him many times through the air vent. Trustee Copeland was supposed to be writing checks and paying bills at night. But apparently, he was having affairs with a few younger ladies. Zeke would watch through the vent as entertainment," said Officer Reese.

"You've got to be joking!" exclaimed Pastor Williams.

"But when Zeke was watching one night, being a peeping Tom, Copeland was in there with one of his regulars when the pastor walked in on them," said Officer Reese.

"You mean Pastor Harris?" asked Pastor Williams.

"Yes. But when Pastor Harris walked into the office, instead of Trustee Copeland freaking out, as Zeke anticipated, he just smiled while Pastor Harris tried to join in on the fun. I guess Trustee Copeland set it up. But Zeke said this girl was not having any of it. They almost raped her, but she fought them off and got away before anything happened. They must have heard Zeke in the walls because the next Sunday, John brought Zeke into his office. Zeke thought he was going to get some money, but there was a gun on his desk, and Trustee Copeland just said, 'Keep your mouth shut, homeless man.'"

"That must have been when Pastor Harris quit the church, and we haven't heard from him since," said Pastor Williams.

"Yes. We are not sure if Pastor Harris left for fear of retribution from that girl, or if he left before anyone else found out, especially us. He was our only other suspect, and we still have not found him yet. I have to keep reminding myself that all this happened in just a few short days," said Officer Reese. He paused with a moment of self-reflection, then continued.

"After that confrontation, Zeke said he gave up on God and church, and one night while on drugs, he said that he denounced God and gave his life and soul to Satan. Heroin and mushrooms made him think he heard directly from Satan and the underworld, and that he needed to burn out the real evil, which he believed was the churches of this neighborhood. He even went out and got a Satan worshipping book and everything," said Officer Reese.

"Wait. What do you mean? So, Zeke wasn't possessed or anything like that?" asked Joshua.

"What?" asked Officer Reese in surprise. "No way. He was talking to us just like I'm talking to you, except with those awful teeth. Drugs make you think, see, and do some crazy things."

Joshua looked down at his arm that was previously injected by Ezekiel. He no longer knew what to think.

Officer Reese had one more note about Ezekiel. "But Zeke did say that he thinks you must have had the Holy Spirit or some angel in you. In his words, 'Josh did the impossible to save the girl.' I think it was just the drugs in him talking," said Officer Reese.

"Did he see any little sparkling lights or spheres around me, in the church?" asked Joshua.

Officer Reese and Pastor Williams looked at each other, thinking Joshua may have bumped his head during the fight. "No. He said nothing about any lights," said Officer Reese.

Joshua thought, *Did I imagine everything in the cave and in the church? Did I really see my mother in the true realm, or was it just a dream? It felt so real. And what about my longtime reoccurring dream? It didn't happen exactly like it, but it was pretty close.*

"I still can't believe all of this. We should let Josh get some rest. Do you want to come down to the café with me and get some joe, Joe?" asked Pastor Williams.

"You just love that old joke, don't you, Pastor? Sure, okay, let's go," said Officer Reese.

Officer Reese walked out of the room, but Pastor Williams stopped and said, "Just give me one minute."

Pastor Williams walked back to Joshua's bed and said, "Looks like we were all deceived, right?"

"I guess so," said Joshua, shaking his head.

"Joshua, there is something else. I can't believe that I am saying this. But when I looked through the church trying to get to you, I saw four silhouettes in there. It was you, Lauren, and Zeke—well, I did not know it was Zeke at the time—but then someone else was just standing in the middle of my pulpit. It was standing there amid the fire, almost like it was watching you three. You three came out, but the fourth did not," said Pastor Williams.

Joshua felt both frightened and surprised. He thought, *That must have been what I felt behind me as we were all taken out of the church by the firefighters.* Their silence was interrupted by Officer Reese.

"Come on, Pastor! I'm still on the clock," yelled Officer Reese from the hallway. Pastor Williams gave Joshua a shoulder shrug and walked out of the room.

Even with all those revelations, Joshua's main thought was still on Lauren. He unhooked the wires attached to himself and quickly walked down the hall with excitement, looking for Lauren's room. He got to the last room, and next to the small wooden dresser, he saw her shoes on the floor. He walked into the room, but it was empty. As he stepped out of the room, he immediately ran into a man that was walking into Lauren's room.

"I'm sorry," said Joshua. He looked up at his face. It was familiar. However, Joshua could not recall who he was.

"I was not expecting you to be down here so soon, Joshua. They told me that they needed to run more tests on you," said the man.

"Sorry, who are you?" asked Joshua.

"I'm a friend of the Bishop. I was just coming back to get Lauren's shoes," said the man.

"Bishop Hines?" asked Joshua. Joshua now recalled his face. He had seen him in pictures at Bishop Hines' house. "I remember now. You are Archbishop Bennett, aren't you? The one that gave Bishop the desk." The man smiled in acknowledgment. "You're almost unrecognizable in regular clothes. What are you doing here, and where's Lauren and the Bishop?" asked Joshua.

"I don't have a lot of time. Let's just say we have taken Lauren somewhere appropriate so that we can really care for her," said Archbishop Bennett.

"What are you talking about?" asked Joshua, feeling that protective instinct for Lauren kicking into gear again.

"Please, keep your voice down," said Archbishop Bennett. "There are a lot of things you still don't understand, Joshua. Go back to your room, get your rest, and in a day or two, we will send a car for you. You will get to see Lauren, and we will explain everything to you," said Archbishop Bennett.

"And you expect me to just be okay with that?" asked an incredulous Joshua.

"Bishop Hines will call you later. He will reassure you that everything is okay. Don't you want to know the truth? Maybe even find out the real reason your mom was always gone and traveling so much?" asked Archbishop Bennett.

Joshua looked back at him in surprise. "If anything happens to Lauren, you will regret it," he threatened.

"Trust me, Joshua. I do not want to cross you. And I know how much you care about Lauren. That is the whole reason why we are here," said Archbishop Bennett.

Joshua knew that in his current state, there was nothing that he could do, especially since he couldn't find Lauren. He had to hope this man was being honest and that he would see her soon. He walked away, gruffly, and went back to his room.

He shut the door behind him and grabbed a blanket off the bed. Joshua laid the blanket on the floor in front of the chair next to his bed. He knelt on the ground and folded his hands on the chair and prayed.

"God, this has been a crazy week. I have never felt so much love, hate, anger, strength, and peace all in such a short time. I do not know what I am doing. And I have no clue what to do next. But I am trusting you to give me wisdom and to guide my steps. Even if I make the wrong decisions, work them out to eventually be the right ones. I thank you for sharing your eternal power with me, providing angels and entities of heaven to protect and guide me, and, most importantly, I thank you for saving my soul and my life in the midst of my sin and the fires. And lastly, thank you for allowing me to experience your true unconditional love through Lauren. She would die for me, and I would die for her. Please help me find her. My soul loves her soul."

Joshua then stood up with his chest out and shoulders slightly back, titled his up and said with loud voice, "I speak peace in my mind. I speak strength in my body. I speak greatness in my actions, and I speak your purpose in my life. In the mighty name of Jesus Christ, I pray. Amen."

At that moment, Joshua's cell phone rang that he left on the meal tray. He looked at the number. It was Bishop Hines calling.

Joshua answered.

"Hello," said Joshua.

"Joshua, it's time," said Bishop Hines.

"Time for what?" asked Joshua, perplexed.

9 781735 872308